MW01473540

TO PAUL:
I PROMISE TO
GET MY
DIGITAL STUFF
SORTED!

SHIV

SHIV

CAMERON S. CURRIE

COPYRIGHT © 2015 BY CAMERON S. CURRIE.

LIBRARY OF CONGRESS CONTROL NUMBER: 2015910103
ISBN: HARDCOVER 978-1-5035-8075-6
SOFTCOVER 978-1-5035-8073-2
EBOOK 978-1-5035-8072-5

All rights reserved. No part of this book may be reproduced or transmitted in any form or by any means, electronic or mechanical, including photocopying, recording, or by any information storage and retrieval system, without permission in writing from the copyright owner.

This is a work of fiction. Names, characters, places and incidents either are the product of the author's imagination or are used fictitiously, and any resemblance to any actual persons, living or dead, events, or locales is entirely coincidental.

Any people depicted in stock imagery provided by Thinkstock are models, and such images are being used for illustrative purposes only.
Certain stock imagery © Thinkstock.

Print information available on the last page.

Rev. date: 07/24/2015

To order additional copies of this book, contact:
Xlibris
1-888-795-4274
www.Xlibris.com
Orders@Xlibris.com
716713

Thanks to:

Chris Parker, Ryan Chedour, Paul Snider,
Britt McKeen, & Steve Cassar,
For their input, additions and complaints
which made Shiv's world what it is.

To my parents, Allan & Wendy, and the numberless
multitudes of my family and friends,
For their support, and for making me
twisted enough to write this stuff.

And the Creator of this world,
For giving me something to plagiarize.

Prologue

The campfire flickered as the Kobodan boy watched across it at his master sharpening his favourite knife. The Amazing Edgison, knife thrower extraordinaire, was also the smith for the troupe, and invariably any of the players, musicians or acrobats that needed a knife or some other tool sharpened or replaced came to Edgison. If it was a job he wanted to do, mostly sharpen or forge knives, Edgison would take on the job himself; repairing pots or straightening bent tools went to the Kobodan boy. Tonight Edgison had little important to do, and when he had free time in the evenings he would sit around the fire, sharpen his throwing knives, and share his special brand of wisdom with anyone who cared to listen. The Kobodan boy always listened.

The boy had joined the troupe four years before, when he was six, and barely capable of carrying a backpack with his own meagre belongings. He had no clear memory of his home; the Kobodans had been a large family, raising chickens and making farming tools, when a plague had struck, and in desperation the ailing father had passed his son into the hands of a troupe of travelling performers. Edgison had told the boy several times that his family was almost certainly dead. He had seen the older Kobodan covered in boils and barely able to walk, and if the boy had not been so obviously untouched by the plague Edgison would have not had pity, but run past and not looked back.

"Finn!" Edgison shouted at the cook, who was stirring a cast iron cauldron of stew. Finn, as usual, ignored Edgison, just like everyone except the boy. "In the name of the Devil's bleeding eyes, why're you putting more of that cabbage in there? We got plenty of meat, plenty of decent veggies... if I ever smell another cabbage, I swear I'll turn cannibal!"

"Jemmi, girl, you tell your black-hearted mother fifty is not too old to make a husband to ye!" he'd shout at the troupe's graceful sixteen year old dancer. She would occasionally smile if the mood struck her, but usually would shudder or stick her tongue out at him. Any response was gleeful music to Edgison.

"Edgison, dammit!" Willie Shersaver, the leader of the troupe and a master bard, would hiss several times a night. "You're handy with iron and a good knife thrower, but if you don't shut your mouth I'll leave you in a ditch!"

This caused both Edgison and the boy to giggle hysterically until Willie stomped off in disgust. Despite the knife thrower's mouth, he was not badly liked, as he did more than his share of the work and did a better job at it than most. And he really was an excellent knife thrower.

Edgison finished sharpening the one knife, and as he put down the stone with one hand he tossed the knife in the air with the other, and the boy watched entranced as the other knives appeared out of nowhere and were juggled through whirling patterns in the air, reflecting firelight in circles and figure eights. Edgison did not even get up from the log he was sitting on, and would occasionally juggle six of his knives (he owned sixteen) with one hand and then take a drink with the other, never stopping. The other players made a point of walking by when they could to get a glance at the whirling knives that never cut anyone, and the wide-eyed boy that watched them.

"That's the secret, boy," Edgison said with a wink. "The secret to life is to know a little about everything, so you're handy to have around, and to know everything about a little, so you're indispensable. And make sure everyone knows it!" He shouted the last bit, and then snatched the knives out of the air with a single pass of his hand. "Well, I'm old and tired. I'm off to bed."

Edgison always went to bed an hour before everyone else. The boy didn't know why, but everyone else did. They watched the boy sneak off into the bundles beside Edgison's tent to steal the field anvil (little more than a many-pronged pole he could jam into the ground), a hammer and a few scraps of the cheapest metal no one would miss. Until everyone else went to bed, the sound of a hammer battering scraps of cold tin or brass out somewhere in the dark would ring out, and then once the others started to retire, the boy would practise throwing or juggling the crude knives he'd made for himself. This night was the same as any other in that way... the various players casting a furtive glance at the boy's hiding spot so they all knew he was safe, and the boy up late into the night. The troupe would take turns as a watchman through the night, but other than the watchman, there were always two awake after all the others- the boy throwing blunt daggers at a tree stump, and The Amazing Edgison, sitting cross-legged in his tent, peeking out in between the flaps at his adopted son and smiling proudly to himself.

****

As usual, the boy woke up a bit uncomfortable... he had fallen asleep sitting against the field anvil; his weight eventually pushed it over, and now one of the metal prongs was pushing uncomfortably into his ribs. He saw the sunlight peek through his eyelids and sprang up immediately, thinking to rush the anvil back to its spot near Edgison's tent before he woke up.
There was no tent.
All of the tents, the four wagons, the horses- none of them were visible through the long grass. With horror, the boy dropped the tools and ran for the camp, looking frantically for any sign of his troupe.
There was a sign.
Sixteen corpses lay in the beaten down grass. All of them. The whole troupe, including his adopted father. Each one looked as if it had been dumped like excess luggage from its tent. Each had the throat slashed wide open, and then the rest of the body slashed to bloody ribbons. All of the troupe's equipment, tools, tents and even some of their clothes had been stolen. Jutting from the bloody gashes in each mangled corpse were the bone handles of the throwing knives of the Amazing Edgison.
The Kobodan boy stared blankly at the scene for most of the morning. He cried until his tears ran dry, waited until he could cry again, and then he did.
That night his crude, cold-forged knives dug sixteen shallow holes in the ground, and into each he dumped a body of a friend and

pushed the dirt back over each with his hands. Last of all he buried Edgison, although he barely recognized what had become of him. Then he took the sixteen throwing knives he had recovered, still crusted with the blood of their only victims. He wrapped all of them in a corpse's shirt, and the smithy tools in another, slung them over his shoulder, and began to walk.

Chapter One

> **Redlock:** a tiny village in the Duchy of Ceborn, Nesland, on the border of Sabosland. Redlock is far enough from the Goblin border that attacks are uncommon. I relocated there late in my second century to care for my aged uncle Karl in his convalescence. Mostly populated by humans and other giant, barbarian species, my family and I are the only gnomes in the area.
> Doctor Unfriendly's Comprehensive Guide to Everything.

Shiv Kobodan gracefully strode into his latest small village, leading his pack mule Cornelius by the halter. Shiv's violently bright clothes and bulky moustache clashed loudly with the poorly concealed leather armour underneath, his prematurely white hair, the lyre slung over one shoulder, and the conspicuous lack of weapons. Unarmed, lone travellers did not wander alone outside towns much these days, and he drew every eye as he strutted like a rooster through the hamlet's main gate- actually just a gap in the large wooden wall.

Redlock was a frontier town, the sort he liked best, away from contested borders but not from wilderness, not too many soldiers but not too soft either. The one soldier who had been sitting with his back to the logs of the town wall leapt to his feet, first looking to make sure his captain had not seen him dozing in the sun, and second to question the newcomer.

"Hey! You there! You're supposed to check in with the guard you know," he called as he approached, rattling his slightly rusty sword in the scabbard and attempting to look official. "Name and business?"

CAMERON S. CURRIE

Shiv made an elaborate bow, sweeping his outer cloak around grandly. Many of the people from across the wilderness wore several cloaks as he did, but in Nesland it was an uncommon practise. His other hand swept the narrow brimmed red hat off to the side, and then flicked it up in the air to land neatly on his head as he stood up.

"Shiv Kobodan at your especially humble service, General. I am a travelling performer, therefore my business is travelling in order to perform. Would there be a place of rest available for hire for a man of simple means nearby?"

"What?"

"An inn, tavern, bar, or trough not too dependent on large amounts of coin, perchance?"

"Oh..." replied the guard, adjusting his stance to appear more official. "Er... you're looking for the Tortoise Toe Inn then?"

"Ah, precisely, professor." Shiv smiled broadly and briefly scratched his huge white moustache. "A place to hang my hat under your useful vigilance. The direction thereto would be...?"

"Er..." said the guard, looking around uncertainly. "Center of town... second biggest building?"

"Excellent, my most informative sir. And this road is the main thoroughfare? Proceeding in an appropriate direction towards this?"

"Er... yes?"

"Astounding, milord. Your canny awareness does your town credit. Then I will take your leave, Eminence, and proceed accordingly. Farewell and good day to you!" Shiv bowed again and swaggered off along the cobblestones, nodding his head or tipping his hat to every passerby with a grin. The soldier stared after him for a moment, uncertain as to whether he had been complimented or insulted. Then, shrugging, he strolled back to his spot by the gate.

Shiv had to walk only a few minutes to get to the centre of town. Past the circumference of the wall, around two dozen single-story wooden cottages squatted beside subsistence gardens and orchards, and small pens held chickens or sheep, even a few cattle. An ugly black stone well stood in the centre, in the small town square, and standing out from the cottages was a three storey stone manor house, and a two storey converted barn. A double door had been cut in the side of the barn, facing the road, and a sign bore a picture of a turtle with one large claw on its right foreleg. Apparently the upper half had also been heavily reworked, as a wooden balcony surrounded the second floor and there were several doors and blurry glass windows which led out onto it.

He quickly tied Cornelius to a post outside and lifted the bulky saddlebags off. Slinging the baggage over the shoulder opposite his lyre, he patted the animal's yellow-brown flank and strutted through the entrance.

Three or four tables were jammed tight across the dusty main room, and a large bar and stone fireplace were on the far side. Slightly dimmed light leaked in through poorly made glass window panes, barely transparent. This light was supplemented by a few fat candles on each table. There were maybe a dozen patrons sipping drinks from clay mugs, and they all eyed him warily through a sudden pause in the conversation.

He strutted over to the bar, smiling broadly at the woman behind it; she was bordering on middle aged, but well-preserved and wearing a long black dress which was far too expensive to wear in such a place. He dropped the baggage at the foot of a barstool, and bowed deeply, flourishing his hat and sweeping his cloaks back.

"Good day my lady, I was wondering if I could purchase one of your fine elixirs to ease the dust from my weary throat... do you have any exceptional wine?"

"No," the woman said, smiling except from her eyes; she brushed some of her dark red-brown hair from her eyes and glanced over his shoulder at some of the patrons. "We have some passable wine; our speciality is the house ale, but it is quite good."

"Then house ale would be perfection itself, thank-you," Shiv smiled broadly again and did not twitch as he heard a few chairs push back and some heavy booted footsteps. He pulled a silver founding out of nowhere and placed it on its edge on the bar top. The coin rolled slowly across the bar into the hand of the barkeep.

"Ahem." came a voice from behind him. Shiv turned to lean back against the bar on his elbows; there were four fairly large men standing behind him frowning. The one who had spoken stood in front of the others, a half-shaven man with his cloak thrown back to reveal enough black lacquered plate armour to nearly collapse whatever chair he had been sitting on. At the right hand of the speaker stood the largest of them, dressed in layers of smelly bearskins, he

CAMERON S. CURRIE

towered over most men by two full heads and outweighed most men three times over with his muscle alone; he also had a single canine tooth that was long and pointed, as if he was part goblin or troll, jutting out over his upper lip. On the other side was a slender man in green who looked as if he could blow away in a stiff breeze, doubtless because of elven blood; and on the other side of the half-elf, perhaps strangest of all, was a man with his hair slicked back, bloody red eyes and long black fingernails that stroked a rapier at his side like it was a beloved pet. All of them had similar reddish hair and mean, narrowed eyes.

"Mother, is this fop annoying you?" said the one with the rapier.

"Now, boys, you can't do this with every traveller that comes into town, or we'll go out of business," said the barkeep. "You'll have to forgive my boys, they're a little overprotective of their sister and me... but still, be sure to cause no trouble while you're here."

She had finished pouring his ale into a large clay mug, and placed it on the bar alongside the five copper ticks left over from his silver. Shiv took a sip in the moment of awkward silence.

"Milady, mischief had not, until it was mentioned, entered my thoughts in the slightest." He took another sip. "The ale is quite good, thank-you, and you may keep the coppers as a joyously surrendered gratuity."

The woman scooped up the coins and turned to the cash-box; Shiv turned on his bar-stool to face the four men casually. Despite their threatening manner, he appeared not to notice and had another sip, pausing afterwards to lick the foam from his moustache.

"So, you four are brothers then?" He asked.

"Half-brothers actually." said the thin one tersely. Shiv slightly rose one eyebrow and rummaged through his pockets for a small wooden pipe. The four waited expectantly for him to say something. He did not, instead busily thumbing a pinch of tobacco into the pipe.

"And the one over there is your half-sister, then?" he said once his pipe was full, nodding towards their table where a statuesque redheaded woman sat watching the exchange. The big one with the big tooth stepped forward and leaned close to his face.

"What's that supposed to mean? You sayin' something about my mum?" he growled. Suddenly his eyes widened and he stepped back from Shiv quickly. Somehow Shiv had clenched the unlit pipe in his teeth, drawn a long, shining dagger from out of nowhere, and put it to the huge man's throat before anyone had seen him move. The point had not drawn blood but was only a hair's breadth from it.

"Hey, just askin'!" the hairy man shouted. "Didn't mean nothin'!"

The three remaining brothers drew swords, the black-armoured one a huge broadsword, the others rapiers. The sister drew two short swords as well and walked over; and soon Shiv was easily surrounded. He smiled widely and looked slowly around the room as if studying it.

"Let Thokk go, traveller, or you'll be dead before all the pieces hit the ground." the red-eyed one said, with the confidence to make it believable.

Suddenly Shiv's unlit pipe shot a flame three feet in the air with a bang, and smoke burst out of it into a cloud, blinding the brothers. There were mutters of surprise, a few shouts, and a series of four rapid knocking sounds. In a few seconds the smoke cleared, and Shiv was standing on the bar, with a long, ivory knife in each hand poised to throw, the half-full mug between his feet. The brothers surged forward briefly, and then stopped, all looking down at the same time. Each of them, except for the sister, had a long, black-bladed dagger sprouting from the toe of one boot.

"Don't make me throw these things!" Shiv shouted. "These ones are rather heavily enchanted, and I'm not sure you won't be injured."

The sister stepped forward, and stopped as a flick of Shiv's wrist sent one of the white-bladed knives into the floor at her feet. With a crunching sound a circle of thick, white ice flashed out from the point of impact, instantly freezing a circle about a half a pace across. The woman jumped back with her eyes wide. The five of them looked up at him, and several seconds passed in silence.

"Lady, don't sneak up on me, I hate that!" Shiv said, shifting his footing slightly, and everyone realized the barkeep was standing behind him with a drawn dagger of her own.

After another few moments five swords and one dagger were lowered, and the daggers in Shiv's hands whirled briefly and disappeared. He pointed at each of the daggers in the floor, and flashing yellow, they one by one they leapt up into his waiting left hand, while he juggled the others single-handedly in his right. When he had all five errant knives, he tossed them up into the air and danced a little jig, with each step catching another knife in a fold of his cloak, a sleeve, or a boot before it disappeared entirely. Then, without pausing, he leapt off of the bar and landed squarely on the barstool, snatched up his mug and drained it.

"Another quaff, please, milady, for my weary throat still aches with the dust of the merciless road..." he said with a smile, and slid the empty mug back across the bar.

The various patrons in the bar who weren't holding weapons suddenly began clapping and laughing; the shortest of them, a tiny man in a blue mantle and robe, whistled approvingly.

"Thank-you, thank-you," said Shiv over the din, "Your discerning eyes and ears have gladdened my troubled and weary heart. Let it be known that seven days hence, a great Show will take place! A Show which will make this mere episode seem pale and everyday by comparison! In one week, I will give you Shiv's Magic Circus!"

The patrons' shouts of appreciation and applause rose until Shiv could no longer make himself heard; around him the four brothers and two women stood stunned in disbelief as Shiv smiled and waved. Yes, this was indeed the sort of town he liked best.

Chapter Two

> ***Baronet Falcior:*** *Falcior is the noble in charge of Redlock. Although human, he has just enough elf in his ancestry to make him unsuitable for advancement to higher ranks. I'm not convinced humans are better at running things than elves, or vice versa.*
> *Doctor Unfriendly's Comprehensive Guide to Everything.*

The foyer of the mansion was made of heavy blocks of plain stone, but was decorated with several large and moderately expensive tapestries, mostly traditional battle scenes featuring units of charging knights. Shiv stood and examined one to pass the time, whistling a slightly off-key tune designed mainly to irritate. He still was carrying his saddlebags, and frankly was getting tired and impatient. He'd made a long journey from Ericstown, and was in the mood for rest, not diplomacy.

"Sir, my lord will see you now," said a voice preceding its owner. The servant who had admitted him went through a large door, this time holding it open invitingly with a mildly sincere smile. "If you'd like I may take your bags and cloak..."

"Thank you for your kindness," Shiv said as he walked through the door. "However my weary feet yearn for rest; I shall hold on to my luggage so as to not delay them unnecessarily. Perchance is there any word as to what milord requires of me so soon upon my arrival?"

"No, sir. I was merely instructed to bring you; I'm sure my lord will answer all of your questions."

"A strikingly accurate prophecy, no doubt, and thank-you for it," Shiv answered with practised nod he reserved for upper-class servants. He was led into a large dining room dominated by a huge oak table and chairs; at the head there was a blonde-haired noble of some sort, seated, with a small lunch for two in front of him. The nobleman was dressed in rich clothes with a shirt of chainmail showing slightly from underneath. Each setting had a miniature bowl of oatmeal with raisins, and there was a plate of several tiny sandwiches and a large platter of fruit in between them. The servant pulled out a chair beside his master, beckoning Shiv to sit. Shiv bowed slightly to the seated man first and then dropped into the chair, dumping his baggage casually in a pile on the floor. The nobleman smirked slightly and poured them both a glass of wine.

"From what I understand your name is... Shiv..." he said. "And I also understand that you single-handedly subdued the Hammerhand Brothers almost without a thought."

He took a sip of his wine and looked expectantly over the rim for Shiv to reply.

"Well, it actually took a fair amount of thought, sir," Shiv said, lifting his own glass. It was real glass, somewhat unusual for the lower nobility. He took a sip himself and was surprised that the wine was fairly good; often the nobility gave only the cheapest wine to commoners. "And no small amount of effort... especially, I might add, to avoid the unnecessary loss of life or limb."

"Yes... so I heard..." the noble replied with a nod and a slight frown. He took one of the sandwiches and gestured for Shiv to do the same. "It might have been easier for everyone if that had not been the case... never mind. I am Baronet Falcior, the local lord... and I've been short of fighting men since a skirmish in the spring cost me more than half my knights. I've been hiring experienced mercenaries lately as a result, and I'd like you to join. You obviously can fight, and the pay is reasonable."

"Well that truly and pleasantly surprises me, my lord," Shiv said. The little sandwiches were actually quite good; some sort of meat paste that seemed to retain its sweet flavour, a scrap of lettuce and pickle rounding it out. "Ordinarily I would expect this to be the 'get out of my town' speech... I have already promised the townsfolk a show in a week, and disappointing them in order to accept a commission of this sort would be a terrible blow to my otherwise sterling reputation..."

"No, no," the Baronet said, smiling around a half mouthful of sandwich. "You can do your little show, so long as you don't charge my people too much money for it... They'll know your position here would only be temporary anyway. I already have several small teams of mercenaries, but there was news not two weeks ago of a force of several dozen knights ambushed by a company of goblins from the battle lines to the north. If a company of goblins got through the pickets, we need all the help we can get until I have more knights sent to me."

"Well, my lord, it is a tempting offer, but I am hardly a soldier. I have some skill with daggers and such, but a master swordsman would, I imagine, outmatch me terribly. I'm afraid also that my wandering lifestyle affords me better wealth than one would imagine- I gathered ninety towers and four foundings last month alone, before expenses... Surely that is beyond the pay of even an experienced mercenary."

"Yes..." Falcior mused, spooning up a bit of oatmeal. "Of course, I could phrase my offer as more of an... urgent request...?"

"Ah... I understand implicitly now... I receive room and board and maybe a founding or two per day, or I receive an appropriate bludgeoning until I reconsider?"

"Something like that, yes," replied Falcior with a subdued grin. "Anyway you won't be able to stay in the Tortoise Toe Inn, it's owned by Mother Hammerhand. The Hammerhand brothers are a nice bunch of boys, but prone to mischief from time to time, and they have a grudge. I don't think you'd want to sleep under their roof unless no other option was available. Fortunately you can stay here, in my guest room. You'll have access to the servants and good food, clean sheets and a founding or two per day. Also, no Hammerhand Brothers beating you to death in your sleep. Of course I must remind you that if you left Redlock, and my protection, Ruzzio Hammerhand is an experienced tracker, and if they were following you, you might be the one caught by surprise."

The rest of the meal went somewhat silently as Shiv considered his options. The food was good, and the money he would save on expenses was something to consider, but even taking that into account, along with a bit of extravagant spending to relieve the boredom for a month or so, he'd be making less than half his usual take. Staying in one place was not useful for his short, or long term goals...

Fortunately the guest bedroom that the butler showed him to was a nice one; a bit small, but cleaner than most inn rooms, and there was a large chest bolted to the floor with a lock to store his belongings. He emptied the trail rations, stage magic kit, tent and field anvil into it, and lastly the heavy canvas bundle containing sixteen old, bone-handled knives still crusted with blood dried twenty years ago. Then he locked the chest, put the key in his belt pouch, and went to sleep on the small but comfortable bed.

Chapter Three

> *Kobolds: These vile creatures are about twice the size of gnomes, or half the size of a human, and combine the worst features of goblin, rat, and reptile with malevolent creativity. They are not a physical match for most of the giant species, such as humans, unless they outnumber them four to one. Which they usually do.*
> *Doctor Unfriendly's Comprehensive Guide to Everything.*

Sir Reginald struggled back to his feet, rubbing his naked legs to remove the dirt from the many cuts. The darkness around him in the huge pit was full of the vile little creatures, their eyes reflecting the moonlight, reddened, back at him. For the hundredth time he wished he had his weapons and armour back, so he could teach these scrawny creatures a lesson... he had stopped wishing for his warhorse; he was certain they'd eaten it already. He shook his head with regret at that thought; his family had bred horses for two hundred years, and this generation had been the finest ever, his warhorse the finest of the lot. Eaten, and likely raw. He growled to himself and looked his questioner in the eye once again.

The kobold was dressed only in a loincloth and belt; the belt was hanging with a dozen various knives, and its hand held a lead-tipped whip. It spoke the King's Neslish with a horrible, bastardized accent, barely understandable. It was short for its kind- its snout about four handspans above the ground, and its sinewy, reptilian arms twitched in anticipation of using the whip again.

"We has asked you many times, and yet you lies..." it hissed, and began walking in a circle around him. Reginald briefly thought of reaching out and strangling the little monster, but he knew he'd have a dozen crossbow bolts through his hand before he ever touched it. Assuming they didn't stop him with a magic spell... his skin crawled. "We hears it that a Neslish knight never lies..."

"That is true," Reginald growled, aware he had not been technically asked to speak. The whip cracked across his hip, drawing blood, and he gritted his teeth, but refused to cry out. Instead he stood up straighter, prouder, in defiance.

"If you never lies then tell us how many knights is in Redlock. How many arrow humans. How many sword humans. Tells us now!"

The creature stopped, and turned to face Sir Reginald, and regarded him coldly.

"I will not lie, nor will I betray my oaths to the Baronet and the King. I choose not to answer." The whip cracked again, and a bigger gash sliced across both thighs. Sir Reginald stumbled back to his hands and knees, and then began slowly standing up again.

"Not tells the truth is same as lies. You tells us now. Last chance."

Reginald drew himself up to his full height, stared blankly ahead, and remained silent. The whip cracked again, across his belly, and he staggered briefly but stayed standing. There was a strange burning in his gut; he had a feeling the whip had cut something internal. The torturer brought the whip back for another strike, and suddenly its hand stopped in place; the torturer struggled with his transfixed hand for a moment, and then stopped and looked over his shoulder fearfully.

"Now, now, Gendill," thrummed a deeper voice from the darkness. "He'll do us no good dead. Well, not as much good, anyway..."

There was a shuffling sound of kobold feet in the darkness, and a faint scraping sound, like horseshoes on the dirt. Sir Reginald groaned slightly, but did not move.

A figure stepped from among the shadows in the pit, into the same column of moonlight that lit Sir Reginald and the torturer. It looked somewhat like the other kobolds, but was larger, maybe chest high, with blue-grey instead of slate coloured scales. It wore no clothes except a long blue scarf thrown over one shoulder, and a crude jade amulet on a thong necklace. The creature carried a rope, which led back to a copper-coloured war-horse. In spite of himself Reginald breathed a sigh of relief. Cobble, his war-horse. He seemed in good health, although the whites of his eyes showed as he looked around at the verminous creatures surrounding him.

The giant blue kobold glanced around the pit as if staring down the others, lastly at the torturer, whose hand was suddenly released. The creatures all backed away a half step. Then it looked up at Reginald calmly.

"This is a fine horse," the creature began, speaking in a wildly different, sharper accent. "I appreciate a good horse. As I'm sure you do...."

"Killing my horse won't make me talk, you realize. I assumed he was already dead," replied the knight. The blood leaking out of the belly wound was blackish. Reginald had seen that before; he was pretty certain he'd be dead soon.

"No, no, you misunderstand me. I'm not going to kill your horse. That would be a waste. In the meanwhile I wanted to let you know something. I am skilled in necromancy; once you are dead, my magic will get whatever answers I need from you. But I'd rather get them from you willingly. Tell me what I want to know, and I'll give you your horse back- not your weapons and armour, of course- and set you free, to warn your village. That's a fair exchange, is it not?"

Reginald's mouth twisted. In a way, it was fair; and there was a possibility someone at the village could heal his wounds. With a warning the village could prepare for a possible attack, and the damage might be minimized... he thought of all the possibilities and dangers for a solid two minutes before answering.

"Falcior has only one knight left alive, and perhaps twenty soldiers. Virtually everyone in the village is trained as militia, perhaps one hundred more- the law says everyone has to own and practise with weapons. This won't do you much good though, since I left, Falcior has been recruiting; he may have another twenty knights by now, and double the soldiery."

The giant kobold stared at Reginald in silence for a moment.

"Now, Gendill. Now you may kill him. Reginald, you are not worthy of your knighthood. I am disappointed." The creature turned to walk away, and Reginald lunged, hands reaching for the creature's throat. Before he reached the thick little neck, three miniature crossbow bolts speared through his wrist, perhaps ten in other places; and he froze in place just like the torturer had. The blue creature looked over its shoulder briefly, and bared its teeth. "Save the skull... I'll need it. Do what you like with the rest."

Reginald kept his eyes focused on his horse being led away, looking over the heads of dozens of scrawny, tough little creatures as they advanced towards him with blades shining in the moonlight.

Chapter Four

> *Goblins: These creatures are two or three times the size of a gnome. Their main industry is eating everything except their own excrement, and their secondary industry is making little goblins, which they do at exceptional speed. They are not terribly strong, but are sneaky and cunning, and have a society similar to the locust. Needless to say, these features make them difficult to get along with.*
> *Doctor Unfriendly's Comprehensive Guide to Everything.*

The town square, set around an ugly black stone well, was surrounded by a thin but interested line of townspeople. Shiv stood by himself near the centre, as the Baronet made a speech to the village as a whole, seeming not to notice that most of the village was absent. The town's other mercenary groups also stood in the square, separate from the others and Shiv, more or less at attention as the Baronet more or less congratulated himself at their expense.

Shiv looked around at the other groups, especially the Hammerhand Brothers, who glared back from time to time. There was also a group of three gnomes standing in the shadow of the well, small enough to nearly escape notice- one of them, wearing a black top hat, nodded as he met Shiv's eyes. Lastly, there was a peg-legged blond Hillman with a weirdly shaped bone staff, standing next to a bleary-eyed but muscular brute with huge, spiked iron gauntlets, and an extremely short figure in a heavy blue cloak. Shiv nodded his head, thinking. As with most adventurers, they seemed an odd bunch, perhaps not all that impressive in a military sense. Despite that most adventurers

Shiv had met had some special skill or bit of magic which made them deceptively formidable... but no doubt the Baronet would have traded them all for half the number of mounted knights.

The one mounted knight Falcior did still have was nearing sixty years old, and although he sat tall in the saddle one could see the weight of the plate armour he wore made it difficult. Shiv shook his head lightly- the old veteran would be sweating and exhausted by mid-day.

"As I've mentioned to you all," Falcior droned on, now addressing the mercenaries (who began paying attention to varying degrees), "Not long ago we received word that a company of goblins ambushed a group of knights headed back from the front lines. Although Redlock is not, obviously, a high value target, it would be prudent to be on the lookout for these and other goblins should they approach our doorstep. I need not remind anyone here what a hundred and fifty armed goblins would do to our village of one hundred and twenty three people. Goblins are also known to attack by ambush or at night, and I do not wish to face an enemy outnumbered and unprepared. So I need the area to the north and east scouted thoroughly. Obviously if you encounter the goblin company, you are not expected to attack them, rather, bring back any information you can so that an attack may be organized with all of the forces at our disposal. In the meanwhile, of course, Sir Mortimer will remain behind, as will Captain Termann's town guards, to ensure our town is still safe. I will see you back here the day after tomorrow. You all have our good wishes, and may the Five Brothers fulfill your needs."

Falcior smiled and motioned several people to follow him, and as the townspeople dispersed the mercenaries began to strap on backpacks and weapon harnesses. The local priest of the Five Brothers, whose name had escaped Shiv, walked by in silver chainmail and multi-coloured silk robes, passing each mercenary with an extravagant gesture of blessing. He gave an extra few moments to the Hammerhand Brothers, perhaps thinking the similarity between the four half-brothers and their sister and the quintuplet demigods was more than coincidence.

Shiv ignored the preacher, straightened the strap of the lyre on his shoulder, and grumbled to himself. This nonsense was delaying the preparations for his show; he'd purchased a temporary pavilion tent for the occasion, and it was already set up just outside of the town walls while two local carpenters were building simple benches, props and a stage inside. There was a notice posted at the tent door offering to hire the town's six best musicians, and a local young tough was posted to keep curious passersby out of the tent and in suspense.

He shrugged to himself and began to saunter along a side road to the village's gateway, and quickly stopped short, nearly tripping over the little gnome with the top hat. The tiny hat came a handspan short of waist height, and he was significantly taller than his two female companions; as a passing thought Shiv judged he might be able to pick up either one of the gnome women with a single hand.

"Doctor Unfriendly, leader of the Wisps of Shadow... pleased to meet you- you are the one they call Shiv, organizing this magic show, are you not?"

"That would be myself sir; you are actually a Doctor of the University?"

"Yes, I am, and thank-you for picking up on the title, most of the locals don't recognize it. I have a well-rounded doctorate in Arcana and other mystical pursuits and am something of an amateur wizard... at any rate, I just wanted to express my relief at the new blood; last month my brother-in-law Lester was lost in combat with kobolds, and I'd hate to feel were losing this town through attrition. Good luck!"

Shiv had no time to reply before the tiny doctor whirled on his heel and scuttled away, looking vaguely like a badly made framework of twigs under a cheap robe. His two partners whirled with him and they all scuttled off as well, each clutching an iron-shod little staff which could not possibly be of much use in a fight. Still, gnomes were known to be resourceful and tricky, if rather strange, and they had obviously survived in this job for a while.

With a quick look around him Shiv shrugged to himself and walked out of the gate, hands loose, relaxed, and ready to flick knives out of nowhere in the blink of an eye.

The Hammerhand Brothers took the main road to the north by northeast- Ericstown was a half a day in that direction- and the group with the peg-legged Hillman headed southeast into some light forest. The gnomes looked briefly at him and started northeast, more or less directly towards the goblin battle lines. Shiv watched them all for a few seconds and then headed due east, into an area of heavier forest and rocky hills.

The area was pleasant enough- although Nesland was known for rain in general, this particular area was fairly dry, and it was a sunny day in early autumn, with the leaves just getting a thin edge of rust. He reached the top of the first large hill in only a few minutes (he stopped and judged the village was just out of bowshot at this range), and then started down the opposite slope into a loose area of woods. He found an area to enter with not too much underbrush and quietly stalked in.

Under the trees the breeze was virtually gone and the sunlight came down in thin beams; birds of a dozen descriptions sung loudly, and occasionally in the distance bushes rustled or a twig snapped. With the lack of a path and the rough ground, progress was slow but uneventful... the border of the official wilderness was supposed to be three leagues away, so no doubt Shiv would be right around the border when he stopped for the night. He planned to cover the area around his campsite for a day or so, depending on the layout, and then head back by a different route. If the Baronet wanted a more detailed search than that, perhaps he'd hired the wrong person for the job.

It wasn't long before he stepped out into an odd clearing. It looked to be a circle perhaps one hundred paces across where all the undergrowth had been trimmed down to knee height; in the centre of the circle was a lone hill with a single dead tree growing up out of it. Shiv frowned to himself. This was most peculiar... why anyone would keep a random area clear of brush was anyone's guess; he noticed a variety of trees from the area had also been cleared, and the long dry wood circled the clearing in neat stacks. So why was the one dead tree still standing, when the rest had been cut down...?

He'd been told once that when something didn't make sense, magic was often involved; while there seemed to be no wizards or standing stones or anything about, it was a definite possibility... with that he sat down cross legged, and took out one of his silver daggers. Humming quietly to himself, he pricked the end of his finger and squeezed a single drop of his blood onto the flat of the blade; then, balancing the blade on an uninjured finger, he let the weapon slowly spin in place. After a few moments, he noticed a glimmer in the droplet of blood; every time the red speck was between him and the hill, the light flickered. It was a trick he'd learned from a blade smith in the far-off Counciltowers; something about the nature of light he quite frankly didn't understand... but it meant there was magic there; a spell someone had cast on that spot years ago, perhaps, or maybe it was a grave of the faeries or something. He had no idea, he wasn't a wizard... but there was something there.

He climbed to his feet, wiping the dagger on the grass in the process, and then spun it lightly before it disappeared into the hiding spot near his armpit... and then warily he approached the hill. Nothing appeared to bar his way, and in a moment he was standing on the hilltop next to the tree. He paused, looking around for some weird spirit creature or a mystical glow... but there was nothing. He slumped a bit, relieved, and leaned up against the tree.

And fell through.

The tree wasn't there... it looked like it was, but his hands passed through it with no resistance. Feeling on the ground, there was a hole several inches across underneath the projection, and... inside, perhaps... tangled roots? He pulled his hand out of the illusion, and the palm was covered in black dust. He brushed the dry dust off, and it came off fairly easily, seeming like ashes or soot. Curious...

He felt around briefly, but found no other illusions- just the tree that wasn't there. Well, whoever had wanted a fake tree did not appear to be around or casting spells on him or anything, so he made a mental note of the location and continued on east out of the clearing and back into the woods. Apparently wizards had nothing better to do than waste his time.

He passed a small, fenced- in graveyard (the sign over the entrance gave the imaginative name 'Redlock Graveyard'), which he stayed the hell out of; and he passed a small stream where he took a drink and refilled his nearly-full water skin. He was on top of another hill when the clouds began to gather. At the bottom of the hill was a thick knot of woods with a heavy canopy of leaves. The wind did not seem to penetrate it, neither did the sunlight, and there were no birds singing in those branches. The sun came out from behind the clouds; as he watched the shadows play around the area he noticed the afternoon sunlight did not seem to even touch the thicket... no matter how the clouds arranged themselves, there was always one between that patch of trees and the sun.

He frowned and took a drink. This area was getting stranger the more he explored. Sighing, he sat down and pricked a second finger, once again doing his magic-detecting test.

The blade spun for a few seconds before it started to tremor and vibrate- he could see that despite the spinning- and then, while pointing at the woods, there was a tiny pop, and the spot of blood vaporized.

He leapt to his feet and stared at the dagger blade- the speck of black where the blood had been was burned into the metal... Shiv cleared his throat and decided that whatever was in that thicket, it probably deserved some privacy. He'd report that thicket, but if they wanted it explored, well, they could send the Hammerhand Brothers.

He stowed the marked dagger with a flourish, adjusted his hat and continued east.

Chapter Five

> *Gnomes: Gnomes are approximately one-quarter the height of a comparable human, but humans have one quarter the intellect of a gnome, so both species can occasionally get along if the humans aren't too stubborn. Gnomes spend much of their time ensuring the other species of the world don't kill themselves with their own stupidity.*
> *Doctor Unfriendly's Comprehensive Guide to Everything.*

Shiv found a larger hilltop with a clutch of a half a dozen trees on top by the time the sun was sinking; it seemed to make for a good camp site; he got his bedroll and miniature tent out of his satchel, and with practised ease quickly set them up.

He'd packed a few meals of trail mix and jerky and a skin of modest wine, and once he'd set up a campfire, he sat down near it, ate, and played his lyre. And when he got tired of that, he threw his knives at a dead tree, from his cross-legged seat, thinking of his boyhood. He'd thrown thirteen of his sixteen knives when he heard footsteps coming from the direction of Redlock.

He was up to his feet in a flash with a knife in each hand, peering into the darkness. It sounded like a group of several people; although there was no clear talking there would occasionally be a low murmur.

"Good evening, noble sirs," Shiv called out into the darkness. "It appears you have seen my campfire from afar... you are welcome to warm yourselves thereof, should you choose to do so..."

CAMERON S. CURRIE

There was no answer, but the footsteps seemed to speed up a bit. Shiv frowned, and walked over to the dead tree to retrieve his knives; he'd just got there when the first of them came into view.

It once had been human, no doubt... now its eyes had gone white, almost entirely rolled back; its teeth had gone ferally sharp and long, bared in a black-crusted mouth; its hands ended in sharpened nails and flexed constantly like they were practising tearing something. As it stepped into the dim firelight it sniffed at the air, growling quietly to itself. It took only a few seconds for it to unroll its eyes directly at Shiv, and the growling rose to a raspy shriek. It leapt towards him, claws outstretched, and one of Shiv's dragon-tooth knives took it in the eye, ice crunching across the monster's face. He sidestepped and the creature tumbled to the ground, claws tearing at the ice.

Four more of them came into view as the first one fell, spread out wide around him in a semicircle. They all glanced briefly at the spasming one on the ground, and in that instant Shiv threw his last dragon tooth knife in the throat of a second and his last cold iron dagger in the forearm of a third... the cold iron blades had funnel-runes engraved in them to drain out enchantments, and the ghoul's arm went limp. The two uninjured monsters launched themselves at him, and Shiv leapt to the side, putting the campfire in the way. The two glanced briefly at the fire, and one circled around it while the other stepped into it directly, its tattered rags smouldering almost instantly. Shiv's hand slipped into his belt pouch, snatched a small clay vial of powder, and tossed it into the fire.

The fire exploded and launched the burning ghoul head over heels, right off of the hill; the circling ghoul had caught fire and clawed what little clothes it had off, never stopping its advance towards its prey. Looking around himself briefly, Shiv saw the four fallen ghouls all climbing to their feet despite their injuries.

Shiv groaned and smacked both of his forearms against his hips, triggering the long, spring-bladed stilettos in his gauntlets; each adamantine spike was maybe a foot long and sharp as a needle at its tip, and packed full of every enchantment to pierce armour that Shiv could procure. Of course, the ghouls weren't wearing armour; at this point a splitting axe would have been preferable...

The first ghoul reached him and clawed across his chest, tearing the expensive silk shirt but not getting past the leather armour underneath. Shiv casually reached past the overstretched arm and stabbed the stiletto into the one remaining eye; as the blinded beast stumbled past him he casually plucked the dragon-tooth from the frozen face and kicked the beast into its closest companion, knocking the two of them down in a heap. The knife barely stayed in his hand a moment before flying into the leg of the burning ghoul; the leg burst into a spray of frozen red dust and that ghoul fell over as well.

Suddenly there was a tug on his cloaks, the limp-armed ghoul had latched onto the cloth with its good hand, and snapped at him with drooling fangs. Shiv elbowed it in the face and turned with the impact, following the elbow with a stiletto to the throat... it struggled and gurgled, letting go of the cape; then he tore the spike free and plunged it into the back of the neck, and again in the ribs. It fell over forward and stopped moving.

The one with the frozen throat had pushed its blinded ally off; as it struggled to its feet, Shiv casually walked over to the fire and selected a heavy burning branch. By the time the monster was lurching towards him Shiv was ready, and thrust the fire into the encrusted ice; it burst with a snapping sound, and the thing's head popped off and fell to the ground in pieces. It was a simple matter to do the same to the blinded one, and then Shiv was left in silence, listening to the crackle of the campfire and the dozens of smaller fires in the grass. He quickly stomped them all out (except for the smouldering ghouls) and then set about retrieving his knives, resolving to never throw away more than half of them in target practise again.

Shiv made sure the wiggling parts of the ghouls were burned thoroughly, and reluctant to stay near the foul-smelling campfire, spent the remainder of the night in a tree a short distance away.

When morning had come he picked out four of the thigh bones from the ashes, and resolved to make a few bone daggers from them- they could be enchanted to kill undead perhaps; he didn't like to be taken unprepared more than once. He mused in silence on the materials he might need for the undead-killing knives, and in the meanwhile wandered off further into the east.

The ground was somewhat flatter now, and the trees a bit smaller and sparser. Some of the wind had returned; he was sure he was near or perhaps just past the border, and decided he'd wander outwards for a few hours to make sure he'd covered the whole area, and then swing around in whatever direction moved him.

He'd been walking only a short while when it started to drizzle; his hat and cloak kept much of the rain off of him, but it still did little to help his mood. He kept to the trees to stay out of the worst of the rain, and had a certain amount of success; in the distance he heard the sound of a river, and decided he'd make for that, and then turn around. As he approached, the hill on one side grew steeper, turning into a vertical wall laden with bushes and protruding roots; the river began to come into view between the end of the wall and a series of bushes. The riverbed was very deep but only running half full, so there was a rocky drop-off twice as tall as Shiv before it touched the level of the water. He stood in the shelter of the wall and looked around for a few minutes when he noticed a sound like a small dog yapping. It was echoed by a dozen or more similar barks in strange unison. He peeked around the edge of the wall towards the sound and saw a rope bridge crossing the river, not far off, crowded with miniature shapes.

They were about half as tall as a human, scrawny like goblins but with scales, short, wiry hair, and toothy little snouts. A long, rope like tail twitched out of the rear of each ragged, heavy robe, and most of them clutched long, crooked spears. Kobolds. They were related to goblins, but seemed to also be part reptile and part rodent, with a nasty streak a mile wide. There were somewhere between one and two dozen scurrying across the bridge; although they were not deadly soldiers, most kobolds knew a few simple spells... not like a wizard or anything, but even a simple spell was dangerous when there were twenty of them aimed at you.

Shiv slunk back around the wall, and as soon as he was sure he was out of sight he began running back the way he had come. He'd done enough scouting in his own estimation, and now he was motivated properly he was sure he could make it back to Redlock by nightfall.

Chapter Six

> *Shiv Kobodan: An interesting human with approximately half the intelligence of a gnome. Probably the most personable giant I have met in this village, he might even be capable of conversing in a rudimentary manner. He has a morbid fascination with knives which would be an impediment in any career other than the one he has chosen.*
>
> *Doctor Unfriendly's Comprehensive Guide to Everything.*

Shiv sat at on a bench in front of his circus tent, whittling on a ghoul's thigh bone and occasionally dipping it in either a small bowl of holy water, or thrusting it into a small campfire of specially selected wood and incense. A frowning Baronet Falcior stood a few paces away, arms crossed. Slightly further away stood one of his servants with three unstrung bows and three quivers of arrows, and the Baronet's two young, pretty daughters.

"So, you saw no goblins at all, yet you came back here early?" the Baronet asked.

"Yes, your worship, your clarity of thought does you credit. Despite my overwhelming desire to throw myself on the spears of a platoon of kobolds and die a heroic death, my mandate was to scout and return alive with useful information-"

"Stop that flowery nonsense!" Falcior shouted. "A yes or no is fine!"

"Certainly, milord. A yes you ask for, a yes you shall receive." Shiv said, letting a tiny hint of smirk touch the corner of his mouth.

25

The two sisters whispered between themselves, and one of them stifled a giggle; the Baronet glanced over his shoulder and they were suddenly silent, if still smiling.

"And all you saw were a couple of shambling zombies and a few kobolds?! The Hammerhand Brothers could have handled that lot easily and kept looking for another day!"

"Alas, the aforementioned Hammerhands outnumber me quintuply-"

"Yes or no!"

"No, then. One or two dozen is not a few. And it was five ghouls, not two zombies. Ghouls are smarter, meaner and they can run."

"I think you're exaggerating. Anyway, you will not be paid for the three day mission, as you did not go for three days. No mission, no pay!"

"Not, milord, that I care about money," Shiv replied, dunking the bone into the holy water again. The water bubbled briefly and let loose a little puff of steam. "But perhaps the morale of the mercenaries might suffer were they to learn their pay may be withheld in this manner...?"

"Fine then, mercenary. You'll be paid, but mark my words, it is not wise to displease your liege lord!"

"I have sworn fealty to no one, nor was I born here, kind Baronet; and I intended no displeasure. At any rate, consider me suitably chastised."

"Father! Let him be for now!" chided one of the girls. She then turned to Shiv, and approached to within a few steps of him. "Excuse me, Master... Shiv is it?"

"Shiv Kobodan, kind lady, that it is; as for Master, only my knives need address me thusly... Shiv will do for you, or Mister Kobodan, if you cling to formality." He bowed his head slightly. She extended her hand.

"It is a pleasure," she said, frowning when he did not take her hand. "I am Recia Falcior, my father's heir."

"Indeed, a pleasure it is," Shiv said, smiling. He raised the half-carved bone in a rough sort of salute. "I regret to not take your hand, however mine is covered in the dust of the undead, and it would be a shame to taint your purity with it."

"Ah, I see," Recia said, smiling again. "Very gentlemanly... I hear you are putting on a show soon... could you perhaps give my sister Temma and me a bit of a peek?"

"Ordinarily, I give no sneak peeks, however in light of you and your father's hospitality, perhaps an exception can be made..." Shiv put the bone down alongside his shaping knife and quickly washed his hands in a bucket he had set to the side. Then he hopped lightly to his feet and snapped his fingers. A steel knife appeared in each hand, and he casually threw them up behind his back, so that they lazily dropped into the seat of his bench, each with a distinct knocking sound.

"As you can see, these two knives are normal, pointy, and no doubt harmful to human flesh- which is much softer than this wood..." He whirled around, scooping up the blades theatrically and, as he turned back to the Falciors, lazily began to juggle the two blades with his right hand. Slowly, he raised his left hand, allowing the loose sleeve to slide down somewhat, revealing the black leather armour underneath. "This armour I wear is called Handspan armour; I won it in a knife-fight with six Si-Anarhan assassins... apparently it was enchanted in the Pharaoh's own court. It is called Handspan armour because although it appears of regular thickness, it functions..."

The two knives flew through the air to drop mid-juggle into his forearm, each blade buried right up to the grip. Both of the princesses screeched out and jumped.

"... as if it were a handspan thick." Shiv smiled casually and tugged one of the knives out, showing the blade was more than long enough to go through both his arm and a layer of leather with an inch or two to spare... yet the matching knife, still buried in the armour, did not protrude from the far side of his arm. The sharp steel knife spun and vanished with a flourish, and then he casually drew out the remaining one, and held his arm out. The armour showed no marks to indicate it had been pierced at all. The two ladies laughed and clapped their hands, and Shiv bowed, the remaining knife disappearing somehow in the process.

"What if you are attacked with a blade more than a handspan long?" said the Baronet, suddenly stepping forward and drawing his long sword. The point hovered in front of Shiv's chest, Falcior smirking behind it. Shiv smiled coolly back at him.

"Perhaps I would have to take other actions to defend myself, milord. If I could not do that, you probably would not have seen fit to hire me."

Falcior continued to smirk, but sheathed the sword and nodded. "Of course."

Shiv sat back down and scooped up the bone and knife, much to the disappointment of the two women, and began shaping the bone once more.

"I think that the thing you'll find most remarkable about the Magic Circus, is that with the exception of what I carry with me when I travel, all of the entertainment will come from your own village... suitably enhanced, of course. I like to think that when I leave a place it has become inherently more entertaining than when I arrived." he smiled broadly at the nobles, his attention now divided between his work and the conversation.

"So, Mister Kobodan, are you some kind of wizard?" Temma asked. "We have a wizard in town, Zimmiman, you may have seen- the Hillman with only one leg?"

"No, no..." Shiv chuckled. "I have learned a few tricks from a few wizards, but my abilities are much more humble. I know everything there is to know about knives, and perhaps a few simple illusions, apprentice level magic really. Most of my tricks are sleight of hand and so forth... I imagine part of the fun is telling which is which."

"I see," Temma replied, exchanging uncertain looks with her sister. "Well thank-you for your time then, Mister Kobodan. And good luck with your show, we will certainly be among your audience."

The two both smiled broadly and turned, walking off with their servant. The Baronet stood watching him intently for a moment, hand resting on the hilt of his sword.

"Don't get any ideas about my daughters, Kobodan. The last traveller with designs on one of them left Redlock with a very high pitched voice." He watched Shiv for a moment, expecting a reaction. When he didn't get one, he spun on his heel and stalked off. "Tomorrow when the others are all here I expect to see you in the square!"

Shiv shook his head as the Falcior walked away, and kept working on his new knife. He had dealt with worse than Falcior before, and he would do so again. He blew the dust off of the emerging knife shape, regarded it for a moment, and then retrieved a slender file, and began sharpening.

Chapter Seven

> *Human Mating Rituals: One of the strangest things about humans... apparently most of these rituals are consensual, with the male as the aggressor. By civilized standards, they are nearly uninterested in mating, with even married couples only partaking once every two or three days. No wonder human females are so touchy.*
> *Doctor Unfriendly's Comprehensive Guide to Everything.*

Despite orders to meet in the town square, upon arriving- last- the Hammerhand Brothers led everyone into the Tortoise Toe Inn, where Julia sat down roughly to remove a stone from her boot and shouted to Mother Hammerhand for a pitcher of ale. Her brothers followed suit, dumping weapons and gear on the floor around the table as they did.

"Excuse me!" Falcior snapped as he entered the Inn. He stood beside the Hammerhand's table in two strides. "Despite certain opinions to the contrary I am the local lord here! Now do you have something to report or do you have an appointment with the stockade for your manners? Forrel?"

The brother in black plate armour looked sideways at the Baronet and nodded. He paused to catch his breath, then gratefully accepted a mug of ale from his mother, which he chugged down entirely before dropping it to the table with a thud.

"We found a gnoll caravan about a day out of the village; or rather what was left of it... the wagons were stripped, one was missing, and the gnolls and their animals were all dead... and butchered thoroughly.

We had barely begun to investigate when we were attacked by a pair of trolls. Big ones- I think a male and a female."

There were some murmurs among the mercenaries present. The female trolls were in general much bigger, meaner, and more cunning than the males. It became apparent that the Hammerhands had a number of fresh injuries; Thokk especially had a huge tear down the front of his bearskins which showed bandages underneath saturated with dried blood.

"They may have been waiting in ambush for us," Julia interrupted. "The female had a pole cleaver that nearly chopped Thokk in half before we realized they were there; the other three boys had to hold them off while I patched up Thokk's chest- he needs to see a proper healer by the way- Forrel killed the male after we got over the surprise- it clawed up his armour pretty good- and once I had Thokk up enough to move I shot her in the eyes with my crossbows." She raised one of her forearms, showing a tiny crossbow built into the armour there. "She ran off then, trying to pull out the bolts, and we retreated to get Thokk fixed up. Still, some trolls can track by scent, and I imagine she'll be after us once she gets those bolts out of her face. She might still have one useable eye."

"I see," Falcior said. He gestured to a servant, who ran out hurriedly. "Very heroic, I'm sure... it has been some time since trolls were brave enough to come into civilized lands..."

"Trolls don't butcher their meat," the half-elf brother interrupted, "And these two were not carrying the remains of the caravan. The missing wagon left tracks headed north from there... trolls wouldn't bother with that kind of thing."

"Well, I hardly care about the troubles of gnoll ruffians. If Duke Ceborn wants to let them into our country from time to time perhaps he should deal with the trouble that results. I think the important thing is that if there were a company of goblins out there someone would have seen them; also, there appears to be a need for increased patrols. Perhaps the Duke will see fit to send me a few extra knights now."

There was a murmur of dissatisfaction through the crowded bar, which gradually dissolved into a murmur of ordering drinks. The Baronet left without another word to the mercenaries, instead busily talking to a small group of his cronies. Shiv sat down at a table by himself, and was quickly joined by the trio of gnomes, who all sat on the table itself, around the edges.

"And what, pray tell me, did you three encounter which the Baronet so obviously has discounted...?" Shiv asked, attempting to signal Mother Hammerhand, who was rather busy.

"A couple of giant spiders, a close scrape with a bear..." chipped in the smaller and younger of the two gnome women. She hopped to her feet and took a couple of steps across the table to shake Shiv's hand, or at least his finger. She had a pretty good grip considering her size. "Dorlah. I'm the Doctor's sister-in-law... and I'm the Wisps' investigator and locksmith. And I'm… a widow... " She kissed Shiv's finger like a man kissing a woman's hand and gave him a smoldering smile until Shiv pulled his hand free with a slight shiver.

"Mrs. Unfriendly," said the last of the trio, brushing her platinum blonde hair from her eyes as she accepted a mug of ale from Mother Hammerhand on a little tray, along with three egg cups. "The Doctor's wife. I'm the tracker and cartographer."

Mother Hammerhand left Shiv with a mug of ale and an annoyed glare. He ignored her and nodded to the gnomes.

"How giant were the spiders? Giant for you, giant for me, or giant for spiders?" he asked, attempting to direct the question to the doctor. Dorlah sat back down, cross-legged, gathering her waist-long blonde curls over her shoulders, and continued with the smouldering looks, giving Shiv the impression she was pondering what was physically possible and what wasn't. The Doctor laughed, seemingly oblivious, and accepted an egg-cup of ale from his wife with a grateful nod.

"Very good... well I imagine they would have not been giant for you, but they certainly were for spiders. They were bigger than a g'nome, fat, white and hairy. One bit Mrs. Unfriendly- I made her some antitoxin- and Dorlah speared that one, and I burned the other with an acid spell so it ran off. The bear would have been an issue but I scared it off with an intimidation spell I learned from Muuntig Greybard. He's an interesting fellow, from this area, actually. Master necromancer, Forest Nomad, creepy. Pretty old for a human... good spell though."

The others took no notice of the Doctor pronouncing 'gnome' oddly, so Shiv ignored it. He took a sip from his mug, briefly analyzing the taste in case Mother Hammerhand had put something nasty in it, and nodded, trying to picture the three gnomes standing off against a bear.

"I tangled with a group of five ghouls and avoided tangling with a platoon of kobolds," Shiv replied, noticing Dorlah's shiver and looking back to the doctor.

"Ghouls?" The doctor's eyebrows went up. "My goodness... did you save any bits of them? I could use something like that for one of my spells..."

"Of course, Doctor." Shiv replied. "I'm carving a set of bone throwing knives- you can have the leftovers if you can make use of them... come by my tent later, I'll gather my scraps for you. So, do you have any impressions about this gnoll caravan? And the kobolds?"

Chapter Eight

> *Human Length Measurements: Humans outside of Sabosland tend to use guesswork and approximation for measurement. The main units are the Staff- as high as a human can reach with his hands- and the Handspan- the span of a human's gargantuan hand as wide as it will stretch. Since humans vary widely in size, this is fairly crude. There are twelve Handspans to a Staff.*
>
> *Doctor Unfriendly's Comprehensive Guide to Everything.*

It was nearing midnight in the village of Redlock as a certain pair of tiny eyes peered through the forest. The eyes reflected the lantern lights from a fair distance away, but if the occasional guard saw the little yellow spots he would probably mistake them for the eyes of an owl or some other nighttime bird. So the eyes peered from an open spot high in a pine tree well within bowshot, noting the small hill-fort and the black stone well which the town had grown up around. The looker took notice of the wooden walls, and how there were, as usual, two guards on patrol, walking the perimeter of the wall holding a lantern, and one on the tower of the hill-fort with a large beacon lantern, shining its wide beam across the town or occasionally into the woods. When the eyes had seen enough, their owner climbed down the tree nimbly to join his two companions, who were vacating trees of their own.

The three of them- short, wiry, and armed only with short bows and daggers- scuttled deeper into the forest where they were soon met by three other groups of scouts; a few minutes after that, the reformed squad of scouts joined up with the other three squads of their platoon.

They walked perhaps another mile before they ran into the first sentry. Although they couldn't see his companions, they knew he would have two of them within eyeshot, and those would each have another in eyeshot, so that the whole squad was nearby but hidden. They all had their own bows and good night vision, so that no one could approach the old mine without getting shot by a dozen different guards.

The mine had been abandoned decades ago and the entrance was entirely grown over with brush; the invaders had cut away the brush, but then wove it back together, into a sort of rickety door. Someone unaware could walk past within arms' reach and never see anything out of the ordinary, barring an abandoned mine cart, which had been sitting so long undisturbed it was grown over with wild flowers that camouflaged the brightly coloured rust.

Of course it helped that they had circled partway around the village, not coming from the northeast but from the south. They had watched with amusement as the patrols had walked by in exactly the wrong direction, then had continued on patrols of their own.

The scout platoon made all the correct signals and walked through undisturbed, the last scout carefully closing the camouflaged door behind him. There was only one chamber in the mine of any size, and that was taken by the officers, so each platoon had laid claim to a particular tunnel, and lay camped awkwardly along one side of it among ratty blankets, garbage, and sacks of scavenged supplies. The scouts had to travel through two platoons of shock troopers to reach the officer's chamber. The heavier troopers were somewhat bigger, and had passable armour, wooden shields, sharp spears, and an assortment of hatchets, knives and clubs as backup weapons. Most of the troopers were eating or playing with dice; a few were making new arrows or sharpening blades.

They did not speak the local language; every so often one of the troopers would say a few harsh syllables in greeting or challenge. As the scouts entered the large chamber, the six officers looked up from the raw remains of a butchered pack animal. Some of the officers spoke in the 'civilized' languages, but they still favoured Ybonnis, the speech they had been raised with.

SHIV

The scout sergeant walked to a point just out of arm's reach of the lead officer and bowed low, his chin touching the floor to the left of his ragged goblin toenails; when the officer nodded, the sergeant half raised and spat several nasty-sounding words in report. Roughly translated, they were:

"Captain, we have an armed goblin for every adult human in the village. Their children are not trained for combat, so we can just kill them after the soldiers are dead."

Chapter Nine

Dwarves: Dwarves are an even odder species than humans. They are about three times a gnome's height, and weigh significantly more than a human. They have an obsession with all forms of craftsmanship, especially those which involve metal or stone. Dwarves tend to be fairly religious, in the sense that most religions have sacrilege, which makes swearing better.
            Doctor Unfriendly's Comprehensive Guide to Everything.

Shiv sat on the stump in front of his tent and had a cork target set into the side of a small haystack. Absent-mindedly he twirled his new bone knives in between his fingers as he chatted with Zimmiman, the town's wizard, and Doctor Unfriendly.

"Eventually," he said, casually flicking one of the knives thirty paces into the bull's eye, "I'll need some kind of undead to test them on... I've never done this sort of enchantment before- I just used all the best cantrips and tricks I know for fighting undead, and I'm hoping for the best."

"That's not much of a method, you know," Zimmiman said, his brow furrowed. "I know you say you're not a wizard, but certain standards must be met or any magical item won't function properly or reliably... I'm not criticizing, it's just basic thaumaturgic law."

Zimmiman leaned on his crooked bone-like staff and turned awkwardly on his peg leg to look down at the Doctor; the gnome was busy adjusting something inside his apparently empty hat, but nodded absent-mindedly.

"I comprehend your most valid point entirely, sir..." Shiv said, throwing another bone knife over one shoulder. It struck three inches to the left of the other knife, just outside the bull's eye. "However, my point is equally valid- I wouldn't know a thaumaturgic law if it snuck up and bit me. My method is to make it, then test it. If it is flawed, then I usually exploit the flaw in some magically interesting manner to make it explode, thereby nullifying the problem. Differing methods, similar result. And, coincidentally, mine does not require ten years of apprenticeship before I begin. I'm a knife smith, not a wizard, and I have little ambition for sudden changes in career."

The Doctor apparently got whatever was in his hat situated properly and replaced it on his head, concealing the tangled, horseshoe-shaped mess that was his hairstyle.

"Master Zimmiman," the Doctor said, now fiddling with a gadget built into his staff which spooled out lengths of thin cord, "I see both of your points, but considering none of us is likely to change we may as well give each other what professional courtesies we can for the good of the town. Can you find a method to test these weapons shy of actual combat, or not?"

"I'm not firing off spells against something I can't predict. That's all there is to it. I've made magical weapons before," Zimmiman said. He lifted up his staff and wiggled it a bit for emphasis. "They're full of destructive energy. I'm not going to unleash something like that by accident. Doctor, do what you like, but I disapprove of hedge wizardry like this. I suggest you bury all of these knives- deeply- before anyone is accidentally hurt."

Glaring briefly at the both of them for a moment, the one legged Hillman wizard seemed to challenge either of them to respond. Neither of them did, but Shiv threw another knife (over his other shoulder) to hit the target three inches to the right of the first one. The wizard shook his head, turned, and limped back into town, his peg leg tapping softly on the cobblestones.

"Well, it was worth a shot," Doctor Unfriendly said, finally getting the cords reeled back into his staff. "I think what you do is remarkable. I'm not experienced with undead stuff, or with enchanting weapons for that matter, but I can tell you theoretically the auras look about right to me."

"Thank-you," said Shiv, and threw the last bone knife high into the air behind him. The Doctor instinctively ducked until he heard a soft rattle; he turned and saw the last knife lying cradled across the grips of its three brothers. Shiv trotted over to retrieve the knives, checking them for any nicks in the blades. He normally avoided working with bone; it was far softer than steel and had trouble keeping a decent edge; but next time he ran into the undead, he'd be better prepared.

"At any rate, I should be seeing to the circus preparations..." Shiv said, nodding to the Doctor. The tiny gnome nodded back absent-mindedly, digging through a satchel he had slung over one shoulder. "Dinner this evening, then, as we agreed...?"

The doctor mumbled something as he scuttled off that sounded vaguely like an agreement, and Shiv smiled to himself before turning and entering his tent. The inside was circular and perhaps forty paces across; much of the outer edge was crowded now with stepped wooden benches the workmen had made. Laid out near the center was a collection of strange equipment he'd commissioned, and in the center of those, bashing one of the items on an anvil, was the Craftsmaster. The Craftsmaster was the town's dwarf merchant, the one who made or procured almost everything in the town; like most dwarves, he was about chest high, incredibly hairy, and usually in full armour. Shiv approached him to inspect his work.

"Methrone's ball-sweat! This doesn't make any sense!" the dwarf roared, spitting a large wad of phlegm to one side. "Master Kobodan- I don't make things that can't be used, and I don't see what use this thing has!"

The object to which he was referring was a sort of double saddle; one half-thickness saddle situated over another and attached by rickety metal rods about four feet long. One of the rods was on his anvil, and after measuring it against one of its brethren and against a paper drawing, he shook his head and began hammering it again, giving it three resounding strikes before plunging it into a bucket of water. Steam billowed out of the water in response.

"It has a use, Craftsmaster, and I thank you for your estimable patience," Shiv said, smiling mildly. "Have you started on the final piece yet?"

"Of course I've started on it," the dwarf said, taking off his metal helmet for a moment to shove his long salt-and-pepper hair back underneath it. He fished out a rolled up piece of paper from a tube nearby and held it out for Shiv's inspection.

"I cannot decipher dwarf plans, but the picture seems about right," Shiv said, nodding.

"Silveraxe's rusty backside- of course it's about right, you paid for the best dwarven craftsmanship, and that's what you're getting. Not my fault you're illiterate- except for those silly scratchings you people call writing... but I still can't tell what you'll use the buggery thing for."

"Well... that's part of the show, Craftsmaster... I'm sure when you watch it you'll see just how each of your contributions fit in. You'll be entertained on a level no one else here can appreciate."

"I should get in free, you know... Shibeth's golden spit- it's professional courtesy!"

"I paid you for your services, Craftsmaster, it's only fair you should pay for mine... at any rate, seeing as how you will be entertained on an extra level, you're getting a better deal than the others on admission!"

The Craftsmaster laughed at this, a deep-throated dwarven laugh which sounded like a wood saw.

"You're savvy, boy- I'd hire you in a minute if you were to take up residence here. Those knives of yours are almost as good as dwarven made... nasty enough for a throw down Tensorah's fanged pie-hole I reckon. You sure you're for the road...?"

"Of course, Craftsmaster- you have your trade, I have mine. Thank-you for the compliment though..."

They talked on for quite a while, the Craftsmaster making small adjustments to Shiv's special gear, the workmen pounding nails into the benches. Despite the dozen or so occupants, all were too busy to notice the pair of goblin eyes peering under the tarp on the side of the tent opposite the village. The goblin only looked for a few seconds, taking it all in, and then dropped the tarp back into place.

Chapter Ten

> *Half-A-Lings: Creatures much like humans, but half the size, they are mistaken for extremely short humans most of the time. Half-A-Lings have no society or country of their own, but live in human towns fulfilling niches no one else wants. They are good black marketeers and con men, and few trust them, but they are at least sociable and peaceful, for the most part. Redlock has one Half-A-Ling: Abner Cadaverous, the undertaker.*
>
> *Doctor Unfriendly's Comprehensive Guide to Everything.*

The gnomes lived in what appeared to be a tiny house crudely carved from a large boulder in the less fashionable quarter of town. Shiv knocked on the square wooden door conspicuously mounted in the shoulder-high rock, and then waited until the door swung inwards. Standing there grinning broadly was a tiny gnomish boy who looked straight ahead at Shiv's knee. The tiny figure was taken aback for a moment before he looked up into Shiv's face and smiled even more broadly before shouting (quite loudly for such a small mouth).

"DOCTOR! THE GIANT'S HERE!"

Without a word he turned and left the door open for Shiv, and scuttled down a circular staircase, gargantuan in proportion to the little gnome's size. There was a commotion of furniture being shoved across a floor, a sound of breaking glass, and the Doctor poked his head around the corner, wild hair unrestrained by his normally present top hat.

"CH'KIVSELTEQ! WE CALL THEM HUMANS TO THEIR FACES!" He shouted over his shoulder, and then turned, smiling to Shiv. "Good evening Master Shiv, I see you're punctual... come on in... it opens up once you get down to the main floor."

Shiv had to sit down first, and crab-walk down the stairway; as it turned the main room came into view, and it was, as the Doctor had said, larger. He got to his feet at the base of the stairs after crawling out a tiny archway; although he could not quite stand up in the room, he could at least walk in a relatively comfortable crouch, and quickly spotted a human-sized easy chair at one side of the cluttered kitchen area. The rest of the room was finished in bright wood panelling, with a large stone fireplace dominating the one side. A large iron cauldron bubbled over the fire along with a small kettle, and in front of the easy chair was a wooden table covered in broken glass and surrounded by (proportionally) high-legged stools. Mrs. Unfriendly smiled apologetically and gestured at the table; all of the glass crashed into a neat pile in the centre of the tabletop, and then stood up in a roughly humanoid shape, hopped off the table and jumped into a nearby tin wastebasket. Shiv's eyes gaped in spite of himself, but he regained his composure quickly enough the gnomes didn't seem to notice. The gnome child was already sitting at the table with a miniature spork in one hand and a wooden sword in the other; beside him sat perhaps the oldest creature Shiv had ever seen... the older gnome was essentially wrinkles and hair wrapped in a leather jerkin; his tiny head was bald and wrinkled enough to be an exposed brain. Standing protectively behind the wrinkles and hair was a huge red-haired bat, which crouched over the gnome's head and hissed softly at Shiv as he approached. The gnome said a few sharp syllables and the bat promptly stood up higher and the hissing stopped.

"Hello, Master Shiv," Mrs. Unfriendly said, smiling. "Our son here- you probably cannot pronounce his real name- Little Unfriendly, and my Great-uncle Karl- ignore the bat- and behind you of course is Dorlah."

Shiv looked behind himself quickly and there was the sultry-eyed Dorlah in a long black evening gown slit up one leg, emerging from a doorway beside the staircase. She looked away from his rear end to meet his eyes and smiled wickedly.

"Hello again, Master Shiv... we don't get many visitors here as... big... as you. I hope you're comfortable...?"

"er... Of course," Shiv said, reaching the easy chair in two quick steps. It was surprisingly comfortable and he wondered briefly how they'd fit it in the door. Dorlah smiled and watched him for a few seconds after he sat down before stalking gracefully over to the table and perching herself on the stool beside him. She smiled at everyone briefly and then began studying his nearest leg like it would be the main course. "er... Little- pleased to meet you, and... you as well... Karl."

"Well, you may as well ask it!" the oldest gnome snapped.

"Pardon?" Shiv asked.

"Sooner or later everyone does, so ask me the first question you wanted to when you saw me. May as well. It'll save a lot of hmming and hawing later on."

"Errrrrr... how old are you...?"

"HA! I knew it." the wrinkles said with a cackle. "I like this one, he tells the truth. Well son, I fought in the Temple-land War when I was ninety-something. I was one of the first g'nomish bat-hangers when young Duke Ceborn fought the Ice War, led a full platoon of 'em... and I saw the Great Wall of Merchantston when they laid the final stone. Of course, they keep on working on the silly thing, repairing and rebuilding and expanding it ever since... gosh-darn silly bugger giants. Ooh, er- pardon me. Humans."

"That'd make you..." Shiv mused, "About six hundred...?"

"Good a guess as anybody's- kinda lost track myself... now no more questions about it, yeah? So, I hear you're some kinda knife thrower, 'zat right?"

"Six hundred... er... yeah, er, ur, yes I am, sir- a master knife thrower and knife smith actually. And an entertainer of sorts."

Steel flashed as two large, spikey knives sprouted from the table's notched surface in front of Shiv's knee. He jumped, startled, and the old gnome cackled, cracking his knuckles with a sound like a bag full of dice. He snapped his fingers and the two huge knives popped up out of the table, balanced against each other, and then walked as if they were legs back over to the ancient, leathery hands. They were big enough to be swords for him.

"I was throwing knives before your great grandfather was a glimmer in his great granddaddy's eye. I'll watch you sometime and see if you're a master or not." He said, before attempting to burst out laughing. His first laugh became a series of hacking coughs that took nearly ten minutes of Mrs. Unfriendly rubbing his back to subside.

During the coughing, the Doctor appeared at Shiv's side lugging a human-sized goblet of wine with both hands; after a couple of unsuccessful attempts to lift it to the table, he just handed it to Shiv, who tasted it and was pleasantly surprised. By the time Shiv put his goblet on the table the others had all been given mugs the size of shot-glasses full of the same wine.

Once Karl had stopped coughing, Mrs. Unfriendly trotted back to the cauldron and began spooning out bowls of some sort of sweet-smelling stew. As soon as Little Unfriendly and Karl got theirs they dug in with their little sporks, one in each hand.

"So, Master Shiv," Dorlah said, "I hear you've been an adventurer for some time... tell me about that."

"Yeah!" said Little, "What was the biggest thing you killed?"

"Well," Shiv said, nodding thanks as he got a human-sized bowl of stew. "That would almost certainly be the ice dragon... although there were seven of us that worked together against it. I made four of its teeth into my frost knives. By myself I fought a troll once, although I didn't quite kill it, I knocked it off a cliff."

The gnomes nodded appreciatively, and in turn each began to relate a story about some fearsome creature they had faced; Shiv was uncertain which, if any, were true, but they were all at least very entertaining. Soon the stew was done, and so was an awful lot of wine.

****

Shiv woke up in the light of a single tiny candle. It was on the other side of the room, so he had to squint to see what was hurting his wrists- there was a mark on the skin as if he had been tied up very tightly. He had the same pain in his ankles. He had an assortment of other mild pains across his body as if he had been doing hard labour, and felt a tiny but painful bruise on his neck. He looked down at himself and realized about half his clothes were off, and the other half were put on awkwardly, like someone else had attempted to dress him and not had the particular talent.

Dorlah sat on the edge of the bed- wide even for a human's- pulling on a tiny pair of slippers. She smiled at him, a trifle less wickedly than usual, and got up off the low mattress and walked over to the little table with the candle. There were two tiny glass vials, empty, standing on it, which she quickly snatched up and hid behind her belt.

"Er..." said Shiv, trying to sit up and finding his head unusually foggy, even considering the wine. "What... exactly happened...?"

"Nothing, Master Shiv. You got drunk so we put you to bed in our spare room. I'm sure you'll be fine in the morning." She smiled sweetly and walked gracefully over to the room's single door. "It'll be night for a few more hours- you'd better get your rest after all your hard work... You... must be tired."

With that she left the room, softly closing the door behind her, and Shiv stared after her, still drunk, foggy, sore and confused.

Chapter Eleven

> *Hold Potion: A simple drug I often brew for disabling monsters, it partially paralyzes the subject and often has the side effect of memory loss. My sister-in-law occasionally pilfers some of it due to a widow's needs... hopefully her subjects' memory loss protects them from anything... traumatic.*
> *Doctor Unfriendly's Comprehensive Guide to Everything.*

The next morning Shiv limped into the Tortoise Toe Inn, looking rather pale. Mother Hammerhand was sitting behind the bar looking over a heavy ledger.

"Hangover?" she said, smiling. "What a shame. My boys would like to see this, I imagine, but they're busy right now. What's wrong with your legs?"

"Nothing," Shiv growled, and he sat down gingerly at a table. "Could I just get some really strong tea...?"

She said nothing, but stepped into the kitchen and soon returned with a teapot and a mug and a small jar of honey. Before she said anything, Shiv dropped a silver founding on the table. She fished in a belt pouch for a moment for some copper, and Shiv silently held his hand up to her to refuse it. She furrowed her brow and frowned slightly for a few seconds, but then left silently.

Shiv poured his own tea, chugged down a cup with just a drop of honey, and then poured another. He sat in silence for a few minutes holding the mug, and then jumped, startled, when the main door opened up, admitting a tiny silhouette in a top hat.

"I... er... sorry about my sister..." the Doctor said as he approached the table slowly. "Apparently she swiped a bit of a paralyzing agent from my lab... I know g'nome women are a bit... aggressive... errrrr... you okay...?"

"I will be once I heal, I imagine." Shiv said, not looking at the doctor. He drained his mug and poured himself another. He sipped it in silence, the Doctor shifting awkwardly atop a tall bar stool.

"You need anything, Doctor..?" said Mother Hammerhand, emerging again from the kitchen.

"I... er... yes, that is... I'll get breakfast for both of us," the Doctor replied, looking at Shiv delicately. Shiv looked at him for a second and the Doctor stammered, "Whatever he likes."

"I have some ham left over from last night- ham and eggs sound good?" Mother Hammerhand asked, now looking at Shiv with a shade of concern over her usual disapproving smirk. Shiv nodded and smiled very slightly, and she retreated. A farmer Shiv didn't recognize walked in and sat at the bar, and she poured him a large beer on her way into the kitchen.

"A bunch of humans arrived early this morning," the Doctor offered, clearing his throat. "They had their faces all wrapped up in scarves- Forest Nomads maybe. They've been waiting at the main gate since."

"If they are nomads, they probably feel they have to be given permission by the Baronet to enter," Shiv offered, leaning back in his chair. "They're officially still at war with Nesland, even if no one has been killed in that war for three hundred years. Have they said what they want?"

The gnome shook his head, but before he could answer further, the door swung open and in strode the Baronet in full armour. Behind him a tallish man in furs followed, with a broad brimmed hat and scarves hiding his face, leaving only a glimpse of eyes uncovered. An iron mace hung at the stranger's belt, brown with dried blood, as were his badly torn clothes and leather armour.

The Baronet gestured to the large table normally reserved for the Hammerhand brothers, and after the nomad sat, he sat himself on the opposite side, and they began to talk.

"What are they saying?" the Doctor whispered to Shiv. "I don't speak much Traban. I'm better with the writing."

"Formal stuff, mostly... introductions. And... sounds like their summer settlement was attacked."

Mother Hammerhand scurried out to stand at the Baronet's table silently. At a pause in the conversation, the Baronet gestured to both himself and the nomad, and she nodded and returned to the bar to retrieve two tankards of ale. The farmer frowned as she ignored him and poured the two drinks, and then began to grumble as she passed him to bring them to the Baronet's table. She placed the drinks, unacknowledged, on the table, and retreated.

"Hey!" shouted the farmer as she returned to the bar. "Don't suppose I could get some service now? All I want is some cheap beer!"

"Shouting is not necessary, Mr. Ticksworth," Mother Hammerhand replied, gesturing for him to be quiet. The two of them received a quick, disapproving glance from the Baronet. "I'll get you a beer, although you already appear drunk. Early in the morning for that, don't you think?"

"I'm ruined... never too early to be drunk when you're ruined. A lifetime's work..."

Ticksworth was receiving irritated stares from everyone now, the Baronet and barbarian chief included. He appeared not to notice, and as soon as his beer was within reach he snatched it and began chugging, his free hand dumping a handful of copper ticks and slices on the bar. He drank three quarters of the drink before stopping to gasp for breath.

"You hear of anyone trying to sell cows or bring them out through the walls?" he said in between gasps. Several heads shook in response. "Someone stole all five of my cattle. The bull, two calves, all of them. How can I feed the family when my livelihood disappeared overnight?"

The barbarian chief jumped up from his chair and was beside the farmer in two steps.

"Fraw jai-esi... emmmm... I have seen cattles. Paar cattles din taki... em... elp please?" he turned from Ticksworth to the Baronet.

"Two cattle staked out," Shiv interrupted. The Baronet looked mildly relieved; apparently his understanding of Traban was also limited. Shiv stepped over to the barbarian, and after a short exchange, began to translate.

47

"He says that the spiders which attacked his camp were lured there by two cattle, each tied to a stake in the ground. They knew about the spider nest and how to steer clear of it, but apparently the whole nest was scattered by something, and critters followed the smell of prey right to the camp."

"We fought some giant spiders out on patrol!" said Dr. Unfriendly. "But what would agitate a whole colony of giant spiders?"

The Baronet rubbed his temple for a moment and sighed heavily. "Ticksworth, I'll see what I can do about recovering any remaining cattle. I don't imagine there will be many left, but no one would sacrifice all of them just to kill some barbarians for no reason. Run along and tell Captain Termann to double the wall guard and remain on alert until I let him know."

Ticksworth's face flickered between sorrow, hope and a dozen other emotions as he nodded and ran outside without finishing his drink.

"Master Shiv, tell the Chief his people will be safe inside the town walls," Baronet Falcior ordered. "They can stay in the barracks until we find them suitable housing. In the meanwhile, I'll tell Sir Mortimer to be ready in half armour should the spiders come any closer to us. Doctor, do you know anything about curing poisons? Your help with the barbarians would be invaluable. Mother Hammerhand, if you could send someone to fetch Brother Carrick and his clerics to help with the healing... and I suppose Rabboni Hareth as well... he may be a lunatic heathen but he can sometimes heal the injured as well."

The people scattered out of the bar in all directions following the Baronet's orders. Shiv limped along with the Chief back to the group of barbarians, getting more information from him and translating for whoever needed it.

No one noticed a pair of eyes looking on from a tree just beyond the walls. The scrawny little spy snickered to himself and watched as the two wall guards were doubled to four, and a half a dozen other armed fighters began strutting around the tiny village looking for trouble. As he watched he chewed on some leftover beef he'd kept aside for snacking.

Chapter Twelve

> *Creatorists: A group of priests, mostly human, who disbelieve in all but one god. Although this pattern of behaviour is not a widely accepted practise, it cannot be denied that they know something about healing and countering magic.*
> *Doctor Unfriendly's Comprehensive Guide to Everything.*

The spiders attacked at dusk, almost as if it was planned. There were two strains it seemed; the smaller strain was maybe a handspan long, but dangerous enough with their poison bite. The larger ones were, without the legs, as large as a small dog; with their fat legs splayed out they were nearly as big as a full grown human, and they had a poisonous bite as well. They were both shaggy, dirty white and grey, and had flat orange eyes arranged in clusters over their fidgety mandibles.

Shiv did not see the first one, but heard the alarm sounded as one of the wall guards stabbed a big one crawling over the town wall. With the one guard shouting, it was only moments before the other three guards on duty were gathering near the first, shouting alarms themselves and stabbing at spiders with their poorly sharpened swords.

Shiv arrived at the same time as the Hammerhand Brothers; Zimmiman the Wizard, who lived on that side of the village, had sat down in his open-sided attic and begun throwing fist-sized balls of fire into the torrent of approaching bugs. Each one burst a fat, hairy body into a greasy, smoking mess. The spiders had already swarmed over the walkway behind the wall by the time the Hammerhands began reclaiming it, every sword stabbing as rapidly as its owner could manage. Soon the walkway was clear of anything moving and spidery, although a carpet of the little ones swirled at the base of the wall and began to spread out to encircle the town. Other townspeople were emerging from their cottages, wearing bits of leather and brigandine armour and holding wooden shields, pitchforks and hatchets, and wandering about the village, uncertain of what to do next.

"Dammit," Shiv spat, seeing several places the smaller spiders had already got past the wall. "Everyone! Shut your doors and man the walls!"

Those that had heard him responded quickly; those who hadn't were prodded into action by their neighbours, and within a few minutes the wall had someone armed every few paces.

On the other side of the village, Doctor Unfriendly and his two companions were standing in the town gateway as the carpet of small spiders enclosed it. Tiny blades or crossbow darts sprang from the ends of their staves, and they soon were stabbing and smashing spiders as fast as they could. Seeing the wall was well defended now, Shiv ran through the village to meet them, each thrown knife pinning a bloated little monster to the ground. The Doctor had his staff in one hand, and was flicking the other like it held invisible darts; two or three flicks would kill a little spider, and when they got too close to him, he would smash one with his iron-shod weapon. One leapt onto his head, knocking his top hat to the side; before it could sink its fangs in, a shaft of bone scythed into it and it fell to the ground, twitching.

"They work on spiders," Shiv said as he took up his place with them. Two more of the bone knives speared into arachnid bodies nearby, and the Doctor nodded his thanks. Dorlah knocked another jumping spider from the air in front of him, just as another landed on the side of her neck. Mrs. Unfriendly swatted the thing off in a wet, red splatter; it took a split second for them to realize it was not all spider blood. By then Dorlah had collapsed to the ground, her eyes rolled back white.

"Master Shiv!" the Doctor shouted, swinging his staff in all directions. "I'm out of anti-toxin! Take her to Brother Carrick!"

"Where's that?" Shiv demanded, scooping up her tiny body in one arm, still throwing knives with his free hand.

"The damn temple! There's only one in town you idiot!" Mrs. Unfriendly shouted. Before she had finished, Shiv was running toward the steeple of the temple of the Five Brothers visible at the north end of town.

Shiv turned past the Inn and ran through the town square, towards the steeple. After the Inn were several smaller houses; as he passed one, a group of three of the larger spiders leapt off the roof and into his path. He flicked a silver dagger at one, which didn't die but folded up into a knot, trying to reach the metal in its flesh. Before he could reach another knife the other two were leaping again. Suddenly one jerked violently to the side; he was too busy dodging the other to see where it went and just concentrated on drawing a cold iron dagger from his boot.

"Bastard!" came a gruff, slurred voice beside him as two of the mercenaries emerged from a side alley. It was the two who had been with Zimmiman on patrol- the brute with the iron gauntlets and the short guy in the blue cloak. The big one had the missing spider by two of its legs, held squirming over his head. The little one pointed a finger at the spider squaring off against Shiv, and it froze in place. Shiv wasted no time in stabbing the cold iron into its back, and when it did not fall, he struck twice more.

The brute gave a loud grunt and a strange crunching noise came from the spider; he threw it to the ground where it lay twitching, two of its legs bent backwards over a weirdly contorted back.

"Gunther..." said the big one, stomping over to step on the twitching spider's neck. He gave a vicious twist and there was another wicked crunch. "And this here is Abner. Keep going, get her taken care of."

And without another word the two turned back the way they had come.

It was a short run to get to the temple, but in front of the double doors was a small crowd of a dozen or so people, either injured or just scared, and Brother Carrick stood in the doors in shining silver chainmail and multi-coloured robes, murmuring as he laid hands on a bleeding young boy.

"Brother Carrick!" shouted Shiv above the din. "Dorlah Unfriendly has a neck wound- she was bit holding the town gate!"

Brother Carrick ignored the shouts and finished his prayer over the boy; it was uncertain as to whether the bleeding had stopped, but the boy seemed less frightened at the least. Carrick stepped to the side and a blue-robed acolyte took the boy inside. Two or three of the townspeople stepped out of Shiv's way, but others barred his path.

"Master Shiv," Carrick said smiling and nodding as he beckoned the tailor's wife over to him. "The gnomes are visitors to our village, I must treat my flock first."

"Dammit, man! It's a neck wound! Most of these can wait!"

"All who are wounded deserve healing, Master Shiv. Both Pial and Dihijazin teach us this. Excuse me." Carrick began murmuring over Mrs. Tailor, who had no apparent injuries but looked shaken. Shiv, infuriated, began to shove his way through the crowd with his free hand. He was stopped by two more acolytes, one in a red robe, the other yellow, as they jammed their staves against him and shoved back.

"Carrick!" shouted a deep base voice from behind Shiv. He turned and saw a slender shape, an elf, in a shining breastplate that looked to be made of black glass. "The town is under attack! Get these people inside, and care for them there- we can't keep the spiders off them in the streets!"

"Yes, Captain," growled Carrick. The elf had already began to turn away, but his tone had told everyone he would not tolerate being disobeyed for even a moment. As he left he gestured Shiv to follow him.

"We'll take her to Rabboni Hareth." the elf said gruffly, and without waiting for an answer broke into a light-footed sprint that didn't rattle a stone or stir up dust where he stepped. Shiv had trouble keeping up, and Dorlah was looking awfully grey and still. He called after the elf, but the Captain just ignored him and ducked in between two cottages. Shiv turned the corner after him and almost immediately they came to a crude looking wattle and daub hut. A grizzled farmer carrying a sickle was waiting for them in front of the door, frowning.

"Put her on the table," the farmer said, and stepped in the doorway.

The room inside was a shambles, full of shelves which were in turn full of books and scrolls and knick-knacks. Shiv stumbled over a wooden chest inexplicably left in the middle of the floor, but recovered and placed Dorlah gently on the table.

"It won't be easy," the old man said to the elf. "She's a non-believer."

"I think the Doctor gave her antitoxin a day or two before the battle-" Shiv began, but was cut off with a dismissive wave of the old man's hand.

"That's nice," he grunted, and turned to examine her tiny, still body.

"Come, there's work to be done," the elf said as he grabbed Shiv by the shoulder and shoved him towards the door.

By the time they had reached the main gate, much of the fighting was over; they kept the walls manned for the rest of the night, however, and whoever was not on the walls spent their time searching out and killing the spiders which had hidden in thatch roofs and holes in the cobblestones.

Chapter Thirteen

> *Skyglass: A strange black crystal that elves use. Elves dislike iron and steel, and use Skyglass instead. Apparently it is made from falling stars and tree sap, although they do not share the process. Although it is remarkably hard, it is not flexible, and thusly more prone to breakage than steel items.*
> *Doctor Unfriendly's Comprehensive Guide to Everything.*

Shiv leaned his back against the black stone well in the centre of the town square, sitting cross-legged on the wide slab of black stone which surrounded it. He frowned to himself as he stared blankly at the front of the Tortoise Toe Inn. Doctor Unfriendly paced in front of him, also frowning, and the elf, Captain Termann, regarded the both of them dispassionately.

"I've heard strange things about this Rabboni guy," the Doctor said. "I wish you'd taken him to Carrick."

"If we had waited at Carrick's temple your sister would be dead, Doctor," said the elf, his deep base voice not matching his slender build. Despite the fact he was as strong as most fighting men, he was half as wide across the shoulders, and like most elves, weighed no more than a small child. "I don't follow the Rabboni's cult either, but he has healed me before. He's good at it, unlike Carrick. Carrick is best at presiding over weddings."

Shiv had remained silent about that; the Captain seemed to be a competent leader of the town guard, and had killed a dozen spiders in the fighting, but the Doctor had been specific.

"I wasn't aware this village contained any elves..." Shiv said, trying to change the subject. "Don't they normally lurk in a forest somewhere, growing orchards and dancing in the starlight or something?"

"Just me and my extended family. Four others. The Baronet's grandfather extended the invitation after I rescued him from a goblin stew pot. The town was pretty much just the fort and a dozen houses back then. And of course the well."

"Don't people normally dig a well after they need the water? Not much point before they're thirsty."

"The well predates the town. The Craftsmaster says it's two thousand years old."

Not sure what to make of that conversation, Shiv attempted to change it yet again.

"Doctor- Carrick said you gnomes are just visitors, but you have a house here..."

"Yes," the Doctor said and chuckled quietly. "We moved here six years ago and hired the Craftsmaster to build the house for us. Returning to the ancestral homelands, I guess... the townspeople don't consider non-humans residents no matter how long you've been here."

"I've been here fifty years," the Captain interjected. "The gnome is right. And Carrick is the worst of the townspeople that way."

Tired of getting into weird conversations, Shiv stood up and began to inventory his knives mentally. The two built into his gauntlets were still there, as were two in each sleeve, one in each armpit, two behind each side, two in each boot, two behind his neck, and the four new ghoul knives still stuck in his belt until he found a hiding spot for them. He nodded to himself, satisfied he'd recovered them all after the fight with the spiders.

"Well, Doctor, let me know when you find out about Dorlah; I have a show to put together for tomorrow night. You sure you have those things I asked for?"

The Doctor nodded, worry still on his face. Shiv nodded to the Captain, who nodded back but stayed motionless leaning against the well.

"My deepest thanks, then, Doctor- assuming your sister-in-law is well, could you bring the items to me at the inn this evening? I'll buy you a drink. You too, if you like, Captain."

They exchanged a round of nodding again and Shiv walked off, determined to get some sleep to make up for the all-night vigil. He changed his mind in only a few steps, and decided instead to visit the barracks.

As usual, the gate was open, and since it was daytime, the guard was beside it instead of up in the tower manning the lantern. Shiv bowed flamboyantly to the guard as he passed, and went into the small courtyard, now cramped with Forest Nomad tents.

Not knowing which one was the chief's, he called out in Traban.

"Chief! I'd like to ask you something!"

There was a slight scuffle from in between the tents and a scarf-wrapped face was visible standing up inside the cluster. He beckoned Shiv to approach.

The tents appeared to be in no particular pattern, but once he walked in between them he realized they were set up to look that way, guiding a possible intruder away from the open space in the center. There was a tiny area perhaps three paces across with a cook fire and a few logs to sit on. The chief was roasting what looked to be a small raccoon on a stick, which rested like a lever on a Y-shaped branch jammed in the ground. Shiv wrinkled his nose at the sight despite being fairly hungry.

"The sun is warm, Chief," said Shiv, again in Traban. It was a typical nomad greeting. "I have a question to ask you."

"The wind is calm," answered the chief, also in Traban. "I am Greybard, Master Shiv."

"As in Muuntig Greybard?" Shiv asked, "The famous swordsman?"

"And necromancer, you can say it..." the chief said. Somehow without removing his face scarves he gave the impression of smiling in amusement. "He is my great-uncle, and still leads a much larger group many days to the south. I am Faarbog Greybard, but we mostly use surnames except with trusted friends and family. Ask your questions."

"You sent two scouts with the Baronet's man to see about Ticksworth's cattle."

"Yes, I did."

"Were there any tracks in the area? Except for the cattle and the spiders, I mean."

"There were not. And my scouts are accomplished trackers. There was secondary sign, though. In several places heavy bushes were moved aside and then back again."

"Did they mention this to the Baronet?" Shiv asked. Faarbog had loosened the lower section of his face scarves, and was now taking bite-sized bits of raccoon and sliding them underneath to eat, never showing any skin.

"They did," said the chief around his mouthful, nodding. "The Baronet wanted proof of something, though, not impressions."

"Impressions of what exactly?"

"Short people of some kind. Gnomes, kobolds, half-a-lings maybe. Or goblins."

"They couldn't tell more specifically than that?" Shiv asked. The Chief motioned him to pick at the roasted raccoon, and Shiv's stomach lurched. "No thanks, I just ate."

"No," the chief said. "They covered their traces too well. I suppose there is someone here who could read the sign better though... the Trapper would know."

"The Trapper?"

"The Trapper who lives in the village. He goes by no other name, but we have dealt with him in the wilds from time to time. I understand he lives beside the gnomes, under the earth."

"Under the earth? What, is he another gnome?"

"No," laughed Faarbog. "No, he's not a gnome, and I wouldn't suggest that to him either. He's a kobold."

Chapter Fourteen

> *Giant Spiders: Disgusting creatures which eat any wet parts of any creature they can catch, unlike the regular-sized spiders which I am led to believe only drink bodily fluids. Their poison is useful in certain potions, and the Wizard Zimmiman made a particularly large one's leg into a magic staff.*
> *Doctor Unfriendly's Comprehensive Guide to Everything.*

Shiv walked along the cobblestones shaking his head. This little village was getting stranger and stranger... it was rare to have anything but humans in a hamlet of this size, but a kobold! That was a new level of strange. Kobolds were not far removed from goblins, perhaps not really at war with Nesland, but smaller, meaner, and more inventive. Shiv was surprised they'd let one in the village at all, let alone to settle.

The Doctor had confirmed directions to the Kobold's lair, and as Shiv approached it, he was not surprised he hadn't noticed it. Even less obvious than the gnomes' boulder, the kobold lair looked like a hole in the ground, with some compost and a few old boards thrown over it in a loose sort of hood to keep the rain out.

"Hello!" shouted Shiv into the hole. "Urrr... Mister Trapper?"

There was no response. The only sound from within was that of faint dripping water. Shiv shouted a second time, and again got no response. Groaning to himself, he crouched down and started to scuttle into the opening. Inside the hole, it looked vaguely like a mine shaft; dirt shored up by bundles of sticks made up the ceiling and walls. Shiv carefully crab-walked down the sloping passage; it was long and curving, so soon he'd lost sight of the opening at the top, and the only daylight he could see was behind him, trickling around a curve in the passage. He fingered a belt pouch and found a candle, and murmured a few magic words and a pass with his fingers until the wick sputtered to life. Crab-walking with a candle in hand slowed his progress immensely, and it took several minutes to reach the end of the tunnel, where it widened into a small room, and a stone wall with what looked like a very civilized front door built into it. There was a small porch, a doorstep, and even a brass knocker. Shiv got up into a crouch, transferred the candle to his other hand, and knocked.

There was a subtle shuffling on the other side of the door. A peephole slipped open and a high-pitched, nasal voice called out.

"Who is you? What does you wants?"

"Shiv Kobodan!" Shiv replied. "On town business! I hear you are a skilled tracker and I need help checking something out!"

"You haves moneys?"

"While I am impressed by your philanthropic spirit, I'm trying to prevent an attack on the village. It's in your best interest to render assistance."

"But you haves moneys?"

Shiv grumbled to himself. "If that is the spark which lights your charitable nature, yes, I do in fact have money."

There was a series of mechanical sounding clicks, and Shiv looked up to see a trio of crossbows retract into panels in the upper parts of the doorframe. In only a glance, they were invisible. There was also the sound of a bar in the door being drawn, and a deadbolt being thrown, and the clinking of small chains being drawn back, and then the door opened slowly. The darkness inside was pierced by two small red eyes, followed by a waist-high dog-faced creature wrapped in leather armour and a chainmail shirt. The kobold screwed up its scaly face in contemplation as it regarded Shiv from the other end of a loaded crossbow.

"Where is moneys?" the creature growled.

Shiv rolled his eyes, and awkwardly contorting in his crouch, managed to retrieve a handful of coins from one of his belt pouches. He showed the kobold- it was mostly silver foundings and copper ticks, and one or two gold-coloured towers. The kobold reached out with his free hand, and Shiv jammed the coins back in the pouch.

"I have the money, my warm and inviting companion. Time is of the essence; let us adjourn to the scene I require investigated and we will discuss terms en route."

The kobold glared at him in silence for only a moment, and then nodded once and slammed the door. Inside there were sounds of thumping and the scraping of heavy objects across a wooden floor. Before he had decided how to react the door swung open again, and the kobold emerged with a bulging sack over one shoulder and the loaded crossbow in the other hand. He nodded Shiv back up the tunnel.

"If you startles me I shoot," said the kobold. He put down the sack for a moment to lock the door. "Arrow is poison. Hurts lots."

"Not the trusting sort I see," Shiv replied as he scuttled backwards. "Perhaps you don't entertain a lot..."

"I is enemy with Storm Kobold. He not sends kobolds into village but sometimes he sends others. Others try to shoot me."

They reached the surface and climbed out into the sun. The kobold pulled a ragged hood over his head, concealing his doglike ears, tiny horns, and much of his snout. His tail curled around his crossbow arm, so only a close inspection would see he was anything but a tall gnome or a half-a-ling. Of course, the loaded crossbow kept people from being too curious.

They left the village quietly, the guard at the town gate obviously familiar with the Trapper and nodding as they passed with a quiet smirk. The arrow-riddled bodies of dead and crippled spiders littered the ground, and Shiv picked his way carefully to avoid the disgusting mess. The Trapper showed no such qualms, and kicked any messy chunks out of his way with a clawed rat like foot.

"You says we discuss moneys." said the kobold, as if making conversation as they headed into the woods.

"Well a founding is standard rate for a day's labour."

"Pfft! Founding-coin for unskilled labour. Tower-coin for skilled. I am skilled tracker. Tower-coin."

"Pfft yourself!" Shiv scoffed, "Look, this will only take a few hours. The spiders should all be gone, two foundings."

The conversation went mostly like that, with the kobold nitpicking over small change and various details of the mission, until they agreed on four foundings, two copper ticks and a near-worthless copper slice. The slice, normally the sort of coin that would buy a piece of string or a small cup of water, the kobold argued over for nearly ten minutes. Despite the arguing they made good time through the light woods.

"Finally, we agree on the price," Shiv said, "So when do you suppose you might begin to apply your masterful skills?"

"Already tracking. You says we look for cow. Been trail of cow smell straight from village. Someone try to cover cow tracks, most gone. And spider tracks. Lot of them. No others though."

"I haven't seen you do anything. Are you perhaps embellishing your skills for the sake of some silver?"

"Pfft. I is smelling mostly. No cow parts left, spiders ate."

"I thought spiders only ate live prey." Shiv said, unsure as to where he had heard that. He did start to sniff though, and smelled nothing.

"Cow parts very fresh, lots of blood, spiders hungry, like blood."

"Okay, fine... so what kind of tracks does a spider leave?"

The kobold pointed casually at a tree as they passed, but Shiv saw nothing. He looked at the kobold, who was looking at him expectantly. When there was no reaction, the kobold hissed and dropped his sack.

"Lets he who has eyes see," the kobold said, and walked over to the tree. Shiv followed.

"What does that mean?" Shiv said.

"It from Creator book. I Creatorist, like Hareth. That why other kobolds not like Trapper and try to shoot. Now look close. See bark?"

The kobold laid his hand on the surface of the pine tree's rough bark. Shiv nodded. Then the kobold pinched two tiny, almost invisible notches and pulled gently, and a hand-sized strip of bark pulled away with almost no resistance.

"Spiders walk on trees. Have to grab with toes. Big spiders, heavy. Bark pulls loose. I looks for loose bark. Lots of spiders, easy to see." The kobold glanced at Shiv to see the expression of comprehension, and then retrieved his sack and walked on. Shiv poked at the tree for a moment, and then jogged to catch up.

"Well, I guess you know what you're talking about then, Trapper," Shiv said when he'd caught up. "So you're in a cult?"

"Pfft. No cult. I get shot, lost hand. Hurt bad. Hareth pray, Creator fix. Kobold goddess no fix, so Trapper talk to Creator now. No more talk about. There first stake."

The kobold pointed to a large, heavy stake stuck into the ground with a ragged, bloody rope leading to what may have been the remains of a cow's carcass. Not much was left beyond the bones and skin, but the remains were scattered across a rough area of flattened underbrush. The kobold walked over and knelt among the remains for a moment.

"Still no tracks from whoever bring cow. Cow not tie itself to stake."

"Very astute," Shiv replied. "I have rarely seen cows skilled in tying knots."

"If no tracks now, either they covered or never made. Yes?'

"Makes sense," Shiv replied, now squatting down beside the kobold.

"If not made, either thing fly or thing magic, yes? But nothing fly with cow that can also tie cow, yes? So either tracks covered or thing magic. What can cover tracks... Trapper can, but I at home then. Something smart, but good with tracks. Maybe good scouts."

"Well whoever stole the Ticksworth cattle got right into the village to steal them, and walked right out with them," Shiv said, attempting to be helpful.

"Saw cow tracks near gate, coming out, going into woods. But no thing tracks there too, just spiders. Spiders too dumb, no use rope. Cows too dumb and can't tie."

"Yeah, I'd figured that bit out actually."

"But covering tracks at village, people see. Take time, but only have a few minutes, yes?"

"That makes sense... at night the patrol passes there every few minutes."

"Then thing ride cows out. Cows no like riders, yes? Either good with cows or must be small." The Trapper began scanning the bushes surrounding the area, and after a few seconds pointed. "There. Yes, thing small. See?"

The kobold got to his feet and scuttled over to the bushes he had pointed to.

SHIV

"See? There branch bent. There leaf pulled off. Thing five handspans high. Crouching when hiding, when hiding tracks. So six handspans high."

He began moving dead leaves and undergrowth around the bushes.

"There... maybe footprint thing hide. Right size for goblin. Goblin scout."

"One goblin scout couldn't bring five cattle out by himself..." Shiv mused.

"Five goblin scout, maybe more, yes?"

"At least, Trapper. Never ridden a bull myself, but I hear it's difficult. One goblin couldn't do it."

"Lots of goblin scouts then. Yes?"

"Absolutely. And where there's a lot of goblin scouts around, there's probably an army. And you know why a goblin army would lure the spiders to attack the village? To soften them up for an attack. Soon. We have to get back right now."

Chapter Fifteen

> *Necromancy: The school of wizardry which deals with summoning dead spirits, animating undead creatures, and the manipulation of life force. Most civilized creatures consider Necromancers to be repulsive, as the grave-robbing habit would suggest. Redlock has one apprentice-level Necromancer in Abner Cadaverous.*
> *Doctor Unfriendly's Comprehensive Guide to Everything.*

The Baronet sat at his table eating a late lunch, frowning despite the good meal. He had a half chicken before him partially eaten, but since Shiv and the kobold had entered he had not taken so much as a nibble. His two daughters, as well as Sir Mortimer and two noblewomen Shiv did not know, also sat at the table in various stages of eating or distaste.

"So you say you saw signs of some goblin scouts, but no tracks of the larger army? A half a dozen scouts is hardly reason to interrupt me. Anyway, I did not order a patrol; I was planning one the day after tomorrow." He frowned and absent-mindedly lifted a chicken leg to take a bite, then glanced at the kobold, made a face and put the morsel down. He did take a large mouthful of wine.

"Your magnanimous lordship," Shiv said, exasperated, "I merely state that the Tracker here suggests the scouts could have obscured the tracks after the army's passage, and scouts are notorious for woodcraft. The goblins are no exception to this universal rule."

"I told you to cease that flowery nonsense around me, peasant. And in future the kobold will stay outside or go back to his hole."

SHIV

"You know, father, he does have a point..." began the princess Recia, nodding towards Shiv. Her sister nodded. The other nobles were watching in silence, except for Sir Mortimer, who had already finished his lunch and was picking tidbits from the plate of the woman next to him.

"Well, what do you suggest we do about it, then?" snapped the Baronet, glaring at his daughters. "I've fought in the field against goblins, but they've never come here before. Tell me what your vast experience suggests will solve this problem for us."

"Put the guards on alert...?" Recia stammered.

"They already are." snapped the Baronet. "You, Temma? Your big idea?"

Temma's mouth moved silently as if feeling for something to say, and she looked around the table at the others, who were all silent, before settling on Shiv.

"Sire, perhaps we could put up some logs across the gate," Shiv said, and all the eyes turned to him. "It's just a gap in the wall, and we know the goblins have used it already. We can lash the logs in place and move them once the attack is over."

There was total silence for a few moments, with the Baronet glaring at Shiv and the rest of the table either looking at the two of them or else pointedly looking away.

"GET OUT!" Shouted the Baronet, and he picked up his plate of food and hurled it at Shiv's head. Shiv ducked, and the plate shattered against the wall, sending chicken and gravy in all directions. Sir Mortimer stood, wiping his mouth with a napkin, and opened his mouth to speak. The Baronet flashed a viscous glance at him, and he wordlessly sat back down.

"Get out of my house, Master Shiv," said Baronet Falcior quietly. "You are not released from my service, but you will have to take your chances in the Tortoise Toe Inn, or sleep in a ditch for all I care. My staff will toss your belongings out the back door in a few minutes, after a thorough search to ensure you didn't steal anything. Take your filthy kobold with you. And if you EVER block up my gate, for any reason, I will have you hanged."

"Very well, Sire," Shiv said, backing slowly towards the door. The kobold turned and scurried out of the room. "I'm sure your plan of bullying young girls will cause the goblins no end of shrieking terror."

The Baronet stood, wiped his mouth, and then snatched up a knife from the table and threw it into Shiv's chest. Everyone at the table jumped, Temma screamed and began to cry, and Shiv calmly pulled the knife out of his leather breastplate and dropped it on the floor before retreating. He closed the dining room door as he left, and then caught up with the kobold, who was already shoving past the butler to get out the front door.

"Thanks for the moneys," said the kobold quietly. "I go home to bar my door."

The kobold scuttled off towards the less fashionable end of town, retrieving the crossbow from his sack as he went.

By the time Shiv strolled around to the back door of the mansion, his mule Cornelius was there and a loose pile of his belongings lay scattered on the ground. Apparently they had a duplicate key to the chest in his room. He laid his own key on the doorstep, and began gathering his things back into the saddlebags.

"Psst!" came a voice from above. Shiv looked up, and the princess Temma was leaning out of a second-story window. Her face was streaked with tears, but she smiled feebly. "Thank-you for taking my father's anger on yourself."

"It was its own reward, my lady, I assure you." Shiv smirked in spite of himself, and checked the straps on Cornelius' pack saddle.

"Where will you stay now?" she asked, an additional look of concern crossing her face.

"I imagine in my circus tent, my lady. It is finished, and most of the preparations are complete; my show is tomorrow evening."

"But your tent is outside the walls! What if the goblins attack us?"

"Then I'll engage as many as I can to keep them out of the village," Shiv replied. The pack saddle was full and secure. "No doubt I'll still see you in the audience tomorrow?"

"I'll do everything I can to be there, Master Shiv."

Shiv made a slight bow and then walked away leading the mule. It took only a few minutes to tie him to a bench inside the tent, out of the way of the workers, and unload all the cargo. He passed an extra copper tick to the man he'd paid to guard the tent. And then he walked back to the center of town to the Tortoise Toe Inn.

He entered and saw the Hammerhand Brothers and their sister at the big table, and Abner, Gunther, and Farmer Ticksworth at another. Mother Hammerhand stood at the bar, putting away a tray of clay mugs. The Hammerhands all glared at him suspiciously. There was an empty table and plenty of seats at the bar, but he walked over and nodded to the three at the other table.

"Sit, Master Shiv," beckoned the farmer. Gunther was drunk enough to be drooling, but he made a vague smile in Shiv's direction; Abner nodded calmly, and Shiv got a good look at the face underneath the blue hood for the first time. Abner looked relatively normal, despite his extremely small size, but his left eye was solid white. Shiv suppressed a slight shudder, but sat down, and gave a slight wave to Mother Hammerhand as he did.

"Mister Ticksworth-" began Shiv, "The Tracker and I followed the tracks back towards the barbarians; I saw nothing of your cattle..."

"I was beginning to suspect that," said the farmer. "Thank-you anyway."

"If you like, I still can use a few extra hands to prepare for the Show, and I pay fair wages. A silver a day for most jobs."

"I shall show up tomorrow morning, and if you don't mind, so will my son."

Shiv nodded, and thanked Mother Hammerhand when she brought him a drink. He silently handed her a tower coin, and when her eyes widened, he just glanced at Ticksworth. She nodded and left without a word.

"So," Abner said, clearing his throat, "Did you see anything else worthwhile with the Tracker?"

"Yes," answered Shiv. "It looks like the goblin company Falcior was talking about is right on our doorstep, and they loosed the spiders on us."

"Well, that would mean they might attack any time now."

Shiv nodded, and then started as Gunther's head dropped on the table with a bang. Ticksworth and Abner both snickered.

"Well, hopefully they'll leave Gunther here enough time to sober up. If he ever does," Abner said. "You too, Ticksworth; you aren't far behind him."

"I have every reason to drink," said the farmer. "And so does Gunther, I suppose. What's your excuse, Abner?"

"I'm the undertaker. Do you really need to ask that?" Abner said ruefully.

"What reason does Gunther have?" asked Shiv.

"He was one of the first bunch of mercenaries to come here, him and four of his friends, all fairly big tavern brawlers, a year or two ago," Abner replied with a morbid smirk. "On his first mission all four of his friends got killed by a pack of kobolds. They were ambushed and apparently the kobolds knew some acid spells. It was pretty gruesome, from what I understand. The bodies were never recovered. Anyway, he quit the mercenary life, except maybe for the odd job with Zimmiman, and took up gathering firewood instead. He's been the town drunk ever since." He drained his mug and waved for Mother Hammerhand.

"And what's your story?" Shiv asked. "If you don't enjoy undertaking, why do it?"

"I'm a necromancer; I already can deal with corpses without getting sick, so it seemed natural. Anyway, I've been learning all I can from Zimmiman, and in the meantime making coffins pays for the beer. Zimmiman only knows a little of my sort of wizardry, so sooner or later I'll move on, find a better teacher, and maybe one day become a Master Necromancer."

Shiv nodded, and began to tell them his story; eventually Gunther awoke, and the four of them drank their sorrows away until late in the evening.

Chapter Sixteen

More Human Length Measurements: Although Staves and Handspans govern most measurements, humans have units for much longer distance. A Stone's Hurl, or just a Hurl, is approximately a dozen Staves long and is the approximate distance a human can throw a pebble. A dozen Hurls make a Jaunt- about a quarter mile- and a dozen Jaunts is a League, which is the distance a man can walk in an hour.

Doctor Unfriendly's Comprehensive Guide to Everything.

Shiv awoke on his bedroll in the circus tent. It was the day of the Magic Circus, and despite the sense he had of the village's impending doom, he was sure everything for his show was ready. His small tent was set up, open at both ends as a vestibule to the main tent. A large chest, full of his freshly made props, sat a foot from his head. In a bundle to his side lay the Handspan Armour, his freshly laundered clothes, his two belt pouches, his lyre, and twenty-two various knives, daggers, and stilettoes. Near that sat a smaller bundle, made of an old, threadbare shirt, which held sixteen bone-handled, rusty knives, coated in carefully preserved, dried blood.

He crawled out of his blankets and stretched the cold out of his bones, and then packed away his bedroll- with any luck he wouldn't need it in Redlock again- and got dressed. Ensuring his armour and knives were all in place, he strutted out of his tent to have breakfast at the Inn. The large notice posted near the town gate listed the show

CAMERON S. CURRIE

time at the fourteenth hour, just after dinner and perhaps an hour before sunset.

The early morning breeze was crisp and there was a slight drizzle in the air; although the clouds were dark and foreboding, there were a great many gaps full of promising blue sky. As he swaggered through the gate and towards the center of town he passed two of the town guards, as one relieved the other just inside the gate. He nodded to both of them, passed through the town square with the ugly stone well and entered the inn through the main entrance's double doors.

Mother Hammerhand was there, talking with her daughter Julia. Julia, like Shiv, was already in her armour, and unlike Shiv, wore her two short swords and two miniature crossbows in plain view.

"Good morning, ladies," he interrupted, as he dropped into a chair at a nearby table. "What wonderful repast is gracing the plates of those breaking fast this morning?"

"Good morning, Master Shiv," muttered Mother Hammerhand. Julia only responded with a low glare. "Just a kettle of oatmeal with apples today, I'm afraid."

"That sounds better than siren songs from Elysium itself, my lady. A generous portion and some strong tea would no doubt make my heart flutter in gratitude."

Mother Hammerhand frowned slightly, as if she had been tempted to smile and then didn't like the idea; she turned without a word and went into the kitchen.

"You know," Julia said in a husky voice barely above a whisper, "My brothers and I don't like you very much. You don't seem to take that seriously."

"Miss Hammerhand, to a traveller such as myself, a multitude of swords pointed at my throat is merely a common form of hello. Aside from the minor kerfuffle on the moment of our original meeting, I hadn't noticed any more aggressive greetings and had come to view them as your standard mannerisms."

"Very funny," she said, frowning, "I suppose you'll be leaving Redlock after your show?"

"Once my promise is fulfilled the road forever calls. Yes, my lady."

Mother Hammerhand returned with a tray containing a pot of tea, a mug, and a bowl of oatmeal. As she left it on the table wordlessly,

Shiv handed her a silver founding and dug in immediately. It was fairly tasty, with large chunks of apple and some kind of spice that gave it an interesting tang.

"And I suppose Redlock will just have to deal with the goblin army with our own soldiers," Julia said, "While you go on to Ericstown or Fort Sabosgate to make more money. Very noble, Master Shiv. I wonder why it is my brothers and I dislike you so."

She glared at him for a moment, and then turned back to the bar, brushing a long strand of red hair over her ear, and then attempted to appear busy, fiddling with one of the crossbows built into her gauntlets. Shiv ignored her as he ate, and after a few mouthfuls, Julia got to her feet and stomped out the main doors.

"You have a lovely effect on my children." Mother Hammerhand said, and returned to the kitchen.

Shiv did not allow their outbursts to bother him, and ate his fill in silence. After he was finished, he relaxed with his second cup of tea while he strummed lazily on his lyre and hummed to himself.

Chapter Seventeen

> *The Friendly War: The country of Talisman lies across the Inland Sea, which has been stocked by their wizard-king with terrible monsters so it cannot be crossed by those without permission; thus the superior armies of Nesland have never had clear access to their foe. Despite the lack of open warfare, the Friendly War has continued for more than a century.*
> *Doctor Unfriendly's Comprehensive Guide to Everything.*

The circumference of the patchy pavilion tent was lined with wooden benches, and all the benches were filled with eager villagers engaged in speculation about the coming show. A few stragglers were still filtering in or finding seating, hurrying as the two toughs at the door, collecting admissions in a locked box with a slot in the top, said the show was about to start.

The circle in the center of the tent, marked out on the grassy floor by brushwood and scraps from the extensive bench-building project, was marked every few paces with an unlit torch, and four small stools sat evenly spaced around the circle where the town's best musicians sat with their instruments on their laps.

The stragglers found their seats, and over a hundred eager customers' chatter rose in volume as the two toughs came in to stand on either side of the entrance. It was only a few moments after the tent flap was lowered that the four lantern stands spaced in between the benches ran out of their carefully measured oil, and the light grew

SHIV

dim. Conversation became even more frantic and yet decreased in volume as casual conversation was replaced by excited whispering.

Suddenly one of the torches burst into life- a flash that quickly resolved itself into a dull red glow; a few seconds after the next torch in line flared and dimmed to orange, and the third yellow. The drummer started up a steady, deep beat like a gargantuan heart as another torch flared green, another blue, and the last purple, completing the circle in weird alchemical twilight. A thin smoke from no apparent source blurred the half-darkness, and as the audience's whispers died to complete silence, so did the steady drumbeat.

There were a few moments of electric anticipation, and then an alien trumpeting sound lanced through the crowded tent- the door curtains parted, and in strode a gargantuan grey beast with a questing serpent for a snout and tusks as long as a grown man. A woman in the audience shrieked and jumped to her feet, and was pulled down and shushed by her excited family; a child or two cried in fear and were comforted on their parents' knees. The gargantuan animal approached the centre of the circle, reared up on its tree-trunk legs, and then thumped back down with another trumpeting roar. Standing proudly on a too-small saddle, a knife balanced on the point of each outstretched finger, was a smiling Master Shiv. With a flourish all the knives disappeared, and he waved to the crowd; those who had recovered somewhat from the appearance of the monster began to clap or whistle in appreciation. Shiv, still standing in the saddle, spread his arms and bowed, sweat beaded on his forehead as he concentrated on his most impressive illusion spell. Then he hopped lightly down to land seated on the saddle, and the elephant illusion shattered into a thousand shimmering specks just as he kicked the struts the Craftsmaster had made, and slid down into a foundation on the back of Cornelius, his humble mule. The applause rose, as much in relief at the disappearance of the elephant as from enjoyment, and the musicians started to play softly.

Shiv stood once again in the much lowered saddle, bowing again, and then motioned for the crowd to quiet down so he could address them, thank them for coming to his show; he knew from the excitement in their eyes the first trick had ensured not a one would ask for a return of their admission.

CAMERON S. CURRIE

****

There were four guards on duty that evening, one in the tower of the fort, one at the gate, and two patrolling the walls. Bernsten, the one at the gate, could overhear the music and thunderous applause leaking out of the tent, and once again cursed his duty to miss the most exciting event yet seen in Redlock. The miserable drizzle had continued all day, deepening his foul mood. He paced back and forth in the small gap, looked again at another outburst of applause, and attempted to curse again.

He found he could not curse, due to the arrow which had just pierced his throat. Bernsten tried to scream, but made no more than a low gurgle. He looked to the guard on the tower, and in the dimming twilight saw instead a goblin scout standing on the battlements next to a hanging line of rope, wrenching a spear out of something lying at its feet.

Bernsten took a few steps into the village, looking for cover and choking on his own blood. He felt another sharp pain lance through his knee, and he spun as he fell against the edge of the wall, impotent against the six goblin scouts who stalked past him right through the town gate. One noticed his struggle to crawl in the mud, drew a knife, and walked over to step on Bernsten's back. He felt one more sharp pain, this time in his eye, and was dead before his head was dropped carelessly to the ground.

****

Master Shiv strolled easily as he strummed his lyre, the other musicians providing accompaniment that, despite the minimal practise, was quite good. However Shiv was strolling across a tightrope, high over evenly spaced planks studded with old, rusty knife blades and sprinkled with broken glass. As he felt the tension lessen among the crowd, he pretended to slowly lose his balance, every part of his body swinging more wildly with each passing moment, although the strumming continued without the slightest interruption, even when an oddly placed foot jerked downwards. Shiv continued to play, this time upside down, and hanging from the tightrope by only one knee. The crowd applauded again, and Shiv let go with his knee, and flipped in mid-fall, landing gracefully on his feet, carefully in between the studded planks as his song came to a smooth, relaxed end.

****

Captain Termann slunk through the twilight around a loose pile of firewood, an arrow nocked in his longbow. Three steps in front of him, facing away, were another three goblin shock troopers with large axes. He let the arrow fly into the back of the first, and then dropped his bow and drew his sword with fluid ease. As the two goblins turned, Termann's black glass sword beheaded the first and parried the first swing of a battle axe. He kicked the goblin in between the legs hard enough to lift him off the ground, and before the screeching creature hit the ground it was silenced by a sword through the left lung. The elf scooped up his bow and scurried back behind the Unfriendly family's boulder, knowing other hostile goblins would have heard the high-pitched scream.

****

Mrs. Thomas, who didn't hold with entertainment of a frivolous nature, was gathering some of the last crop of apples from her family's tiny orchard when she noticed a movement in the branches above her. Thinking of the large white spiders, she took four steps back before the goblins dropped out of the tree, spear points leading. One of the goblins pried the basket of apples from her dead hand, and turned to the cottage where her two youngest children had just gone to bed.

****

Shiv stood tied to a large stake in the middle of the tent, and each of six volunteers took a turn throwing a short, heavy knife at him. The first missed on purpose, the blade hitting a board set up behind the living target... she walked away, looking rather squeamish. The second, Forrel Hammerhand, threw the blade hard enough that it sunk into the Handspan Armour up to its handle. Shiv laughed and taunted the next one in line to do better. Marvin Tailor got a glancing hit on

Shiv's left arm, the knife barely slicing into the leather armour and then dropping to the ground. The last volunteer, Julia Hammerhand, threw the knife at Shiv's unarmoured face; somehow he managed to slide one arm free, snatch the blade out of midair, and in the same motion throw it into the dirt a hair's breadth in front of her toe.

"Damn, I missed!" Shiv said to the crowd as the ropes slid off of him, his careful slip-knots going slack and falling to the ground. There was more applause, which drowned out the scream of a goblin dying on Termann's sword outside.

****

Baronet Falcior had not gone to the show on principle, instead dressing in full armour for a few patrols with Sir Mortimer before having a late supper. They had made several circuits outside the town walls, and having seen nothing, decided to return to the town gate and investigate the scream they had heard. Sir Mortimer's sixty-year old spine was already sagging in the saddle. Falcior sighed, and caught up to the old soldier's huge grey war-horse.

"Sir Mortimer!" the Baronet said, nearly having to shout over yet another burst of cheers and applause from the tent near the gate. He paused long enough for a brief glare in the direction of the circus. "Perhaps you should retire for the evening- I can check on the scream myself. It was likely just an accidental injury anyway."

"No, milord," said Mortimer, lifting his visor to reveal a wrinkled grin and several missing teeth. "I can deal with a few more minutes. Say, how many guards are supposed to be on duty?"

"Four, why?"

"Well, there should be one at the gate and there isn't... and there should be one at the beacon lantern in the tower, but I haven't noticed the light move in a while."

"True," Falcior said, although he was drowned out by a small burst of the applause. "Come to think of it, we should have seen more of the wall guards passing by now. Very well, we'll investigate the scream first- it was at the northeast end- and then the barracks are near there."

They both spurred their horses to a lumbering gallop, and rode through the main gate. Bernsten's body had been moved, and the drizzle had washed away much of the blood, so other than the fact the guard was not there, nothing appeared amiss.

Their heavy hooves thundered along the cobblestones, past the Inn, the Baronet's Mansion, and several houses to the northeast corner. The treehouse the elves lived in marked this corner, and was dark and silent. Considered the least fashionable part of town it also had the kobold's lair, the gnomes' boulder, and Gunther the wood cutter's shack and wood pile. Three goblin bodies were hidden behind the woodpile, but they couldn't see those in the dim light. All was silent, apart from the drizzle hitting the ground; there was no sign of the screamer.

The fort was in sight, so they turned to investigate that as well, when the sound of a horn pierced the twilight. Two short notes, one long- the signal the town was under attack. The signal repeated itself.

****

Shiv was juggling six burning torches while bouncing them off of three iron shields set up around him. Each torch would launch outwards, trailing fire, and set off a small burst of sparks when it hit a shield, then bounce back into his hand, and the trails and bursts of fire were setting up wonderful patterns of different colours and shapes, all in time to the musicians. When the alarm horn sounded, he nearly dropped a returning torch.

"What does that mean?" he shouted to one of the attending guards.

"We're under attack!" shouted the guard, both in reply to Shiv and in the line of duty. He stood up and drew his rusty sword. "Everyone in the town, and to the barracks!"

The Hammerhand Brothers jumped up and ran out immediately, drawing weapons. Most of the townspeople had daggers, knives and staves which came out as they also leapt up and in surprisingly good order, marched briskly towards the tent exit. There were four other town guards present, so that all five took up a lead position at the column of townspeople as the women and children were shuffled as well as was possible towards the center.

Shiv and his musicians gathered together, as did Doctor Unfriendly, Old Karl and the little gnome. All six torches leapt in turn from Shiv's hands to land in a nearby bucket of water. The small group made for the side of the tent, which Shiv slashed open with one of his steel-bladed knives, and as they hopped out they were joined by Zimmiman, Gunther and Abner.

"We have to get inside; the gate will be full for the next few minutes," Shiv exclaimed. Already it was obvious the fort had no soldiers in it, and several of the cottages had already been set on fire.

"Dorlah and my wife are still at home!" exclaimed the Doctor. He pointed his little staff at the wall and with a snapping sound a hook and cord shot out over the battlements of the fort. He scuttled up the cord like a spider as soon as the hook was set, and one by one they followed so as to not snap the cable. By the time Shiv got to the top, all the others had assembled, but the Doctor had run off into the rain, alone and unarmed.

Chapter Eighteen

> *Master: A commonly referred to level of skill, a Master has passed the point where he can learn much from anyone he can find, and now can earn a respectable living teaching his craft to others. Typically a Master has trained in and successfully practised his art for at least a decade. Master swordsmen or wizards are extremely dangerous.*
> *Doctor Unfriendly's Comprehensive Guide to Everything.*

In the courtyard of the fort, the Forest Nomad tents were still clustered, although more than half of the barbarians were still in the crowd of returning spectators, over by the main gate. Near the entrance to the fort fought a bloody Captain Termann, surrounded by four goblins with axes. His signal horn was in his off hand and his black glass sword blade was wet with goblin blood.

Most of the Nomads were out fighting in the drizzle as well, aided by the Baronet who was still on horseback, unlike the exhausted Sir Mortimer. All of them were surrounded, and there were nearly as many human remains as those of the goblins; clearly many of the villagers had died attempting to find shelter in the unmanned fort.

"Musicians! Get into the tower!" shouted Shiv over the noise. "There should be weapons in there- shoot at the goblins from up high..."

Old Karl whistled with his fingers in his mouth, incredibly loudly despite his withered, tiny form. Gunther had already dropped in among the barbarians, and was using a ragged goblin body as a club. Zimmiman had begun throwing fire into the goblins, each fist-sized chunk bursting a sinewy body into several pieces. Abner had already disappeared into the rain.

"Karl- you keep Little Unfriendly here with you, and stay out of sight!" Shiv said, and drawing two knives, began to run along the wall.

"Sorry, young fella!" shouted Karl, and a gigantic bat swooped out of the sky to snatch him up. "I got to rescue my nephew. Look after the boy!"

Shiv caught a brief glimpse of Karl arranging himself on some kind of harness hanging from the bat's belly as he soared into the drizzle, smoke and darkness. Looking over his shoulder, the barely visible form of Little Unfriendly stood wide-eyed and alone between him and the retreating musicians. Shiv slid to a halt on the wet stone, and ran back to the tiny child.

"Sorry, my friend, you're so sneaky I barely saw you there!" Shiv said as he crouched down. The boy was silent despite the tears on his face obscuring the rain, and motionless except for a panicked shivering. The knife in Shiv's left hand vanished with a snap of his fingers, and he let tiny boy climb into his open palm. "Come help me find your parents, now- sit on my shoulder and hold onto my hair... yes, like that. Here- put your leg down beneath my breastplate- it'll help keep you on there. Good... are you ready?"

The boy nodded hopefully, and crouched beneath the rim of Shiv's hat, as the giant ran along the battlements to the front of the fort.

"MASTER SHIV!" thundered the voice of the Baronet. "Get down here and help! We're surrounded!"

Two ivory knives flicked out into two of the goblins around Falcior, and they dropped, as Shiv in turn landed on top of another, each hand's stiletto buried in the side of another little monster. Shiv smacked his forearms against his sides, and the stiletto blades retracted, and he was instantly running out of the gate, scooping up the two ivory knives as he passed.

"DAMNATION! GET BACK HERE!!" Falcior shouted at Shiv's back. Despite his anger, he dropped the only remaining goblin near him, and rode over to help the beleaguered Sir Mortimer.

The Unfriendly boulder was only across the street, and Shiv ran up to a pile of bodies- three dead goblins stood tangled with the

SHIV

remains of Old Karl, the crumpled form of his giant bat smattered against the rocky side of his home and studded with arrows. Little Unfriendly shuddered, and a new wave of tears began with a wail.

"Shhh!" Shiv said, patting the boy's leg. He dropped to his knees and started crawling down the stairs into the boulder, and the boy's wail lowered to a whimper. "We have to help your father, too, don't we?"

The tiny boy said nothing, but Shiv felt the nodding in his hair. He passed up a tiny glass vial to the boy, and then whispered to him.

"Your father made that- it was supposed to be for my show. If you get really scared, you throw that as hard as you can at some goblins. That'll teach 'em to mess with gnomes..." he wriggled around the corner on his belly, and saw the main room in a shambles... books and broken glass covered the floor. He held a finger up to his lips, glancing at the boy with an encouraging grin, and then drew two knives and slunk into a crouch. There was a sound of breaking glass from Dorlah's room, behind the stairs, and a sound like a muffled whimper; Shiv shoved open the little door, and saw a small group of goblins- two held the Doctor up against the wall by his arms, and another group crowded around the bed, showing only the protruding legs of the two gnome women. Two of Shiv's silver knives lanced into the mass, and in response one of the two holding the Doctor let go to draw a small, curved sword.

The Doctor dropped most of the way to the ground; the goblin holding him was still twice his size, and held him up by the wrist so his toes scratched at the floor. The gnome struggled for a moment, attempting to get free, and then spat an unintelligible word and touched his captor with his free hand. The goblin held still for a moment, before twitching uncontrollably as black smoke poured out of his ears.

Shiv met the advancing goblin with a pair of black iron knives, parrying each sword stroke, but unable to strike back as yet in the cramped quarters. The three surviving goblins on the bed turned to meet Shiv as well, and were set upon by frenzied punching, kicking and biting from their would-be victims.

One of them managed to crawl out of the mess and land in a heap on the floor. As it got to its feet, the Doctor's hand, smoking and sparking, poked it in the eyes and stayed there until it stopped twitching.

Shiv crossed his daggers and pinned the goblin's sword against the wall, and while the creature struggled for a moment, he kicked it in the groin. Without pausing to finish off the creature, he turned and let one of the iron knives fly, pinning one of the goblins on the bed to the wall through the side of the neck. While it twitched violently and soaked the bed with blood, the two gnome women grabbed their last attacker, and began to bash its head repeatedly against the wall.

Shiv slumped in relief; the Doctor had a massive collection of cuts and bruises, but no serious injuries, and Little Unfriendly hopped lightly off Shiv's shoulder to run to him. The two hugged fiercely, and then turned to the two victorious gnome women and hugged them as they got off the bed, leaving the goblin with the broken skull in a mangled mess behind them.

They all took a moment to catch their breath and check each other's injuries, and then Dorlah extracted herself.

"This is twice you've saved my life, Master Shiv..." she said, her mouth somewhere in between a smile and an embarrassed frown. "I'm sorry I took... liberties with you before."

Shiv nodded awkwardly, but said nothing, and Mrs. Unfriendly shooed them out of the room as she retrieved a sword and regarded the goblin which was still clutching its groin. Shiv made sure he closed the door behind him before he heard the sound of the sword chopping into flesh, followed by a short but emphatic goblin shriek.

Chapter Nineteen

> *Hobgoblins: Goblins practise selective breeding, choosing the best-bred mates based on how high their social class is. Thus the upper classes become stronger, faster, smarter and taller, while the lower classes become less so. Hobgoblins are this upper class- nearly as tall as a human, they tend to physical prowess, cunning, and a bizarre honour system.*
>
> *Doctor Unfriendly's Comprehensive Guide to Everything.*

The four gnomes emerged from their boulder as Shiv stood guard nearby; although no goblin soldiers were within immediate view, the sounds of fighting now sounded over the village, and the smoke and glow of burning thatch and wood filled the air. The gnomes had got themselves armed with little staves, and the two women and the boy had all put on leather armour with metal studs. Little Unfriendly now carried one of the goblin swords, clearly far too big for him, and a little wooden shield.

"Master Shiv!" called the Baronet. He was still on horseback, and approaching with a badly wounded Sir Mortimer and a small group of the Nomads. "I trust you're done here?"

Shiv nodded, as did the gnomes, in response.

"Good. Then let us retake the gate, that's where most of the fighting is now, and many of the people there are unarmed."

They got back to the gate quickly, and a swirling mob of human and goblin combatants sprawled over the whole area. Some of the fort walls were visible over the rooftops, and Zimmiman and the musicians had gathered there, picking off goblin stragglers with fire or crossbow bolts, but avoiding shooting near the humans. The ground was littered with human bodies: men, women and children, who, despite being two or three times the size of a goblin, had been overmatched without armour or decent weapons. The Baronet and Sir Mortimer charged into the mass, each taking down several goblins before getting bogged down; Sir Mortimer was almost immediately impaled on a goblin spear and dragged off of his horse.

The gnomes stood at a distance, protecting the boy but throwing darts and minor spells; soon some of the humans began to break off from the melee and rally around them. Shiv dropped several goblins with thrown knives before four of them broke off to engage him with axes and swords. Slowly the goblins were being shoved to one side of the fight, reforming a sort of battle line just inside the gate. Although the goblins were specialists at surprise attacks they were not used to a prolonged toe-to-toe melee; humans who had been previously unarmed had begun to scavenge weapons from the fallen, and the goblins were being driven back slowly out of the gate.

It was around the time the villagers had begun to regain hope that several goblins started to climb out of the black stone well in the town square. Shiv was down to his last attacker, a little monster that was good with its miniature sword. He looked to one side and hand-sprang out of reach of a sword stroke, and noticed a group of goblin soldiers emerging and forming a circle around the well. Two goblins in heavier armour, with staves bedecked with various animal skulls, took up position on either side of the circle, and then began shaking their staves, producing a rhythmic rattle sound.

Slowly the fighters began to take notice and the fighting died down somewhat; the goblins outside the gate actually began to slink away from the fighting entirely, and the noise faded away, except for the rattle-thump of the goblin sticks shaking in time and then thumping into the ground- rattle-rattle-thump... rattle-rattle-thump.

The goblin soldiers around the well parted, and a large hobgoblin emerged, in hide and plate armour, with a curved two-handed sword over one shoulder, and a black iron helmet festooned with spikes. The rattles stopped.

"Nessslish peoplesss," the creature said, its voice harsh and raspy. It looked over the crowd, and stretched itself up to its full height- perhaps as high as Shiv's chin. "Thisss attack has clearly not worked out asss well asss I had hoped. But there isss something you should know. Already a sssquad of my goblins hasss left the village, with several of your treasuresss... and seven of your children."

There was a murmur from the crowd and one or two shouts. The Hammerhand Brothers pushed their way through to the front of the crowd.

"SHUT UP!" shouted the Baronet, glaring at his people. A short, wrinkled goblin emerged to stand beside the goblin captain, and whispered in its ear. The captain nodded briefly. When everyone was quiet, the Baronet turned. "What do you want?"

"We will walk out of here," replied the captain, "And when we are an hoursss' walk away, we will free the children. Otherwissse, they will be eaten."

"What if we kill you all and then chase down the kidnappers?" asked the Baronet.

"Can you chassse fassster than my sssoldiers can ssslice them? And killing usss all that quickly will be difficult; thessse are my bessst troopsss."

There was silence as the Baronet glared at the captain for several seconds. Then he loudly spoke a single word.

"Zimmiman?"

A ball of fire streaked out from the fort towards the goblin leader's head... and stopped a few paces away. Then it slowly drifted into the wrinkled, older goblin's outstretched hand, and hovered there while the miniature sorceror examined it curiously.

"Very well," said Falcior, and his shoulders slumped a little. "Since goblins rarely keep their word anyway..."

He raised his sword and charged his horse at the hobgoblin, who in exchange stood still and smiled, showing a jagged set of needle-like teeth. Three goblins on either side of him lowered spears, planted the butt ends in the ground, and watched as the horse impaled itself. It collapsed, crushing one goblin soldier beneath it, and trapping the Baronet's leg underneath its flank.

"Ssstupid humansss," said the goblin commander, half to himself. "Anyone elssse? Your children are getting clossser to death while we wait."

Shiv stepped forward and shouted to the crowd of townspeople.

"We need time to regroup and help the injured!" There was a murmur of anger from the townspeople. "We let these ones go and I'll gather a group to go out for the children!"

"SHUT UP!" shouted the Baronet from under his horse. "Look, they'll eat the kids anyway. ATTACK!"

The townspeople began kneeling among the wounded and gathering fallen weapons. Others helped up those that could move, and soon a path was cleared of bodies and injured which led straight to the gate.

"Townspeople! We need patrols to ensure all the goblins are leaving!" Shiv spoke loudly over the murmur of activity. "Groups of six or more, cover every street and building, starting with the far side of town! Hurry, we haven't much time!"

The Hammerhands walked over to the protesting Baronet Falcior, moving the dead horse and helping him to his feet. Shiv watched for a few seconds to make sure everyone was moving as best as they could, and then approached the hobgoblin captain.

"You'd better honour your word. You won't have the advantage of surprise this time." Shiv said, glaring at the little villains. The captain's platoon of goblins began moving slowly toward the gate, still clutching weapons and baring pointy teeth.

"Yesss," replied the captain as he passed, grinning wickedly. "I will. A Captain'sss word isss hisss ssstrongessst weapon. I'll sssee you in an hour."

Shiv watched the goblins scuttle out of the village as two of the Hammerhands helped the Baronet approach him. Apparently one of his legs was broken in several places.

"Master Shiv, if any of those children are harmed in the slightest," Falcior said in a low, steady voice, "I will personally see you drawn and quartered."

Without another word, the Baronet was helped back towards his mansion, and Shiv began to gather his rescue party.

Chapter Twenty

Hob-gar-est: The Hobgoblin honour system. A hobgoblin's honour is concerned with three things: the superiority of his race and himself, efficiency, and a legalistic form of honesty. To a Hobgoblin, lying only counts when you are caught.
Doctor Unfriendly's Comprehensive Guide to Everything.

Doctor Unfriendly and his sister-in-law stood by Shiv's side in the town square as the others in the rescue party gathered around them. Gunther and Abner Cadaverous were there, as was Zimmiman the wizard, the Kobold Trapper and two of the Forest Nomads. The Hammerhand Brothers stood guard nearby, in front of the Baronet's mansion, observing but not participating. There were no horses to be spared in the town except for one, which Zimmiman was sitting on; he had agreed to let the gnomes ride along with him.

"We need to hurry- the goblins are about twenty minutes ahead of us, and we have to catch up to them by the end of an hour," Shiv shouted to the group. "The Kobold and the two Nomads will track for us, Zimmiman and the gnomes will keep a look-out from up on the horse, and the rest of us will guard them. Let's go!"

Several of the villagers had finished checking the town and stood by to see them off; Captain Termann was guarding the gate personally (all his remaining guardsmen were on the wall). He nodded solemnly to them as they passed.

"My baby's name is Sherry!" shouted a woman from the crowd, her eyes watery and red. "She has red hair! She's too young to walk!"

Other shouts came from the villagers as well; a few of the men had volunteered, but Shiv and Zimmiman had felt only experienced people should go, in case anything went wrong or if the Hammerhands and guards needed help guarding the village. The party trotted ahead quickly, and didn't look back or waste time answering the cries.

Shortly after losing sight of the village, the sound of footsteps came from behind them. The Doctor called to Shiv and pointed backwards, and the whole procession slowed, alert.

Julia Hammerhand's red hair was visible through the trees briefly before the rest of her was, and she sprinted quickly into view. They all looked at her in mild surprise.

"That kid Sherry is my cousin," she said gruffly.

"What about your brothers?" asked Shiv.

"Through my father's side."

"Ah," Shiv said, and decided not to pursue the issue. Without another word, they all set off at a brisk jog.

The signs of the goblins' passage was obvious, now, even to those who could not track. The monsters had given up on all pretense of stealth, and in addition to the tracks there were gouges on trees from casual axe swings, and birds shot through with arrows and left to rot.

After perhaps a quarter hour, they entered the clearing Shiv had passed several days earlier: the empty circle with the hill in the middle, and the unreal tree.

"Hey!" shouted Abner, riding on Gunther's shoulders since he had run out of breath some distance back. "This is my place... I have to fetch something; you guys all run on, we'll catch up!"

Gunther slowed and approached the hill as the others left the clearing, apparently deciding unanimously that whatever Abner thought might be helpful was worth delaying him, but not the rest of the party. They all jogged on for a while longer, passing the graveyard (which had been terribly vandalized), and soon, Shiv felt, they were nearing the one-league mark where the goblins and their hostages would be waiting. They slowed down to a regular walk to regain their breath and to allow for Abner and Gunther to catch up.

"By my guess we will catch up in only a few minutes," Julia said, loudly enough for the group but not so loud as to be heard from a distance. The Kobold Trapper, ahead with the two barbarians, looked over his shoulder and nodded. "I think we should all have our weapons readied should we need them."

They all complied, except for Shiv, who knew his knives would be ready as soon as he needed them.

"Somethings is wrong!" called back the Trapper. "They has sped up and is running!"

The group sped up again in response to a slow jog. All eyes were now on the Trapper and the two barbarians. Footsteps behind them prompted them all to whirl around, but it was just the approach of Gunther, Abner on his shoulders carrying a long staff made from some huge creature's thigh bone, and a leather sack. No one bothered to ask what he needed the things for, and the two fell into place alongside the others.

"They is only few minuteses ahead," called the Trapper, "And they is running as fast as they can... they knows we are catching up!"

The group sped up as fast as they could as well, exchanging worried murmurs, but not daring to turn back or slow. They ran for nearly a half an hour, many of them panting for breath, before the Kobold held up a hand and began to slow. He signalled for quiet, and let the group approach him.

"They has slowed down and is just ahead. I hear their talkings and I thinks some childrens talkings."

The Kobold got down on all fours and crept ahead, his crossbow in one hand, into an area of bushes. Soon a lazy gesture with his rat like tail beckoned them forward. Apparently the goblins had not set up an ambush and were waiting for them.

"Psst!" Shiv hissed. "Zimmiman, Doctor! You stay with the horse and cover us with some spells. The rest of you, come with me and look intimidating."

The six of them passed the Kobold's hiding spot and into an open area between two hills. Just within sight, the tight thicket of trees Shiv had noticed several days ago lurked, still looking dark and foreboding. Between the thicket and the rescue party stood a military formation of around thirty or forty goblins, all with weapons out, in a half-circle around the group of seven children. The two oldest of them carried the two youngest, and they all looked terrified, and relieved to see their rescuers. They made not a sound, however, for the hobgoblin captain stood beside them with his wicked sword held ready to strike.

"Are you going to keep your word?" called out Shiv.

"Yesss, humansss, ssso long asss you keep yoursss." He nodded, and the youngest child who could walk started towards the group of rescuers, trembling. As she reached them, Dorlah Unfriendly took her hand and gestured for her to go back through the bushes to the others. One by one, the children walked back to them, lastly the two who carried the babies. Gunther took the two babies from the exhausted children, and then walked with the last of them back out of the clearing.

Shiv, Abner, Julia, and the two nomads stood their ground nervously facing off against the goblins.

"Well?" shouted the hobgoblin. "Isss our contract fulfilled?"

"Contract?" shouted Shiv. "What do you mean?"

"Nearly!" said Abner, drawing the looks of the whole group. He stepped forward, using the bone staff as a walking stick while he approached the goblin commander. He did not look at any of the rescuers. "Do you have what I asked for?"

The captain nodded, and about half of the goblins rushed forward, dragging filthy sacks on the ground. At Abner's gesture, they dumped them on the ground- piles of human corpses, in various states of decomposition- either brought from the town, or scavenged from the graveyard along the way. Abner dumped his own sack into the pile.

"What is going on here?" snapped Julia. "Abner, you little runt, what have you done?"

Abner looked over his shoulder, almost surprised at her shout. He smiled broadly, and for the first time since Shiv had met him, he pulled his hood down. His head was totally bald, his bad eye stark white and his good eye so yellow it almost glowed.

"Well, Julia, I had wanted the goblins to wipe out the village. But I always have a backup plan. All the mercenaries the Baronet has been hiring were too skilled, there may have been too many survivors. But now most of the best mercenaries are out here, aren't you? Now we can take you on separately, on our own ground. All that's left to guard Redlock now are two or three town guards and your brothers, and maybe half of the regular villagers."

SHIV

"WHAT?!?" Julia Hammerhand shouted, her face going red. "Abner, I've known you all my life! Why would you do that?"

"Oh, yes... that would be confusing to you, wouldn't it?" Abner laughed. "Actually Abner has been gone for nearly a year."

Abner's figure shimmered like the surface of water, and the heavy cloak and robes dropped off. Then the figure shook his whole body like a dog shaking himself dry, and the illusions surrounding him dissolved. Standing there holding the bone staff was a huge bluish kobold with a rough jade amulet.

"That's better," came the figure's new, deeper voice. "You see, Redlock was wilderness only a century or two ago. My ancestors built that well in the center of town. Right on top of their own little gold mine. The Neslish came and chased us away, but they never did climb down the well and find the gold... Anyway, Captain, kill them, and our contract is done. Oh- I almost forgot."

He lazily swung his staff over the pile of dead bodies, which immediately started to quiver. As the goblins began to approach, the chunks of flesh pulled themselves together into near-human shapes and staggered to their feet. The ghouls, like those Shiv had seen nearby, now outnumbered the goblins.

With the staff outstretched, the blue kobold shouted a few ancient words at the ghouls, and their eyes all turned to focus on the rescue party.

"Kill them." ordered the Storm Kobold, and then turned and walked towards the thicket.

Chapter Twenty-One

> *Ghouls: Ghouls are like zombies, except they are smarter and they can run. They have long, filthy nails and their teeth have grown into sharp points; none of these are used for socially acceptable pursuits. Rumour has it that ghouls are descended from humans who willingly hunted and ate other humans for sport*
>
> *Doctor Unfriendly's Comprehensive Guide to Everything.*

Shiv's ghoul knives flew through the air before another word could be spoken; each one exploded, blasting a ghoul to scraps and maiming a half a dozen others. Julia Hammerhand fired two bolts from her crossbows, putting out both of a ghoul's eyes, but not slowing it down; the pair of Forest Nomads hurled several of their tisken knives, maiming, but not stopping, two more. Gunther emerged from the woods, bellowing curses at the retreated Storm Kobold and brandishing his huge axe.

The Kobold Trapper put a single shot through the head of the wrinkly goblin sorceror. The twisted creature fell without a sound, although the captain beside him spat out a curse and flung himself out of the line of fire.

As soon as the sorceror hit the ground, a streak came out of the woods, shimmered at a point in the air just past the ghouls' heads, and exploded into a sheet of flame. Ghouls and goblins alike caught fire and ran around screaming as they blackened and fell apart.

The five companions on the battle line hesitated for a silent, stunned moment, and then a dozen or so of the ghouls clambered through the blackened carnage. Around the sides of the ashen heap, scattered goblins were visible fitting arrows to bowstrings.

"Retreat!" shouted Shiv, and the five turned and ran into the woods as the first arrows began to fall. A few paces in, they met the Kobold Trapper, awkwardly winding his crossbow as he ran; a few more paces and they came upon Zimmiman in an awkward stance with his hands over his head like claws. He dropped the odd pose as soon as he saw them, and fell in, snatching up his staff and limping along as fast as he could.

"Why the hell didn't you do that earlier?" Shiv snapped.

"Takes time to prepare, and had to wait for the shaman to drop, or he might have countered it. Also the aim was a bit tricky. Glad to see you got rid of those knives in such a beneficial way."

"Thanks," Shiv replied. They had caught up with the horse, which was carrying a heap of four of the children, including the two babies. The other three trotted alongside, occasionally nudging a slipping child back onto the saddle. The two gnomes were there as well, staves held at the ready as the group came into view. "They'll catch up to us soon; we can't run fast with Zimmiman's leg. Best make a stand here."

The arrows had trouble getting anywhere near them through the trees, but the ghouls were only a few paces behind, howling and trailing smoke as they clambered through the underbrush.

"Kids! Go on, follow the path! Dorlah, go with them, we'll hold the line here!" Shiv shouted, and turned just as Gunther's axe lopped off an undead arm reaching for his face. The ghoul, unperturbed, simply reached with his other arm, which met Shiv's ready ice-knife. A second swipe with the huge axe cut the head and a third of the body off in one viscous upstroke, spraying black goo and red dust.

Zimmiman's little balls of fire began to slam into ghouls and trees; the ghouls burned fairly well but the trees, luckily, were too green to catch fire. The Doctor threw smaller spells of his own, near invisible shimmers that shrivelled an arm or leg of a pursuing ghoul each time one hit.

The ghouls were beginning to surround them; although Gunther kept them at bay along the path with wide swipes of the greataxe, several crashed through the underbrush to either side much faster than Zimmiman or the gnomes could run. Knowing what was needed, the two Nomads met with the monsters on one flank with hatchets and tisken knives; one of them let out a gurgling scream after his first stroke, as an armless ghoul latched its teeth onto his neck. Julia and Shiv took the other flank with knives and short swords proving somewhat less effective than Gunther's axe. The Kobold had finally loaded his crossbow, and the bolt took a ghoulish head half off; the ghoul kept coming, smoke trailing behind it.

"Just thought you should know," shouted Zimmiman, still hurling fist-sized chunks of fire, "I'm almost out of these!"

"Me too!" shouted the Doctor, who now was swinging his little staff at any who got too close to Gunther. He took a chance at a glance over his shoulder, and was relieved to see his sister and the children were a long way off. He looked back in time to see sharp fingers latch onto his face.

The Kobold lopped the arm off with a little sword, and dropped his crossbow at his feet. The fingers kept digging in, so he dropped his sword as well, put his foot on the gnome's face for leverage, and yanked the claw off with both hands. He flung it into the woods as hard as he could, and turned back to see the Doctor's face a bloody ruin.

Gunther's axe lodged in a ghoulish spine, and immediately two of the creatures hurled themselves at him, pulling him down beneath them. Zimmiman swung his crooked bone staff at one ghoul, its face disintegrating with a loud bang as it flipped over backwards; then he went down as well as the next one leapt on him.

There was a sudden moment of weird silence, and Zimmiman's suddenly immobile ghoul was dragged off of him by the Forest Nomad. Gunther nearby was struggling to his feet from underneath two ghoul bodies which looked like they had been tied together with their own limbs.

"That's the last of them I think," Shiv said, breathless. Zimmiman looked around as he struggled to his foot; seven of them were alive but covered in claw marks (except the Kobold Trapper, who was inexplicably untouched). They all stood there panting for a moment, still looking for ghouls. All of the wounds were already infected with some kind of unnatural rot; the Doctor had only one eye left and it was badly swollen.

"So we won?" Gunther said, looking around for more ghouls.

"Well, except for the twenty or so goblins still after us," said Julia, "And the fact we are low on weapons and spells, and one of the Nomads is dead. Yes."

Shiv pointed at his knives each in turn as they flew back to hand; he was missing one of his silver knives, and his face was clawed a bit; the Handspan Armour had protected the rest of him well, but his clothes were filthy rags.

"We have to catch up to the little ones," he said, and ran off after them without a word. The others ran after him immediately, except Gunther, who helped the Nomad recover the body of his fallen comrade, and then slung it over one shoulder. Despite the weight of the body he caught up with the limping Zimmiman and the others quickly.

Chapter Twenty-Two

> *Moons: There are fully twenty-eight moons, although many appear rarely, or are hard to spot given their colour or size. They all have different cycles, appearing as much as once every few days or as rarely as once every fifty years or so. The moon highest in the sky at the moment of birth is considered a person's astrological sign, and each moon has a mystical link to one of the Stargods.*
>
> *Doctor Unfriendly's Comprehensive Guide to Everything.*

The group caught up with the children only a few minutes afterwards. The three walking children were too exhausted to run any more; and even the two oldest on the horse could barely hold the babies they carried. The procession carried on as best as they could, the adults taking turns carrying the babies despite being exhausted as well.

The goblins were waiting for them at twilight in the clearing with Abner's house and the illusionary tree. There were nineteen left, eleven of them archers, with arrows waiting in half-drawn bows. The archers had fanned out in front of the hill; the eight others had spears, swords and axes, and knelt in a line in front of the archers, ready to leap up should they be approached. The hobgoblin stood on the hill with an ornate composite bow of his own.

Shiv motioned the children behind them.

"I have to sssay you have done much better than I exsspected," the captain said to all of them. "It would be a shame to kill you all, you are worthy opponentsss... but I mussst be paid. Essspecially now that my army isss almosssst gone."

"What, pray tell, do you propose? You know we will not give up the children without a fight." Shiv said.

"Exssactly," replied the hobgoblin. "I have no doubt we would kill you, but I'd lose many of my goblinsss. This land is hossstile to my kind, and without an army I would never collect my reward. Ssso, I will let you all go ssso long as you leave usss your armour and weaponsss. Essspecially yoursss, Masssster Shiv."

"Haaa, of course, and once we were disarmed you could kill us without losing half your men!" shouted Julia. "No deal!"

"Have I not proven my sssincsserity? My word wasss good with our previous agreement."

"And yet the children are still not home safe," answered Shiv.

"Are you ssso anxiousss to die?" said the hobgoblin, shaking his head.

"The setting sun is at our backs and in their eyes," whispered Zimmiman. "If we are going to attack, now's the time."

"Give me a minute to confer with my colleagues," Shiv called back. They turned to each other and lowered their voices, one eye still mostly on the treacherous goblins.

"A half a minute, Masssster Shiv."

"Miss Hammerhand," Shiv whispered, "Your crossbows are loaded again. Can you take out two at once?"

"Maybe. One at least, but the aiming will be tricky if we aim to surprise them."

"Doctor? Dorlah?"

"We can each take out one, I think." the Doctor replied.

"Crossbows is loaded, one," said the Trapper.

"I have a stun spell left that'll delay one, that's about it," Zimmiman whispered.

The Nomad nodded and held up one heavily gloved finger.

"I can take two," Shiv said. "Aim for the archers. Children, run as soon as we attack. Redlock is only a mile or two that way."

"Masssster Shiv? Your anssswer?" called the Captain.

The answer came in flying metal. Six of the goblin archers fell, and one staggered back from Zimmiman's spell. The remaining four archers loosed arrows. Shiv was hit in the chest, but the arrow did not sink deep enough to pierce his armour's magic. Gunther was hit in the arm and dropped his axe, and Zimmiman took an arrow to his wooden leg. Shiv and his companions charged. Before they had taken more than a few steps, the goblin captain drew an arrow and shot Gunther in the neck; he dropped like a stone, gurgling blood. The rest of them reached the goblin line, clubbing with staves and stabbing with swords and knives. The goblin archers, unable to clearly sight their targets, stepped back to stand with the goblin captain, drawing their bows.

Julia downed a goblin with a sword to the throat almost immediately, and then faced off against another. The Nomad had somehow lost his hatchet and was grappling with one of the spear-goblins; despite the barbarian's greater size, he was exhausted, and the wiry goblin latched onto the his arm with both legs, the spear with both hands, and snapped at him whenever his teeth came close to anything he could bite.

Shiv was squared off against a goblin with a sword with which he was very nearly a master. His two stilletos together could catch the little sword's strokes, but he couldn't get past the blade or the goblin's shield to hit anything. The swordsgoblin was hitting the Handspan Armour with tiny jabs, never quite penetrating, but sooner or later he would, and Shiv had no room for error... over the goblin's head he saw the captain and his archers circling around them. A few seconds later he noticed one of the children, the little red-haired girl, standing transfixed, apparently left behind by the others. He glanced over his shoulder, realizing the captain would reach her in only a moment, and as he did he got a wicked slash across the side of his face, widening his mouth by several inches and knocking out two teeth and a lot of blood. He staggered back, drool and blood in one eye.

"CAN ANYBODY GET TO THAT GIRL?" Shiv shouted, immediately regretting it from the pain in his face. He parried as best as he could with his impaired vision; the swordsgoblin was big for his kind, nearly up to Shiv's shoulder, and the constant flurry of sword slashes was driving him back, away from the group. The goblin grinned.

"You magic armoursss can't cover you face, yesss?" it sneered with a chuckle. "I is bessst with sssword in thisss army. Have killed lotsss of human with more armoursss than you!"

Shiv caught the blade again on his crossed stilettoes, and the goblin suddenly changed his grip, sliding the blade forward in between the knives to jab at Shiv's leather breastplate. Shiv tried to steal another glance toward the girl, but the goblin was expecting that, and this time drove the sword into Shiv's forearm. The steel slid deep enough that it bit into flesh, and Shiv cried out in pain as it twisted and his fingers spasmed. The stiletto clicked and slid back into his gauntlet, and Shiv dropped to his knees.

"HEY!" came a cry from behind the goblin, who looked over his shoulder to see Zimmiman's shimmering staff meet its teeth. The swordsgoblin flew end over end, smoking, and landed on its neck a few feet away with a loud crack.

Shiv took a breath of relief, and glanced over at the captain and his archers approaching the little girl. He rolled and twisted into a standing position with acrobatic ease, despite the sword hanging from his crippled arm, and let one of his frost knives fly into one of the archers; one of the Trapper's crossbow bolts appeared in the forehead of another.

Julia was the first to place herself in the path of the goblins. Despite the fighting she had only two small cuts, both on one hip; her two short swords were bared and drenched in goblin blood. Several of the archers slowed at the sight of her.

She was quickly joined by the two gnomes and the Nomad; the kobold was reloading his crossbow, and Shiv and Zimmiman, despite their wounds, were approaching the goblins directly. The remaining archers, no longer having superior numbers, began to back away slowly.

The captain, furious, shouted at his troops and drew his curved sword, facing them instead of the companions; the archers paused for a moment until another of the Kobold Trapper's crossbow bolts knocked one to the ground. With that, they scattered in all directions, some dropping weapons in their haste. The hobgoblin beheaded one of them with a shout as they passed, but the others ignored him and fled in all directions into the woods.

The hobgoblin let out a shriek of rage and turned with his sword at the ready; he found himself facing six opponents. They were all wounded to some degree, but still moving and still armed. There was a moment where the only sound was the creak of the Kobold's crossbow winding back a short distance away.

"Perhapsss we can rene-" the hobgoblin began, before a goblin arrow sprouted from his throat. He dropped his sword, eyes wide, and grabbed at the shaft, coughing and choking.

At the edge of the woods one goblin archer stood, fitting another arrow to his bow, its face blank. It aimed carefully and waited for the captain to turn around, and then it let another arrow bury itself in the captain's eye. It watched the hobgoblin fall, and twitch on the ground for a moment. Then, without a word, the last goblin stalked back into the woods. The companions let it go, instead gathering around the girl to make sure she was uninjured.

They staggered into Redlock as dusk fell, meeting nearly the whole village at the main gate.

Chapter Twenty-Three

> *Healing: Most of the major priesthoods have some knowledge of healing, whether by supernatural or scientific means. The Stargod priests, such as the Followers of the Five Brothers, sometimes charge a fee, but prefer to exchange the service for a favour to be named later. Refusing to repay can result in the return of the original injury. The other religions- Creatorists, Druids, or Keepers- have different traditions.*
>
> *Doctor Unfriendly's Comprehensive Guide to Everything.*

"Funny how whenever a lot of people are injured, you're involved," said a voice, and Shiv opened his eyes. He was lying on a table, in Hareth's hut, only half clothed and awfully sore. The goblin sword had been removed from his arm, leaving a magnificent scar near his wrist and a less impressive one on the other side near his elbow. Somehow, the odd preacher had healed the injury, although, his other cuts and scrapes had been dealt with more traditionally. He had several small lines here and there made from cat-gut stitching in his skin; no doubt they would be extraordinarily painful to remove later.

Shiv slowly sat up, flexing his hands and arms as if to test them; it was not an enjoyable experience.

"You used some kind of magic to heal me, why couldn't you have given me something for the pain?" he grumbled.

"I asked Creator to heal you and your companions, and he healed what he would. And pain is a gift, it teaches you not to get stabbed so much. It seems you really need to learn that," Hareth said with a

CAMERON S. CURRIE

slight smile. "Your gear is in the corner, although you need to replace your clothes, they were kinda torn up."

The preacher was right. Shiv's shirt was torn in a dozen places, his outer cloak was covered in mud and blood (from whom or what was not apparent) and a large section was missing from the brim of his hat. However the Handspan Armour was intact, as was the large heap of knives on top of it, and the belt pouches with the remainder of his other gear. Shiv piled it all into his one good cloak and tied it together to make a sack, and belted on his pouches and two of his daggers.

"So, errr... Father Hareth, how much do I owe you for your painful but thorough services? I only have a little cash, due to my humble occupation."

"We use Rabboni, not Father. You actually carry a lot of coin, Master Shiv," Hareth replied, "I understand you may have noble uses set aside for it, I only ask that you give me what you think is right, and know that it will be put to good use."

Shiv sighed a bit, but dug in his pouch (there was nothing missing), and put about half of his coins on the table. It was never a good policy to annoy someone who might have just saved your life. Or who might again someday.

"Thanks, Rabboni... I'll make sure to mention you to all my incapacitated friends," Shiv said awkwardly, and limped outside with the crude sack over one aching shoulder. It was a cold, bright morning outside, his lack of a shirt giving him gooseflesh.

Doctor Unfriendly sat on a pile of firewood nearby, wearing an eye patch, with Dorlah and a gnome-shaped pile of bandages, splints, and possibly glue which apparently had been used to rebuild Old Karl.

"Karl! You're okay!" Shiv said as he approached. "I saw you all mangled after the goblins attacked, thought you were dead four times over!"

"Six at least," Karl rasped, looking at him with his one functioning eye; the other was swollen shut. "But I was pretty near dead twice over before the fightin' started. I got me two goblins at least before they nailed my bat, poor fella, when I woke up in bits an' on the ground I managed to grab one of the stragglers too. Little bugger squirmed pretty good, so I broke his cruddy little neck."

SHIV

"Good to hear... how about breakfast at the Inn? And beer- I need both, and I'm buying." The three gnomes hopped off of the woodpile, Dorlah giving Shiv's leg a quick hug before they set off to the Tortoise Toe Inn.

It was barely after dawn, so it came as a surprise that there were already a number of people at the Inn, and the only seats left were at the bar. Virtually everyone in the place was injured, the Baronet especially was heavily wrapped in bandages with his left arm in a sling. The chatter died down as Shiv and the gnomes walked through the crowd to their seats.

"Half, Master Shiv," said the Baronet loudly. Shiv ignored him long enough to ask Mother Hammerhand for breakfast for the four of them, and then lifted Dorlah and Old Karl onto the end of the bar due to the lack of seats. They both sat cross-legged with their backs to the wall, relatively comfortable.

"What was that, your eminent worshipfulness?" Shiv said, turning on his bar stool and dropping his sack on the floor beside him. He gestured casually to the mess of catgut stitching that stretched from his ear to his chin. "I'm having a bit of trouble hearing out of the side of my face I lost yesterday."

"I said half. Half of our village died while under your protection yesterday. Sixty-nine souls. You were just lucky that none of them were the kidnapped children."

"Odd, I don't recall being paid the wages of a general. I seem to recall one founding per day, some of which is still past due. At last count I was paid nothing for the whole day of fighting."

Baronet Falcior jumped to his feet, recalling his injuries halfway up and stumbling a half a breath before one of the villagers steadied him.

"But you swindled the village out of more than a hundred foundings in wages for your ridiculous show! Which you never performed, I might add. A hundred foundings is easily the worth of a general. And yet half our village is dead."

Shiv looked blankly at the Baronet for a few seconds.

"Milord, if you want to hang me because of your lack wit incompetence, you can go ahead and try." There was a murmur of surprise throughout the room. The Baronet was silent, but breathing heavily, his face going red. "Perhaps if you hadn't fallen under your horse like a buffoon the minute your life was threatened, you might have contributed as much to the fight as one of the little girls. Regardless, you can order your subjects to arrest me if you like, and hope none of them have children I rescued. Maybe that will make you feel like less of a farcical swine, but I doubt it will convince them. And I doubt mercenaries anywhere will work for you when you hang those who do the best job."

Shiv turned his back on the puffing Baronet, whose mouth was moving without making any words. Mother Hammerhand stood, still at the bar, eyes wide and mouth agape.

"Breakfast?" Shiv said again, and she scurried off suddenly into the back room. He cleared his throat. "Damn my throat is dry..."

Before he had finished speaking, one of the patrons had put a full tankard in front of him. He smiled gratefully, reached for it and stopped. Shiv's reaching hand suddenly had a curved ivory knife in it, and it thudded into the surface of the bar, a circle freezing around the embedded point.

"BARONET!" Shiv shouted. "If you are going to stick that in me I'd appreciate you not doing it like a coward."

Heads turned to the Baronet, whose sword was half drawn. His mouth was twisted in rage, his hands were shaking, and in his purpled face one eyelid twitched madly. The sword was released without ever leaving the scabbard, and Falcior made at least three totally unintelligible attempts to begin a sentence, and then shoved his way out of the bar, stumbling with every other step.

Shiv's breakfast consisted of bacon, fried bread and potatoes, and cheese. It was delicious.

Chapter Twenty-Four

> *Bathangers: A Bathanger is a gnome, half-a-ling or small human who is trained to hang from a harness suspended from the belly of a giant bat. These clearly unstable individuals (such as my uncle Karl) are used by the military forces of Nesland as scouts, skirmishers and outriders.*
> *Doctor Unfriendly's Comprehensive Guide to Everything.*

Despite the painful remainders of his wounds, Shiv had worked up a heavy sweat with a pair of tisken knives bought from one of the Forest Nomads. He and Old Karl had started off sitting on Gunther's wood pile discussing knife throwing tricks; the conversation soon had them standing, showing off various stances, grips, and backspins, and then had progressed to throwing knives at the wood they had been sitting on.

Now they were into their most bizarre maneuvers, Karl teaching Shiv how to make a tisken return to the thrower, and Shiv explaining how to grip two or three knives in a single-handed throw.

"Young fella," Old Karl chuckled, "Looks like you're already putting on another show." A small group of onlookers had indeed gathered to watch, from a safe distance.

"Errrr..." said a quiet voice from the audience. A smallish, wiry man in a heavy quilted vest was approaching tentatively. "Master Shiv! I, er, wanted to thank you. My, er, son Liam was one of the, er, well, you rescued him. Marvin Tailor, er, that is, I am."

"You're welcome, Master Tailor." Shiv said. He plucked his tiskens out of the mangled target log and stuck them in his belt, and wiped his sweaty hands on what little remained of his shirt. Once they were dry he shook the man's hand. "I was overjoyed at the opportunity to offer up my humble talents."

"Yes, well, er... I'm a tailor by trade as well as name, er, runs in the family. I made you a new set of clothes, by sight instead of measurement I'm afraid." He produced a fair-sized bundle of clothes from under one arm, which turned out to be a fairly decent replica of Shiv's old suit of clothes, only slightly more bulky. "They should be a good deal warmer, er, and are mostly the sort of quilting used in armour undersuits: very sturdy, and somewhat more protective than normal clothes. It all should fit under your armour quite nicely, except for the cloaks, and the overshirt, which go over... er... thank-you, as I said."

"No, thank, you!" Shiv said, smiling. He tried the shirt on as he was talking, and it fit quite comfortably. The hat fit snugly, and felt almost like a helmet. He flexed his arms back with a wince, and started whirling knives between his fingers as if to test himself. The tailor started to back up slowly. "You are a gifted craftsman, sir, something I always recognize and don't forget."

Shiv made all the blades disappear, except for one, a silver, straight-bladed dagger with double edges, which he held out hilt first towards Marvin. "One good gift deserves another; this blade is enchanted to touch what can't be touched. That, combined with the silver blade, means it is effective against werewolves and ghosts and the like. It needs a lot of sharpening, but should help keep the little Tailors safer from things which go bump in the night," Shiv smiled and bowed, waiting until the hesitating man accepted it. Marvin made a few attempts at thanks, but made no more successful sounds than several 'er's and a bit of stammering.

"Master Shiv," came a voice from behind. Shiv straightened as he turned to face the Baronet's older daughter, who was bearing a mischievous smile. "I'd also like to thank you. Please come to dinner tonight."

"Your father might not be enthused." Shiv replied.

"My father has shut himself in his bedchamber, Master Shiv. I don't think his opinion will factor in, actually. He hasn't spoken to anyone since your... conversation yesterday."

"How uncharacteristic of him."

"In the event that my father is unwilling or unable to fulfill his responsibilities, my sister and I are both trained to take his place. We have some ideas about that we'd wish to discuss with you."

Shiv stood grasping for something to say, and came up with nothing.

"Dinner begins with the twelfth hour. Be prompt, and dress appropriately."

Princess Recia gave a sly smile, and without waiting for a response, turned on her heel and walked away.

"Well, that was odd," Shiv said to no one in particular.

"True, son, very odd. Keep your wits about you around that one, and her sister, too. I don't know 'em personally but I always thought they looked like they're up to something," Karl interjected. "And generally I don't trust women to begin with. Human women are just like the g'nome variety, always neck deep in trouble. Only humans have higher necks!"

Shiv looked at the grinning gnome and laughed, then he threw one of his borrowed tiskens high over the town's wooden wall. It arced around widely, then whirled back, thudding into the dirt two or three paces in front of them.

"I think I'll have it in a few more throws," he said, and Old Karl nodded, smirking as they noticed the onlookers giving them a bit more space. "Then I'll see if I can combine the two tricks. I want to see if I can throw two of them with one hand and have them both return."

"You better have a few extra hands for that, 'cuz you're bound to lose a few," Karl joked. "Catching them is tricky. Either way, might be an idea to go ready yourself for that dinner. Not wise to keep the gentry waiting."

One of the onlookers, a scowling Julia Hammerhand, stayed and glared as Shiv retrieved his thrown knives and other gear.

"Excuse me, Miss Hammerhand? I suppose your family's establishment offers hot baths and other such thorough means of cleanliness?"

"You... what?" she snapped. "Er, yes. If that's what you want go ask my mother. I don't handle that kind of thing." And she whirled around and stomped off, lacking as much grace as the princess had displayed.

"A lot of people are doing that today," Shiv remarked.

"Just like I said, neck deep in trouble." replied Karl.

Chapter Twenty-Five

Rank: In Nesland most positions of power are hereditary, and pass on with the death or incapacitation of the noble in question. There are many ifs, ands and buts which unnecessarily complicate the process as giants tend to do. They are especially concerned with the noble having an heir, as this sometimes prevents a bunch of giants stabbing each other over who gets the job.
Doctor Unfriendly's Comprehensive Guide to Everything.

Shiv used the door knocker a few minutes before the twelfth hour. It was a large, round face and shoulders with a hoop made of two matching arms locked at the hands, and Shiv noted with amusement that the knocker's arms could be made to hit the brass face in the chin, as opposed to the breastplate as was clearly intended. The sun was low, but still bright, and the shadows had moved a tiny, but perceptible amount before the door was opened in response.

The same servant answered as had before; he was a middle-aged, thin man with close-cropped hair, dressed in grey with his master's red and yellow crest over the heart. He did not say a word to Shiv, instead regarding him coldly for a half a second, but then assumed a politer face and beckoned him inside.

"Good evening, kind sir, and thank-you for the hospitality," Shiv said as he entered. "I didn't catch your name the last time I was here, actually, but I recall the steely professionalism."

"Ironfield, Master Shiv. Harris Ironfield," replied the servant as he shut the door and beckoned Shiv towards the dining hall. "And actually, calling me Sir is somewhat inappropriate."

"Of course you are correct, Master Ironfield," Shiv answered absent-mindedly as he glanced at the various tapestries on the way. One was missing, although he could not recall what it illustrated; he noticed it mainly due to its absence on the otherwise heavily decorated wall. "I offer my humble apologies, rank is burden enough without it being thrust on an unwilling recipient."

Ironfield seemed to be working through that as he opened the door to the dining hall; the heavy table dominated the room and clearly had space for a dozen people, but only two places had been set, side by side, and the other chairs had been removed. In one, in a simple yellow gown, sat Recia Falcior. Her reddish-blonde hair was tied up in a complicated knot at the back of her head, with two long, thin braids running down over each shoulder, framing the slight glance of pale cleavage between them. The princess let Shiv look at her for a moment with a slight smile until Ironfield closed the door behind him.

"Please, Master Kobodan, sit down." She said, nodding to the chair beside her. He paused only a second before following her instructions. She gestured to a glass pitcher full of a dark red nearby. "Could you pour me some wine, please?"

"Er... certainly, my lady. You're looking... very regal today." he said, and poured the wine. She nodded for him to pour for himself as well, and watched him intently through the whole process.

"Thank you... Shiv," she said, and took a sip slowly. Shiv took one as well, the wine was quite good. "You didn't spill a drop, although that pitcher is unusually heavy..."

"It would be a pity to waste even a drop," Shiv replied.

"Thoroughly taking care of details... and strong hands. Useful traits," the princess said. "You have many of those."

"Thank-you, er... Princess."

"Call me Recia, Shiv."

"You mentioned you and your sister wanted to discuss some ideas with me?"

"Well, I suppose I did, although we don't necessarily need Temma here. Try those little pastries with the cherries in them. They're quite good. What I had planned to discuss would be more productive in as... intimate a setting as possible."

"I see," said Shiv carefully. He took a somewhat longer sip of the wine.

"Since the managing of the land needs to be done, and no one is doing it, I am the legal heir, and am taking it up."

"I gathered that. They are quite good," said Shiv, munching on a bite-size pastry.

"Of course, there is nothing to prevent my father from recovering and taking up his responsibilities again. Unless..."

"You want me to kill your father?!?" Shiv said incredulously, putting down his wine.

"No, no." said the princess, putting her delicate hand on Shiv's thigh and looking intently at him. "But people would have more confidence in me continuing my rule if I had my own heir. And a noble husband."

"Uh, well... I hadn't thought of that," Shiv said, relieved at not being hired as an assassin. A variety of mixed emotions competed on his face as he searched for a reply. Before he found one, Recia leaned over and kissed him. Her lips were unbelievably soft, and tasted of the wine. He drew her towards him and kissed her back, tasting the wine on her tongue as well. After a few minutes she pulled away slowly.

"Well?" she asked.

"That was a surprise," said Shiv. "Er, I hadn't thought about marriage any time soon..."

"I see..." Recia said, frowning. "So, you'd prefer my sister instead?"

"What? I never-" Shiv stuttered.

"One of us has to get married and with child. If it is you, that will keep my father feeling... under the weather... until I (or my sister) have been ruling for some time. I know you have become accustomed to the roaming life, Shiv, but," here she gripped his thigh tighter, "I'm sure I can offer you plenty of compensation."

"Listen, princess, it's not that I don't like you, and your sister for that matter, but I only met you a few days ago," Shiv said, now pulling back.

"Oh, I see," Recia said, frowning thoughtfully. "Well, one of us would have to be the legal wife, but otherwise I think we'd be fine; Temma has some unusual tastes I'd have trouble getting used to but..."

"No!" said Shiv. "That's not what I meant at all! Not that I'm not intrigued, of course-"

"Dammit, then, what do you want?!?" she shouted at him. "It's not that Hammerhand slut is it?"

"What?"

"Julia Hammerhand. I've seen the way she looks at you. Pretends like she's mad but she just can't look away. There's no way you can have all three of us Shiv. Two princesses should be plenty for any man."

"Now you listen here," Shiv said, standing up and knocking her hand away.

"It's not Mother Hammerhand, is it?" Her face twisted in disapproval.

"No! Will you just-"

"It is Julia! That bitch, I'm going to kill her. Get out!"

"What?"

"Ironfield!" Recia shouted, standing up herself. Ironfield opened the door almost instantly. "Escort Master Kobodan from the premises please. He won't be staying for dinner after all!"

Shiv left the hall feeling confused, irritated, and still hungry. Ironfield had to rush to keep up with him as he opened the door and stomped partway through it.

"Master Shiv!" hissed Ironfield, grabbing Shiv's sleeve to stop him. Shiv whirled around, ready to shout. "Master Shiv, I know that must have been tempting. I have to say, I respect your integrity. I know I am a man of humble means, but if you ever need anything, remember to ask. Honestly."

Shiv left the mansion feeling even more confused than before.

Chapter Twenty-Six

> *Duels: A silly practise in which giants try to kill each other to settle an argument instead of arguing about it. Whichever one gets stabbed loses.*
> *Doctor Unfriendly's Comprehensive Guide to Everything.*

Shiv sat in the Tortoise Toe Inn, munching on roast rabbit, onion soup and a huge chunk of bread; his face flitted between hungry, irritated, and overwhelmed. Across the table from him sat Doctor Unfriendly, also eating and occasionally chuckling at him.

"Look, Shiv," he said. "People have worse problems than two princesses fighting over him. Any g'nome I know would be happy to trade places with you."

"Human women don't normally encourage this sort of thing. One woman is difficult enough to keep happy, two would be impossible. Anyway, I have reasons I keep moving."

"What are those? Are they better than two beautiful rich young women?"

"Well, I don't know about better," Shiv said, snickering in spite of himself. "There are things I have to find out. More important might be a better way of saying it."

"How important could they be?" the gnome asked incredulously.

"Monumentally important, Doctor. Concerning my background. Matters concerning the fates of my family, my surrogate family, and my birthplace."

"Why, where are you from?"

"I have no idea. Somewhere in Nesland, I think, but no idea specifically, which is essentially bulk of the problem."

"Where is your family, then?"

"Also no idea. But undoubtedly dead from plague."

"Which leads me to the surrogate family. Where are they?"

"Definitely dead, in the wilderness about seventy leagues from here, near Resude and Talisman, though their murderers remain at large, so far as I know."

"How long have you been looking for your answers, then?"

"About two decades, more or less." Shiv had finished his rabbit, and was now sopping up the last of his soup with the remains of the bread. "Truth be told, I'm not even sure how old I am."

"Well, before I went to the University, I lived in the northern parts of Resude."

Shiv looked up in surprise, but then shook his head.

"From what I understand, there were no survivors, and I'm pretty sure I never saw a gnome until after I left my troupe."

"Perhaps," mused the Doctor. "Still, I remember around that time there were some border wars going on between the Duke of Resude and Talisman. As I recall, the King of Nesland was considering drawing the whole country into it. That actually figured into my reasons for leaving. After all, Mrs. Unfriendly was pregnant at the time."

"You had another child?" Shiv said, popping the last bit of moistened bread in his mouth and leaning back.

"No, it was with my son. He was born just over a year after we left. He's eighteen, now."

"Little Unfriendly is eighteen." Shiv said skeptically.

"Of course. A g'nome isn't full grown until he's maybe fifty or so."

"Unbelievable." Shiv said, taking a sip of his tea, which was long since cold. He briefly made a face and gestured to Mother Hammerhand to replace the teapot with some ale for the two of them. "So then, what do you remember about plagues?"

"Well, not much, exactly. But I remember the King of Talisman (there they call him the Zanquitor, a rather nonsensical title) was accused of employing dark magic against our side. He was always a sorceror of the worst sort, and is dramatically insane by most accounts. He caused hailstorms, sent monsters from the Inland Sea, I even recall him poisoning an entire river at one point, which wiped out several villages in one stroke. I'd bet any plague around that time was caused by him, or by one of his vassals."

Shiv sat back and took off his hat; he covered his face with his hands for a moment, deep in thought. Mother Hammerhand came placed the two drinks on the table, and had to clear her throat to get Shiv's attention. He recovered, smiled apologetically, and handed her three silver foundings, with which she scurried away before he could change his mind.

"I'd heard about the war, but no one ever pointed all that out." Shiv said. "I'd assumed it was a natural disease."

"I don't think that's likely."

"Well I suppose I have to go to Talisman, then." Shiv said. Before the Doctor could protest, the Inn's doors flung open, and in stomped the Hammerhand brothers and Julia. They were all armed and armoured, and they crowded around their favourite table, dropping heavy backpacks and other gear.

"Well, Master Shiv," shouted Forrel Hammerhand as soon as he had taken off his heavy black helmet. "It appears you've been shirking your duties since the Baronet became indisposed. We've been out on patrol, and those ghouls you mentioned are everywhere! We killed a lot of them."

Mother Hammerhand had got to the table quickly with a tray full of pitchers and tankards and a smile for her boys and daughter; Forrel cleared his throat and drained a tankard gratefully. The others were not far behind, and when their mother left to return to the bar after only a moment, she carried two empty pitchers on her tray.

"I see, Master Forrel, and I can only assume the blind, injured troll you brave fellows left out there has been suitably dispatched, and the Storm Kobold was no doubt defeated, and on your journey back you took a few minutes to slay an errant dragon or two?"

Forrel clambered to his feet and stomped over, plate armour clanking, to tower over Shiv with a vicious smirk on his face.

"You know, while you were out chasing children, before the Baronet put himself away he knighted me as a reward for my selfless defense of the village. You should address me as 'Sir Hammerhand', peasant."

"I see," Shiv said with a frown. He stood up, still a handspan shorter than the newly made knight. "It appears the Baronet is still making decisions with his usual munificent wisdom. Congratulations, *Sir* Hammerhand. I hope your own munificent wisdom will one day outshine your benefactor's."

Forrel frowned to himself, apparently surprised at how Shiv had reacted. One of the other patrons of the tavern, Farmer Hapsed, chuckled softly, and then quickly lifted his mug to hide the smirk. Still working it out, Sir Forrel walked back to his chair, deciding on a superior grin as he sat down.

As he did so, Julia got up and approached Shiv's table. She looked first to make sure her brothers were engaged in their own conversation, and then leaned over him in the same manner her brother had.

"You know, one of these days, I'm going to tell my brothers you're insulting them." she said, regarding him with a disdainful smile. "So, have you decided which of the princesses you'll marry?"

"Actually, Miss Hammerhand," Shiv replied, "I've decided to move on. The village got three quarters of my show and very nearly my life, I consider us even; I believe I'll head south in a day or two."

"What?" Julia said; her mouth twisted awkwardly and she stood up straight, arms crossed. "What about the kobolds, and the... I mean, I thought..."

"We don't need his help!" boomed a voice from the doorway. There, framed in the last breath of daylight, stood the Baronet. He was in full armour, his injuries apparently healed. He walked in confidently, stepped over to Shiv, and then took off his armoured gauntlet. Without a pause, he swung the metal glove at Shiv's face, although Shiv twisted out of the way as he scrambled to his feet.

"Tomorrow at dawn. In front of the well." the Baronet said evenly. Then he turned, and walked out as confidently as he had entered.

"Maybe you should leave, Master Shiv," said Julia quietly. "Leave tonight."

Chapter Twenty-Seven

> *Koriebi: The Stargod of strength and sportsmanship, he is always depicted with bared arms and a white shirt with black stripes. His followers are fairly easygoing and don't mind picking sides, unofficially, so long as games are kept fair enough for people to keep playing.*
> *Doctor Unfriendly's Comprehensive Guide to Everything.*

The sun was threatening to peek over the horizon as the entire village assembled around the town square. Shiv sat on a stool he had brought, adjusting the chainmail shirt he had rented from the Craftsmaster over top of the Handspan Armour. Unusually, his knives had not been concealed, and were brazenly strapped to his arms and legs, or to the small of his back over top of the chainmail. The shirt would not quite settle correctly over his shoulders, and the Craftsmaster was making a few last minute adjustments to the various straps which held everything in place without impeding Shiv's arms or legs.

Doctor Unfriendly stood nearby, frowning, with his wife and Old Karl. Some of the benches and torches from Shiv's circus tent had been arranged around the square by the villagers, but even still it was packed so tightly, shoulder to shoulder, that no one saw the Baronet approach until the crowd parted for him.

He sat on horseback in full armour, a lance and shield in his hands and a long sword scabbarded at his side. In his wake hobbled Zimmiman, also frowning, and looking bleary-eyed like he was not used to early mornings.

"Shiv," whispered the Doctor, while everyone watched the Baronet's entrance. "Let me cast a few protective spells on you. I have one that will make you appear a half a step to one side of where you really are."

"No, Doctor. If it comes down to it, I'll use my own magic, but I'll do it during the fight, and on my own."

"A little help is fine, I imagine he's had blessings from the priests or something."

"And I'll defeat him anyway. He's an elitist bully who needs a good beating."

"I didn't think you were the prideful type."

"I've put up with his nonsense from the minute I stepped into this village. This needs to be resolved, or he'll just go on harassing me until one of us is dead," Shiv grumbled, and then shouted over at the Baronet. "Are you going to ride that thing in a duel, your courageousness? That's not very traditional."

"Brother Carrick? Do the Five Brothers condemn the use of horses in a duel?"

"No, milord," replied Brother Carrick, standing up in one of the choice seats. He was dressed in a more formal robe than usual, green with multi-coloured embroidery, and wore a silver mace at his belt. "None of the Brothers' writings suggest horseback duelling is either a virtue or a vice."

"Thank-you, Carrick. There you are, Master Shiv," Falcior replied. He trotted the horse around the edge of the square, his glare never leaving his opponent. "Any other cries of protest?"

"No, sir, I'll leave the crying to you." Shiv said and stood up. "Use the horse then, it'll help you to run away faster. You'll need a head start to compose your usual list of excuses."

The crowd was silent, save for one or two snickers, which silenced as the Baronet glared around the circle. He then turned the horse and walked back to his entry point, a few paces out of the square proper, to give him a running start with his lance. Seeing his intention, a bench was moved to one side at the other end to allow him an unobstructed exit. Falcior nodded in approval as the villagers climbed back onto the repositioned benches, and lowered his visor. The silence turned into excited whispers as the Baronet lowered his lance, pointing at Shiv who stood openly in the gap at the opposite end of the square.

SHIV

The knife thrower stood lazily with no weapons in his hands as the sun's first rays broke over the eastern edge of town, and placed an open-faced helmet on his head, tossing his hat to the side of the circle. The ugly stone well stood in between them in the center of the square, casting its shadow towards the Baronet's pawing war-horse.

With a kick, the horse broke into a lumbering trot, and the crowd broke into a loud, excited murmur as Shiv crossed his arms and waited.

The lumbering trot turned into a slow gallop as the huge grey horse approached the well, veering slightly to the right. Shiv uncrossed his arms and slowly walked outward, away from the well to the Baronet's right side; the crowd's reaction was one of surprise, as most had expected the knife thrower to take cover behind the stone well to avoid the lance and the brunt of the horse's charge.

Falcior's horse was thundering forwards unstoppably, as Shiv pulled a square of heavy canvas from one of his belt pouches, perhaps twice as wide as a handkerchief, and squarely faced the approaching horse. Then he held up the piece of cloth with both hands, as if to shield himself from the lance point only a few steps away.

The lance impaled the cloth, and Shiv jumped and twisted in midair, the cloth wrapping like a net around the shaft of the weapon, and both of his feet came down directly on the Baronet's armoured hand.

Despite the steel plates, Falcior yelped and let go of the lance, riding past as Shiv landed lightly on his feet nearby where the lance stabbed into the ground between the cobblestones. The horse stumbled a bit but managed to steer back between the benches and wheeled around, Falcior roaring as he drew his sword.

Shiv calmly took out one of his frost knives, and hacked at the shaft of the standing lance once; the magical ice crunched along a section of the pole, and then he hacked a second time, and the pole snapped in half.

Falcior began another approach as Shiv tossed the two pieces of lance to the side of the square, and then began idly tossing the frost knife into the air, careful to catch it each time by the grip instead of the blade. This time, as the horse approached Shiv did step behind the well, the Baronet's sword uselessly on the opposite side, and the frost knife slammed into the ground close enough to touch the side of the horse's hoof.

The horse shrieked as its leg yanked to the side, frozen to the ground in a solid chunk of ice and soil; the chunk came free, but not before the animal was tumbling to the ground in a heap. The Baronet was luckier this time, not trapped beneath his horse but lying in a crumpled heap a few feet away.

Shiv picked up his blade, lying among bits of ice, earth and loose cobblestones, and then watched the horse get to its feet. Satisfied the horse was walking away with little more than a serious limp, Shiv turned to the Baronet, who was on his hands and knees, struggling to his feet despite the weight of his heavy armour.

Shiv walked over and kicked him in the side, and Falcior fell flat onto his back.

"Coward!" shouted Falcior, tearing off his helmet, and struggling up again. "That's dirty fighting! How dare you!"

"Oh, I see," said Shiv, sheathing the frost knife. "But running down a pedestrian on an armoured horse is very courageous. Thanks for enlightening me, milord. Perhaps you could show me, by your fine example, what else a gentleman ought to be doing."

With that he kicked the Baronet over again.

"Perhaps," said Shiv, turning his back on the struggling Falcior, "A gentleman should be spending his time harassing his allies when his village needs him? Or sulking while lesser men put out the fires burning across the town, rescue prisoners, and help the injured? Tell me, your worshipf-"

At that moment, Shiv turned around to the point of the Baronet's sword as it thrust into the chainmail over the left area of his chest. The links slowed down the blade, but did not stop it, as the steel slid into the leather underneath. Shiv looked up, meeting the Baronet's triumphant eyes, in shock. A tiny trickle of blood dripped out along the sword blade as the crowd quieted, and Falcior chuckled, still on his knees, and then let out a hearty laugh.

Shiv, shaking, struck his left arm against his thigh, and the sharp spike hidden in his gauntlet clanged and slid out into the daylight. Its dark adamant blade did not glimmer or flash despite the light from the rising sun; however, it had been enchanted with every spell and trick of armour piercing Shiv had ever encountered.

With one quick jab the spike lanced right through the Baronet's armoured glove, his hand, and the hilt of the sword.

The Baronet shrieked and collapsed to his knees, trying to drop the sword and not succeeding. With his right hand, Shiv took the sword blade in his leather gauntleted hand and yanked it out of his chest. The last half an inch of the blade was stained with the knife thrower's blood. It clattered to the paving stones. The Handspan Armour had a small cut in it, barely noticeable under the torn chain mail. Shiv staggered a few steps away, clutching his chest for a moment, and let the sword clatter to the ground.

"Ow, that hurt!" he shouted. Then he approached the Baronet, still huddled as close to a fetal position as his restrictive armour would allow, and kicked the bloody sword away. Once he was sure the weeping Baronet was not trying to get up, he gave him one more kick in the head for good measure, knocking him over once again. "That's for trying to kill me. I take that personally."

He waved Carrick over and pointed at the Baronet's crumpled hand.

"Can you do anything with that? I'm concerned he'll never play the harp again."

"Clever, Master Shiv," said Carrick, setting aside his silver mace to kneel and inspect the Baronet's wound. "I'm not sure I approve of your methods. His hand will recover, but only somewhat. In perhaps six months."

"Do the Five Brothers disapprove of what I did?"

"No, very little is a virtue or a vice in the eyes of the Five. But it was poor sportsmanship. Next time you encounter a shrine to Koriebi you might want to make a small act of penance."

"Of course, Brother, but to do that I'd have to be sorry. My apology and penances will have to wait until I am older and wiser, I'm afraid."

Shiv smiled to himself and walked away, dramatically bowing to the crowd. About half cheered or clapped, and the other half looked nervously at their lord. The Doctor came trotting towards him, smiling broadly.

"You know, the theatrics were probably unnecessary."

"True, but he was right about one thing. I did owe the town the last few minutes of my show. That was about the same thing, and I normally don't take a sword to the chest during the process. Now I just need the money the Baronet owes me."

"What?" the Doctor snorted, in the middle of scratching at his eyepatch.

"And perhaps an apology. I ended up out a lot of money over this village." Shiv wriggled out of the chainmail shirt as the Craftsmaster stomped over to them. The dwarf took the shirt from Shiv and held it up to the light, shaking his head.

"I'm keeping your deposit," he growled, and stomped away.

"See what I mean?" Shiv said, and went to look for his hat.

Chapter Twenty-Eight

> *Liquid Fire: A mixture relatively common among alchemists, liquid fire is an oily compound that bursts into flame when exposed to air. It is usually kept in tiny glass vials sealed with wax, and can be thrown so that the glass cracks and sets it off. I usually carry some myself. Warning: Do not attempt to drink it.*
>
> *Doctor Unfriendly's Comprehensive Guide to Everything.*

Shiv had nearly finished packing his circus gear back into the mule's saddlebags. A few people from across the village were helping him pack, bringing supplies, or just watching him go with various states of pleasure or disappointment.

Julia Hammerhand stood twenty paces away, arms crossed and a scowl on her face. Marvin Tailor had brought him a couple of skins of wine for the trip, and the Craftsmaster brought him a bill for a few odds and ends he hadn't yet paid for.

"You never got to use my liquid fire," Doctor Unfriendly said, handing him a small bundle, "But I thought you might find a use for it; there's a half a dozen vials in there."

He thanked them all, adjusted his hat and the strap of his lyre over one shoulder, and then noticed the two princesses walking towards the group. Julia Hammerhand rolled her eyes and stomped away as they approached.

"Master Shiv?" Recia called out, "Wait a minute."

Shiv regarded the two sisters silently. Recia held out a small leather pouch.

"This is the money my father promised you, we realize he was going to welch on his agreement, and we didn't like that."

"Oh, thanks," Shiv said, looking in the pouch. It was a generous handful of silver foundings, perhaps a bit more than the agreement had called for. He smiled a bit and stuffed the pouch into one of his saddlebags.

"You have further considered our offer?" Temma asked, her deep blue eyes meeting his.

"Somewhat... I frankly think I am many years from settling down." he answered, frowning and looking away. He noticed Julia was still watching him, albeit from further away, and leaning perhaps too casually against the Inn.

"Then we have another for you," Recia answered with a businesslike frown.

"I don't know..." Shiv said, looking out of the town gate.

"The kobolds are still out there, there's a mad, blind troll the Hammerhands have not tracked down yet, and our village is down to under seventy people."

"Listen," Shiv interrupted, "I'm glad you at least paid your debt, but frankly, your father coerced me into accepting that little. I got to put on my circus, but then I spent more than I earned on healing at the Rabboni's house, and renting the Craftsmaster's chainmail for that stupid duel, and on the expenses I had during the time I wasted here. Your people have been pleasant and hospitable, but I'm about seventy towers poorer than I was when I came here, and I didn't choose this lifestyle to lose money."

"We planned to pay you as an adventurer of your status deserves."

Shiv scoffed, and walked away shaking his head.

"Ten towers per day, plus expenses. And room and board!" Recia called after him.

Shiv stopped, and his shoulders sagged for a moment. Then he straightened, and turned to face them.

"Fifteen per day, paid in advance, weekly," Shiv said. "Today is Chepday, I need five foundings per day for expenses at the Inn, also in advance. That's one hundred and eight towers, five foundings, in my hand now, otherwise I am behind my lofty schedule. And another one hundred and eight and five every Chepday morning."

"Fifteen per day, and you pay your own expenses." Recia responded.

"I believe that kobold said you have an undiscovered gold mine under the town. Perhaps a share in the gold would be more advantageous to all concerned?"

"Excuse me, boy," Recia said to one of the village children. "Would you be a dear and fetch Ironfield from the Manor for me? Tell him we need the iron chest."

The boy looked briefly at Shiv, and then back to his princess, and held out his hand with a smile. Recia glared at Shiv, all pretense of affection gone. Then her smile returned in a somewhat forced fashion, and she handed the boy a copper tick.

Shiv sat down on a bit of wood and began whittling, blatantly ignoring the princesses, until the boy and Ironfield returned with the chest. A few snickers were heard among the bystanders when the princesses weren't looking, and the Doctor was openly smiling with amusement. The princesses huddled over the chest for a moment, counting and squabbling quietly. Then Recia turned and walked over to Shiv with a fat pouch of coins.

"One hundred and eight and five," She said, frowning. "And I am beginning to understand why my father had such difficulty with you."

Shiv stood up, and his knife flickered and vanished.

"Then I graciously accept," he said, taking the pouch and bowing flamboyantly. "I hope our relationship is long, professional, and mutually satisfying."

Shiv led his mule back towards the Inn, smiling mildly. As he passed Julia Hammerhand, he bowed slightly to her.

"Miss Hammerhand, I'd like to know everything about the encounter with the troll, and anything you know about these local kobolds. The Storm Kobold especially."

"I suppose," she said, smirking slightly in spite of herself. "But you'll need to buy me breakfast to reimburse me for my time."

"Not a problem," Shiv said, nodding. "Apparently the Baronet is buying."

Chapter Twenty-Nine

> *Gimlet: Gimlet was a Dark Elf (those are nasty buggers) who had a career as an assassin roughly a century ago. Hired by kobolds to kill a certain group of adventurers, he failed several times before being chopped in half, lengthwise, by Duke Ceborn.*
> *Doctor Unfriendly's Comprehensive Guide to Everything.*

Shiv sat at a table in the Tortoise Toe Inn, amid a steadily growing group of the local mercenary crowd. Julia sat at his left and Doctor Unfriendly at his right, and they were also joined by two of the Forest Nomads, Zimmiman the Wizard, the elven Captain Termann, and the Kobold Trapper. Mother Hammerhand was busy keeping them all supplied with scrambled eggs, sausages, fried bread, and drinks; she was also busy keeping tally of the bill on a slate near the bar, for later delivery to the Baronet's mansion.

"So we have the one wounded she-troll," Shiv said, "And the Storm Kobold. Does anyone know anything about his resources? What are we up against?"

"Well," Zimmiman answered through a mouthful of eggs, "We know he hired the goblins; he might have had the resources to pay for them, or he might have just promised them a share of the mine, at which point he would have needed the force to keep them from making off with all of it. So, he has the means to hire an army, or an army of his own. Or both."

"Probably both," said Doctor Unfriendly. "There have been stories in this area for the better part of a hundred years about the

Storm Kobold from what I understand, and before that there were accounts of the kobolds of this area hiring assassins to deal with powerful rivals."

"Gimlet the dark elf," confirmed Termann. "I lived not too far from here about a hundred and forty years ago. They hired Gimlet to kill Sir Larry MacTaroh, the Duke, and maybe a few others."

"Let's not forget he's a sorceror. He raised all those ghouls without too much trouble, and he disguised himself as Abner for who knows how long. This is ridiculous, he appears to have every advantage." The Doctor drummed the table with his fingers as he thought.

"I see," Shiv said, shaking his head and taking a sip from his mug. "So he probably used the goblins to avoid wasting his own army. Maybe that means his army is not big enough to take the village easily."

"There is stories in Gnoll Passage of Kobold castle," said one of the nomads. He was one Shiv had not met before, perhaps one who had been wounded; most of them could not speak Neslish.

"Kobolds do not build castles," interrupted the Doctor. He was shushed at by several listeners.

"Kobold castle different. Dug into hills, mostly in ground. Only one road to go there, is magic. Man walk off road, cannot find again. Road full of traps and spells. Dangerous," answered the Nomad.

Shiv looked over at the Trapper.

"You've been awfully quiet about all of this."

"I is hoping you not asking," the Trapper answered. "I knows about Kobolds of Terikota, used to live there."

There was a commotion from everyone as all attention focussed on the Trapper.

"Why didn't you say something?" snapped Julia. "You like wasting our time?"

"No," chuckled the Trapper. "I escapes. Stole moneys from... Estofith... who works for Storm Kobold, then I gets caught. Before I have... trial... I escapes down One Road. They changes traps since then, but I know rules, so I can say to you. Not enough moneys to make me go, though. I say rules, but I stay in Redlock."

"Estofith?" asked Zimmiman.

"It's a term for a leader of a team of sorcerors. A sorceror-lieutenant. " the Doctor answered automatically.

"This is ridiculous," Julia said, addressing the Trapper. "You've been there, but you won't show us the way? What if we make you come?"

"Then I tell you wrong rules. You lose road, maybe you disappear, maybe you fall in hole. I still escape."

The commotion arose again.

"So, clearly we can't trust anything you say," said Captain Termann.

"This why is hope you not asking."

Shiv gestured everyone to be silent.

"Why would you tell us the truth, then? Why should we trust you?"

"Storm Kobold want Trapper dead. I tells you where he is, maybe Trapper safe."

"We'd be more likely to succeed if you came with us."

The kobold made a barking noise that might have been a big, belly laugh, spilling his tea and knocking a half a sausage onto the floor. It took him a moment to recover.

"If Storm Kobold catch you, some escape, some die," the Trapper said. He drew one finger across his throat. "If he catches Trapper, I loses finger every day, then toe every day, then tail, then arm, then eye... Storm Kobold use magics to keep bloods in. He does when really angries. Before I die, he catches Trapper's life in a bottles and put on shelf. Storm Kobold has lots of shelf, lots of bottles. I stays here."

After a second or two of silence, most of them nodded agreement.

"I can understand that," Julia replied reasonably.

"Alright then," Shiv replied. "Tell us these rules."

Chapter Thirty

> *Trolls: Trolls are the smallest and most animalistic of what the giants call giants. Although not terribly bright, they are not half as stupid as they appear. A troll is about a staff tall, weighs around a ton, and looks like a humanoid cross between an alligator and a gorilla. Be very polite to them.*
> *Doctor Unfriendly's Comprehensive Guide to Everything.*

The world was dark, and she was alone.

She had run for a long time; although she could not see the sun, she could feel it, and like any of her kind, she did not like it one bit. Humans believed it would turn her to stone, it was said, and although she had found out that was not true, it was still unpleasant. She had hidden after she had run, though, and she was sure that outside of her shelter the sun was going down. Her sensitive ears could hear the sound of a very light rain beginning.

Now she was in a cave, she could tell by the smell. It also stunk of goblins. They were long gone now, but they had left some provisions, fresh beef jerky mostly, in sacks thrown into a corner, along with thick bundles of arrows. She wolfed down all of the jerky, sacks included, and began to sniff around the cave for what else she could find. The stench was overpowering; goblins did not go outside to defecate, but left their spoor in piles in any out-of-the-way crevasse. She had nothing on her but a huge hide poncho, the legs of whatever the animal it had been tied off like tube-shaped leather pockets, mostly empty. So she searched, and also rifled through her pockets as she went, identifying the few remaining contents by feel and smell.

Several rocks she had liked for various reasons, good for hammering. A bit of raw meat the size of a large raccoon (she wolfed that down too). A cord she had made herself from the bits she found inside a bear, very handy. A knife which had once been a human's dinner plate: one of the others had rubbed the edges on rocks until half of it was sharp, and then rolled up the rest of the metal to make a crude sort of grip. She sniffed, and smelled the one who had made it for her, and the tears began to fall again, and a noise like a tree falling in a storm came out of her throat.

"Gesh!" she sobbed. That had been his name. "GESH!"

She shuffled through the cramped cave for some time, kicking aside goblin garbage absent-mindedly as she cradled Gesh's knife. She did not know how long it was, but thought the sun would have set by now.

Then she found a pile of damaged goblin armour and weapons. Most were poor metal, such as bronze, tin, or copper, but she found a steel breastplate that had a small arrow puncture in need of repair. She snuffled and wiped the tears away with the back of her arm.

This was perfect. She smiled a little in spite of herself; an assortment of jagged teeth and two longer tusks made the smile frightening. She put away Gesh's knife, retrieved one of her hammer rocks, and with the breastplate in the other hand she stomped back towards the entrance of the cave. As she neared the outside air, she smelled the rain and the cool night air, and ran more quickly, now eager, knocking a barrel of some goblin drink to the side like a chicken's egg.

She burst out into the rain, and spread her arms, looking into the sky with her ruined and sightless eyes. She smiled to herself for a moment, then got back to business. She smelled the trees nearby, and walked up to one. It was a bit too small.

The next one was better, and the third one perfect. It fit into her hand like it was made for it, perhaps as big around as a human waist. She chuckled to herself and knocked the tree down with one swing of the rock, breaking it off at the base. She then grabbed the top of it and rammed her hand down its length, breaking off branches, until she had a huge, heavy pole, still oozing sap. The top half snapped off easily (it was too thin anyway, and she only needed it so long) and then she slammed the end into the breastplate. The steel curled around partway at the first stroke, and then she used her hammer to bend more of the metal around the pole, making a socket out of half of the plate, the other half jutting out like Gesh's knife.

Her smaller rock-hammer, the one with the pointed end, came out, and she laid the crude pole-axe along the ground. The pointed end scraped a complicated shape on the blade of the poleaxe- a rune her mother had taught her, one of only three she knew. It looked like a crooked rectangle, with an extra line poking out of two of the sides. It took a long time to scrape the rune into the metal, and that was not enough. She worked a long strand of drool into the lines with her thumb, feeling the spark growing within it; Gesh's knife slit a tiny line on her finger, and she let a single drop of her blood fall on each point of the rectangle. It fizzled, like it had been smoldering and then hit by a raindrop.

A boulder nearby was rough enough for her to begin sharpening the narrow blade. She smiled again as she began grinding.

"Gesh," she said to herself. "Tor," that had been the name of the other one. She had never been able to say her own name, it was too complex. But she knew it. She thought of it as she scraped the blade, over and over. She would soon need to think of another name; that was taxing, but she would come up with one.

"Gesh, Tor. Gesh, Tor." She repeated the names as she scraped, keeping rhythm. As the rain stopped and the moons came out, the third name came to her.

"Dek!" she called out. She paused in the sharpening, and put her hand on her midsection. It was a good name. Her bloated belly moved. "Gesh, Tor, Dek."

She could not say her own name, but she knew it, and so would Dek. She began sharpening again, and thought of it.

Her name was Mother.

Chapter Thirty-One

> *Iron: Iron does not work well in conjunction with magic, which is, from what I understand, why elves don't like it. Cold-forged or raw iron will occasionally even disrupt magic, although forged steel apparently does not work that way. I use powdered iron occasionally to mess with certain spells. It sometimes works.*
> *Doctor Unfriendly's Comprehensive Guide to Everything.*

It was overcast and drizzling when they walked out of Redlock. Once again, the Hammerhand Brothers stayed behind to guard Redlock; however, knowing that the Storm Kobold no doubt had an army, Shiv had raised a small one of his own. Doctor Unfriendly, Dorlah Unfriendly, Zimmiman, and Julia had gathered four of the Forest Nomads, and Captain Termann had gathered all the remaining, unwounded guardsmen, six of them, for what amounted to, all told, a decent-sized platoon.

All who had needed new weapons or armour had got them at the Craftmaster's shop (sending the bill to the Baronet's mansion), so that all but Shiv and the two wizards had new shirts of chainmail, and more than half of them had bows or crossbows, with plenty of ammunition. They had also gathered enough food and water to fill a small backpack for each of them, and Shiv had calculated they had enough in them to last a week, maybe ten days.

In perhaps a half an hour they entered the clearing with Abner's weird hideout: the hill with the illusionary tree. It was there that they made their first stop, huddling under the edge of the nearby treeline while Shiv, Zimmiman and the Doctor approached it.

"So, Doctor, you're the expert in illusions," Zimmiman said. The Doctor scoffed a bit but did not argue. "Can you figure out where the entrance is hidden?"

"Of course," the Doctor replied. "It'll just take a minute."

The gnome took off his backpack and set it down, retrieving a small pouch from inside it. He left the backpack there, for the moment, and walked over to the miniature hill. With a mumble and a waggle of his fingers, he took a pinch of powder from the pouch and flicked it at the hillside, and then watched it settle.

"What's that?" asked Shiv. "Some kind of magic dust?"

"If you like," answered Doctor Unfriendly. He tossed another pinch at the hillside, so that it fell a pace or two to the side of the first. He reached for a third pinch, and stopped as he noticed Shiv and Zimmiman looking at him expectantly. "What?"

"If we like?" Zimmiman said.

"Fine," growled the Doctor. "If you must know, it's powdered iron. Probably a few other metals in there, but mainly iron. I got it cheap, as leftover scrap from the Craftsmaster."

"And you did what to it?" asked Shiv.

"Nothing. Iron doesn't work all that well with magic, but mainly it's relatively heavy. I toss it on the hillside, and if it lands of a spot masked by an illusion, it'll fall under the projection and disappear." He threw the third pinch, and Zimmiman shook his head with disapproval. "If you two didn't already know something about magic, I would have lied and made something up, so count yourselves lucky. If you want to preserve the mystery, don't ask. There we are."

A few grains from the fourth pinch had vanished, showing a faint straight line through the grass; on one side of the line was the powdered iron, on the other side, there wasn't. He took a fifth pinch, and sprinkled it around that area, and soon had a rough circle marked, comfortably wide for the Doctor to walk through, but only large enough to crawl for the other two.

He reached towards the center of the doorway, and his hand sunk into the image. Had someone not been looking for that effect, they probably would not have noticed the grass did not part so much as

CAMERON S. CURRIE

fade where it was touched; he felt around for a doorknob, jiggled it and pronounced it locked.

"Do we have anyone who can pick locks?" the Doctor asked.

"I can," Shiv replied, rummaging through one of his pouches. "I pick open manacles all the time in my show."

He retrieved a couple of thin wire tools from his pouch, and felt around where the Doctor indicated; the lock was not especially difficult to pick, even blindly, and in a moment they heard an audible click.

The Doctor stepped in front of Shiv and vanished into the hillside.

"Come on in, it's safe," he shouted. Shiv got on his hands and knees, and shuffled into the side of the hill; it felt like stepping through a beaded curtain, and inside was a cool, dry room.

It was cramped, being built for Abner's size, and Shiv had to crouch even once he was in through the doorway. It was mostly empty, and the comfortable furniture was smashed into firewood and piled in a heap by the central fireplace. The rest of the circular, one room house was wide, but low ceilinged, and essentially empty, looted by the kobolds. Other than the firewood, the only supplies were three large barrels stacked to one side; on the far side of the room was a floor length two panelled mirror.

"Well, that's odd," said Shiv. "Abner, or the Storm Kobold, whichever he was at the time, never struck me as vain, and that thing looks expensive."

Zimmiman crawled through the door at that point, but could not crouch properly on his peg leg. He contented himself with shuffling around on his knees as he looked around.

"Er... what were the rules again?" Zimmiman said, spotting the mirror.

"First rule: go east. Not north, not south, straight east," Shiv replied, mimicking the Kobold Trapper's voice. "Do not turn to right or left, or path will be lost."

"Second rule," interrupted the Doctor, also attempting to mimic the Trapper, but having an entirely inappropriate voice for much success. The doctor's voice was nasal and squeaky, whereas the Trapper sounded like he was growling even at his most cheerful. "Do not look on the sun, do not look upon water, do not look upon fire or path will be lost."

"Third rule," continued Shiv, "Keep on going. Once you are on path, you must get to end before sun rises, or path will be lost. And fourth rule, follow Mark of Terrikota, do not follow other mark or path will be lost."

The Kobold had showed them the Mark of Terrikota; it was a small rune that looked like two triangles, one overlapping the other, both pointing up, and a circle beneath the both of them. The top triangle, pierced by the lower, was the rune for fire; the lower triangle, looking vaguely like a mountain, was the rune for earth, and the solid circle, which was usually written in black if colour was available, was the rune for darkness. The three runes were joined, straight up the middle, by a single thin line.

The Mark was etched into the upper frame of the mirror.

They had discovered the path.

Chapter Thirty-Two

> *Magic Words: Spells cast by wizards are closely guarded secrets; they occasionally trade them or sell them, but they are not given away. Some wizards try to gather spells by watching other wizards closely. For this reason, magic words which contribute to a spell are traditionally mumbled.*
> *Doctor Unfriendly's Comprehensive Guide to Everything.*

"Well, what do we do now?" Julia asked, looking at herself in the mirror with a mild frown. She touched the reflection, and it seemed solid enough. "It's mounted on the wall, we can't go around it."

"We go through it," Shiv replied. He knocked on the mirror and it made a hollow sounding tap. "The Trapper said the passage was here before Abner moved into this place. Maybe he wanted to keep an eye on it."

He felt around the edge of the frame, and quickly found a small latch that clicked loudly. With that each panel swung out, like a set of double doors. Behind the mirrors was an underground passage, shored up with ancient-looking planks. Although the floor was dusty, there was a path cleared by many recent feet. Shiv stepped through into the darkness.

"Do we have some light?" he asked, rummaging in his belt pouches. There were a few sizzles behind him, and each of the two wizards lit up the end of his staff. Zimmiman's was a dim, yellowish flame like a torch, and the Doctor's was a pale blue light that shone without a flicker. They all entered the passage (Zimmiman now had enough room to stand up) with the lights to guide their steps, and they headed east into the earth.

There was no sound other than their footsteps and the occasional bit of earth falling from the ceiling; other than the roughly cut passage there was nothing else to see. They walked two by two, chatting in harsh whispers, eyes open for any sign of danger.

Shiv and the Doctor were first, with Julia and Captain Termann just behind them. Zimmiman and one of the Nomads brought up the rear, the nomad nervously looking over his shoulder at almost every echo.

"First rule: go east. Not north, not south, but straight east." the Doctor was whispering to himself, going on with each rule in turn. When he finished, he would start again, repeating them with what may have been a nervous habit. "Does Zimmiman's light spell count as fire?" he asked no one in particular, but before anyone could speculate, he simply began reciting the rules again.

They had walked for over an hour before they came to a T-shaped junction. There was a passage going right and one going left, both identical, but ahead was nothing but a blank earthen wall held up by the same dusty planks. Shiv looked at the paths in the dust, but there were identical paths going down each passage. He took off his hat and scratched his head.

"Well this doesn't make any sense," Shiv said. Julia cursed under her breath.

The Doctor said nothing, but tossed a pinch of his dust at the wall. It vanished. He smiled, and reached his arm right through the wall.

"Pay attention next time I teach you something," he said, smiling, and then stepped through the wall.

They all followed, and the passage continued on much as before; it took nearly another hour for them to reach a large, irregularly shaped chamber with benches along the walls. There was a darkened alcove to one side from which came the sound of trickling water. The passage continued uninterrupted from the other end.

"This looks like some kind of rest area," offered Termann. "We should probably take advantage and eat while we can."

"Third rule!" interrupted the Doctor. "We'll eat while we walk."

The others grumbled, especially Zimmiman, but as there was no obvious alternative they kept on going, a few of them snacking on jerky or drinking from water bags as they went.

"Errr... how many of the Nomads came with us?" asked Dorlah from a few ranks back. The column stopped.

"Four, why?" asked the Doctor.

"Garell and Jotin are missing, I think," she replied. The rest of the group, most especially the two other nomads, hurriedly looked around, but there was no sign of them. "What do we do?"

"We can't go back," Shiv said. "Rule one, we'll lose the path."

"Well we can't just leave them either," answered Zimmiman. "The rule said no right and no left, it didn't say no going back."

They argued for a few minutes, until it was decided Berest, one of the other nomads, would run back for a few minutes while the others continued on. Berest was a decent tracker, he would no doubt be able to see if any foot prints diverged from the path, and if he saw no sign of them by the time he reached the illusionary wall, he would catch up to them. Grumbling in his own harsh language, he ran back into the darkness, first lighting a torch to see his way.

"Well, this isn't a good start," Julia said, but she shoved Shiv aside and walked ahead with the Doctor anyway. "We've only got thirteen left. At this rate we'll all be gone before we get there."

Their legs and feet were getting fairly tired after another hour or two. The Nomad runner had not returned, and the lot of them were all nervous. Once they passed a rickety door on the right, which they all wholeheartedly ignored, and another time they passed another rest area much like the first, a similar watery drip hinting vaguely at what might have happened to Garell and Jotin. They ignored the rest area and the alcove with the dripping sounds, and continued on without stopping.

They soon reached a third rest area, only instead of the passage continuing on from the opposite end, three identical passages did so. They were located one on top of the other, so none were to the right or the left.

"Boost me up," Julia said, beckoning Shiv over to her. He picked her up by the waist and set her upon his shoulders, and from there she scrambled to her feet and looked into the middle passage. "I don't see anything!"

Dorlah Unfriendly pointed her staff at the wall near the topmost passage, pressed a hidden trigger, and a dart trailing cord shot out, sinking into the wall with an audible crack. Before anyone commented she began to scuttle up the knotted cord, reaching the passage in only a moment.

"I don't see anything either," she called back down.

Shiv looked in the lower passage while he acted as a stepladder.

"Well, there's a mark here, near the opening. It's the rune for 'under the earth'," he said. "Might mean it doesn't go up, to the sun."

"Fourth rule- follow Mark of Terrikota, do not follow other mark or path will be lost!" called the Doctor. "We can't follow the rune. It has to be the middle one or the top one."

Zimmiman had sat a few feet from Shiv, sketching a circle on the ground with a small knife. He just now had finished, got up, and stood in the circle. He tapped the center of the circle with his peg leg, mumbled something, and the circle tore free of the ground, rising up to a level with the floor of the middle passage.

"You could have mentioned you could do that," Julia grumbled as she climbed off of Shiv's shoulders and onto the middle passage's floor.

"Yes, I could have," Zimmiman said absent-mindedly as he scanned the walls. He stepped off of his platform and it gradually drifted back down to the floor, fitting perfectly into the shallow recess it had left. "Errr... Doctor! Can you bring some of your powder up here?"

The Doctor stepped onto the circle, which rose back up to the second passage, and then joined Zimmiman, sprinkling powder over the walls as he went.

The circle kept on rising and falling without Zimmiman paying it any attention, so after a few repetitions, Captain Termann hopped lightly onto it as it began to rise.

"Everyone, we may as well get up to the second passage. We know it isn't the lower one, it'll save time later." they all followed his suggestion.

"Well," Zimmiman said as the last load of people stepped into the second passage. "I'm sure there are no marks anywhere near the entrance in here, visible or invisible."

"I haven't seen any up here," called Dorlah Unfriendly from the upper passage. "I've been looking the whole time!"

"We're wasting time!" snapped Julia. "Let's just pick one and go, or we'll miss the rising sun and get lost."

"We still have a few hours," said the Doctor. "If we pick the wrong one we'll get lost regardless. I'd like to live the next three or four hours if you don't mind."

This started everyone to bickering and offering suggestions. The last Forest Nomad, whose name was Hazbar, made a loud hiss at them to be quiet. It took a few moments, but once they had all quieted down, he pointed to his ear and then down the passage. After a moment came the sound of trickling water.

They unanimously decided to go to the upper passage.

When they had all been lifted up by Zimmiman's platform, he lowered it back into its original place, and then made a sweeping motion with one hand, and the circle disappeared. Then he turned, again bringing up the rear, and they continued their journey into the upper passage.

Chapter Thirty-Three

> *Tensorah: Goddess of the dark and things that go bump in the night. Not a very nice deity, she tends to attract worshippers with an overdeveloped sense of revenge or a dark sense of humour. There is a shrine to her in the dark thicket to the east of Redlock.*
> *Doctor Unfriendly's Comprehensive Guide to Everything.*

This new passage was different, carved into rock instead of earth, with only the rare bit of wood for support. There were a lot of passages branching off to one side or the other, but the group stayed on the path as the Kobold Trapper had instructed. The floor was smooth as well, and they travelled quickly, until after a few hours of walking they emerged suddenly from the tunnel into the moonlight.

The tunnel exit was high up in the side of a steep, grassy hill; a path continued on down the slope, between two other hills that loomed ahead, silhouetted by the moons behind them, each only a narrow sliver against the sky.

"The moons of Tensorah, two of the Five Brothers, and Dornovigorn," stated the Doctor as if reading from a textbook. "Rather inconclusive omens, astrologically speaking."

No one replied to that, as they shared the moons' consensus. They continued on down into the valley between the two hills, however, knowing the sunrise was only an hour or two away.

The two hills ahead actually became the sides of a valley, the gravelly path rising up on either side to steep scree slopes that were almost walls. The top of the slopes began to be littered with boulders, fallen trees and other detritus, silhouetted against the brightening sky.

"This would be an excellent spot for an ambush," remarked Termann, gazing into the darkness with his keen, elvish eyes. "A few guards up there with bows could kill almost anything before it made it up to the top."

"And then we'd lose the path," said the Doctor. His eyes went wide. "Zimmiman! Lights out!"

Both the wizards' staves fizzled out, leaving the group in blackness until their eyes began to adjust.

"Errr... why?" asked Zimmiman, when no disaster happened.

"This is why the kobold said to not look upon fire! Guards up there would see us!" the Doctor responded. "We'd be sitting targets, night-blind and unable to even see where the arrows were coming from!"

"Shhh!" hissed Shiv. The all quieted down, ears straining for the sound of kobold guards or anything else hostile. Especially at the top of the slope. Nothing sounded for a few minutes, but then a loud, trumpeting sound came from far ahead. "Termann! Can you see in the dark?"

"Of course," came the hushed response.

"What made that noise from ahead?" Shiv asked, but Termann had already come to the head of the column, his shadowy form crouched, squinting, into the distance.

"It's a troll. A big one." Termann said quietly. "I think the guards found it."

"How many guards are there?" asked Julia.

"I can't see them," Termann said, "But the sound we heard was the troll shouting, a boulder landed on it. Her. There's already another rolling down the slope at her. The guards must be pushing them down."

"Lucky she went in ahead of us," the Doctor said. "The guards were focussed on her long enough to maybe miss our fire. I guess the moons were favourable after all."

"You can tell it's a she? In the dark?" Shiv asked the elven captain.

"More the sound of her voice, really. She's howling again. My goodness! She caught the boulder and is throwing it up at them. Good for her!"

SHIV

There was silence for a moment as the group listened to the faint sounds in the distance, a trumpeting bellow now and then, a nearly inaudible rumble from several rolling boulders, and possibly a chittering sound that could be kobold guards.

"You know," said one of Termann's guards, "I don't like trolls much, but I'm rooting for her." His comrades murmured consent. Julia hissed at them for quiet.

"The boulder she threw didn't reach the top," Termann whispered. "It almost looks like she's juggling now, catching rocks and throwing them up again. They've rolled three or four more down... now I think they are just waiting to... one's got her. I think her leg is broken. She's still trying to throw. Maybe... no. That's it."

There was another bellow, and another, quieter. There was a third noise, which could have been another attempt at a bellow, but it didn't last quite so long as the others, and then silence. The group sat in the darkness for a moment.

"Well," said Dorlah, "We should probably get going. We might catch a few guards at the bottom trying to recover the boulders or loot the body."

"And they'll have fewer boulders to lever down on us," the Doctor said.

By now the fire had been gone long enough their vision was not bad in the dim moonlight. The path was smooth and relatively featureless, easy to navigate, and they all walked without tripping, weapons at the ready.

"Shiv, the walls are getting awfully high. Could you throw a knife that far up?" Julia asked, a bit of fear uncharacteristically seeping into her voice.

"Not usefully, milady. I might get it up there, but at that range it would be unlikely to accomplish much except supply them with ammunition."

"Milady?" she said. He shrugged.

"Hush," whispered Termann. "The spot where the troll died is only a few minutes ahead."

The carcass came into view in the extreme distance, not so different to their night vision from the boulders which lay clustered around her. Smaller shapes skittered around her, the odd sound of kobold laughter echoing along the valley. Soon one of the rocks was

143

slowly moving up the slope, and the kobolds began to tie ropes around a second rock.

One of the guardsmen, holding a longbow with an arrow nocked, scrabbled to the front of the column.

"Captain, should we try to take them now while they are down here, or sneak past after they leave?" he asked.

"Now," Terrman said, looking at the sky. "We don't have time to wait."

All six guardsmen made a cramped firing line, bows drawing back to the ear. Termann unslung his bow as well, kneeling in front of the line.

"The main thing is quiet," he whispered. "If you can, aim for the throat or the head. And no noise afterwards."

With that there was a sharp twang, and Termann's arrow flew silently through the air, watched by them all, until it stopped in the throat of a kobold. The guards all let fly, trying to follow the Captain's aim, but their human eyes could not make out details of the tiny creatures in the dark from this range. A cacophony of kobold screeching began instantly, and they scattered, half dead or injured from arrows, the other half scuttling up the slopes.

The guardsmen kept firing into the panicking group on the valley floor, but Termann picked off the slow-moving climbers, one by one, before they got very far. Up above, along the crest of the walls, there were screeching sounds of kobolds calling down to their comrades, but no sound came back to them in answer. Then came the rumble of boulders; the guards at the top of the walls were taking no chances. After a half a dozen or so boulders had come to rest at the site of the massacre, there was silence for several moments.

"They are maybe a bit reluctant to come down," said the Doctor, smiling. "Should we sneak though yet?"

He was answered by another boulder rolling down the slope; however, this one was coated in burning oil, and lit up the valley for several paces around it. It crashed into the boulders and gore at the bottom, splashing gobs of the oil around and lighting up the whole area in dim firelight. Shiv and his companions were still a long distance away, but in the area of firelight, there was no place to hide thirteen people. The guards would see anyone trying to sneak past, and there were probably more boulders up there. Their path was blocked, and in the east, along the horizon, the stars had vanished in a swiftly brightening sky.

Chapter Thirty-Four

> *Scrying: This is looking at distant things by magical means. Usually it employs an enchanted mirror, or a pool of water, or a crystal. Usually a wizard requires the name of who he wants to see, or maybe a bit of their hair or clothes. There are lots of other rules, which make it an awkward way to find things out.*
> *Doctor Unfriendly's Comprehensive Guide to Everything.*

The shallow pool of water shimmered as if a dim light source was beneath it, lighting up the cluttered room with just enough light to pick one shadow from another. Abner watched silently, hanging limply from his shackles, as he had for longer than he could guess.

The Storm Kobold had put on a black robe with runes traced out on it in silver, and he held a short staff tipped with a clear blue crystal. As he leaned over the pool intently, his rough jade amulet, always present on a leather thong around his neck, dangled just above the rippling surface.

Other prisoners were there as well, hanging in much the same way as Abner. Most had long since died, from time, the Storm Kobold's rage, or merely no one remembering to feed them; those hung there unnoticed until their captor asked them a question. Even the dead ones spoke, when the monstrous necromancer demanded it, so he cared little whether they were alive or not.

"Reginald!" called the Storm Kobold's weirdly deep voice. "Tell me, who or what do you suppose the Baronet will send against me?

He has these mercenaries, those Hammerhands, maybe half of his town guards left."

Sir Reginald's corpse, mostly bone and rot, now, identifiable only by the knightly colours upon his rags, said nothing. The stocky blue kobold waited for a moment, then his face suddenly twisted in rage and he covered the wide room in three athletic leaps. His free hand jammed into the tattered meat that hung on the corpse, and grabbed a rib like another might grab at a man's shirt. The kobold lifted himself up on the handhold, clawed feet finding purchase in the open cavity that had once been Reginald's belly. Under his breath he hissed three short words, and without pause Reginald's empty eye sockets lit up with a dull red flicker.

"Yes, my lord." came the passionless voice, unchanged by death.

"You heard the question, fallen knight."

"I suppose nothing, not since I died." came the hollow response. Although the skull was incapable of smiling and the voice had no emotion left in it, the corpse somehow radiated a smug mirth.

"Very funny. I will rephrase: what force will the Baronet's reprisal most likely consist of?"

"Armed men, most likely." said the dead knight. The Kobold roared and leapt down from the hanging corpse.

"You realize I can make you suffer for being evasive?" the creature said over his shoulder.

"I have realized nothing, not since my mind died; and my body is beyond suffering." said the corpse. The kobold was quiet for a moment.

"Again evasive. And you surprise me by your lack of imagination."

"I have imagined nothing, not since my-"

"Shut up," spat the kobold. He was facing the knight now, but his eyes suddenly narrowed and his voice lowered. "How about this: do you think... *Caroline's* body is beyond suffering...?"

"N-no..." came the corpse's voice. It came out as more subdued, now. From the other side of the room came a whimper. The kobold smiled wickedly.

"I wonder if you would suffer, for example, if I tore off her arm. Perhaps then I would burn the wound closed, and then let her starve to death." The kobold strolled over, relaxed, to gaze at a huge, round glass jar. It was the only thing lit other than the pool; dozens of fireflies flew about inside, about the huddled form of a little girl wrapped in rags. The corpse was silent.

"Once more: who will the Baronet send against me?"

"I... c-c-can't..." came the voice of the corpse, no longer smug. "I d-don't know the mercenaries. He would send mercenaries if they were skilled, but... he trusts the Hammerhands."

"I know," said Abner, his voice hoarse from lack of water. "I know what he'd do."

Surprised, the kobold turned to face Abner.

"Really?" said the Storm Kobold. "I was under the impression you were something of an outcast- half the size of a normal human, undertaker, amateur necromancer, I rather thought you'd know less than the Baronet's lieutenant."

"I used to-" Abner broke out in a series of hacking coughs. His voice came out in a strangled croak as he struggled to speak but could not. The Storm Kobold growled again, threw down his staff, and snatched up a rather filthy skull. Eyes never leaving Abner's coughing and spasming form, he scooped up a skull-full of water from the pool, stalked over and held the dripping eye socket to Abner's lips.

The water tasted foul and metallic, being polluted with any number of magical ingredients, but it was wet and cool, and Abner sputtered as he drank a mouthful. The coughing subsided. He panted, trying to catch his breath.

"Go on," growled the Kobold, his deep, base voice gaining a razor's edge.

"I used to play chess with him, a few years ago. Before he had lost so many knights. He still talked with me then."

"Very well, who do you think he'll send?"

"The Baronet loves the Hammerhands, but won't risk them, so he'll send two parties. He'll send the mercenaries to deal with you, and the Hammerhands will sneak behind, at a distance, to watch. They can learn from the mercenaries' mistakes, report on how well they did, and if they nearly succeed, the Hammerhands could take over and finish the job."

"Good answer," said the kobold, gazing into the air thoughtfully. He started to wander off, deep in thought.

"Can I have more water?" Abner said. "I helped you, can I please...?"

The Kobold turned around, eyes narrowed.

"That is... I can probably answer questions better if I am alive. The dead are sometimes evasive."

The Kobold burst out laughing, a deep, booming laugh that sounded like a human, not a kobold. It lasted several minutes before he shook it off, and with a smile, scuttled up to give Abner the rest of the skull-full of water. Abner gulped it down greedily, and then threw up about half of it immediately. But he felt better.

"Very well, Abner," said the blue Kobold. He walked over to one of many cluttered tables and found a mouldy heel of bread. He held it up for Abner to look at. "I can't locate the mercenaries. To see them in the pool I need a name. For this, I would like you tell me one of their names."

"You won't kill me, like Reginald, will you?"

"Of course not. He swore an oath, you are an outcast. Your honour is unimpinged either way."

"Zimmiman. The wizard with the peg-leg. His name is Zimmiman."

"Very good, Abner," said the kobold. He stepped over and poked the chunk of bread into Abner's mouth. "Very good indeed. You know, I thought at first you were just a convenient person to replace, maybe a good source for bone and organs and so on... you know, we just might become friends."

Abner choked down the stale chunk of bread, chewing hard lumps of mouldy crust that stuck in his teeth afterwards. He nodded, and smiled.

"I know more," Abner said. "The gnome- is there a gnome with him?"

"There are two," said the kobold, finding a half-eaten fish, mostly bone. Abner's face lit up, and in spite of himself began to drool for the first time in two days.

"The first one is Doctor Unfriendly. He's kind of a beginner wizard, an illusion specialist I think. The second would probably be his wife, Mrs. Unfriendly. I think she's a scout or something."

The Kobold stuffed the fish into Abner's mouth. Abner choked and half of the morsel fell out as he crunched the thin bones between his teeth, trying to grind them up into something digestible. Despite the gagging and the scratching as it went down his throat, it was the most food he'd had in days and he got it all down, immediately looking around eagerly for more.

"Tell me," said the kobold, a magical gesture causing a nearby rat to float into the air. He caught it by the tail, and without looking, smashed its brains out on the table, and then held up the ruined remains for Abner's inspection. "Does the gnome doctor have any children...?"

Chapter Thirty-Five

> *Illusions: Another type of magic, this essentially deals with things which are not real, but appear to be, and similar concepts. Projections are the most well-known type, although I personally favour Impression-based illusions, which directly create effects in the mind of an opponent, such as my 'shove' spell.*
>
> *Doctor Unfriendly's Comprehensive Guide to Everything.*

"I heard you the first time!" hissed Shiv, trying to whisper and shout at Zimmiman at the same time. "Greater Second Rotation of the left hand. I don't know what that means!"

They were huddled behind a boulder, as close as they would dare to where the troll had been flattened. Thirty or forty paces off, the burning boulder had been joined by two more, and was lighting up that part of the valley floor brightly.

"This is why I didn't want to teach you any magic. You don't know the basics! Show me your spell book again, such as it is." Zimmiman's voice was a harsh whisper. Shiv pulled a small leather sack out of his largest belt pouch and fished out one of several worn pieces of cloth with notes scribbled on both sides. It had been rolled into a ball and needed to be flattened out against the side of the rock. Zimmiman scowled as he tried to make out the rough diagrams in the dark. "I can't learn anything from this, not in the dark. You'll still have to cast the spell. But the Greater Second Rotation will extend the duration by-"

"Verily I say unto thee, milord, I knoweth not what that pithy phrase means, despite the pedantic manner in which it is expressed. Perhaps your wisdom can produce a more colourful illustration of your profound thoughts?" Shiv whispered.

"Look, none of that!" snapped Zimmiman. "Give me your left hand."

Shiv's hand was seized by the old Hillman wizard and pried into an awkward position with the ring finger jutting out at a painful angle.

"Ouch! I'm not double jointed you know," complained Shiv. "Okay, I have it though. Does it have to be this way exactly?"

"Of course it does. Now do it when you see the fog," Zimmiman growled and crawled away into the dark to rejoin the main group. Shiv grumbled a bit to himself and rubbed the stiffness out of his knuckle. Once Zimmiman had crawled back far enough, Shiv peered around the edge of the boulder, and then again up at the top of the ridge to his left side. The two gnomes were up there somewhere, getting into position.

It was only a few minutes before the Doctor's illusionary fog began to creep along the ridge towards the kobold guards. When it got close to them, Shiv began casting his spell.

Shiv's illusionary elephant walked silently out of the darkness, the oil fires making it stand out instantly. Shiv made it pause, like it was sniffing the air for predators, although he had no idea what an elephant doing that might look like. He settled on the long trunk making a kind of sniffing motion and swinging back and forth like a spyglass scanning the horizon.

There was a chittering from the top of the cliffs; the kobolds had taken the bait. To a tribe that lived on hunting, ten tons of meat was too great an opportunity to pass up. The sound of boulders being rolled into position for another volley was audible despite the kobolds suddenly going quiet again, and Shiv made the elephant walk forward hesitantly. An arrow from one of the over excited kobolds flew down at the elephant's back, and there was a sound of a high pitched reprimand, no doubt from the squad leader.

Shiv jammed his fingers into the Second Greater Rotation as the arrow sailed through the image, trying to incorporate a copy of the arrow into his illusion, but failed; his powers were already stretched to the maximum. He'd just have to hope the kobolds didn't notice the lack of an arrow sticking out of the beast's hide, or maybe they'd think they missed. The Rotation did help, though, the image was maintaining itself somewhat more easily than usual.

In the darkness a dozen paces behind Shiv, the rest of the party was now scaling the valley wall on the rope left behind by the gnomes. Hopefully the distraction of the elephant, along with the fire spoiling the kobolds' night vision, would allow the group to reach the top without spoiling the trap. Shiv winced as another pile of gravel was dislodged and sent scattering down the wall, but he could not afford to look. He had an elephant to maintain.

The illusion of the elephant got to within a few paces of the fire and the troll corpse, and Shiv made the elephant hesitate, as if it was looking for a way around without getting too close to the fires. He selected a route for it after a few moments and nodded at the rumble of the first boulder. It was joined quickly by two or three more, and Shiv made the elephant look around worriedly. He chanced a glance up to the valley wall, and saw the fog reaching where the kobold guards were surely hiding. He smirked briefly, and then turned his right hand slowly, watching the elephant turn in response. Its eyes widened at his command, and then the beast turned back towards the far end of the valley and ran, narrowly avoiding the first boulder. He knew he would not be able to fake a boulder injury if he could not manage an arrow, so the elephant dodged and ran far more quickly than was strictly believable, leaping like a grasshopper over the next two boulders, once hanging a handspan above the ground for a split second before he remembered to make it fall.

At the top of the cliff, Termann was in place, hidden in the fog, as the kobolds with one mind turned away from them, following the increasingly unbelievable progress of the elephant. The illusion started to shimmer, reaching the end of Shiv's abilities, and one if its colossal legs popped off, reappearing three or four paces to the creature's side. Before the kobolds had any time to react, he shouted for the archers to release.

The kobold guards were about twenty in number, but were looking in exactly the wrong direction as nearly half of them were shot in the back. The screaming started as the creatures either turned to figure out what was going on, or ran clutching at wounds. Before they could do anything meaningful, the town guardsmen, one Nomad, and Captain Termann had drawn more arrows and were firing, as the two gnomes tried to load more darts into their trick staves. Most of the remaining kobolds dropped, and the remaining two or three with no injuries turned to flee along a path behind the boulders, but were shot down before they had made it a few paces.

Down by the floor of the valley, the elephant's head turned upside down and then bright red, before the whole image dissolved into nothing. Shiv let the image dissipate, and got up from behind his boulder. Further back into the darkness, Zimmiman stood up on his good leg only a few paces from the valley floor, his peg leg having fallen off near the beginning of his climb. Shiv smiled and went to retrieve it for him, thinking he had never got the elephant to last half as long as it had. Perhaps there was something to this Greater Rotation stuff after all.

Chapter Thirty-Six

> *Slaves: Although slavery is technically illegal in most countries, it is widely practised in wilderness areas, or with prisoners of war, or enemies of the state, who, generally speaking, don't count.*
>
> *Doctor Unfriendly's Comprehensive Guide to Everything.*

The valley floor began to rise shortly after the ambush point, moving towards a cluster of hills. The group from Redlock, having reassembled, ran along the path, all pretence of stealth abandoned, racing the first glimmers of sunrise.

Zimmiman was lagging far behind, his peg-leg simply incapable of anything resembling running. The two gnomes were also somewhere in behind the main group, their short legs moving impressively fast, but not fast enough to make up for their size. The main group, though, appeared to be keeping ahead of the rising sun; Termann ranged far ahead, only looking over his shoulder periodically to ensure his companions were still on his trail.

In the dim light, runes were visible, carved into stones along the path. They would have been indistinct in the dark, but now flickered between the colour of smouldering embers and the black of coal. There was no need to scan about for the path as it was marked, and they followed it at a full sprint. Shiv, Julia, and three of the guardsmen scrambled up to Termann's perch at the top of a gravelly rise. Panting, Shiv looked behind him.

"They're gone," Captain Termann said before he had seen. He was right; the lagging members of the party had vanished from sight.

"Six of us is not enough to take on a whole tribe of kobolds," Julia said, scowling.

"Well, neither was the whole group," Shiv replied. "I think we were always planning on some kind of trickery once we got there. I was hoping the wizards would be able to help with that."

"So where have the others gone?" asked one of Termann's guards. His squad-mates nodded in agreement.

"Probably it is actually us who are gone," replied Termann. "From what I understand, the kobold fortress is in some kind of... not sure how you say it in Neslish... an extra space...? At any rate they are in the normal world, we are in the Storm Kobold's lands."

"That's good, I think," said another guardsman.

"Well, let's see what we're dealing with," Shiv said, and with that he crept up the path until it peaked at a ridge. The others followed, looking with him over the lip into the valley of Terrikota.

It was small, smaller than Redlock, and circular. The hills formed a ring around the valley floor, which was dominated by a dark pit big enough to hold a building. At its edge, a stone platform marked the top of a smooth ramp of flagstones that ran around the circumference of the pit, down into the darkness.

Surrounding the pit in small groups were a few dozen kobolds, and an equal number of slaves in chains, mostly human, but with a couple of goblins, and a dwarf. The slaves were working small gardens, hoeing the earth with their bare hands, picking weeds, and harvesting the various vegetables and herbs. Nearby a few were bringing buckets of water from out of the pit to fill troughs for the goats and sheep.

Around them, the kobolds stood holding weapons or did any of the jobs which required tools, and as far as possible from the slaves were groups of tiny creatures they guessed were kobold children, chasing each other in tight circles.

Although much of the valley was in the shade of the hills, it was far too bright and open to sneak down. Julia frowned and reloaded the crossbows fitted to her forearms, and Shiv began to twirl a dagger between his fingers.

"We could take a hostage," Termann offered. "If I had one of the kobold cubs in my sights with an arrow, perhaps they would allow us to pass."

SHIV

"No," Shiv snapped. "I won't be a part of that."

"Well, we can't just walk down there!" hissed Julia.

"We could free the slaves," said one of the guardsmen. "They might fight with us, maybe overpower the kobolds."

"Brilliant plan, sir, perchance you can stroll down there and pick the locks of twoscore of manacles before the guards happen to notice," Shiv said. "And while we wait for your triumphant return we can plan your funerary rites."

"Can you magic some of the manacles open?" Termann asked Shiv.

"Well, I suppose if we got close enough, I could get one of them. I've had to escape manacles in my show, but never twenty sets at once. I could maybe manage four sets over a few minutes before my magic dried up."

"Just one at a time?"

"Well, it's complicated, I'd have to magic-hand some lockpicks down there and then do it by feel. I'd still need to be within maybe twelve paces or so. Pretty close."

"The dwarf." Termann said, squinting over the ridge.

"Pardon?" Shiv asked.

"I've been running the town guards for years. I can spot a thief by the way he stands, the way he looks at things. He's casing the area, maybe looking for something he can steal to escape. The dwarf is a thief, and dwarves are good with tools. Perhaps if you free him he can take your lockpicks and free some of the others."

The group crept back until they were fully out of sight, and then circled around to roughly where the dwarf had been working. As Shiv consulted some of the notes from his haphazard spell book, Termann wrote a few words with a bit of coal on a scrap of cloth. It said:

"FREE YOURE SELF AND THENN AS MANEE OF THE OTHRES AS YOU CAN. IFF YOU ARE SPOTTED WE WILL DEFENDE YOU AND AID IN YOURE ESCAPE"

Shiv smiled at the poor spelling, but used the cloth to wrap up his small collection of lockpicks into a neat little bundle. Then, holding the bundle between his teeth, he crawled on his belly up over the ridge.

The dwarf was a bit further away than Shiv would have liked; he was digging rows in the soil with his manacled hands, no doubt

CAMERON S. CURRIE

making a new plot for planting, and did not notice as Shiv crawled through the shallow grass, stopping perhaps fifteen paces away in the shade of a small pile of rocks. The cover was terribly meagre, and if the kobolds had been looking for intruders Shiv would have been spotted with little effort; as it was, Shiv was uncertain of how effective it would be, or for how long.

He spat out the bundle on the ground, and pronounced a few magical syllables, mimicking a scuttling, crablike motion with the fingers of his left hand, and a subtle spinning, cranking motion with the middle finger of his right. His magic-hand spell flickered to life, being barely visible apart from a vague yellow shimmer. He had always felt a minimal bit of decoration was perfect for his escape artist routine, which was fortunate now, as he had no idea how to change its appearance. Luckily, the growing sunlight made the shimmer stand out somewhat less, and the little bundle lifted itself a few inches above the ground and slipped smoothly towards the dwarf.

The bundle got perhaps four paces from the digger and stopped as if it had hit a wall. The spell would go no further. The dwarf still had not spotted it, as he was intent on his work and putting the odd glance behind him towards his masters a short distance away. Shiv began to sweat as he crooked his little finger uncomfortably, but it would twist no more to increase the distance. Frustrated, he began to jiggle the little package, hoping to catch the dwarf's attention without drawing the attention of the kobolds who were gradually strolling nearer.

Finally, in desperation, he threw it. Shiv had never thrown anything with his magic-hand spell before, and frankly had no idea if it would work, but had nothing else to try. It did work, somewhat, as if thrown by the hand of a small and uncoordinated child, and not entirely in the right direction; the magic hand spasmed with the effort and vanished with a tiny wisp of yellow smoke.

The package landed not far from the dwarf, and the sudden movement caught his eye. He immediately glanced behind him at the approaching kobolds, obviously gauging whether they had seen the bundle or were going to. The two guards were continuing their slow meander, conversing in the chittery babble Shiv was becoming used to.

The dwarf scuttled, crablike, sideways a half a pace, and began a new line in the dirt parallel to the last one, and a half a pace closer to the bundle. The kobolds glanced vaguely in his direction, dismissing his motion almost immediately, and continued past him. As soon as they looked away, the dwarf's hand darted out and snatched the bundle, jamming it in amongst his rags and continuing his work uninterrupted.

Shiv breathed a sigh of relief. After a moment, he began to wriggle backwards into the grass, and away from the small pile of stones. One stone, barely larger than a pebble, was nudged from the pile, and drew the eyes of one of the kobolds.

The sinewy creature let out a loud hiss, and tapped its companion with one hand while he drew a short bronze sword with the other. Its eyes locked in Shiv's direction, and it ran past the dwarf. His companion raised a spear and joined him, pausing only to screech over his shoulder at a further-off group of guards. Soon half a dozen were sprinting closer, bearing weapons and knocking the slaves or livestock aside, each screeching to call the attention to more of their companions.

More kobolds erupted from the pit in the center of the valley, and the slaves and kobold cubs began to withdraw towards the pit, eyes scanning in every direction for whatever the trouble might be. Bows were bent, arrows were drawn and pointed, and with a groan, Shiv raised his hands and stood up.

Around him maybe twenty kobolds converged, all with weapons pointed, and all hissing wickedly. Shiv recognized a few simple magical gestures among the kobolds' hands and guessed that several rather hurtful spells were aimed at him along with the weapons. He maintained his gaze directly forward as he stood up, primarily to not give away the position of his companions, but also to mark the progress of the dwarf slave as he scrambled with his peers down into the pit.

"I'm unarmed," Shiv said in the chittery kobold language, hands held high and open. This was totally untrue; he had eighteen various knives on him, but they were all cleverly concealed in the leather panels of the Handspan Armour.

Chapter Thirty-Seven

> *Enchanted Pathways: There are a lot of enchanted pathways in the world; these are areas that exist only when a given condition is met, such as a time of day, or a certain type of person steps on them, or some other condition. Often, interpreting these rules is a combination of guesswork and gambling. They are a pain to deal with but the only way to enter many areas safely.*
> *Doctor Unfriendly's Comprehensive Guide to Everything.*

Zimmiman stood, stooped over and panting, as the two gnomes, one nomad and three guardsmen gathered about him.

"That was interesting," said the Doctor. "I assume they made it to the kobold lair."

"Of course," replied one of the guardsmen. "They followed all the rules. You notice those runes are gone? Hell, the whole path is. We saw there's nothing on the other side of those hills."

"Dammit. I suppose we have to head back to Redlock," Zimmiman said, finally catching his breath. "I imagine they could have used our help."

"You'll have to explain that," said a voice from behind them. They all turned away from the hills to spot Ruzzio Hammerhand walking towards him, somewhat ahead of his three brothers. They couldn't help but notice his bow was out and strung, and an arrow was casually hanging half-loaded in the same hand.

Forrel stomped past his brother, his heavy black plate armour clanking. He stopped to mop his brow with the edge of his cloak.

Daryd, missing his brothers' heavy gear, strutted around to the group's flank, his weird red eyes scanning them as if they were prey. Behind them all Thokk leaned heavily on his poleaxe.

"The enchanted path disappears at sunrise, we hadn't quite made it," answered Doctor Unfriendly. Forrel pretended he hadn't heard.

"Zimmiman?" he asked.

"The enchanted path disappears at sunrise, we hadn't quite made it," Zimmiman said. He had regained his breath, for the most part, and stood up straight, looking between the gnome and the plate-armoured man. "What's this about?"

"Enchanted path? That's the path right there!"

"The unenchanted one, yes. The enchanted one is gone unless we start at the beginning again," the Doctor interjected.

Forrel pretended he hadn't heard. His three brothers snickered.

"The unenchanted one, yes. The enchanted one is gone unless we start at the beginning again," said Zimmiman, scowling as he caught on.

"I see," said Forrel. "Well the Baronet is going to want to talk to you before that is decided. We'll have to head back to Redlock. You five come with us."

"Does he have a problem with you, or all g'nomes?" Dorlah asked her brother-in-law.

"I would imagine all g'nomes," the Doctor replied. Then his voice lowered to a whisper. "That's okay, if he wants to overlook us, we can start back to the path as soon as he isn't looking."

The nomad and the three guards broke off from the rest of them to see if they could find out what had happened to Captain Termann and the two missing nomads. Once they had left, the Hammerhands kept up a pace deliberately difficult for the gnomes, so the Doctor and Dorlah quickly fell behind. When Zimmiman had difficulty keeping up, Thokk Hammerhand picked him up like a sack and carried him over one shoulder. As the gnomes fell entirely out of view the last sight they had of them was the wizard's outraged but resigned frown.

"It's just after dawn, and we have to backtrack a whole night's travel," said Dorlah, once she guessed they were out of earshot. "Perhaps we should take a short rest, let them make some distance, and then we'll go straight to Abner's hideout."

The Doctor agreed, and they found a sheltered spot out of sight and had a light meal, their legs weary from constant use and the lack of sleep. After the meal, it was agreed they would each take a turn at an hour's sleep while the other kept watch. If there was any more time to spare, they would take it in Abner's house.

****

The Doctor was sound asleep under a bush, his face in a tiny sunbeam, when Dorlah heard a sound like a deep, throaty growl from a short distance off. She had been sharpening the spring-out spear in her trick staff, and quietly put away her rags and sharpening stone. Thinking to replenish their supplies with a bit of hunting, she crept slowly out to the edge of the bushes and peeked out slowly.

She looked in the direction of the Hammerhands, and saw nothing; as she turned to look in the other direction a wall of elephantine skin slammed to the ground in front of her.

"Gesh, Tor, Dek," came the growl. The troll stood, newly-made poleaxe over one shoulder, and sniffed at the ground. The beast's shaggy head turned to face her hiding spot and sniffed again; swollen and sightless eyes passed her hiding spot impotently, but the toothy muzzle pointed at her smell all the same.

Dorlah froze on the spot, meeting the troll's ineffective gaze with eyes wide. A mouth debatably large enough to take her in one mouthful opened slowly in a wet, drooling snarl.

"Gesh, Tor, Dek," it said again. It appeared to wait for some kind of response, but when it heard none, the huge snout gave a wet snort, and the troll was suddenly moving again, nose to the ground. "Gesh, Tor, Dek."

Dorlah was frozen until a moment after the troll had passed. Her breath started again in near-panicked gasps as she looked at the footprint that was large enough for her to sit comfortably in. Then she sprung to her feet, and scrambled back to her brother-in-law's hiding spot.

"Doctor!" she hissed, torn between being loud enough to wake him, and being quiet enough to avoid tempting the troll to return for a snack. "Doctor! We have to warn the Hammerhands!"

"No," groaned the stirring gnome. "We have to save Shiv. Did you fall asleep?"

"That troll has come back to get the Hammerhands! Zimmiman is with them!"

"Even when they're somewhere else they find a way to bother me," the Doctor groaned, but slowly sat up. "Very well, we warn the Hammerhands, not that they'll thank us."

They quickly gathered their packs and supplies and staggered after the troll, still bleary-eyed and exhausted.

Chapter Thirty-Eight

> *Shamaleah: A Grandmaster human wizard and ruler of the Counciltowers, who died nearly a century ago in a magical duel in the Realm of Ashphault. He was known for his penchant for fine horses, and spells which imprisoned souls in precious stones and other vessels.*
> *Doctor Unfriendly's Comprehensive Guide to Everything.*

"Ouch," complained Shiv when the kobold behind him prodded him in the back with the point of his spear. It hadn't really hurt, the Handspan Armour had easily absorbed it, but he wasn't about to advertise that fact. "Stay your mighty hand, grandmaster piker, for my flesh is tender and prone to bleeding."

The kobold hissed at him to be quiet and jabbed him twice as hard. Shiv's dozen kobold guards- six in front, six behind- led him down the ramp in the massive hole in Terrikota's valley floor. The cleverness of the design became apparent as they descended; although there were no walls or railings along the ramp, the bottom of the pit had a low stone wall that circled the perimeter; crouched behind the wall watching them descend were at least another twenty kobolds, each clutching a loaded and aimed crossbow. The earthen ramp had to circle the wide pit three times to reach the bottom; an invading army would have to march single file down the ramp for several minutes while being peppered with darts from every direction, while the kobolds' wall gave them nearly impenetrable cover. Six times on the way down, there was a gap in the ramp bridged by a series of rickety planks; the defending kobolds could yank a rope or two and trap someone at any point during the descent and then finish them off at their leisure.

Shiv became somewhat more aware of the number of crossbows trained on him and swallowed nervously. Still, the kobolds had searched him and hadn't been able to find any of his knives; sooner or later they would figure out his trick but for the moment he was still heavily armed.

The spear jabbed at him from behind again. This time Shiv distinctly heard the tap of the metal hitting one of his knives, hidden in an invisible slash in the Handspan Armour. Even with the weird handspan of leeway, there was only so much space to go around a single suit of armour, and most of it was full of knife blades.

They reached the bottom of the ramp, and Shiv noticed all the kobolds with crossbows had retreated into little tunnels that led into the wall. Each was only as high as Shiv's hip, room enough for an angry kobold, but too cramped for a human to pursue. He shook his head in wonder.

"I guess this place would hold out against an army for ever," he said to no one in particular. "Do you critters have many enemies?"

"No. Mostly deads they are," said one of his captors. They turned into a rough passageway that lead away from the pit; it was huge, by kobold standards, looking something like the great hall. The ceiling was about as far up as Shiv could have reached with his fingertips, if his hands had not been tied behind his back. The walls were decorated with dried skulls, broken weapons, and hundreds of runes that glowed blue bright enough to dimly light the chamber without the use of fire. Each rune was the now-familiar double triangle, circle and line of Terrikota, each smaller than a finger in size.

At the end of the room was a raised platform; on it stood a knight's war-horse, in full armour and well-made heraldry: blue with a yellow double triangle, pointing down, almost like two stylized lightning bolts.

Standing in front of the horse on a stool, whispering and purring in its agitated ear, was the Storm Kobold. He was not dressed in the robes Shiv had seen him in earlier, just a brown leather loincloth. A crude jade amulet hung from his neck on a leather thong.

"Master Shiv," said the creature loudly, patting the horse on the side of its metal-plated head and then turning to regard him. "You have given me no end of trouble, you know."

"Thank-you for noticing," Shiv replied. "A craftsman always rejoices to find his work serving its purpose."

The large blue kobold turned to regard him. Despite his heavily scaled skin, corded muscle rippled underneath with every motion, his stomach rigidly divided into knotted sections. His toothy mouth cracked open in a wide crocodilian smile.

"Yes, I suppose you would be pleased in that. Of course, I've wiped out half of your little village, and my own losses have been minimal. The goblins were always expected to take the brunt of the Baronet's counterattacks, and falsely expected to receive an equal share of the gold. I've lost very few kobolds, considering. But you found your way into my land. That concerns me."

The kobolds which had been guarding and jabbing him began to back away, blocking his access to the entrance and leaving Shiv in a clear circle several paces across. Shiv nodded.

"Don't insult me, by the way," the Kobold continued. "I know you can slip out of those ropes at any time. And if you feel the need to carry that ridiculous number of daggers about to feel safe, by all means do so, but take notice of the slits in the walls."

Shiv tried not to look surprised at the squat beast's knowledge, and looked about the chamber carefully. There were a number of cross-shaped slits in the wall, each perhaps two handspans wide. In several of the gaps the increasingly familiar glimmer of kobold arrowheads was present. There were dozens of gaps. Shiv shrugged and wiggled out of the ropes with little effort, dropping them on the floor at his feet. He absent-mindedly picked them up and began arranging them into a coil.

"Always thinking, aren't we," said the Storm Kobold, still watching him. "I have two questions for you. If you answer them honestly, I'll let you go."

"I was just thinking how I had always been struck by your honesty and integrity," Shiv replied. "In fact, after the blue scales and posing as Abner that was the first thing I noticed."

"Droll, as I expected," replied the blue creature. He began to stroll towards Shiv, regarding the trophies on the walls as he did so. "Of course, I don't suppose you have a better idea for escaping. I think you may have to take my word regardless. Question one: Who told you how to get here? Question two: what defenses does Redlock still have in place?"

"Answer one," Shiv replied, "Is that once we found out you had replaced Abner, his house seemed a logical place to search, and you hid the passage with less cunning than was strictly advisable."

"Yes?" mused the Storm Kobold.

"Answer two is that Redlock has more or less the same defenses it always had, minus a few civilian casualties. You'll find that although your flunky goblin army has been scattered, all they really managed was to decimate the women and children, the aged and sick. You've gained nothing, whereas we have gained both experience and wisdom, and the weaponry of the goblins, of course."

"Very clever," said the Storm Kobold. "So answer one tells me nothing useful while being, strictly speaking, honest, and answer two tells me nothing which could be easily confirmed. And, of course, you subtly discourage me from attacking again. Clever, but predictable. You remain a prisoner."

"Truly a surprising decision," replied Shiv. "Not very clever, a bold-faced lie never is, but I was truly shocked that a villain would not keep his word. Wow."

"Have you found his companions yet?" The blue creature snarled. "I imagine, at the very least, a certain gnome doctor and perhaps a deserter from our own community?"

There was a collection of chitter from several kobold guards near the entrance, generally answering in the negative.

"Very well, make sure the slaves are secured for the daytime. Double the night patrols, find the trespassers. And properly disarm this one, give him thirty lashes, and put him in with the others."

The Storm Kobold turned back to the horse, and the crowd of guards began prodding Shiv with the spears again. He was pushed toward one particular side tunnel, and had to get on his hands and knees to enter it, spear points pricking his feet to make him crawl faster.

The passage curved this way and that, left, right, up, down, and Shiv was certain it had gone several times in complete circles in the darkness until it opened up again. As soon as he was clear of the little tunnel, Shiv rose to his feet, and saw a circular chamber whose walls were lined with crude cages, all full of the slaves which had been outside. He looked them over, getting another poke in the backside from a spear as he hesitated, and thought he saw a dwarf nod carefully in his direction.

The kobolds once again surrounded him. One rank stayed back several paces with their spears pointed at him, while the others skittered over to him to strip off his armour. Watching from behind both ranks, another kobold, unusually tall and thin, glared at him and toyed with the tails of a wicked, lead-tipped whip.

Chapter Thirty-Nine

> *Elf Knot: A somewhat magical knot some elves know how to tie which, if properly done, can never be untied, only cut. The Dark Elves of the Sidhe forest enjoy using elf knots to tie a human to a tree by the hair, a stunt they find unbelievably funny.*
>
> *Doctor Unfriendly's Comprehensive Guide to Everything.*

Shiv's left hand was tied in a massive tangle of rope, which then led to a metal ring set in the wall. His right hand was tied in a similar fashion, leading to the opposite wall. Several kobolds were pulling the ropes tight while others tied them tightly to the rings, so that Shiv was held more or less in the center of the room. Nearby in a pile were most of his clothes and armour, Shiv being stripped to the waist. They had found a number of his knives (most had fallen out of his armour while they were shaking it, and the ones in his gauntlets were not terribly well-hidden) but he still had four knives hidden in his boots, leather greaves, and codpiece. They were the four steel ones, not his favourites, but still pretty dangerous. Although he could slip the ropes with relative ease, he could not take on more than twenty kobolds by himself.

So he waited as the kobolds finished their knot-tying, watching the caged prisoners while the tall kobold with the whip stalked back and forth glaring at him. He was sure the dwarf had nodded deliberately in his direction, although he was beginning to wonder what that had meant. He couldn't see the dwarf at all, now.

The other kobolds backed away into a wide circle, satisfied they had him immobilized, and the taller one stopped its pacing and chuckled at him. It didn't say a word, but displayed the whip to Shiv, carefully showing each wickedly barbed tail to best effect. Shiv shut his eyes, attempting to steal the creature's fun and avoid building up the anticipation so much; it didn't work very well.

The whip cracked, and the first lash cut through all his defenses; the sharp lead barbs tore through his skin like the claws of a tiger. Shiv shrieked in pain, and began twisting his wrists hurriedly to escape the ropes. Before he had made any headway, though, the second lash hit and he lost what little progress he'd made on his bonds. His eyes were open now- he couldn't bear not seeing when it was coming- and he began to twist his wrists again.

The third lash crossed over the cuts from the first one; his chest was beginning to look like something that belonged packed in a sausage. One of the barbs stuck in the flesh on his stomach; the torturer yanked the whip to dislodge it and a strip of skin the size of Shiv's thumb came off with it. He fell to his knees and wondered if anyone had ever survived thirty lashes.

The torturer smiled steadily as it circled around behind him; Shiv followed its gaze until his neck wouldn't turn any more, noticing the torturer was missing its left ear. Realizing he had a few precious seconds before the next lash came, Shiv ferociously began to twist his wrists, prying hard against the rope on his right wrist. He felt it slip a hair's breadth before the lash came, and over his own shriek he realized the other kobolds were cheering. He hadn't noticed when that had started. Shiv's vision was swimming and he was coughing for some reason he couldn't grasp. His wrist slid another hair's breadth before the next one hit, and he hung from the ropes for the uncomfortable respite it seemed to give him. Droplets of his blood decorated the ground around him, like it had just started to rain. Shiv couldn't see much else, though; when the torturer walked back in front of him, he was little more than a blur with too few pointy bits on the top.

His vision cleared for a moment, and he saw his one-eared torturer parading for the crowd, the whip held high above his head, and his sinewy back facing him.

SHIV

The rope on his right wrist slipped just a bit more, and with a long-practised twist his hand slipped free. Shiv collapsed to the ground and the crowd gasped and went from cheering to a quiet murmur.

The torturer turned around in surprise, looking for what had taken his glory, and saw Shiv shakily getting to his hands and knees. With a growl, the creature turned, raised the whip, and then shrieked himself as a steel knife plunged into his wrist. Shiv was already staggering to his feet, another knife in his hand and a murderous glare in his eyes.

The crowd quickly remembered they were soldiers, after all, and quickly drew swords and knives and recovered spears. In the moment it took them to get their weapons out, Shiv had hacked through the rope holding his other wrist, and his left hand suddenly held a sharp steel dagger as well. The circle began to tighten as the guards crept closer, cautious, but confident in their superiority of numbers.

One of the wicker cage doors opened quietly behind the circle of guards, and a ragged dwarf slipped out, followed by a steady stream of fellow slaves. The dwarf went to the next cage door, while the others crept silently to the pile of Shiv's possessions against the wall. As the first kobold spear poked at Shiv, testing his defenses, the first three armed slaves roared, and struck.

The guards turned at the shout, and Shiv threw a single knife, dropping one opponent, and drew his last spare.

Three kobolds were writhing on the floor from the slaves' first attack, and the ragged prisoners had already began to swing their plundered knives at new opponents. Meanwhile, one of the other slaves, a young woman, had picked up a spear dropped by one of the kobolds. In her hands it looked far too small, like a walking stick with a bronze point, but the kobolds stayed out of reach as best as they could all the same.

The first prisoner fell fairly quickly to a thrown spear. For all their bravado and the element of surprise, they were tired and malnourished, and the kobolds were heavily armed. Shiv tried to stay out of reach of the nearest kobolds, but lashed out with one of his knives any time one of them turned to deal with the slaves. He managed to drop one with a slash across the neck, but the majority were keeping him at bay with the somewhat longer reach of their miniature spears.

In between swings, his vision cleared somewhat, and he could assess the situation. The kobolds still had a massive advantage, and unless something changed the prisoners would all be killed, including himself.

"Prisoners!" Shiv shouted at the ragged escapees. The dwarf had apparently picked the locks on the other cages while the guards were focussed on the armed opponents. "You'd better get out while you can! If you know the way to the surface, take it while these ones are busy with us!"

Some of the kobolds obviously understood human speech, for there was a murmur through the guards. The freed prisoners now had more or less even numbers with the kobolds, and most of them were much larger than the jailers; as the few armed prisoners squared off against the kobolds, several of the unarmed prisoners slipped quietly out one of the side passages.

Shiv began to press the attack, trying to gain ground towards his pile of weaponry, but the kobolds surrounding him had gone on the defensive, poking at his hands and wrists with spears whenever he got too close; so he threw his left hand knife, striking one kobold in the eye, and then rushed past him as he fell. One of the other guards managed to nick him in the side with a long-handled bronze hatchet as he passed. His vision was swimming again, and he spat a curse under his breath. Another spear hit him, but luckily hit the Handspan Armour still on his leg, and he wasn't hurt. He lashed out with his one remaining dagger, and hit something, but whether it was a kobold or just the shaft of a spear he could no longer tell. One guard had snuck up behind him, and instinct had somehow guided Shiv to swing back with his empty hand and catch on to one miniature wrist. His catch squealed and tried to wriggle free, but Shiv yanked the arm upwards as far as it would go, keeping his prey at an angle facing away from him.

And another spearhead sunk into his back.

Shiv gasped and fell down onto his knees again, this time noticing his blood pooling beneath him. He looked around desperately for aid, but saw nothing more than a blur of kobold skin and sharp bronze. He felt a heavy thud on his shoulder, and coughed out what should have been a call for help, an order for his allies to run, something... but nothing more came out than a low groan. Another kobold screeched, and Shiv's vision went black.

His last steel knife dropped from his fingers.

Chapter Forty

Healing Potions: A relatively simple form of magical healing, these little bottles of nasty stuff multiply the body's ability to heal injuries. They usually last only a few minutes, but in that time the body will recover as much as they would in several days or more. They won't regrow organs or replace lost blood, but are still incredibly handy to those in violent professions. Expensive.
Doctor Unfriendly's Comprehensive Guide to Everything.

"... coughing it up, you idiot," came a voice out of the blackness. There was a taste in Shiv's mouth of burning alcohol and something like licorice root. He had trouble breathing, and some of the vitriolic, stinging mixture came out through his nose. He had a tremendous fit of coughing, causing stabbing pains in his stomach on top of the acidy burn in his nose and eyes.

"I said stop that, this stuff is expensive!" came the voice of Julia, and a thump on his back that could have been aid for his cough or punishment for his spilling whatever she was talking about. His eyes tried to sort through the blurs, and managed to make out Julia holding a small flask before she pinched his nose and forced the flask in his mouth again. He forced it down, some of it down the wrong pipe, and began coughing and choking again. Despite his discomfort, his vision began to clear.

Julia was standing over him, and he was curled up in a foetal position on the cold stone floor of the kobold jail. Nearby stood Captain Termann and two of the Redlock town guards; further off sat the dwarf thief, busy fiddling with a pile of leather and bronze. Standing over the dwarf were six of the kobolds' prisoners. One of them, a human, had a crude leather-and-bronze breastplate made of bits of kobold armour, and all of them held various miniature kobold weapons and small wooden shields. Piled in the cages were kobold bodies stripped of all their gear.

"Ouch," said Shiv, making a mental catalogue of all his aches, pains, and injuries. "How am I still breathing?"

"Healing potion," explained Julia. "I got a recipe from... well never mind, but it does a pretty good job. How do you think I helped Thokk when that troll nearly cut him in half?"

Shiv sat up, fought off a slight dizzy spell, and looked himself over; although all of his injuries were still there, they looked as if they had spent a week or so healing. The bleeding had stopped, and although the injuries were dry it looked like any serious exertion would rip them open with ease.

"Thank-you," he answered. "You should market this stuff. We could sell it alongside the tickets at my circus."

"I don't think so," she replied, a slight smile curling up one side of her mouth. "It's expensive and difficult to make. I don't relish spending the rest of my life over a cauldron to make a few coins."

He staggered to his feet and brushed himself off; the missing portions of his armour and clothes were neatly stacked at the side of the room, along with his knives. Shiv looked through it briefly and then began to dress himself again. The dwarf looked up from what he was doing from a few paces away.

"Thanks, human. Those lashes must've stung like the molars of Yahbeb. A lot to go through, even for a dwarf." Without another word he returned to his work, which appeared to be making another suit of patchwork armour.

"Agreed, knifemaster," said another of the recently freed slaves, a pale-skinned human boy of perhaps eighteen years. "You were remarkable. Are you perhaps in the market for an apprentice?"

One of the prisoners, the only female, approached, nodding at the word 'apprentice'.

"A bit early for that. We're still in enemy territory, and we have quite a few more battles to win before we can escape," Shiv chuckled, doing up the last of the many straps on the Handspan Armour. He looked around for a moment. "Looks like our numbers are back up to a dozen, and our hosts have been generous enough to supply us with weapons."

"I can only make three suits of armour big enough for us out of the kobolds' stuff," said the dwarf. "We'll need more as soon as we can manage."

"Very well," Shiv said. "Captain? Do you know the way out of here?"

"Yes," Termann replied solemnly. "But it should be used as a path of retreat; we have done little more here than give the Storm Kobold a bloody nose thus far."

Julia and Shiv frowned at each other.

"I suppose so," Shiv replied, holding an armload of knives. He looked briefly around the group for a moment, hesitating, then shrugged and cut a slit in the armour on his side. With an ease born of long practise he jiggled the knife until it slid into the armour entirely and disappeared. He ignored the looks of surprise from the others. "But we are hardly in shape for a frontal assault, and we certainly can't wipe out another hundred kobolds or anything."

"I suppose we need a target," Julia said, shaking her head at the simplicity of Shiv's trick. "We find something valuable and important, smash it, leave the Storm Kobold a message that we can hurt him, we know his defenses. Then we run off before he can mount a counterattack, and get out of here and back to Redlock."

There was a moment where everyone was silent, except for the sounds of Shiv strategically inserting knives into his armour.

"His laboratory." said the dwarf. "I know where it is. We smash everything there, I would imagine his powers would be at least somewhat reduced. And perhaps we can find some loot there as well."

"As good a plan as any," agreed Termann. "Your name, Master Dwarf?"

"Still but a journeyman," snickered the dwarf. "Shorik. The human boy there is Enwerd, the four human men are Jon, Istav, Kasser, and Berrit. And the human lady there is Shantel."

Shiv finished packing away all of his knives, and then helped Enwerd finish up the armour, while Termann and Shorik began to sketch out a map of the complex in a little book Termann carried. The other eight stood with weapons at the ready, four at each of the two doors which led into the room. It only took a few minutes for their preparations to be complete.

Chapter Forty-One

> *Bypass Wand: An unusual form of wand that can make a section of wall or other obstruction vanish. Their effects are easy to reverse but temporarily make a mockery of security. Eventually they burn out if used a lot.*
> *Doctor Unfriendly's Comprehensive Guide to Everything.*

The group slunk along the cramped passage. It was easily roomy enough for two kobolds to walk side by side, but only wide enough for the humans to walk single file. Shorik took the lead, being the only one of them who could stand fully upright in the passageway, and the only one who could see in the underground darkness. Termann brought up the rear; although even his eyes could not pierce blackness this heavy, his alert pointed ears would be able to detect any pursuers.

"It seems odd that they didn't hear the big fight in the prison," said Shiv, close on the heels of the dwarf. "I would have imagined they'd be shooting at us already."

"This kind of rock absorbs sound," muttered Shorik, his hand brushing the roughly carved wall. "Probably they were thinking they could use it to sneak up on invaders without warning. Their whole army could approach through these tunnels; a couple of hundred kobolds tiptoeing in full armour would make a fair amount of noise under normal circumstances."

"How far is it?" Shiv asked.

"If you keep on chattering they'll hear you regardless of the walls. It's close. Shut up." Shorik said, consistently using the same muttering tone and volume with just a hint of annoyance. After a few minutes, the tunnel became light enough to see a bit, and Shorik held his hand back to bring them to a halt. Once they were all stopped, Shorik crept ahead to look out of a doorway in the left side of the tunnel. After only a moment, he returned and beckoned them to continue the way they had been going.

They came to another opening after several more minutes of travel; this opening made far less light, and there were the sounds of quiet shuffling and scraping coming from it. Shorik again stopped them, and crept ahead.

After a moment he stepped out of the tunnel entirely, and a moment after that, he stuck his arm back into the passage and beckoned them out.

The large round chamber was lit by a soft glow from the pool of water in the centre; around it was a clear path several paces wide, but clutter of every description obscured most of the walls beyond that. There were tables, mostly, full of bottles and pipes and the remains of partially dissected animals. There were shelves stuffed with books and scrolls and all manner of knick-knacks stored in little wooden boxes and baskets. Behind much of the clutter hung the remains of prisoners in various states of decay, bones and rotting meat loosely clinging to manacles, some with bits of entrails or disembodied limbs forming piles beneath them. One pair of manacles was empty.

"Who are you?" came a quiet, high-pitched voice. There was a globe which looked like it was made of a solid piece of glass, perhaps as wide as Shiv was tall, and somehow trapped inside was a little girl. Around her fluttered several fireflies, the only source of light in the room other than the pool. "Did you come to rescue us?"

As the group emerged from the tunnel, Shiv strode over to the globe, examining it and the large wooden frame that held it in place.

"As a matter of fact we did," Shiv said. "Your name, miss?"

"Caroline." said the little girl, standing straight to show her filthy rags to best effect, as if they were the robes of an aristocrat. She looked to be about eight years old at the most, and was a slender as a girl could be without being emaciated. She gave a formal curtsy, and Shiv bowed in exchange. The others began picking through the detritus, looking for valuables or anything that looked like it was worth destroying. They had agreed not to begin smashing until they had finished scouting, so as to avoid alerting anyone nearby.

"Do you know how we get you out of this thing? I'm not sure we can just smash it without hurting you," Shiv said.

"I don't know. You could ask Sir Reginald, though."

"Who?" asked Shiv, although he noticed that Julia and Termann had both stopped searching and looked towards him at the name.

"Sir Reginald. He's hanging over there." she said, pointing. Shiv looked over his shoulder and saw one of the corpses, or rather, the upper half of a corpse, hanging in greasy tatters from the wall. Shiv's face twisted in response, but the girl explained. "No, you don't understand. He's still alive, the wizard comes and says three words to him once a day, and he stays alive enough to speak. He can't move though."

"We are in a wizard's lair," Julia offered. Shiv nodded in response, and walked over to stand before the corpse. It did not react, only hung there with flies buzzing about it and the odd maggot dropping out of its open chest.

"Sir Reginald?" Shiv asked.

"Who are you?" came a voice, oddly fleshy-sounding despite the lips being long gone. The jaw only moved slightly, and Shiv hoped the thing which moved around behind the few remaining teeth was a tongue. "I don't know you."

"My name is Shiv Kobodan. I'm here with a group of mercenaries from Redlock."

There was a sound of quiet chuckling. It got louder and more enthusiastic, erupting into a booming belly laugh, or what would have been one had Reginald still had a belly. The group ducked and began waving their hands and making shushing noises at the corpse, sure its cackling would bring a kobold army in to investigate. After only a moment though, the corpse calmed down.

"Thank-you. I don't care what you are here for, just know you have brought what is left of my soul more joy than I can remember having. Whatever you need to know, you have but to ask."

"Uh..." said Shiv, still unnerved at talking to the corpse. "I would like to know how to get the girl out of the glass ball."

"What for?" asked the corpse.

"Well, I'm sure she doesn't want to be in there. Also, I know whatever she is in there for, it'll bother the Storm Kobold."

"You could not have given a better answer. There is a tiny wooden box on a shelf near the globe. Open it, and there is a miniature wand. Trace a doorway with the wand and it will open. May I speak with someone from Redlock?"

"Of course," Shiv replied. He beckoned over Julia, who approached timidly with her eyes bright.

"Who is it?" asked Reginald.

"H... Hello, Reginald, it's Julia Hammerhand."

"Ah, Julia. I wish I could look upon you again, but my eyes were taken from me. You still have a beautiful voice. How is your mother?"

"I... she's good... doing really well." she said, tears now running down her cheeks.

"Did the goblins attack Redlock yet? Is it still there?"

"Yes, they did, but we fought them off. Shiv here helped. Redlock is still there, but a lot of people died."

"I see. Well, it could have been worse, despite my betrayal."

Julia burst into tears, and tried to say something, but could not pronounce words through the sobbing.

"I did betray them, at the end. I would ask you two things, please." The corpse's muscles flexed, a few rotten strands broke, and the head lifted up to look her in the eyes. Julia nodded, and looked back through her tears, but was still unable to speak. "First, I would ask your forgiveness. I might have spared the village some pain had I kept my vows. Second, when you leave here, I ask that you would burn my body. I don't deserve a proper burial, but perhaps it would end my betrayal and give me some peace."

"Yes," Julia said, nodding vigorously. She had got the sobbing under control enough to talk. "I f-forgive you. You were always so... good to us."

Shiv attempted to put his arm around her, but Julia shrugged it off and gave him a push. Uncertain, he hesitated before crossing the room to look for the wand. He stopped halfway, and got one of the little glass vials Doctor Unfriendly had given him. He handed it to her.

"This should do it. Just throw it at the wall over top of him." he said, and then walked away. She nodded, and took it from him, and as he walked away she resumed talking with the corpse quietly.

The wand was not difficult to find, and the girl was ecstatic upon seeing it.

"That's it!" she cried. "I remember he'd use that to trace something on the outside of the globe when he let me out."

"He let you out?" Shiv said, tracing a large rectangle on the glass.

"Oh yes, several times. He needs to let me out now and then so I can take some time with me back into the globe."

"Take time in? What do you mean?" he asked. The glass wasn't opening. Shiv tried again, tracing a smaller rectangle; he kept his face plain so as to not alarm the girl.

"There's no time in here, I think he said. Magic keeps it out. So if he wants to talk with me, or see anything happen, he has to let me out for a few minutes, so I can carry a few minutes' time back in with me."

"How long have you been in there?"

"Oh, I have no idea. Days. Maybe. Or weeks. I remember when Reginald was all-the-way alive. There were fewer prisoners then."

"Er... this isn't working. Do you think Reginald would know any more about this?" Shiv asked, keeping his expression hopeful.

"No, Reginald doesn't know anything about magic, he just watched the Kobold do it. Reginald was a knight, he wouldn't even know basic magic."

"The basics..." Shiv mused to himself. Then he put the wand in his left hand, and used it to make an approximation of the Greater Rotation. The tip flared to a dull green light, and left a mark like a translucent green thread as he drew a square shape on the glass. There was a soft popping sound and a hiss, and the square he had marked out disappeared. The girl jumped with a squeal of delight, knocking the top of her head on the globe a bit. Rubbing her head, she stepped out of the globe onto the wooden frame, and then hopped lightly down.

"Thank-you!" she said, giggling. She seized Shiv and hugged him fiercely, and then waved past him to the other side of the room. "Thanks, too, Sir Reginald!"

"You're welcome, child. Go now, go home." the corpse said. Julia had backed away from Reginald, and after remaining silent for a moment, she threw the vial. It smashed, scattering a dark liquid across the wall and the top of the rotted head; as the liquid ran down his gruesome face, it suddenly erupted into blue flame, spreading quickly among his tattered rags and the pitiful remainder of his hair. There was a howl in Reginald's voice, a howl that broke into laughter, even louder than before, an insane, overjoyed cackle that began to shake the corpse.

"Go now, run!" he shouted. "They will be coming for you! Run, Miss Kobodan! Run and never come back!"

Shiv Kobodan's jaw dropped as he watched the others crowd back into the passageway. Some were heavily laden with junk, others were beckoning, but he stood like a statue, amid the echoes of the cackling corpse.

"RUN!!!" screeched Reginald, as one of his blazing arms fell out of its socket. His remains fell to the floor, but his booming voice shouted as loud and clear as it ever had in life. "GET HER OUT OF HERE, MASTER SHIV!!! YOUR BIG SISTER NEEDS YOU!!!"

Chapter Forty-Two

> *Elves: An odd form of giant, elves used to be the dominant form of life thousands of years ago. It is said that they were the first race created, whereas the dwarves were the last. Elves live practically forever, until they are killed, which happens a lot as they are often contemptuous of others. They like anything that can be viewed as art, and dislike anything that can't. The average elf is nearly as tall as a human but weighs less than half as much, being exceptionally skinny and of lower density.*
> *Doctor Unfriendly's Comprehensive Guide to Everything.*

Shiv scurried along the passageway in a daze, all the others ahead of him, including, apparently, his big sister. He was barely aware of his surroundings as he worked out how that might be true, or why Reginald would have said it, if it was not. Suddenly realizing he had fallen further behind than he had intended, he scurried to catch up to the others, and collided with a shape in the darkness.

"Er...Termann?"

"Yes, Master Shiv."

"So what is our plan now?"

"You helped devise it. Was the news about the girl a shock?"

"Yes, one might express it thusly, were sufficient adjectives not available."

"I see. Well put it out of your mind for the moment. We need to escape, and the only way we know out of here is through the main gate. I assume the guards will be in place in the stairwell, and that area looks like a slaughterhouse."

"Slaughterhouse?" asked Shiv, still having trouble concentrating.

"You probably couldn't tell, but the blood of hundreds stained those steps. No fortress is impregnable, but I've rarely seen closer. We need some way to either remove the guards from the entrance or to sneak past them, and I cannot think of anything with a reasonable chance of success."

The group emerged back in the prison, fanning out into a large circle. Most of them started dumping the loot from the laboratory on the floor to better sort through it. A few of the prisoners had found better weapons or armour, and were going through the process of re-arming themselves; Julia was staring off into space clutching an empty sword scabbard, her own blades still sheathed. Shiv stood, much like Julia, deep in thought and still clutching the miniature wand he'd used to open the globe. It looked to be made of a thin sliver of grey stone as thick as his finger and maybe a little over a handspan long. Tiny streaks of white moved around its surface, like they were living creatures or maybe ripples of water.

Shorik had just dumped his armload of booty to one side, and had begun adding to his map. Soon he was joined by Termann, and they began discussing plans and details fervently.

Caroline walked over to Shiv and stood before him. He snapped out of his reverie, startled, and crouched down to look her in the eye.

"Hello there, again, my lady," he said.

"Did you hear what Sir Reginald said? About your big sister?" she asked.

"Yes, do you know what he meant by that?"

"I wanted to ask you. Do you have a big sister?"

"I don't remember. Do you have any?" Shiv replied, fiddling with the wand and looking away from her.

"That's a silly thing to not remember. You can't just forget your brothers and sisters. And no, I have no sisters, but I have brothers. I used to have three, but the baby went away when we all got sick, and the other two died."

"You all got sick?" he asked.

"Yes. We all had some kind of plague. Except my baby brother, so when we thought we weren't going to get better, my Dad gave him away. But my father and I did get better, so maybe one day he'll come back."

"That would be nice," Shiv replied, looking at her intensely. "I'm sure your baby brother will be happy to come back to a big sister like you."

Suddenly, there was a soft popping sound, and Shiv fell into a small hole that had just appeared beneath him. Caroline screeched, and jumped back. The hole was about waist deep, and looked like it had been carved out of the stone floor with a razor in a roughly rectangular shape. Shiv staggered to his feet, more dazed than hurt, and met the gaze of everyone in the group who were staring back at him. He wiped a bit of dust off his forehead with the back of his hand, and Julia pointed at him in response.

"The wand," she said.

Chapter Forty-Three

> *Ceborn's Sky-Ship: Duke Ceborn has a large wooden ship that, like many elf creations, is fashioned in the shape of a tree. It is enchanted to fly instead of travel on water, and the Duke uses it to drop things on people he doesn't like.*
> *Doctor Unfriendly's Comprehensive Guide to Everything.*

Ruzzio Hammerhand crouched behind a dense copse of trees in the treeline which surrounded Redlock. The late afternoon sky was clear, except for one unusual sight. Hanging in the air above the village was a massive wooden ship which looked like it had been shaped out of a living tree; roots made up the stern and spreading branches made up the prow, and a complicated arrangement of sails and branching masts festooned the decks. He had heard the Duke had a flying ship, but whether he would be pleased with the state of the village was anyone's guess. He raised two fingers in a motion he had told his brothers meant 'wait'.

****

Thokk Hammerhand peered out from the thicket he and the rest of his brothers had hidden in. Forrel had his steel-laden arms crossed and tapped his steel-shod foot impatiently, and Daryd, as usual, was flexing the long-nailed fingers of his sword hand, red eyes narrowed to slits. Thokk raised his considerable bulk from hands and knees, and retrieved his poleaxe from where he had set it down. Zimmiman,

CAMERON S. CURRIE

no longer a piece of luggage, sat a short distance away with his peg leg off, rubbing his heavily bruised stump.

"He just is watching something. I can't see what it is through the trees though." Thokk looked to his older brother as he always did for a decision.

"It can't be that important. We're at home," Forrel snapped.

"We always defer to each man's expertise," purred Daryd. "Ruzzio is the scout, let him scout."

****

The troll lay as flat as her protruding belly would allow at the top of the bluff; the four men she had been tracking were down there crouching in a copse of trees. The light was dim enough to cause her no discomfort, clouds obscuring the worst of the sunlight, but her ruined eyes had no need to squint. One eye would eventually heal, although it was still swelled shut; the four had a unique enough smell that she had followed them with no difficulty. The brother with elf blood occasionally circled back to obscure their tracks, but he did not think in terms of smell and she ignored his best efforts. The brother with the goblin blood stank enough to follow easily, as did the one in all the armour. The last one smelled… unnatural. She didn't like the smell of that one; it made her want to kill him even more. The female who had been with them, who had smelled like their sister, had thus far been undetectable, so Mother waited to make sure it was not some kind of cunning human trap.

****

Dorlah Unfriendly peered out of an abandoned animal den at the nearby wall of troll flesh, and put away the tiny bottle of musk she had been rubbing on her skin. Then she crept silently back down into the main chamber, where the Doctor comfortably reclined, squinting in the dark at one of his books and stinking of badger musk. They had spent considerable effort getting ahead of the she-troll, and since they had found this spot to wait the Doctor had been entirely too comfortable. She held her finger to her lips as he looked up, and pointed to the entrance.

"She's right there," she mouthed silently.

****

The Storm Kobold, seething and grinding his needle-like teeth, kept trying to focus on the location of the knife thrower, and kept getting darkness. While his night vision was particularly good, it did not function through the pool. He growled and tried the location of the Hammerhands, but kept getting blurs, as though the pool was trying to focus on multiple areas at once. He struck the surface of the water, scattering what little image there was, and began pacing his lab again as several of his apprentices put everything back in order. Much of his equipment was missing, and no matter how many holes he poked in Abner, the only culprits the half-sized wretch could come up with were the gnomes, the Hammerhands, and the one-legged wizard. Abner knew even less about this Shiv they had captured than he did. He ordered his kobolds to re-shackle the half-a-ling, and decided to try again.

"Kef tora'eth Doctor Unfriendly," the blue creature said to his pool, dropping in six drops of blood from a tiny vial. The pool shimmered, swirled, and showed blackness again. He shrieked at the pool, then turned and gestured at the nearest kobold. His target had only a moment to register its surprise before its head burst in a shower of sizzling sparks.

****

A mirror in an opulently decorated, far-off chamber displayed an image of the Storm Kobold's tantrum, and the white-cloaked man chuckled quietly to himself. As he watched, he cracked his knuckles one by one; despite his fingers appearing normal, he cracked at least six knuckles in the thumbs and each of the first two fingers, and yet ignored the remaining two fingers as if they weren't there. The hand shimmered as if it was attempting to return to its accustomed shape, but a glance and a gesture so small it was imperceptible restored it, without its owner wasting a conscious thought.

The white-cloaked man looked almost out of place in his richly decorated laboratory; it was constructed of different coloured blocks of marble, and the shelves and tables, while superficially similar to the Storm Kobold's, were also of exquisitely detailed stonework. The man's appearance, by comparison, was almost strangely ordinary. He was of slightly less than average height, of average build, and had brown hair of a middling length and eyes of an indeterminate colour. His robes were little better than rags, only seen to when he bothered to think about them, thread-bare and worn to the point that their colour, apart from the cloak, was also hard to discriminate.

With another low chuckle and a few whispered syllables, the image of the Storm Kobold faded and was replaced by someone else. The white-cloaked man studied his new subject, the one who carried all the knives. The mirror showed the knife-master in unerring detail as he used a bypass wand to carve a tunnel in utter darkness. Behind the knife thrower, the false light of his spell showed a number of lesser people, unimportant to the greater plan, except, perhaps, for the older sister. She might be essential.

"Hello, my boy..." said the white-cloaked man softly. "It is good to see you are doing so well... you have nearly reached your goal..."

With a gesture the mirror shimmered and then returned to displaying the room, and the scaled creature that wore the white cloak, and a powerful illusion, over its huge and twisted form. In the mirror's surface the creature held out a withered arm which sprouted a vestigial wing from the elbow, and a bat-winged little gargoyle flew over to perch there. Also in the mirror's surface, dozens of other deformed monsters of various shapes and sizes rustled from cleverly disguised hiding places amid the tapestries, bookshelves and carvings.

Away from the mirror's surface, there was just a white-cloaked man, with a pleasant songbird perched on his hand. He whispered something to it as he left the room, and with a single word extinguished the one hundred and eighteen lanterns that illuminated it.

The door swung shut behind him, leaving the room in blackness. In the blackness, the rustling of the hidden gargoyles seemed somehow louder.

Chapter Forty-Four

> *The Year: The Human calendar says it is the year 1006 of the Neslish Reckoning. This is wildly incorrect, that happened 1031 years ago. It also says the year is 12 months long, and that each month begins at the dark of the moons, lasting 4½ weeks, which is more or less correct if you count on your fingers. Any discrepancies with real life are traditionally glossed over by the nobility.*
> *Doctor Unfriendly's Comprehensive Guide to Everything.*

The hillside was quiet in the darkness. The sounds of kobold soldiers running up their staircase could be heard from the opposite side of the hill. Soon after that began, a barely-visible greenish light appeared in the grass, the size of a fingertip. Once there, it began to elongate into a line, as if an invisible artist was drawing the glow with a pen on the surface of the ground, in glowing green ink. This was not far from the truth.

Soon the line bent at a hard angle, and continued for a short time before bending again. It bent once more, meeting up at its starting point and forming a square. There was a quiet popping sound and the square of ground disappeared, replaced with a tunnel opening. There was the sound of several people coughing as quietly as they could manage.

"I'm sorry the ceiling fell in. I'm not a coal miner," Shiv hissed, suppressing a cough of his own as he crawled from the tunnel. The stubby wand was still clutched in his hand, the tip glowing an angry red. "We're lucky the wand didn't run dry halfway here."

The dwarf followed him, beating the dust out of his scavenged clothes.

"Well, I have been a coal miner, among other things."

"Well, granted. But I didn't have anything to shore up the sides, so you're just going to have to live with that. Anyway, you don't know anything about using wands."

"Quiet. The kobolds are already searching for us. I can hear them coming out of the stairwell," said Termann. He helped the little girl out of the tunnel and into the growing crowd of escapees.

As soon as they had all emerged, they headed down the hillside as quietly as they could, the slaves making a few whispered exclamations of joy despite the danger.

"Which way back to Redlock?" asked Shiv, stowing the wand in one of his pouches and drawing two black iron daggers.

"West is that way," replied Termann, pointing with one hand and unlimbering his longbow with the other. He stopped a moment to string it and notch an arrow. "However we should stay away from the path. It'll be easy enough for them to track a group this big without us going exactly the way they expect."

They were less than halfway down when the first kobold crested the hill. Termann shooed the others ahead of himself, motioning for them to keep down as well. He crouched and drew his bow, eyeing the kobold intently; the creature scanned out into the darkness, but luckily appeared to be looking out toward the horizon instead of down the slope.

Shorik stayed behind with Termann, also watching the kobold.

"They can't know how we escaped quite yet," the elven captain told the dwarf. "He most likely came to the top of the hill to get a wider view of the entrance valley."

Sure enough, the kobold turned his back to them after only a moment and shouldered a large crossbow. With a nod, Termann relaxed the draw on his bow and scurried lightly down the slope, with Shorik close behind.

The group met at the base of the hill; as Termann and Shorik approached the others were already arguing in harsh whispers. Termann smacked one of the loudest, one of the escaped slaves. As they all turned to face him Termann made an emphatic gesture of his hand over his mouth. Up at the top of the slope there were now three kobolds, milling about in a little group chittering to each other.

"We can argue about where we are going once we are safely away," Shiv whispered as quietly as he could. They all followed Termann carefully, Shiv stopping to take Caroline's hand and repeat the 'quiet' gesture to her. She nodded and followed in silence, and they ran along parallel to the path, but a few hundred paces away, in the brush and occasional trees that were there. They avoided the valley with the troll entirely, and although the terrain was far more rugged off of the path they made good time considering the group's increasing fatigue.

As the sun rose they rejoined the path, and scanned the way behind them for some time before entering the tunnel to Abner's hideout.

"We should rest here," Termann said, no longer whispering. He sat down in the doorway, laying his strung bow across his lap. "I'll take the watch. We can see kobolds pursuing for some distance at this point, and you all need some sleep. In a few hours I'll wake you and we'll split up the last of our food. I'm sure you prisoners can take refuge in Redlock for a day or two while we decide what to do with you."

"Hold on a moment!" said the man called Instav. "I was a prisoner there for a couple of years. I have a family in Sabosland, and a farmstead. I don't have any desire to hang out in some Neslish backwater while my family thinks I'm dead. What if my wife remarries?"

The other prisoners nodded.

"Go if you want," Termann said, and shrugged. "I was just thinking of the safety in remaining as a group. If you get captured, I would take it as a personal favour if you did not reveal who we were or where we were going."

Enwerd nodded, as did Shantel. Instav shook his head and gestured to Jon, Berrit, and Kasser; after a pause the four of them walked off into the tunnel, leaving the remaining nine there to make a ramshackle camp just inside the doorway.

They had arranged their meagre possessions into a few piles for makeshift pillows, and were getting as comfortable as they could when Caroline, lying down asked a question aloud.

"What year is it?"

Chapter Forty-Five

> *Dukes: In Nesland, the rank just below the King. Nesland is divided into four Duchies and one separate County. Each of the Duchies are divided into Counties and/or Baronies and even smaller estates, each under the power of a noble of appropriate rank. Despite all this organization, they still have trouble running things.*
> Doctor Unfriendly's Comprehensive Guide to Everything.

"So, we wait here until the Duke is gone?" Thokk asked Forrel, and then took a huge bite from the slab of salted meat he'd been saving. He chewed in noisily with his mouth open. Ruzzio and Daryd shared a knowing look and both shook their heads at him, long since over attempting to teach their half-brother any sort of refinement. His appetite always interfered. They each nibbled on their own trail rations in a more measured way while they listened to Forrel's answer.

Zimmiman had finally quit complaining about his sore leg, and was lying a few paces away with his head on his backpack. He stubbornly pretended he was sleeping, pausing just long enough to glare at the brothers every time they spoke.

"Look, if the Duke has brought soldiers or knights or whatever and is happy with the Baronet, he'll be happy and treat us well when we get back. If the Duke makes trouble, we'll show up after the smoke clears, the Baronet's loyal subjects, and he'll still treat us well. If we show up while the Duke is giving him trouble, we might share in it."

"So that's a yes?" Thokk mumbled through a half-chewed mouthful.

"Yes, ape. Yes." Forrel said levelly, and sat down with a growl. "Can we have a fire, now?"

"No," Ruzzio said flatly. "The less sign we leave the better. No point showing up late if they think we were here the whole time... Shh!"

There was a slight rustle in some nearby bushes, and one of the gnomes, the doctor with the ridiculous hat, stepped into view, crouching as if he was hiding from someone.

"Oh, I thought it was something important." Forrel said. His brothers snickered.

"Very nice," whispered the Doctor. "And it is something important. There's a troll tracking you about two hurls back the way you came."

"Nonsense," Ruzzio snapped. "I'd hear a troll a mile off, they're loud and stupid."

"You're the loud and stupid ones," hissed the Doctor. Dorlah Unfriendly emerged, also in a sneaky crouch, just behind her brother-in-law. "She's on the move now, I think she wants to attack before you can get to the village."

"She?" asked Daryd. His long-nailed hand moved unconsciously to the hilt of his rapier. "You don't mean it's the one from before?"

"Probably. Either way, it's a female. You know they're more dangerous. It's injured, and it's angry. It's coming this way, and it'll be here in a few minutes."

"Zimmiman?" asked Forrel, standing up and drawing his sword despite the unbelieving smile on his face. "Do you want to go scout out this troll for us, maybe blow it up?"

"Zimmiman can't sneak to save his life!" snapped Dorlah, earning a glare from the wizard. Zimmiman growled to himself, sat up, and began strapping his peg leg on.

"We could use some fireballs or something," growled Thokk, slowly getting to his feet, using his poleaxe for leverage. "So how far-"

A deafening bang came from only a few paces off as one of the outer trees in their hiding spot was chopped in half in one swing. The upper half, heavy with evergreen branches, bounced heavily to one side before starting to fall. As it fell it revealed a swollen troll face, jagged fangs bared and one remaining eye open just a watery slit.

"GESH, TOR, DEK!" the monster roared, and blindly swung her huge poleaxe into the midst of them; they all dove away from the deadly blade, which looked like retooled breastplate mounted on a half a tree, and drew their weapons. The troll yanked the blade out of the ground, spraying clods of earth, and swung the flat backside like a hammer into Forrel's chest in the same movement. With a loud clang, Forrel flipped end over end into the trees, landing curled up in a steel-plated ball.

Daryd's slender sword was already poking at her face, narrowly missing her one swollen, leaking eye, but leaving two tiny holes in the troll's cheek. She snarled and hit him with a backhand, knocking him flying, and then howled again as she realized the rapier was stuck like a sliver in her wrist.

Zimmiman, not finished with his leg, discarded it and crawled away from the fight, gathering up his staff as he did so. Once he was behind the largest tree he could find, he began rifling through his pockets for spell components.

A tiny dart appeared in the troll's forehead, and the Doctor twirled his staff, revealing the second end to be hollow as well. With a click it fired his second dart, which hit her shoulder. The troll roared again, but otherwise seemed unaware of the darts at all. Her glare turned to Thokk, and she charged into him, shoulder knocking him sprawling, but getting the largest brother's own poleaxe caught in her hide poncho as she did. Blood trickled down along one of her tube-shaped pockets, but she ignored the injury. She had suffered far worse.

"GESH!" the troll shouted, swinging her axe and narrowly missing Ruzzio. The momentum flung Daryd's rapier end-over-end into the bushes. She ignored it, swinging again at Ruzzio, who had a sword and buckler out. He leapt back out of her reach, trying to circle around to her flank. "TOR!" The troll roared and stepped forward, swinging the axe again and forcing Ruzzio to jump back further. He jumped over the curled up body of his older brother, and spared a glance to see if he was breathing, looking up just in time to duck under a fourth deadly swing.

Dorlah Unfriendly's spear jabbed into the troll's foot from behind, but the troll ignored it, no more than an insect sting. Daryd, bloodied, staggered towards the troll's back, poking his recovered rapier at her stumpy tail and hindquarters, but his lithe agility was gone, along with three of his ribs.

A tiny ball of fire, the size of a fist, shot out of the woods and splattered against the troll's flank. Her head whipped around to glare at the one legged wizard leaning awkwardly against a tree a short distance off. While she was distracted, Thokk leapt onto her broad back, legs hooking her neck and hands trying to free his axe from the tangle of animal hide.

Another click sounded, the Doctor firing another dart out of his staff. In his off-hand he held a narrow steel bar, which he hurriedly inserted down the barrel to re-cock the mechanism inside. His eyes went wide as he realized he was in the troll's path as it charged at the equally shocked Zimmiman.

Thokk finally freed his axe, the strength of his last pull knocking him loose, and he fell backwards off of the troll, sprawling again.

Another fireball streaked from Zimmiman's outstretched fingers, bursting on the troll's shoulder; she staggered but didn't slow down much, the remains of one eye focussed on the increasingly wide-eyed wizard.

"DEK!" came a shout from the trees. The troll skidded to a halt, suddenly, great clawed feet digging up undergrowth.

"Dek?" she said, a low, menacing, growl. She looked over her shoulder and squinted her blurry eye to regard an elf. It wasn't the elf from the village, the smell was wrong, but it was holding a sword pointed at her.

The Doctor pointed his staff, and was gestured to halt by the newcomer. It was a male elf, much bigger than Termann, in a fur-lined leather cloak and shining plate armour made of a dark crystal substance. Barely visible were hints of a moustache, almost unheard of on an elf of any age. In one hand he held a sword, pointed at the troll, and on his back was a bundle which looked like it contained at least six other weapons.

"Dek!" snapped the elf a second time. His free hand patted his flat, plate-armoured belly. "Teff nuk go-ath!"

From the same direction the elf had come, ten soldiers appeared, each carrying a long-hafted spear. They stood behind the elf, neither threatening nor cowering, spears pointed at the sky.

"GESH! TOR!" howled the troll. She waited, as if expecting a response from the elf. She raised her poleaxe and shook it. When that didn't get a response, she slapped her open hand against the two large burns Zimmiman's fireballs had left. "Go-har tee nuk! GESH! TOR!"

"Gesh. Tor," replied the elf. He raised the sword and sheathed it in the bundle on his back. "Go-ath."

The troll roared again, with no particular words, and then snorted loudly, spitting blood and phlegm, in a huge wad, onto the ground. It stared at the elf for a long moment, then turned and walked away growling. The elf stood still, watching her stomp away, at then turned to the recovering Hammerhands.

"Idiots," he growled softly to himself, and turned back towards Redlock, his entourage following him wordlessly. The two gnomes snickered.

"Who the hell are you?" shouted Forrel as his brothers helped him stagger to his feet. The elf and his guards froze in place for a moment, and then the one of the guards turned back and approached. He regarded the injured Forrel for only a moment before suddenly punching him in his face, knocking his helmet off with one stroke. Forrel collapsed, once again, to his knees. The other three Hammerhands drew weapons, and were totally ignored by the guard.

"That's better," said the guard, pointing angrily at the prone Hammerhand. "That's the posture one takes when addressing His Grace, Duke Ceborn. Any one of us will take great offense if you ever fail to show him respect again."

"Especially after I saved your lives," said the Duke, who had approached without the slightest noise. He looked down at Forrel for a moment, lips pursed as if he was assessing something about him. As if making a decision, he turned suddenly to regard the panting Zimmiman. "I hate to have to kill someone I just saved, it's counterproductive. You- wizard. I'll want to speak with you."

He turned and walked away, again without the slightest noise despite his heavy armour and collection of weaponry. Without looking back, he made a signal over his shoulder, like he expected to be followed. Zimmiman hopped along as quickly as he could, leaning on his staff, and the gnomes came close behind, still stifling chuckles.

Picking up their brother between them, the Hammerhands followed the Duke and his men, and made no argument or protest.

Chapter Forty-Six

> *Knights: Knights are the lowest significant rank in the giant upper class. Generally speaking they exemplify the stereotypes of humanity: big, somewhat stupid, and violent, and convinced they are more honourable than they really are. A typical knight is equipped with as much plate armour and weaponry as he can carry without breaking his war-horse's spine.*
>
> *Doctor Unfriendly's Comprehensive Guide to Everything.*

It was past dark when Shiv and his party approached Redlock; from a distance they saw the huge blackness that was the floating ship above the town, blotting out a great swath of stars and two of the seven waxing moons that had been lighting their path.

"What is that?" asked Julia, pointing to the black shape while they were still far-off. Before anyone could respond, there was the sound of a signal horn blaring two long notes, and then two short.

"We only have three signals, and that's not one of them. There was never a need for more," stated Termann, frown visible despite the low light. "Although recent events might indicate that has changed. There are horses coming." By the time he had said it, the others could hear the hoof beats as well. They all began casually reaching for weapons at the same time, as if it had been rehearsed.

Despite the shadows a rider soon was visible; he approached without any attempt to hide or use the sparse brush as concealment, and simultaneously all of them relaxed their sword hands. Caroline stepped behind Shiv and the rider slowed to a halt in front of them.

The rider was a soldier, but not one they knew from Redlock; he wore a half suit of plate armour over chainmail, although the horse itself was unarmoured. A long, steel-tipped lance was in his right hand, pointed at the sky.

"Are you the mercenaries returning from the Storm Kobold's lair?" the rider asked, not addressing anyone in particular.

"Some of us are, Sir Knight," said Shiv, stepping to the front of the group. "The rest are escapees from that foul location or residents of this very village. To what emergency do I owe the honour of your surprising presence?"

"His grace, the Duke of Ceborn, ordered you to an audience with him as soon as you returned," said the horseman impassively. He was a bit lightly equipped for a typical knight, but did not react at the title.

"Well," said Shiv, looking past the horseman at the village, still a few minutes' walk away. "We haven't quite returned yet, have we?"

"The Duke wants you in front of him. I can escort you or drag you, but finding a sack to stuff you in might take a minute. I'd rather not waste the minute."

It was impossible to see the knight's facial expression with his helmet's visor down, and with the bored sound of his voice it was uncertain whether he was joking or not. Shiv shrugged, and stepped around him, and the others followed. The walk took only a few minutes, despite their weariness from the journey.

At the gate, one of Termann's soldiers had apparently recovered from his injuries and stood guard; instead of leaning he was rigidly at attention, a freshly forged spear in his hand pointed straight up. He stared straight ahead, not moving even as the group approached him, and his armour shone in the light of a nearby lantern. In front of him were four arrows stuck in the ground as if the bow slung on his back might be needed at any moment.

Captain Termann raised his eyebrows as they walked past, inspecting the guard as if some detail might jump out of place.

The town square was only a short distance from the edge of town, and it was crowded with people who looked as if they had just arrived there. At the opposite end of the square one of the benches from Shiv's circus tent had been set up and a single figure sat there, with an honour guard of a dozen heavily-armed soldiers standing behind him. Around the perimeter of the square, brass lamp-stands had been erected, all lit, with their shutters opened to focus the light into the square, just in front of the bench.

As the group entered the square a few paces behind the horseman, the figure on the bench rose. He was an elf, although it took a second glance to determine that, as he was easily the largest elf Shiv had ever seen. Only a half a head shorter than the human guards behind him, his shoulders were just as wide, and his slender arms and legs projected wiry strength. He was dressed in black glass armour and wore a heavy cloak of leather and fur, and a bundle of a half a dozen or more sword hilts peeked over his shoulder. As he stepped into the brightest of the lamp-light, a slight moustache was visible, despite the fact elves were generally believed to be incapable of growing them.

"Your grace, the mercenaries you asked for," the horseman said as he hopped down off the horse directly into a deep bow in front of the standing elf. The elf nodded without a word, and the horseman turned and stood to face the mercenaries. "His grace, Ceborn Duke of Ceborn, Lord-General of the Air, Protector of the North, will now receive you."

Captain Termann bowed on one knee, as did Julia Hammerhand, Zimmiman, and the gnomes. The others, most of the escaped slaves and town guards, followed their lead only a moment later. Shiv, the dwarf Shorik, and Caroline all stood.

"You all heard me say time was an issue," said the horseman, frowning. The honour guard all matched his frown, as if they had been personally insulted. Shiv frowned back, and exchanged a glance with both the girl and the dwarf before going down on one knee as well. The soldiers' frowns dissipated somewhat.

"I don't know if you are my subjects directly, so I'll forgive that. Be thankful I have a sense of humour," the Duke said. He didn't smile. "I understand you are among those I have to thank for Redlock still standing."

Shiv, still on one knee, looked around himself, and seeing no one else was answering, spoke.

"Yes, er… your grace. We just returned from the Storm Kobold's stronghold, although we did little more than irritate him I think."

"And you were instrumental in fighting off the goblins," the Duke said. He paced back and forth in front of them, his face appearing mildly irritated. Each step gave the impression that his foot landed exactly where he intended, and not a hair off in any direction, as if he had rehearsed this exact meeting for years. He gestured for Shiv to stand. Shiv did, trying to slouch a bit so as to not tower over the Duke too much. "This would be exceptional from any of my subjects. However, you, Master Shiv, are not my subject. Also, you were paid a pittance and kept against your will for a time. Although the Baronet's daughters settled accounts with you, I feel somewhat indebted regardless."

"Um... thank-you... your grace?" Shiv said, uncertain as to where this was headed.

"I owe you a favour. I am rather pressed for time, as I had to wait here nearly a day, but anything I can manage before I go, I'll do to settle up that debt. Does anything come to mind?" The Duke stopped pacing, and stood facing Shiv. Despite looking upwards at him, he still gave the impression of looking down. Shiv paused only a moment before slightly nodding to himself.

"About twenty-five years ago there was a plague near the border of Talisman, in the duchy of Resude, down south. I heard a rumour that a Talismanian wizard caused that plague. Do you know who that wizard was?"

"I'd tell that to anyone, regardless of whether I owed them a favour," the Duke said, the corners of his mouth hinting at a smile. "I don't know for certain, but I'd bet mixed metal it was the Zanquitor himself."

"Zanquitor?" Shiv asked.

"Ugh... their king, of sorts. Zanquitor Zachary Talisman, sometimes known as Talisman the second. He's a wizard, beyond a grandmaster, but insane as you can imagine. Perhaps crazier than that. Why? What's so important about that plague?"

"It killed my first family, or at least some of them," Shiv said, looking at Caroline, whose jaw dropped as she looked back. The Duke nodded in response.

"Well, although you have as much cause as anyone for revenge, I wouldn't go up against the Zanquitor. I'm beyond a master swordsman, and a master wizard, and I wouldn't go up against him myself, unless I had an army with me. What did you mean first family?"

"My second family was an acting troupe that was murdered about twenty years ago, in the Gnoll Passage outside of Sabosland. I kept the murder weapons, but the trail is long since cold with them, and I don't know how likely it is I'll ever catch the murderer at this point."

"That I can help you with. It so happens someone owes me a favour, someone who can solve that mystery for you, so long as you haven't done anything with those weapons."

"And you can arrange a meeting before you leave?" Shiv said incredulously. "I… I… thank-you, your grace!"

"Don't thank me, your work isn't done yet," the Duke said. "I offer the path to a clue, nothing more."

Chapter Forty-Seven

> *Inter-species Diplomacy: A point of interest for me personally is the fact that every race in Dylactae is convinced that they are the only civilized one, and that all the others are ignorant savages. If they were really interested in being properly civilized, they would all learn about it from the gnomes.*
> *Doctor Unfriendly's Comprehensive Guide to Everything.*

Mother stomped angrily through the thin brush, growling to herself. The elf had threatened her and Dek, something she would not normally forgive. However, he claimed he had killed many trolls, and he offered her a chance to leave unharmed, something which did not fit with her experience. She was not sure whether she was mad at the elf, or at herself for believing his threats.

In frustration she knocked over a fairly large pine tree with a casual backhand, and then took hold of the uprooted wreckage and tossed it over some nearby treetops and into the darkness. Mildly out of breath, she paused and realized she felt a little better. She had not got her full measure of revenge, but she had given the four brothers a fairly good beating. It was something. She sneezed a bit and wiped her oozing face on the back of her arm, and realized her one eye was healed enough she could see somewhat clearly through it.

With a deep chuckle she sat down and put her poleaxe down beside her, looking at it briefly. It was well-made for being forged without the use of her eyes. The toothy smile only lasted long enough for her to retrieve Gesh's knife. She sat and stared at it, uncertain what to do; the elf and his herd of soldiers protected the brothers, now, so her revenge was out of reach. She thought for a long time, nearly until morning. That was when she heard the elf's voice again.

He was shouting her name, and some other words, poor approximations of proper trollish words, but obviously ones designed to get her attention. More curious than anything else, she got up, stowed Gesh's knife, and followed the sound of the shouting.

The elf was standing in a clearing, with only one human and what looked and smelled like a pile of meat. This only increased Mother's curiosity, and she emerged from the brush slowly, looking and smelling for ambush. The elf and human both stood there, arms crossed in a trollish sign of non-aggression.

In front of the two was a raw side of beef, a pile of tanned leather, and four large chunks of raw iron. Mother eyed the two suspiciously, but they did not smell aggressive, and there was no smell of others with them. The human made some quiet human noises, and the elf nodded, but otherwise they stayed motionless. Slowly, Mother approached, her ever-present hunger adding to the curiosity. When she was close enough she sniffed the pile.

"Yes. Yours. For trade," said the elf in terrible trollish. His pronunciation was so awful it took her a moment to understand. Mother was surprised, she had not heard any of the small people talk so much before. Certainly not about anything so complex as trade.

"Lie. Your herd killed Gesh and Tor," she replied, speaking slowly so the creature could maybe understand. She snarled a bit, showing a few inches of tusk for emphasis. "You are troll killer."

"No lie. Trade. No more killing," replied the elf. The two small people made more human noises between them, and a few subtle gestures, but then returned their arms to crossed position. Mother sniffed the pile again, and then each of the small people in turn. The human stank of fear (Mother chuckled at this, and tapped one finger, as thick as the human's leg, on the top of its head, as a warning to keep calm). The elf, oddly enough, smelled a little tense, but not of fear at all. Apparently he had been telling the truth about killing trolls, anyway. Somewhat satisfied, Mother sat back on her haunches and crossed her own arms over her bloated belly. "What trade?" she asked.

"Human," the elf said, pointing to his companion, "Want to see Grandmother."

Mother laughed. The thought of this mute human meeting the all-knowing Grandmother was ridiculous. Grandmother would eat this tiny human before she even discovered the reason for his intrusion. It seemed a waste of Grandmother's wisdom, a visit from a mute, ignorant animal.

"She eat human." Mother replied, curious as to what dispute the elf had with the human to send him to Grandmother.

"Human make trade with Grandmother," said the elf. This caused even more laughter from Mother, who couldn't help but uncross her arms to use her hands for balance.

"This is for me?" Mother asked, pointing to the pile. It was quite a lot of trade for just an introduction.

"Yes," the elf said nodding to his companion. He made a few gestures and the human picked up the hides (evidently it was a large, sturdy leather sack) and began heaving the meat and iron into the sack for her. It was funny to watch, the human struggling with such a small weight, so Mother relaxed and chuckled to herself while she waited. When he was finished, Mother snatched the sack roughly out of his hands and slung it over one shoulder.

"Done," she said, and turned to leave. She hoped the human was smart enough to follow her. The human and elf made a few human noises at each other, and then the human did follow.

Chapter Forty-Eight

> *North: Lodestones and compass needles point north, which is the direction to a spot on the Ice Mountain, a place so inhospitable it is only inhabited by some human wizards from the Counciltowers, who think they can find out how north works. It has taken them nearly 200 years, and so far they have discovered they do not like the cold.*
> *Doctor Unfriendly's Comprehensive Guide to Everything.*

Shiv hurried along behind the troll, looking briefly over his shoulder at the Duke. The imposing elf was already headed back towards Redlock, and soon was out of sight. He was still unclear as to how he was supposed to talk to this half-troll Oracle, or for that matter, what exactly a half-troll Oracle was, other than someone who might know the answers he needed. The troll seemed to know the direction, and the Duke had said it would take a couple of days to get where they were going.

They soon came to Abner's hideout, and the troll stopped to sniff the air. Shiv wondered at how many places the little hill seemed to lead to, but said nothing. He was certain the troll wouldn't understand any kind of speech anyway, apart from the animalistic grunting and bellowing it had shared with the Duke.

After only a moment's pause, the troll headed southeast; there was no path, but the troll seemed unconcerned, flattening anything smaller than a tree without a thought, and anything tree-sized or larger with little more than a casual shove. After a few hours of travelling through increasingly rocky terrain, he was sure they were

CAMERON S. CURRIE

in the huge tract of wilderness called the Gnoll Passage, and out of Nesland. Shiv had crossed the edge of the Passage before, in order to make small shortcuts, but now they were headed into the heart of it. They could expect nomads, packs of wolves or bears, no doubt more trolls, and of course caravans of gnolls. After thinking of this he briefly checked a half dozen of his knives to ensure they were loose in their hiding spots.

They made good time, but soon the sun was high above the jagged horizon, and the troll was squinting and hissing at the light. She quickly found a rock with scrub bushes growing over it, which looked big enough to shade her bulk, and half dug, half crawled in underneath. Without a word, she curled up into a ball, looking not unlike a huge boulder herself, and glared a brief warning at Shiv, before quickly falling asleep.

Shiv stood watching until she was asleep before unlimbering his freshly-filled backpack and setting up a little tent. It was nothing on his pavilion, but was light, sturdy, and most importantly, cheap. With regret he wished he could have brought his mule, Cornelius, but Duke Ceborn had assured him it would have lasted only until the troll needed breakfast. Mother Hammerhand had packed him a pair of bulky sandwiches in cheese cloth, and he greedily devoured one, reflecting he had not had any sleep since Abner's hideout with the escapees the day before.

He had eaten most of the sandwich and drank heavily from his water bag when he heard the approach of several pairs of feet. Grumbling and tired, he got up and drew two of his dragon-tooth knives.

"Oh, there you are," said the squeaky voice of Doctor Unfriendly as he rounded a small hillock nearby. The gnome turned and beckoned behind him, and was soon joined by Julia Hammerhand, and two of the escaped slaves, Enwerd and Shantel. The two slaves each had a new suit of clothes, but otherwise were still equipped with scavenged kobold weapons and Shorik's makeshift armour.

"What are you all doing here? What do you think will happen when the troll wakes up?!?" snapped Shiv. "Julia, you shot out her eye!"

"Don't worry," the Doctor replied, interposing himself between them and Shiv. "When we told the Duke we wanted to come he said the troll would probably be fine with it. Anyway, I speak trollish, and that might come in handy."

"Shouldn't you two be off enjoying your freedom or something?" Shiv asked the two escapees.

"You'll recall we both expressed an interest in being your apprentices," answered Shantel. "Not to mention we owed you a debt for saving our lives, thought maybe we could return the favour."

Shiv looked them up and down irritably. Both of them still looked underfed and sickly, albeit slightly less so, but their eyes were full of determination. Enwerd had broad shoulders which would fill out as he recovered, and ragged brown hair that would go unremarked in almost any town Shiv had ever been in. Shantel had the potential to be pretty, eventually, with dirty blonde hair finally brushed out to shoulder length, and slightly heavy hips that narrowed to a wasp-like waist. They both waited silently for Shiv's approval.

"Anyway," interrupted Julia, "you left a little girl back in Redlock with a lot of questions that need answering. You left rather abruptly, actually. I mean to keep you alive to answer them."

"I had to leave abruptly, the Duke was leaving and we had to catch the troll," Shiv said, rewrapping the last bit of sandwich. He got up and started looking for firewood. "This is the first progress I've made in decades, I'm not going to stop to teach my older sister her family history. Most of which I don't know anyway."

"You weren't that flippant when she was in front of you," said Julia, watching his face closely. He ignored her as he found his first few scraps of dead wood.

"So what is it exactly you two want to learn from me?" Shiv asked, not looking at any of them.

"Knife fighting," said Shantel, herself stooping to pick up a small branch. She went to the side of camp opposite Shiv, collecting sticks and dry bark as she went.

"Anything you can teach me," answered Enwerd, watching them both with his arms crossed. "I want to be an adventurer like yourself."

"I'm a travelling performer," Shiv growled. Julia snickered quietly to herself, and sat cross-legged opposite the sleeping troll. She drew a half a dozen damaged crossbow bolts from one of her quivers and began removing the steel arrowheads. "This journey is about my family, not adventure. When I have followed this lead to its end, then I am heading to Fort Sabosgate for my next show. They have a thousand people there; I can make up for the time I wasted in Redlock."

Julia threw a broken shaft of wood at Shiv, which bounced off his hat. He paused just long enough to give her a brief glare. The Doctor, meanwhile, had dug a small fire pit, and was filling it with dry grass. Shantel dumped a small armload of sticks by his side, which he began carving up for kindling.

In a few minutes there was no more loose wood to be gathered, and the Doctor had built it into a decent fire. He, Enwerd and Julia sat around it and began producing food for cooking; the gnome had a tiny, blackened metal teapot that soon was nestled in the flames. Shiv sat comfortably and began lobbing knives at an old tree stump, throwing them in a high arc so they lazily dropped into it from above. Shantel watched for a few minutes, and then drew a pair of knives she had acquired in Redlock and threw them as well, missing badly.

Shiv groaned softly, and began telling her about the problems with her stance. It would be some time before he could, in good conscience, go to sleep.

Chapter Forty-Nine

> *Gnolls: These are lanky giants, taller than humans but related to goblins. They are barred from settling in any country except for one small county in Nesland. They use creatures called* darangas, *huge shaggy things with sharp teeth, to drag their wagons full of junk and contraband. Unpleasant in the extreme, gnolls are said to prefer eating anything that can beg them not to.*
> Doctor Unfriendly's Comprehensive Guide to Everything.

Soon after the sun touched the horizon to the west, the she-troll stirred. Blearily she looked around her, sniffing, and then growling a bit at the newcomers. Doctor Unfriendly had last watch, and was absent-mindedly poking the smoldering coals with the last stick from the woodpile. He gave a start when the troll suddenly lurched out of her shallow hole, shaking the dirt loose.

Shiv was the next to wake, his head poking out of his tent as the troll stomped around the fire, ignoring the gnome doctor, to where Julia was nestled under her bedroll. The troll sniffed, a louder growl building in her throat.

Julia awoke to a face full of sharp tusks and drool as Shiv stumbled out of his tent half-dressed. The gnome doctor had scrambled to his feet as well, and ran over, shouting a guttural word several times.

"Goor-fah! Goor-fah!" he repeated, as he converged on the troll with Shiv. The troll stopped, and looked up in surprise at the gnome, as if noticing the tiny figure for the first time.

"Goor-fah ter bont!" he said, unsure whether shouting or quiet was better, and ending up squeaking halfway in between. He hurriedly swept off his top hat, revealing a bald spot nearly the entire breadth of his head. The troll growled again, somewhat quieter, and raised one monstrous hand to make a fist the size of a watermelon. The growl might have contained a few crude syllables, but everyone's attention was on the troll's upraised hand.

"Cho tunk," said the gnome, waving his free hand around in a circle.

"What are you telling her?" hissed Shiv.

"Shut up, I'm busy," hissed the doctor. He ignored Shiv, but gave a quick glare to Enwerd and Shantel, both approaching with weapons drawn. "Put those away!"

The troll looked calmly at each of the group in turn, seeming unperturbed by Shantel and Enwerd's kobold spears. Apparently deciding they were not important, she turned back to Julia.

"Tunk," the troll rumbled, looking intently as Julia pulled her tangled red hair out of her widened eyes. Julia stammered, staring at a fist that could wrap around her waist, and jaws that could bite her in half. She twitched her hands and legs, trying to get up and finding her limbs would not obey her.

"Repeat it!" hissed the doctor. "Repeat it!"

"T-tunk?" whispered Julia. The troll's steady rumble ended with a grunt and a snuffle, spraying her with drool; the fist lowered to the ground, and the troll stomped away on all fours.

"We're going, now!" snapped the Doctor, and ran to scoop up his staff and ready backpack. The humans frenziedly tore at tent, bedrolls and clothes, throwing everything into backpacks as the troll walked away into the dim light.

It was twenty minutes before they were all packed and caught up to the troll and the gnome. Each of them continued to do up buttons and straps, and adjust clothing, as they marched.

"What was it you said?" Shiv asked, falling into place beside the gnome.

"I said Julia watches her brothers, like an adopted mother."

"You said that in four words? And it talked back?"

"It's a rough translation. She says I'm an eloquent speaker, but she thinks you humans fiddle around with your knick-knacks and clothes too much. Your tent annoys her for some reason," the Doctor smiled. "We had a bit of a chat while you four caught up."

The travel that night went quickly, the hills smoothing out somewhat and the underbrush thinning out; it was a clear night with twelve moons out, so the moonlight was bright enough to show the majority of roots, rocks and other minor pitfalls. The troll lead them at a brisk pace, stopping only rarely to pull a chunk of meat out of a pocket in her hide poncho, or to relieve herself against a boulder or bush. The gnome kept chattering away to the troll, and the troll would occasionally reply with one or two rough syllables. The others stayed well back, glad to have the gnome keep their guide relatively docile. Enwerd complained once or twice about having to eat while walking, and Shantel of sore feet.

Julia walked at the rear, at least thirty paces behind the troll. Shiv seemed to rotate between them, checking to ensure the doctor hadn't been eaten, ordering the apprentices to keep pace, and checking to make sure the surly redhead was not going to shoot the troll in the back.

Once they saw a gnoll caravan at a distance: eight huge, wooden wagons with rickety roofs, covered in pots and pans and anything else the filthy creatures thought someone might buy, and their huge, shaggy *darangas* scavenging nearby for rabbits or whatever else they could catch. The troll gave them a wide berth, which no doubt the gnolls appreciated.

All of them were trudging along half asleep by the time the sunrise began to glimmer on the horizon, all except the troll, who gave no indication she was tired until she stomped into a small copse of bushes, and fell asleep before her head hit the ground. The Doctor had to check to make sure she hadn't hurt herself, and then turned to the others.

"Apparently we stop here for the day," he said, and dropped his baggage a few paces from the troll's elephantine flank. The others breathed a sigh of relief, dropping bedrolls and backpacks without a second word.

Julia, unwrapping a package of dried meat, walked over to the Doctor, and stood over him for a moment. He stopped arranging his bedroll and looked up at her in response.

"So the troll said it wouldn't eat me, right?"

"Obviously," the Doctor replied. He placed his miniature backpack so that he could use it as an improvised pillow.

"Why? What's to say she doesn't change her mind?"

"Like I told Master Shiv," the Doctor said, climbing into his little nest of blankets. "I told her you were looking after your brothers, like a surrogate mother, and that it was their idea to start killing trolls."

"It was Forrel. So she'll still kill them, just not me?"

"Best I could do. That assumes you don't pick a fight, and you aren't there when she finds your brothers. You only get the one pass."

"Well, at least I understand it… sort of. Er, thanks."

"You're welcome. Oh, and please don't give her a reason to change her mind. It'd look rather bad on me, vouching for you, and I'd rather not be swallowed whole." He smiled oddly and then rolled over on his side and pulled the blankets over his head. Julia walked back to her gear and sat down, chewing on dried meat. From where she sat, the curled up gnome looked like a small sack one of them had dropped.

Chapter Fifty

> *Hellhounds: Big, black animals that look like a cross between a rabid dog and a running steam engine, covered in spikes. I know of nothing in particular that can defend against them, but my best guess would be a dozen or so heavy cannon loaded with grapeshot. For each one.*
> *Doctor Unfriendly's Comprehensive Guide to Everything.*

Shiv woke up while it was still light. Although it had been a longer night of travel than the previous one, he'd had a whole day to rest. The Doctor, as usual, had taken the last watch, and was studying a heavy book in the light of the setting sun.

Shiv frowned to himself, and silently crept out of his tent. The Doctor did not look up; he was engrossed in what he was reading, and his right hand was contorting in rhythm to the words he was mumbling; he was no doubt practising magic. Shiv took an empty sack from inside his tent, held it open, and crept closer to the gnome, grinning. His pace slowed as he approached the gnome from behind, each step more careful than the last. The Doctor appeared not to notice, even when Shiv had got within arm's reach. The knife thrower reached slowly out with the sack.

"You know gnomes can hear a lot better than humans," Doctor Unfriendly said, not looking up. "And I have a spell ready that'll blow the bottom out of that sack if you try it."

Shiv's shoulders slumped and he walked away to get some breakfast, chuckling.

This time he woke his apprentices and Julia before the troll got up, and they had a meal of bread, salted pork, and dried apple; by the time the troll was stirring, they had packed up camp and were sitting around a low campfire, chatting contentedly as the sun went down. The loud, rumbling yawn of their monstrous guide broke up the conversation, and Shiv doused the fire as the others slung their backpacks into place.

"You know," commented Shantel as they settled into a pace slightly quicker than was comfortable. "Adventuring is not so bad. This is actually quite pleasant."

"Of course," Shiv replied. "Only that part of adventuring which involves adventure is unpleasant. I particularly dislike those times someone else's goals do not align with my own."

"How often is that?" she asked.

"Most of the time, actually," answered Julia. "You might have heard that this particular troll was busy a few days ago, trying to hack up my brothers and me. In between goblins and kobolds and anything else that had time on its hands. Probably that gnoll caravan would have had a go at us if the troll wasn't here."

There was a moment of awkward silence, which was broken by Enwerd.

"Excuse me, er... Doctor? Does the troll know how long it'll take to get there?"

The gnome Doctor made a few guttural syllables at the troll, and was answered in kind. The gnome's high-pitched, nasal squeak made a sharp contrast to the she-troll's gravelly base.

"She says we'll be at the Grandmother's house sometime in the middle of the night. That would be tonight."

"Master Shiv?" Enwerd asked. "This troll Grandmother is supposed to know who killed your troupe?"

"From what the Duke said, she's supposed to know damn near everything worth knowing," Shiv replied. "I can't imagine that being true, or if it was, what kind of favours she might need, that she would owe him for."

"From what I have heard, the Duke is not the sort to say something he isn't sure of," the Doctor said over his shoulder. He was having trouble staying within a few paces of the troll, yet far enough back that he could take part in the conversation.

"You know a lot about the Duke? Why didn't you tell me?" Shiv asked.

"Karl has lived in this area since before the Duke arrived. Why wouldn't I know something?"

"Of course," Shiv said, half to himself. "Say, do you know something about this troll Grandmother, or Oracle or whatever she is?"

"The Oracle of the Gnoll Passage was first reported by a group of adventurers two centuries ago. Even then she was probably one of the best diviners (er... wizards who specialize in finding things out). She worked as a sort of information mercenary, discovering lost secrets, and that kind of thing. A Grandmaster, back then, and she's had two hundred years of experience since. Female trolls are smarter and somewhat bigger than the males, and they often have some minor talent with magic. But they get bigger and smarter with age. Oh, and rumour has it, she's only half troll."

"And half human?" Shantel asked.

"No, half something else." The Doctor said. He did not elaborate.

"That's a little disturbing." Shiv said. "Do we have to worry about this meeting? Is she dangerous?"

"Yes," answered the gnome, and he trotted faster to catch up to the troll.

They followed the troll in silence as the darkness grew deeper. Only two moons were up tonight, and neither particularly bright, so soon they had to light torches and lanterns. The troll seemed irritated by the light, but had slowed somewhat, sniffing the barren ground more often.

The hills were extremely rocky, and weirdly shaped peaks decorated with stunted and warped little bushes appeared closer together. The troll paid them no mind, beyond an occasional glance, but kept in the relatively level gaps between. Some of the rocks began to suggest shapes, as if they had been carved into columns or statues and then worn smooth again with weather, their indistinct mouths and eyes moving with the flickering of the torchlight. Soon they reached an area where the strangely shaped rocks appeared in piles, crudely leaning up against short cliffs or set up like primitive signposts. Soon after that, the piles became more elaborate, simple lean-tos or giant archways. The lot of them were silent, and instead of lagging behind the troll, they now stayed only a step or two behind.

"I hear footsteps," muttered Doctor Unfriendly. "Something big, an animal maybe, is following us."

Shiv nodded, having had that feeling for some time, if not the senses to be sure of it. The others said nothing but stuck even closer to the troll, who now was advancing cautiously with her head and tail down like a skittish dog.

The stone archways were now clustered together, looking like crude stone booths made for something twice as tall as a man, and between them and the sheer-sided hills the area took on an appearance of a dark, crude labyrinth. The footsteps behind them were audible now, the soft, padding steps of a large predator, or perhaps more than one.

Julia began to draw her swords, and the troll's head whipped around at the sound of scraping metal. She barked a command from behind bared fangs.

"Put those away, dammit!" translated the Doctor. Julia slid the weapons back into place. "We're here."

The troll had stopped, and sat on her monstrous haunches. She laid down her huge poleaxe, and looked back and forth as if expecting something to appear from any direction. Something did.

From an archway behind them, a huge animal emerged. It was something like a dog or wolf, but taller at the shoulder than any of them, and covered in black spines, like wrought iron bristles of a metal brush. It had no eyes, exactly, so much as eye sockets, which looked like pits filled with burning coals. All of them, even the troll, whipped around to avoid the thing being at their backs; and then another identical creature crept from an archway on the opposite side. The creatures made no sound other than their footsteps, but stared single-mindedly at the lot of them. Once the two monsters had fully emerged, they stalked around the group lazily in a wide circle, studying them; each time the creatures sniffed at them, sulfur-smelling smoke puffed out of their nostrils.

"Don't pay them any mind," said a loud voice, unmistakably female but also deep and gravelly. "They look terrible but won't hurt anyone who doesn't hurt me. And you couldn't hurt me if you tried."

The voice seemed to come from all directions, but behind the stone columns to their right, something large moved in the darkness. The troll guide bowed, her lower jaw touching the ground and her eyes shut tight. Doctor Unfriendly quickly followed suit, although his bow appeared insignificant next to the troll's bulk. There were no instructions exchanged, but the others bowed as low as they could as well.

The giant black hounds laid down on the right and the left of the group, forgotten in the face of much larger footsteps, footsteps that made crunching sounds despite the fact that the ground was almost entirely rock. The archway in front of them, the one the huge dog had emerged from, suddenly seemed to contain something, a motion in the shadows within.

"Alright, alright, that's enough. Get up," said the voice. "I like seeing groveling as much as the next person, but it makes conversation difficult."

They all looked up as a huge pile of animal hides squeezed through the great archway like it was a foxhole; the shape underneath the crudely stitched together furs and leathers dwarfed the she-troll, who now looked up like a timid puppy greeting a stern master. The shape slowly resolved itself into something vaguely troll-shaped, apparently backing out through the archway, dragging a bulging sack the size of a small cottage. With a satisfied grunt, the newcomer dropped the sack and stood roughly upright; a spinal ridge like bony swords stuck out through the furs, piercing the patchwork robe in a line from a huge, misshapen hunch down to the halfway point of a shaggy, stumpy tail. Then the immense creature turned and smiled at them, a smile so full of jagged fangs and pitted tusks it was difficult to see much else of the face. Where the creature's face was visible, it was mostly long folds of sagging, slate-coloured skin beneath long rope-like strands of uncombed, filthy hair.

"Now," the voice came from the mass of horrifying teeth, the creature's face suspended twice Shiv's height above them. "I know the young Duke sent you, Master Kobodan. Tell me, since I don't think I'm going to eat you all right now, what it is I can do for you."

Chapter Fifty-One

> *Blood: Blood is useful in a number of necromantic or divination rituals, in that it is believed to be the vessel of the soul. Anything which effects the soul effects the blood, and vice versa. In my experience most wizards need to get out more.*
>
> *Doctor Unfriendly's Comprehensive Guide to Everything.*

"Well, er..." stammered Shiv, "I am looking for whoever killed my family... or rather, two of them. I was told you might know... something?"

"Yes, yes, I know all that," snapped the Oracle. She scowled and narrowed her eyes, examining Shiv in a way none of them were comfortable with. "You've had your family wiped out twice, shame, that, and have been looking for the murderers ever since. I knew the Duke sent you to me, so I did a bit of research to prepare. What *exactly* do you want from me?"

Shiv's jaw dropped, along with most of his companions'. The troll guide, seeming to want the Grandmother's attention, playfully nipped her ankle. In absent-minded irritation, the Grandmother knocked the troll sprawling with a single huge backhand.

"I'd like to know who the murderers are. The Duke told me the Zanquitor might be behind the plague that hurt my first family... I don't have any idea about the second, but I have evidence that might help."

"Evidence? Do tell," replied the Oracle, appearing bored.

"Er... yes," Shiv said, gaining confidence somewhat. He unslung his backpack and withdrew a heavy bundle made up of a threadbare old shirt. "There were sixteen of them, and whoever did it left a knife in each corpse."

"You left the blood on them?" interrupted the Oracle, sniffing and rubbing her nose on one sleeve. She appeared somewhat more interested, however, and raised one eyebrow as she watched Shiv withdraw the collection of tarnished blades. "And you did not use them? For anything?"

"Yes, my... lady... I just kept the shirt a bit oiled so they wouldn't rust too much; the blood dried, but most of it is still there."

"It will have to do," said the Oracle thoughtfully. The she-troll nipped her again, and this time, the Oracle's backhand threw Mother end-over-end out of the stone circle. There was a crash and a yelp from a surprising distance. "It was thoughtful to do that much. Lay them out on the stone slab over there. In a circle, points inward."

Shiv did so, the others keeping back to give him, the dogs and the Oracle as much room as possible. The Oracle leaned over his work and watched as if already learning volumes from how he placed them. Occasionally she would reach over him and adjust a knife's position a hair's breadth in one direction or another.

"Very good. Now leave a space, here." The Oracle said, pointing. Soon the circle of knives was complete; it was obvious from even a casual glance that the circle was perfect, each knife exactly the same distance from the next, except for the gap at one end, as if one was missing. The Oracle nodded. "There were seventeen victims of this crime, we need blood from the seventeenth."

"What, me?" Shiv asked. "I wasn't there."

"Nevertheless, you were a victim." Suddenly she lashed out at Shiv, her clawed hand latching onto his left arm, nearly covering the whole of it, but leaving the wrist and hand exposed. Holding Shiv up in front of her face for inspection, she gently removed his leather gauntlet with her other hand and discarded it. She smiled like a crocodile. "Let's see. This little piggy went to market..."

Between thumb and forefinger, she ripped the smallest finger off of Shiv's hand and tossed him aside. Shiv howled in pain, and the others gasped. The Grandmother ignored them all and squeezed the finger, dripping the blood into the gap in the circle of knives.

CAMERON S. CURRIE

Humming to herself softly, she popped the pulped remains into her mouth, and chewed as she traced a rune in the blood with one thick claw.

"WHAT WAS THAT FOR?" Shiv shouted, clutching his dripping hand. The huge black dogs glared at him, but did not get up.

"Knowledge always comes at a price," the Oracle said, not entirely paying attention. She had produced a leather pouch the size of a pumpkin, and was taking pinches of some sort of powder from it to sprinkle over the knives. "You've given twenty years for this information, surely your finger is little in comparison."

Sputtering in protest, Shiv could think of nothing better to do than to watch what she was doing. He said nothing, but the pain made noises in his throat. The blackened powder clinging to the knife blades began to smoke, a reddish cloud forming above the stone slab, swirling in response to gestures from the Oracle. Shiv noticed at least one Greater Rotation from her left hand, but most of the other gestures were infinitely more complex, her knuckles making cracking sounds as they bent into unnatural shapes. The Oracle peered into the cloud, watching intently, although what she could see was invisible to the others.

"You've had a lot of problems regarding... a blue kobold recently, have you not?" the Oracle mused, half to herself.

"Y-yes," answered Shiv, shaking a little, but paying attention. "The Storm Kobold. It couldn't have been him..."

"The Zanquitor. Zachary Talisman... Hmmmm."

"What!?!" Shiv shouted. "What about him? Did he pay the Storm Kobold or something?"

"No, no," the Oracle chuckled, still staring into the cloud. "The Zanquitor created the Storm Kobold (is that what they call him now? Hmm.) in a manner of speaking. The Zanquitor caused the plague as part of the Friendly War, and then... er... harvested you from the aftermath. Then, years later, the Storm Kobold was sent with several underlings to remove your troupe. You were not far enough away, the kobolds did see you. You were spared. The knives were specially chosen, and left for you, a sort of message."

"What? Why? What's the message?" sputtered Shiv, suddenly forgetting his hand. The Oracle chuckled. "That doesn't make any sense!"

SHIV

The Oracle picked up one of the knives and examined it carefully; as soon as it was moved the cloud sparked and dissipated.

"Funny," she remarked. "I never noticed, but these are quite pretty. Just the sort of wickedly sharp weapons to catch a boy's budding interest... Of course it doesn't make sense, it's Talisman. He never makes sense. But he is a clever boy, apparently."

"Why? Why go to all this trouble? What does he want?" Shiv demanded.

"You'll have to ask him. That's what you want anyway, isn't it? To confront him, ask him why?"

Shiv, taken aback, was silent for a moment. He began clutching his bleeding hand again, and then nodded.

"How do I get there?" Shiv asked. "I know I have to cross the Inland Sea, and that's maybe ten days travel south of here... Is there anywhere I could hire a boat?"

"You can't cross the Inland Sea, whether you have a boat or not. Zachary Talisman conjures and crossbreeds monsters; anything vicious enough he dumps in the Inland Sea. Unless you have his permission, the sea monsters will make sure you never reach the Talismanian shore."

"So how do I get there? Fly?" Shiv asked.

"I can get you there," the Oracle mused, "but I have discharged the Duke's favour, I think. This will cost extra. I have no desire to have the Zanquitor angry with me."

"Wait a minute!" interrupted Julia, approaching despite the looming Oracle. "Shiv, everything anyone knows about Talisman II is terrible, he's a Grandmaster wizard twice over. What are you going to do, try to kill him?"

"I just want to talk to him," said Shiv, not looking at her.

"And what if he doesn't want to talk?"

"I'll persuade him to." Shiv said, one of the dragon-tooth knives appearing in his hand. "I can be persuasive."

"The man breeds sea monsters for fun, Shiv. I hear the army of Talisman is made of undead soldiers, most of the land is a jungle of poisonous plants, and his Golden Tower is surrounded by a maze that somehow eats people," interrupted Doctor Unfriendly, approaching as well. The rest of the group was approaching too. "You have a family! Caroline is waiting for you in Redlock, and her presence would suggest some other members of your family might be alive."

"If Talisman is that dangerous, bringing two brand new apprentices into it might not be the best use of their abilities," Enwerd interjected. Shantel nodded in agreement.

"Twenty years," Shiv stated, scowling. "I have looked for this for twenty years. Now, I am this close, and you tell me to just give up? Are you serious?"

"I am," Julia said. "When the goblins took the village children, you made a big show of saving them; now you are going to leave your own sister alone while you go off looking for revenge? This is suicide in the name of stupid pride, no more. You go into Talisman, you go without me."

"Revenge, huh?" Shiv said, and was quiet for a long time. "This Talisman person has gone to great expense and effort to kill everyone around me. If I don't resolve this, are you going to feel safe? Should my sister feel safe? How long will she have before the Zanquitor tries to wipe out my third family?"

Everyone was silent, eyes downcast, as Shiv glared at them.

"Oracle, I want to go to Talisman. Name your price. And just to be clear, I want a way out as well, I don't mean to die in there."

"Name my price?" the Oracle. She snickered a bit, letting loose a long string of drool from between jagged fangs. "Name my price… my goodness… give me a moment. I know. A year."

"A year?" Shiv asked. "What do you mean?"

"One year's service. I should be able to find a use for your skills. For one year, you do everything I ask you to. At the end of the year, I'll release you, debt cleared."

"Alive?" Shiv asked, and the Oracle burst into a belly laugh loud enough to hurt their ears.

"Oh, very well, then, alive. Free and clear, no further obligation, and alive."

"I won't be an assassin." Shiv said. "No assigning me to kill my own family, or chop off my own arm or anything like that?"

"That would not be a very effective use of my resources." answered the Oracle, shaking her head. "Honestly, I may be a horrible monster, but even I have my limits. One year."

"Done," Shiv said, "But I go to Talisman first. AND I go to tell my family what I learned. Then a year's service."

"Two years, then. I am risking Talisman's wrath even if you die while you're there. And a return trip is more difficult," the Oracle said, snarling uncomfortably close to Shiv's face.

"Fifteen months," Shiv replied.

"Eighteen," the Oracle growled, the dripping fangs closer still. It was immediately evident that Shiv's head and torso would fit comfortably in the Oracle's mouth should she wish to snap at him.

"Done," Shiv said, with a smug look on his face. He turned around and regarded his companions. "Who is coming with me?"

Chapter Fifty-Two

> *Teptkins: Rather rotten parrots that live in Talisman. They come in two varieties: the leader parrots, about a tenth of the flock, which lead their weird sing-alongs, and the followers. They are rather unpleasantly tempered and extremely numerous.*
> *Doctor Unfriendly's Comprehensive Guide to Everything.*

Reluctantly Julia and Doctor Unfriendly raised their hands; Enwerd and Shantel did nothing except look nervous. Shiv frowned in response. The Oracle ignored the lot of them, and instead held out a small metal disc between thumb and forefinger.

"Take this, Master Shiv. It shall be your way back here. When you are finished in Talisman, press this side and this," she said, pointing a taloned finger at two sides, each marked with a plain square. "Squeeze as hard as you can, and it will show you the way back to the archway."

Shiv nodded and took the disc; it was just large enough to fit comfortably in his palm. The Oracle pointed at him and narrowed her bloodshot eyes.

"Two warnings: first, it will only work once, so be certain you are truly done. The enchantment only lasts for a day at most once it is activated. Second: it will not work at all in the Zanquitor's Golden Tower, or in any temple; and if the Zanquitor knows what you are doing, he may be able to stop it from functioning."

"Isn't that three warnings?" Shiv asked. He received a toothy grimace in response, and the troll guide growled at him.

"Just remember what I said. I mean to collect my payment, and I cannot if you die," the Oracle smiled sweetly, or attempted to, but the effect was not pleasant; she pointed towards one of the archways. "That doorway leads to Talisman, there. It exits a half a day south of the capital city. Leave when you are ready."

Grumbling to herself, she threw the sack over her shoulder and squeezed back through the archway she had emerged from; as soon as she was out of sight, the giant black dogs rose silently and padded after her, without a glance at the five of them.

"Well?" Shiv said, shoving the metal disc into a belt pouch. "What, pray tell, are your plans, my stalwart apprentices? Follow into adventure or retreat, injured only in pride?"

"I'll go under one condition," Shantel said. "If I'm to be your apprentice, I'll want a proper set of knives of my own. A dozen of them, and I know you're supposed to make the best."

"How about I teach you how to make your own? Then you can make as many of them as you like," he answered. Shantel paused for a moment, then nodded. Shiv turned to Enwerrd. "And you? I suppose you want something as well?"

"Just a full share of the plunder," said Enwerrd. "I'll need some decent weapons sooner or later, but I can supply that out of my share."

"Plunder?" Shiv scoffed. "Lately there seems precious little of that. But certainly, we find something, you get a full share. Shantel, you're getting training and materials from me, so you get a half share."

"Hey!" she protested.

"All settled," Shiv said, and beckoned them to follow; then he turned and stepped into the archway.

Although the archway appeared to lead only to a shallow alcove, as they entered it seemed to deepen; the further they marched into it, the deeper and darker the alcove became.

"This is sort of creepy," the Doctor said aloud. He got the distinct impression someone had nodded in response, but in the darkness he had no idea who it was. His voice and their footsteps echoed in the deepening silence.

It remained totally dark for a few footsteps, and then, in the distance, a gloomy light began to show. They soon could tell where each of them was, and the silence was soon penetrated by some sort of complicated music, muted by distance.

"What is that?" Enwerd asked.

"You're the adventurer, you go find out," said Julia. A dry smirk was just visible on her face in the gloom. They all continued at the same cautious pace nevertheless, and the greenish light in the distance began to take shape as a rectangular archway similar to the one they had entered, and long, dim shadows danced back and forth in time to the music.

"It's birdsong," said the Doctor. "It must be hundreds of birds, although I don't recognize the type."

As soon as he had said it, the others could make it out. The music was weirdly synchronised, as if the birds were working together. It resembled no human music ever, and yet a bizarre rhythm began to take shape within it. About a tenth of the birds would pipe a short series of five or six notes, and then the remainder of them would sing back the same tune, but magnified in volume by the greater numbers. Then the leader birds would sing a slightly altered tune, and the flock would repeat it again.

"It could be teptkins," mused the Doctor, listening carefully.

"So? They're birds!" replied Enwerrd.

"Oh, look, another totally harmless statue!" said Julia dryly.

"What does that mean?" asked Shantel quietly.

"It's a common saying among veteran adventurers," said Shiv. "It means 'never expect anything to be harmless'. There's your first lesson."

"Seems like a defeatist attitude," said Shantel. The doctor cleared his throat.

"Sorry, Doctor," said Shiv. "What are teptkins?"

"It sounds like the birds are counting. I've never been to Talisman, but I've read about it. Teptkins are a kind of small parrot. It's said they have the intelligence and personality of a small child."

"Oh, good, they're harmless," said Enwerd. The rectangle of light was large enough they could see it was another archway, and there were trees swaying in the breeze visible through it.

"What did I just say?" Shiv said.

"What are teptkins?" Enwerd said with a sigh, now visible in the increasing light. Before anyone else could say anything, the Doctor cleared his throat.

"You obviously have no experience with small children. Picture two hundred or so bored children with no adults to teach them right from wrong. This group of kids doesn't tease each other, or pull hair, or poke at people that annoy them, because every one of them has a sharp little beak that can snip off a finger. They can fly, although not terribly well, and they are smart enough to mimic speech. They like songs about numbers."

"How do you know it's a song about numbers?" Julia interjected. "It could just be a bunch of peeps."

"Each verse has one more peep than the last."

The group stopped walking, and listened in silence.

The lead birds peeped five times in a perky but simple tune. Then the rest peeped five times. There was a pause, and then the lead voices peeped six times, the tune slightly longer.

"Oh, look, some harmless birds," Shiv said, "Let's walk out into their midst unprotected, where we will surely pass unscathed!"

"Oh, I get it," said Enwerd quietly.

"Do you have any magic that can deal with two hundred birds?" Shantel asked the Doctor.

"Actually my sources say 'several hundred', not two. And no, I don't."

"You're not much of a wizard, are you?" said Enwerd. "Come to think of it, I can't remember you ever casting a spell that I saw."

The Doctor casually made a flicking motion with one hand, there was a quiet sizzle sound, and Enwerd jumped.

"Ouch!" he shouted. "Okay, fine, you're a wizard."

"Can everyone whistle?" the Doctor asked. They all did a single discordant note. "Good, from what I understand they like it when people sing with them. Let's hope they're in a good mood."

They approached the doorway, the bright sunlight filtering through a jungle canopy hurting their eyes. In the trees, hopping and climbing and whistling, were several thousand dull grey birds, maybe twice as long as a human hand. About half of them had bright red tail feathers.

The group followed Shiv out cautiously into the light, and the cacophony of whistles and cheeps stopped suddenly. They were carefully watched by nine thousand, eight hundred and forty-four tiny green and black eyes.

After a short moment of quiet, four hundred and twenty throats, in perfect unison and perfectly tuned to the same sharp note, gave a long, clear whistle.

Chapter Fifty-Three

> *Panic: A practise of most giant races, this involves doing the least appropriate thing at a critical moment. A properly trained giant should be weaned off of this behaviour as quickly as possible.*
> *Doctor Unfriendly's Comprehensive Guide to Everything.*

There was a pause where everyone was quiet. In only a few seconds, the birds started rustling feathers in irritation. Quickly, the Doctor backhanded Shiv on the leg, and the two of them whistled back the same note; the doctor was off key by a hair, and Shantel joined in halfway through. Julia started to whistle a bit after that. Enwerd had frozen, silent, and then jumped, as if startled, when the note ended.

The silence was broken by a cacophony of angry squawks and croaks, and many of the birds jumped off of their branches to swoop around in short, clumsy circles. The commotion died down as quickly as it had begun, and after a moment, the leader birds repeated the same long note, a trifle louder.

"It seems they didn't like our performance," mused Doctor Unfriendly. Shiv hit him back, knocking the gnome's tiny top hat askew. "One... two... three... go..."

Their second attempt was better. All five of them got the note right, and only Enwerdd ended it slightly later than the others. The birds stared silently at them, as if considering.

Then the birds responded with two notes. They were shorter than the first, and the second note was slightly higher in pitch. Enwerrd breathed a sigh of relief, and the group copied both shrill notes. Shiv gestured to the lot of them, and made a walking fingers gesture. They started walking slowly, cautiously. A few of the closest birds, only a few paces away, jumped as if they were slightly startled. There was a slight murmur among a few of the birds, although whether it was approval or not was difficult to judge.

The leader birds called out three notes, slightly quicker than the last, low, middle, and high pitched. The rustle of discontent had stopped, and the group whistled the notes back, seeming to meet with the birds' approval. They walked very slowly and carefully towards the edge of the birds' area. Enwerd was smiling now, daring to relax somewhat.

The leader birds sang out a single note again, but before pausing, repeated the two-note group and the three-note group; there was a much shorter pause than usual, and the whole swarm whistled one, two, and three notes. Then the swarm was quiet, staring at them.

"Uh oh," Enwerdd whispered, but the group whistled back the one, two, and three notes. Without a pause, the leader birds whistled back one note, two notes, three notes and then four notes; the fourth series of whistles was high-pitched, low-pitched, medium, and then high. The group nervously copied out the increasingly complex tune.

The whole series of tunes began to get confusing by number five; it was high, medium-high, low-medium-high, high-low-medium-high, low-high-low-medium-high-high. The group whistled again, but Enwerrd whistled high instead of low in the four-note group. There was grumbling and croaking from the swarm. They repeated the whole song, first the leader birds, then the flock as a whole.

The birds repeated the one-two-three-four-five series, with a lot of murmuring and croaking in the background. The group tried to get all fifteen notes, but the erratic tune came out even worse than the first attempt. In response, dozens of the birds jumped and flew between branches, and three of them actually swooped at the group, diving aside at the last moment. Most of the group ducked, and Enwerd covered his head with his hands.

"This isn't working," Shantel said warily. The Doctor nodded.

"We might be able to make it back to the archway if we run," he murmured, eyeing the birds as they cawed and shrieked and screeched angrily.

"I'm not working for that witch for nothing," Shiv growled. The birds repeated the song, barely audible through the cries of anger. "Make one more try, and be ready to duck."

The group tried the song again, except for Shiv, and all of them made mistakes, their fumbles making each note a little bit worse. Shiv mumbled a few words and made a few gestures, paying careful attention to the Greater Rotation of the left hand. The swarm of birds shrieked angrily, making such a loud variety of offended noises they could not hear anything else. The final note was still being whistled when the first bird knocked Shantel in the head, and it was followed by dozens of birds, each swooping and screeching at one of their group. One of the birds actually landed on Enwerd and latched on with both its beak and claws; the former slave shrieked back and tried to tug the bird off, causing a long, bloody strip of his scalp to tear loose before the bird flew away with its prize.

Suddenly the five of them were enveloped by an opaque grey bubble, and they lost sight of the birds. The shrieking and screeching of both the birds and Enwerd drowned out any sound they might have made, but Shiv gestured a follow-me sign with a crooked finger, and as the group began to run the irregularly shaped grey bubble moved with them. One bird swooped down into the bubble, suddenly attempting to change direction as it entered as if surprised, and it crashed in front of Julia, who stomped on it with a crunch before it recovered. Enwerd began to pull ahead of the group, holding his bloody head with both hands, his kobold spear long since lost, his screams unheard among the noise of the birds. Shiv tried to call out to caution him, but none could hear, and the wrinkly grey bubble shimmered as Shiv's concentration wavered.

Enwerd ran out of the front of the bubble wild-eyed, and they lost sight of him; they all quickened their pace, although Shiv murmuring and adjusting his hands to maintain his magic could only go so fast. Another bird swooped through the bubble, this time smoothly entering one side and exiting the opposite. Fortunately, the shrieking sounds were quieter, if just a little, and it became clear they were leaving the center of the swarm.

They kept a quick jog so that Shiv could keep up, now sweating from the effort of maintaining the shimmering, irregular bubble, and the sound began to die down, until Shantel tripped on a wet pile of red and screamed louder than any of them had. Julia clamped her hands over Shantel's mouth and yanked her to follow, leaving Enwerd's shredded corpse behind. They ran as fast as they could manage, jungle trees and underbrush popping into the bubble and disappearing out of the rear, and it became clear after a minute or so that the birds were far behind.

They all stopped, panting, tears streaking down Shantel's face, and the grey bubble vanished.

"What was that bubble?" asked Julia, in between gulps of air.

"My elephant spell," Shiv gasped in response, more tired than the others from the extra effort it had taken. "I put it right over top of us, so you saw the inside. I hoped the birds wouldn't figure out the trick until we were out of there."

"We'd better keep moving, it looks like a few of them followed the elephant," said the Doctor, pointing at a dozen or so birds behind them. "I don't know if they can return and report but I don't want to find out."

"But what about Enwerd?" shrieked Shantel.

"If you want to join him, go ahead. I want to live," snapped Julia, and she continued on into the jungle.

Chapter Fifty-Four

> *Talisman City: The Capital city of Talisman, also the home of Talisman II, their ruler. Talismanians have little imagination when it comes to naming things.*
> *Doctor Unfriendly's Comprehensive Guide to Everything.*

The sunlight which had filtered down into the teptkin swarm appeared to be an exception. Ever since then, the four of them had encountered cloudy conditions above the jungle canopy, with an almost constant drizzle, and occasionally, despite the heat, fog.

"Do you think we are still going north?" Julia asked. "We should have brought a compass."

"What's a compass?" asked Shantel, trying to distract herself long enough for her eyes to dry. She jumped as she avoided a spider bigger than her fist.

"A magnet or lodestone," piped in the Doctor. "They always point the same direction when hung from a string, so you mark one end north and you'll always know the direction. We make handy little ones in Sabosland that fit into a sort of big locket. But we are going the right direction, I think."

"We will have to stop and rest soon," Shiv said, "We've been up since yesterday afternoon, walking most of the time. I don't want to arrive there exhausted."

"Agreed," the Doctor replied. "There's a rocky spot a stone's hurl over that way, we can probably stop there."

They all turned a bit to the east and in a few minutes were climbing up to the top of a small hill, with a huge rock that jutted out at an angle to nearly double the formation's height. They scrambled up to an impression in the top that despite the drizzle remained somewhat dry, draining through two large cracks. From there they could see both slightly above the canopy and down to the jungle floor. They had barely time to sit down before Shantel had swung her pack off her back and extracted her little bag of food.

"I would kill for some green-berry jam," she said regretfully, as she bit into a small loaf of bread, "And something other than dried meat and bread to eat."

"Then become a wizard," Shiv said, leaning back onto a smooth slab of rock and pulling his hat down over his eyes. He gave a start, and then looked over at the Doctor, who shook his head.

"I'd suggest you pick some fruit, we are in a jungle, but I don't think I'd trust Talismanian fruit I didn't know." The doctor paused regretfully. "I do have a bit of wine, though."

Shantel sat up quickly, and nodded with enthusiasm.

"We should drink to Enwerd," Julia said. "He held on all that time as a slave, only to get killed as a free man, by a bunch of birds."

The others nodded; they had no cups, so they passed around the Doctor's little wineskin and each took a mouthful.

"A bunch of damned birds," said Julia again quietly, staring off into the morning sun. "Shiv, when we get whatever it is you are looking for, you had better get back there and look after your sister."

"Yes," Shiv said quietly. "Why did you come, anyway? I know Shantel and Enwerd wanted to learn, and I can understand why the Doctor here came, but you have no reason to be interested, and every reason not be fond of me."

Julia scowled at him without saying a word, and then shook her head as if disgusted. She rolled over to lie down on her side.

"I don't know why myself. Perhaps I made a mistake coming at all."

They only rested for a few hours, the rising heat and damp becoming increasingly uncomfortable. Julia and Shiv said no more, but the tension between them was palpable. Shantel, after eating as much as she could, fell into a deep sleep in which she snored softly. The Doctor had a short cat nap, and then spent time paging through miniature books from his backpack, idly conjuring a tiny illusion of himself to dance, to a teptkins' counting song he whistled in his teeth.

Their rest was interrupted by a crash from in the jungle. Doctor Unfriendly looked up, his illusion fizzling. The others woke up to look in the direction of the crash, in time to hear another, and this time, to see a tree shudder and lurch to one side as if it had been torn halfway from the ground.

"You know, that's not that far off. Perhaps we should get going," Julia said, stretching quickly and then slinging her pack into place. The others followed suit, even the Doctor packing his books like it had been rehearsed, and soon they were trotting down the side of the rocky slope.

The next crash was closer; if not headed exactly towards them it was certainly not veering away. The four of them scurried into the trees, luckily north being the direction away from whatever was making the noise. Whatever the thing was, it passed behind them, making more crashes when it knocked trees aside, and when it didn't, a quieter but equally violent rustle of brush being trampled.

They walked for only an hour or so until the jungle began to thin. There was a wide murky pond they avoided, and a great many small but menacing animals they saw, but nothing barred their path. As the brush gave way to small pathways and hunting trails, the trees began to spread further apart. Here and there was a cluster of tree stumps from a woodcutter plying his trade.

Suddenly the last of the trees gave way just as the sun came out; past a few paces wide of cleared ground was a high wall of yellowish stone. It rose to three times the height of a man, and standing on top at rigid attention, were guards in hooded red robes, each with a spear pointed directly up, and each looking out into the jungle unwaveringly.

"Excuse me, gentlemen!" shouted Shiv. "Which way is it to the town gate?"

The guards made no indication they had heard him, indeed no motion of any kind. One could almost believe they were statues which had been dressed in red robes, but the iron-tipped spears looked real enough.

"Gentle lords! We weary travellers wish to enter your palatial town for good-natured yet unwise throwing about of coinage! Pray direct us in this noble mission!"

"Shiv," said the Doctor, "I don't think they'll respond, no matter how much you insult them."

"I can insult them a lot more than that," Shiv mused.

"Yes, but do you want that kind of reaction?" answered the Doctor. They looked each way along the curving wall, and for several dozen paces in each direction the same guards stood, each a spear's length apart from the next. There were at least twenty of them in clear view, and the curve of the wall suggested many more hidden by the structure or the encroachment of jungle. "Let's just head that way."

They turned left and followed the direction the doctor pointed, along the perimeter until they came several minutes later to a wide gate with a thick wooden portcullis down, barring the way. Behind it stood two more of the silent red-robed guards, and a short, nondescript man in a thin black robe, with faint purple and red lines at the hems. The man carried no weapons, and regarded them with an insolent smirk.

"Welcome, travellers, to Talisman City," he said. "What made you dare to come here?"

Chapter Fifty-Five

> *Talismanians: An odd human subspecies, the Talismanians are generally hostile and have the unusual trait of all looking pretty much the same. Virtually all Talismanians are seven handspans tall and weigh a stone less than average. They all have brown hair, brown eyes, and olive skin. Talismanians are known to be good at anything that does not require physical strength.*
>
> Doctor Unfriendly's Comprehensive Guide to Everything.

The nondescript man stood regarding them as if they were some sort of vermin, with a look of distaste and scorn. The red robes, however, stood motionless, no emotion evident, and no clue as to whether there were human occupants within them.

"Open the gate," said Shiv. "I have business with the Zanquitor."

"Oh, my goodness, I certainly apologize for the delay," said the man, grinning malevolently. He called over his shoulder to raise the portcullis, and then regarded them with an eager smile and a steady stare as the gate slowly rose. "It is but a short walk to the Great Maze, and the Golden Tower is at the center. I'd advise you not to wander about town; you'll be noticed rather quickly, and possibly accosted. We wouldn't want the Zanquitor to wait too long for his amusement."

Smile never fading, he bowed elaborately and gestured towards the center of the town. Julia frowned and hesitated, but Shiv strutted by the standing red robes without pause. After looking about warily for a moment, the Doctor trotted to catch up with him, and then Shantel and Julia followed reluctantly.

The road was paved in faded red bricks, and the buildings to either side were narrow and tall, some ramshackle to the point of collapse, and others carved out of a single piece of sand-coloured stone. The streets were sparsely populated, people going about their business hurriedly.

"That's odd," Shiv said as they caught up. He pointed at the nearest group of people. "They all look like they could be the gatekeeper's family."

It was true; the small huddle of five people in front of a merchant's stall were all of similar height, somewhat shorter than average, and all had the same thick brown hair. As Shiv walked by them, five similar pairs of brown eyes regarded him, each face bearing a similar arrogant smirk. The shortest member of the group was a woman, perhaps a quarter-head shorter than the tallest. They wore a variety of clothes: robes on some, shapeless pantaloons and ponchos on others, seemingly regardless of sex, but every scrap of clothing was either black or grey, with at most a few threads of red or purple for decoration.

They passed that group, and looked into the merchant's stall. The merchant, who stopped in the middle of a sentence proclaiming the superiority of his cups and goblets, was of a similar height to all the others, with tousled brown hair and a thin goatee, a crooked nose, and nondescript brown eyes. He wore a black tunic with a thin grey dust cloak and thin black linen breeches. He smiled as they passed, wickedly, and nodded to them.

Further on down the road, a woman was sweeping the stone patio in front of a large wooden inn. She was dressed in a black linen gown, and wore her thick brown hair loose, barely to her shoulders. She smiled knowingly at them as they passed.

"These people are creepy," mused Shantel.

"I had heard people in Talisman looked similar to each other, but I had no idea," agreed Doctor Unfriendly. "I wonder if there would be the same effect on a gnome if he lived here, and how long would it take?"

There was no baldness, and no people were especially tall or short or thin or fat; the darkest hair was slightly dark brown and the lightest hair was slightly light brown.

"Imagine trying to find someone by a description here," said Julia, returning a nod to a porter who rushed by carrying a small crate.

The town was rather small, and in only a few minutes the winding streets opened into a plaza, the opposite side of which was bordered by a grey stone wall. It was smooth and featureless, and appeared to extend in either direction for some distance. Shiv frowned and waved to a woman with a cart, selling what appeared to be pie filling in folded over shells of unleavened bread. She was as alike as all of the other inhabitants, and dressed in grey and black with a black linen shawl.

"Excuse me! I'm looking for the Great Maze. It was supposed to be in this direction," he asked. She appeared startled for a split second.

"The Great M- oh, I see. Guests of the Zanquitor?" she said, approaching. "I don't suppose you'd like a final meal? Four ticks for one, three for a founding?"

"Give us one each, keep the change," Shiv said, and handed her a tower coin. As she spooned the ground meat and red and purple peppers into the hard bread, she looked around warily, handing the odd sandwiches to each of them. When she had finished, she whispered.

"If you run now, you might escape. No one escapes once they enter the maze." Shiv looked into her brown eyes and saw abject terror. She looked at each of them in turn. "The guards never run."

"What?" Shiv said. "I don't think you understand, we just want an audience with the Zanquitor, I just need to talk with him."

The woman's jaw dropped, and the tower coin fell from her hand, forgotten. She backed away wordlessly, and if anything, her otherwise nondescript eyes showed even more fear. Three paces away, she turned and ran, pushing her cart as fast as she could.

"What a strange reaction," said the Doctor, watching her frenzied retreat.

"You know, I don't feel especially confident in this mission," remarked Julia. "Shiv, perhaps we should leave."

Shiv shook his head, and took a bite of the odd sandwich. He nearly choked at the searing hot spices, and immediately began looking for a drink that wasn't there. Finding nothing, he dropped the sandwich and rifled through his backpack to find his water bag, and greedily chugged down half of it without stopping.

"No, I'm not working for the Oracle for nothing," he said, panting and eyes watering. He stuffed the water bag back in his backpack and slung it back into position beside his lyre, and panting and wiping his face, walked over towards the grey stone wall.

As they followed him, Shantel noticed a half a dozen passersby walking after the woman with the cart with grim smiles on their faces. One of them stopped to pick up the coin, and then gestured to a red-robed guard near the edge of the plaza; it wordlessly followed.

As Shiv approached the wall, he looked along its length in either direction. Before he could discern how long it was a loud, deep voice boomed out from beyond the wall.

"Who goes there?" it said. There was no clue as to where the voice came from.

"I am Shiv Kobodan. I have questions for the Zanquitor. With me are three of my friends: Doctor Unfriendly of Sabosland, and Julia Hammerhand and Shantel..." He paused suddenly, and turned to whisper fiercely to Shantel. "I don't know your last name!"

"Robberan," said Shantel dryly.

"-Robberan of Nesland," he finished. There was a pause, an uncomfortably long one.

"Greetings, Master Shiv," boomed the voice. "Long have we awaited your presence. You are welcome, as are your friends. Enter."

The wall suddenly sprouted two cracks from top to bottom, and with a grinding noise, the whole section between the cracks pivoted slowly. The wall was a solid slab a pace thick, and no gears or other means behind its rotation seemed evident. Behind the slab was a roadway of the same grey stone, flanked by more grey stone walls identical to the first. There were no side passages or doorways, simply a featureless path, on the other end of which was an open courtyard filled with a thick grey fog. Rising out of the fog, and shining in the sunlight, was the Golden Tower.

The tower looked smooth as glass; although it no doubt was gold molded over stone, no scrap of the stone was visible, nor were windows, doors, or balconies.

"Well, the Golden Tower deserves its name, but I can't say much for the Great Maze." said Shiv, and he walked confidently down the featureless road. There was no sign of life, but as the others entered they all felt the peculiar sensation of being watched.

They had gone a stone's hurl down the road, about half its length, when there was a grinding noise behind them. They all turned, and saw that the entrance was gone. The gap in the walls where it had been was again featureless stone, with no seams or cracks. The only way out, unless one knew how to fly, was the far end, still wide open. Far off in the distance, there was a barely audible sound of several people screaming. It only lasted a moment.

"You know, I don't like Talisman much. I don't think I'll come here again," said Julia. She frowned at Shiv. "This had better be worth it."

They reached the end of the road, and the corridor opened up into a wide plaza filled with thick fog. Just ahead of them, the fog cleared as if it was held back by glass walls, and against the smooth golden surface of the Tower was a platform of the familiar grey stone, rising out of the plaza floor as high as a single stair. It was shaped like a crescent formed to the curving golden wall, and was easily wide enough to accommodate all of them.

"I agree. I don't much care for Talisman," said the Doctor. They all stepped onto the platform, and as the last foot, Shantel's, reached it, the stone began to rise steadily. Once they had cleared the fog, the Doctor looked out over the edge. The clear passageway they had entered by was gone, and all the way to the outer wall, the surrounding area was indeed a maze of unbelievable complexity. Leaving without permission would be near impossible. As the ground fell far beneath them, the gnome shuddered, and stepped back hurriedly. "I wouldn't advise doing that, if anyone else is curious."

The stone platform soon reached the top of the tower; on the other side of the golden wall were golden steps which encircled the entire top of the tower, and which led down to a grey stone floor. There was a plain-looking, iron-bound stone trapdoor in the very center. Standing on the golden steps were a dozen of the red-robed guards, motionless, in a near circle with only enough room in between for the visitors to walk down from the crescent to the stone floor. Shiv led them all down the steps, smiling oddly as if he were eager instead of intimidated like the rest of his group.

CAMERON S. CURRIE

As Shantel stepped off the crescent, she happened to look back; it had disappeared without warning. The drop to the fog was about two hurls, thirty times her height at a minimum, and she suddenly swooned, arms wheeling crazily until Julia caught her hand and dragged her forward.

"Shiv! Your apprentice nearly died back here!" she snapped, guiding a shivering Shantel forward in between the motionless guards. "That'd be the second of them today!"

"Sorry… she's okay, right?" Shiv said, looking back absent-mindedly. He nodded, and didn't wait for an answer; he had reached the trapdoor, and gripped the metal ring in the center of the stone slab. It opened easily, as if it were weightless. The circular hole the slab revealed was pitch black, and the bright sunlight disappeared as clouds suddenly covered the sun once again. Doctor Unfriendly looked up, and there were no gaps in the clouds, as if there never had been.

Shiv looked up at them, smiling eagerly, and then back down into the hole. He stepped into the darkness, and began to descend the steps inside.

Chapter Fifty-Six

> *Magic Wards: These are notoriously unreliable spells that are designed to keep a wizard safe from attack. They must be cast well in advance of the attack, and must be designed to block a particular substance; therefore one might stop a sword blade but be useless against a well-aimed boot. A Master can usually make a moderately effective shield, but they are only formidable in the hands of even more skilled wizards.*
>
> *Doctor Unfriendly's Comprehensive Guide to Everything.*

The staircase Shiv descended was tight, barely allowing room for a few thin rays of daylight to squeeze past him. The stairs curled tightly, so each flight narrowly cleared his head when he reached the next flight below. The walls, only just visible in the increasing darkness, were of the same grey stone he'd seen on the roof and walls of the poorly named Great Maze.

The stairs curved around in seemingly endless circles; Shiv quickly lost track of how many flights there had been, but despite that they soon ended in a closet sized vestibule; light seeped in through the cracks around the only door. He looked briefly to ensure the others were behind him, and then tried the latch.

The rickety wooden door opened easily, with a slight creak. Apparently the staircase had descended through a tight stone tube in the center of a large, circular chamber. Surprisingly, it was brightly lit, from a multitude of golden lampstands and hanging lanterns. The chamber had a high arched ceiling, and the walls were made of blocks of many coloured pale marble. Shelves covered every surface that did not bear a lamp, and huge, heavy stone bookshelves sported an almost limitless collection of scrolls, books, loose papers and miscellaneous knick-knacks.

The room was empty of people except for a single nondescript man in a shabby black robe and a white cloak. Like all the other Talismanians they had seen, he was moderately short, and had nondescript brown hair and eyes. He patiently watched the group enter with a mild smile, cracking his knuckles. Shantel came in last, hesitantly, and as soon as she passed the door it swung shut with a clatter.

"Hello, there, Master Shiv," said the white-cloaked man. His voice was soft and he had an odd habit of breathing heavily, appearing slightly out of breath. He absent-mindedly glanced over at a mirror on one wall, and then deliberately took a single small step to the side. Nodding slightly as if pleased with himself, he looked over the group. "Doctor. Miss Hammerhand. Miss Robberan."

"You know us?" Shiv said with a surprised frown.

"Of course! Well, you, Master Shiv, I have known of for some time. The others, you see, I found out about recently. Except, of course, for your uncle, Doctor. It seems I knew of him, or rather, his exploits. A long time ago." He smiled broadly and toyed with an amulet, a dull metal circle on a leather thong. "I suppose, being here, young Kobodan, you have a few questions for me."

There was a collection of scattered rustles from somewhere high above them, although nothing was visible there. The white-cloaked man frowned and scratched his head, then considering, began to crack the bones in his neck while they watched.

"Er... yes," said Shiv, a little disturbed by the long process of cracking. "I wanted to speak with Zanquitor Zachary Talisman."

"Oh, yes, of course. Maybe a bit rude of me, I suppose," the white-cloaked man said, appearing slightly surprised. He continued cracking his neck, twelve or thirteen times along one side, and then the same number along the other. "I don't engage much, of course, in the social graces. Yes. You've found him. That is, me. I am him. He. The Zanquitor." He finished cracking his neck, and then held out his hand as if to shake Shiv's hand. Before Shiv could respond, the

Zanquitor seemed to suddenly reconsider, and pulled his hand back with a grin, wiping it on his black robe.

"I... did you order the deaths of my family and my troupe?" Shiv asked, meeting the odd man's eyes.

"Well, as a matter of fact, I did, actually," he replied, smiling both proudly and shyly at the same time. Suddenly he grasped his jaw in both hands and wrenched it roughly to one side. There was a loud crunching sound like a snapping plank. "Oh, that was it. Much better, that's been bothering me forever."

The group shifted nervously, all of them looking to Shiv, although he did not seem to notice.

"Why?" said Shiv, his look becoming more intense. He crossed his arms, and his fingers twitched.

"Well, it is sort of a project for me. You are, actually. The project."

"Wha- excuse me?" Shiv demanded. Within his crossed arms the others noticed his fingers closing on something in the leather plates of his armour. "What do you mean?"

"Well, you understand, you are an artist, of sorts. I am. As well," said the Zanquitor. His smile increased, and he started cracking his knuckles again.

Shiv's hand flickered and one of his dragon-tooth knives was suddenly in his hand. His frown became almost a snarl. He nodded slowly.

"Your... art... is those wonderful knives that you make, and what you do with them. Other things, I suppose, as well, but mainly the knives. My art is more, sort of, the world. I make... terrible things. The Inland Sea, my father made, although I improved upon it, eventually."

A small reddish songbird fluttered over to him and he absent-mindedly held out his hand for it to perch. Shiv's anger was combined now with confusion.

"Your art is terrible things? I don't understand. What does that have to do with my family?"

"Of course. You have my apologies, modern Neslish is a bit imprecise. I make... monsters, Master Shiv. Things like that. I actually make a wide variety of monsters. I am, by trade, a conjurer, mentalist... translocative multidimensional psychodevelopmental metabreeding, I suppose you could call it."

"I know you're a wizard. What are you saying, this was some kind of experiment?" Shiv said impatiently.

"No," replied the Zanquitor. "Or rather, yes, I am a wizard, to put it crudely, yes, although I am a Grandmaster in two unrelated fields of study, and a Master in essentially all the others, so 'a wizard' is sort of, well, understating it. But no, it wasn't an experiment, not as such, I do what I do for... artistic purposes."

"You kill people for art?!?" snapped Shiv.

"NO! No, you misunderstand. Murder is not creative. No, I create monsters. Sometimes this requires some deaths, but that is... incidental. No. You, Shiv. You are a monster, and I created you."

"That's ridiculous!" snapped Shiv. The ivory knife was out openly now, along with another that matched it. Shiv's knuckles were white on the bone handles, and his hands shook. "I am as human as anybody, I was born, not created. Tell me the truth!"

"Heh, no, rather disappointing actually, you still don't understand. No, I created you, but not that way. My canvas is your mind, your life, your skills. And you are still not finished. Your home village was selected. I hit four other villages as well. The plague that struck it was tailored, if I can call it that, to exempt anyone with the requisite skills. I planted a rumour so the troupe would pass by. A troupe with a knife thrower in it, a Master, the Amazing Edgison. You were the fertile ground, and he planted the seed in you. But you may have just been another knife thrower, another blacksmith. No... I needed more impetus, so I removed the troupe with another little project of mine, the Storm Kobold."

"YOU'RE INSANE!" shouted Shiv, and both ice daggers whirled at the white-cloaked man. While they were still in the air, two more ice daggers were out and flying. Not one of them hit. They stopped, hanging in the air an inch from the Zanquitor, motionless. The Zanquitor burst out laughing, laughing so hard tears began to run down his cheeks. Before he recovered, Shiv threw four black iron daggers, sending the Zanquitor into deeper hysterics. The red songbird grew annoyed at its unstable perch, and flew away as the white-robed man dropped to the floor, laughing helplessly. Shiv threw his three silver knives. They all hung in the air as well, as the Zanquitor struggled to his feet.

Julia growled and fired both her crossbows; the darts stuck in the same barrier the knives had. This made the Zanquitor laugh even louder, and he paused in getting to his feet, unable to go on until the laughing passed.

"Maybe," the Zanquitor continued, ignoring the knives and darts, "Maybe once you are finished you'll be able to hurt me, but I doubt it." He wiped the tears from his face with the back of his sleeve.

"Still, you are doing exceptionally well," the Zanquitor mused, watching Shiv draw the pair of tisken knives and throw them. They rebounded off of the Zanquitor's shield, spun out to either side, and then circled back to strike from the man's rear. The shield stopped them there, as well. He grinned and snickered a little at the tiskens. "You arrived here on schedule, and your murderous rage right now is what I was hoping for."

Shiv threw one steel dagger, his last for throwing, and then knocked his forearms on his sides to spring the stilettoes from his gauntlets. He held his rage in check though, glaring at the Zanquitor as if he could find the shield's weaknesses if he watched closely enough.

"So now," continued the Zanquitor, rubbing his hands together with a smile, "What we need is another tragedy, a terrible event that shall scar you worse than the previous two."

Chapter Fifty-Seven

> *Words of Power: The goal of most wizards, a Word of Power is a spell that can be cast with a single word (normally other words can still be added for detail, but aren't necessary). Much magical research is the gradual removal of gibberish from a pre-existing spell, and a Word of Power is the final result of that.*
> *Doctor Unfriendly's Comprehensive Guide to Everything.*

"We'll stop you," growled Julia, drawing both her short swords. The Zanquitor grinned awkwardly and shook his head.

"No, no, that's not your part, you see, you have to be bystanders. Bystanders? No, witnesses, I think, is a better word. You have to be witnesses."

She rushed forward, swords ready, and Shiv did with his stilettoes; Shantel carefully circled around to the side, kobold spear at the ready, and the Doctor began murmuring a spell.

The Zanquitor was faster than all of them, speaking a single word. It seemed to echo and reverberate, and the syllables slurred into each other in a way no human mouth should have been able to pronounce.

All four of them were thrown backwards to land, gasping, on the stone floor. They regained their breath, and then slowly struggled to their feet, looking around for where their gear had clattered to the floor. Shiv's stilettoes, having been mounted in his gauntlets, were still at hand.

"You recognize that spell, Doctor? Similar to that apprentice-level stun spell you're so fond of, but cast with a bit of finesse. A bit more refinement and I think it'll be a true Word of Power. Not even in my area of specialty, really, I am more skilled with spells of this nature..."

Four magical syllables rolled off of his tongue as if they were part of the sentence, and in an odd gesture with his left hand, his fingers bent backwards in a way that should have broken them. The Zanquitor didn't flinch. A half a dozen fizzling red sparks appeared on the floor between them.

There was a pause of only a second, and the sparks exploded in growth that hurt the eye to watch; by the end of another second each spark had grown into a black-skinned gargoyle, bigger than a man and sweating sulfurous black smoke. Before any of them could reach their weapons, one of the creatures had latched onto each of them with taloned fingers, and they were wrenched into helpless positions. Except Shiv, who punched a stiletto into a gargoyle's short ribs. It barely flinched, and swung a glossy black claw, tearing strips out of the Handspan Armour. The Zanquitor started laughing again, clapping his hands and watching Shiv with delight.

There were two unengaged gargoyles, however, and as Shiv sparred and punched holes in his opponent, they circled around and snatched his arms from behind. Shiv was slammed to the floor and pinned between the three of them. The white-cloaked man's laughing continued for a moment, and he clapped his hands in appreciation.

"My goodness, Shiv, you are a master. I am rather pleased," he said. "It almost is a shame I have to do this, but sacrifices must be made, you know. You others may enjoy watching this, actually, being his friends and all. This spell roots out the subject's greatest fears, and attacks him with them. It's usually rather, unpleasant, as in lethal, but I have faith our knife smith here will manage admirably. Master Shiv, are you ready?"

Shiv snarled at him as he struggled with the gargoyles, but didn't answer. The Zanquitor nodded as if the response had been a polite nod, and retrieved a speck of something from a pocket of his robe; once again his voice reverberated and his hands contorted unnaturally.

Chapter Fifty-Eight

Fear spells: These are difficult to master but extremely nasty. They stimulate the target's mind to produce a fear sensation, sometimes with and sometimes without a projection of something that frightens them. I don't like using them, they are a bit too cruel.
Doctor Unfriendly's Comprehensive Guide to Everything.

Terrence Kobodan got up from his hands and knees on his front porch. His family lay in their beds, in worse health than him, except for young Terry, his son. Terry, still too young to walk anywhere by himself for help, regarded his father with a faithful smile, and said encouraging words that had grown stale with repetition.

Interrupting her younger brother, Caroline staggered out onto the porch, and shook her head.

"Mother is gone, I think," she said hoarsely, and stopped to vomit at her feet, holding the door handle for support. She smiled sadly at her brother and wiped her face as best as she could. Then her eyes lit up. She pointed out over her father's head, and the three of them turned to see a train of wagons trundling up the dusty road. The colourful vehicles were pulled by healthy-looking horses, and handled by drivers who looked equally robust. Caroline waved at them to stop, trotting towards the road, but her own momentum knocked her sprawling. As she struggled to get to her feet, her father, showing strength unseen for weeks, snatched up young Terry and ran to intercept the wagons as they passed. He reached the third wagon in the row, a wagon with multi-coloured knives and daggers painted on the sides, and held up his son.

There was a flicker, and the illusion floating above him changed, a teary-eyed Shiv struggling all the harder between the three gargoyles.

"Interesting," said the white-cloaked man, cracking his knuckles again.

The Amazing Edgison got up out of the tent he was sitting in, smiling to himself. The boy was finally asleep. He stepped towards him, only once, and stopped. Something was wrong. He was not sure what, but he gestured to Willie and drew two of his sharpest knives. Sure enough, the grass to the south was shivering as if something was crawling through it. A lot of somethings. He crept towards the disturbance, silently, and Willie followed, brandishing his walking stick like a cudgel. The grass burst apart in shapes of slate-coloured kobolds, holding knives themselves, and soon, Edgison was fighting for his life. He had never actually hurt anyone with his knives, and he muttered under his breath as one of the kobolds drew first blood from his left arm.

"Stay asleep, boy, just stay asleep." he whispered to himself, as the last of the three or four dozen kobolds came out of the grass, a larger one with odd blueish scales and a jade amulet.

Edgison never saw who it was that stabbed him in the back of the neck, but he saw the reddened blade come out from just beneath his jaw.

"My goodness, I am so glad I made an impression!" said the Zanquitor, smiling and chuckling to himself. "You three can let him go, now, the spell has him for the moment."

He made a twisting motion with one hand, and another which looked vaguely like a downward push, and a hissing syllable, and the three gargoyles shrivelled back into red sparks that skittered on the floor for a moment before vanishing. Shiv's three companions still struggled at their captors' grasp, but Shiv lay motionless on the floor, whimpering, his eyes wide with terror.

Shiv, alone and weary from his long journey, returned to Redlock. He had been gone for nearly two years, now, having served the Oracle for his full term. Surprisingly, the labours had not been grotesque, so much as gruelling. He did not know if he would stay or not, but at the least he had to recover his gear and his mule, Cornelius.

CAMERON S. CURRIE

The town wall had been repaired, and a gate finally built in the entranceway, an impressive thing made of iron and marked with the names of those who had died in the battles with the goblins and the spiders. The gate was unguarded, however, and no one walked in the streets. Concerned, he trotted more quickly, looking left and right for townspeople who were not there. The town was abandoned.

He began searching the buildings, finding one after the other empty, until he entered the Tortoise Toe Inn; when he entered there, it was a charnel house. There was barely enough room for the door to open before the pile started, a pile of arms, legs, and other pieces of townspeople, young and old. They had all died in gruesome fashion, blood covering every surface, obscuring any detail of which part belonged to which person; the only thing that was clear and easy to identify was the look of pain and horror frozen on each face.

Shiv collapsed to his knees. The blood was all fresh, as if he had missed the attack by hours; there were no killers there, now, only thick clouds of flies feasting on the stinking remains.

He began dry heaving as he saw a long red braid attached to a disembodied scalp, and a few body parts that were a quarter of the size of the others. One arm was even smaller, and clutched a wooden sword with white, bloodless knuckles.

"Shiv! It's not real! Fight it!" screeched Julia for the fifth time. The white-cloaked man ignored her, studying Shiv for one moment, and then the floating illusion that hung in the air above him. His hands occasionally made discreet movements to adjust the spell, but largely it sustained itself.

Shiv looked up proudly at the front of his shop, and the new sign which read 'Shiv Kobodan, World's Greatest Knife smith, serving you for ten years!' His wife put her arm around him, although her face was blurry, he knew she was beautiful, especially her smile. A group of three children emerged from the shop to begin setting up for the morning, each carrying baskets of knives to set up on the tables along the front of the sturdy wooden building.

He quickly kissed his wife and then entered the building to start the forge fire. Poking at the carefully banked coals, he added a large sack's contents to them, and then went to retrieve a slab of pig iron to begin heating. His smile vanished as he heard a scream from the *yard out front. Dropping the slab at his feet, he was running before it hit the ground.*

Empty baskets lay in the lawn, but no one was there; at the sound of a whimper he turned, and saw his wife and children nailed with his own knives to the front of his shop.

The Zanquitor burst out laughing, nearly dropping to his knees as he did. Tears streamed down from his eyes as he attempted to stand. He wiped his eyes with the back of his sleeve, and the laughter stopped. The gnome doctor stood in front of the gargoyle that had been holding him, a rune of holding somehow carved into the thing's arm, preventing it from moving. As the Zanquitor struggled to get painfully to his feet, the doctor retrieved a small packet from a belt pouch and held a handful of the contents up for the Zanquitor to see. It was powdered iron.

"NO!!!" shrieked the white-cloaked man, still on his knees. He pointed, wide-eyed, at the gnome, and the flitting songbird dropped to the floor, smoothly becoming a large fox as it landed. It launched itself at the gnome.

"I... don't understand..." said his oldest child, gasping his last breath and coughing up blood. Shiv followed the child's eyes to the basket he had, unnoticed, under his arm. A basket half full of his own knives. In his other hand he held one, still slick with fresh blood. As was Shiv's shirt and smith's apron.

Shiv gasped and held the left side of his chest; his back arched so far that only his ankles and shoulders touched the floor. Blood trickled from his nose, and the strangled sound that came from his throat was too crude to form words. Beside him the gnome wrestled with a bristled red fox whose teeth had clamped onto his arm. Beside them both was a small packet surrounded by spilled iron shavings.

Shiv knelt in the doorway of the Tortoise Toe Inn, in front of a pile of body parts. He had lost track of when he had started screaming. He held his hands up to shield his face from what he saw, and his hands clutched two butcher's cleavers, covered in the same wet blood that he was kneeling in. His clothes and armour were rent from dozens of attacks, and the blood and viscera of his victims was ground into the cloth that had been gifted to him by Marvin Tailor. He tried to scream, and realized he still was when he saw Marvin's upper half, partly skinned, sitting an arm's reach to one side.

CAMERON S. CURRIE

Shiv's left eye had rolled back to expose the white, and the left side of his body had gone limp, but the right side was still arched above the floor, and his right eye still stared at the cluster of pictures floating above him. The Zanquitor had regained his feet and stomped towards the gnome; the floor shook with each step as if he weighed vastly more than was apparent.

The gnome and fox rolled over to where a miniature staff lay; on his side, the gnome's eyes widened as he saw it; his hand grasped a certain part of the wooden shaft, and a blade sprang from the end. Painted onto the miniature blade was a concoction of his own creation, something that made the fox stiffen like a board as soon as the blade scratched its side. Dropping the staff and kicking off the fox, the gnome climbed to his feet, and saw the white-cloaked man standing between him and the iron shavings.

The Zanquitor smiled and pointed at the gnome, wagging his finger in a 'no-no' gesture. But his eyes went wide again as the gnome leapt to the side, landing sprawled beside Julia and her gargoyle. His finger began to spark as he drew a simple rectangular rune on the creature's foot.

The Kobodan boy woke up, the field anvil digging into his back. He stood, worried, to look over the grass, and saw sixteen dead bodies lying with bone-handled knives protruding from them. Knives like the two bloody ones he held in his own hands. He screamed again, and realized his throat was painfully raw, and would no longer make noise.

Shiv collapsed to lie flat on his back, struggling for breath and not finding any. A small pile of iron shavings lay beside him, and the white-cloaked Zanquitor stood nearby. He saw Julia and Doctor Unfriendly nearby, still alive, and he tried to see what they were doing, but his eyes were wrenched back to the thing floating above him. His weakly flailing hand clutched on something that sifted through his fingers.

Young Terry Kobodan sat on the wagon beside a large man with a sympathetic smile, who said his name was Edgison. The man cleared his throat, eyes moist, and did something with the reins to make his horses move. As the wagon pulled away from the only home he had ever known, he looked over his shoulder, to see a man and a girl collapsed near the side of the road, each covered in knife wounds.

"It's okay, boy," said the Amazing Edgison. *"You can put those down now."*

He did not want to look. He knew what should be in his hands, two of his mother's kitchen knives, but he did not want to look. If he looked, he knew he would surely die. But he could feel them. His left hand grasped a wooden handle, worn smooth from years of use. His right hand... that was odd. His right hand did not feel like it held a knife. It felt like it held... powder.

He looked down at his right hand, careful not to look at the left, and saw the hand of a grown-up. It was wearing a dark leather gauntlet, with an arrangement of straps and metal that held a stiletto onto his wrist. He remembered such a stiletto; there was a lever in the forearm of the armour that could be slammed against his side to pop the stiletto in and out. And in the palm of the gauntlet, there was a handful of dark grey powder. There was a glimmer of memory there, too. Something about a powder like that...

He looked up at Edgison, who smiled encouragingly, and threw the powder in his face. The face shimmered, and vanished like smoke, revealing a block of white marble in a ceiling above him.

Shiv, writhing on the floor and barely in control of his muscles, numbly flung some of the powder above him. Some of it landed in his face, stinging eyes already empty of tears. Though it was hard to see through the iron in his eyes, he could see enough to know where he was. Beside him loomed a huge, blue-scaled creature wrapped in black rags and covered with a large white cloak. Shiv choked and smiled, spitting up blood and iron shavings. There were two blurs on the other side of the blue monster that looked like Julia and the Doctor, and another blur that looked like a woman in the arms of a gargoyle.

But she was alive. They all were.

Chapter Fifty-Nine

Grandmaster: The highest rank attainable in most cases, this implies that a person has been training and practising their trade for at least twenty-five years; sometimes it requires far longer. A Grandmaster is the equivalent of a Master even in areas of their profession well outside of their specialty.
Doctor Unfriendly's Comprehensive Guide to Everything.

The man in the white cloak was gone; the cloak was still there, but it was far larger and draped over a blue-scaled monster three times as tall as Shiv, despite bending over nearly double, so the sound of its voice would come out of the right spot. Between the scraps of black rags that once could have been a robe, serpentine features blended with human behind pebbly scales the colour of a night sky. A disk made of adamant, the same metal as Shiv's stilettoes, hung from the thing's neck like a medallion. Its arms each split at the elbow into two parts: one a shrivelled forearm with two seven-knuckled fingers, the other a vestigial and ineffective-looking bat wing. The creature's legs and face looked equally withered and sickly.

"You stupid peasants!" spat the monster, in the same voice as the man had used. "You can't win! This is just mean-spirited, and meddlesome!"

Shiv struggled painfully to his feet, still gasping, and wiped the trickle of blood from his nose. His body shook as if he was freezing to death, although in truth he felt hot. He could not see much beyond a blur, although blinking his stinging eyes repeatedly seemed to help a little.

Julia stood to the side, reloading her crossbows, and the Doctor walked over to Shantel and the last moving gargoyle. All of them watched the bulky creature in the white cloak warily.

"Shiv, just let me work. I'm covered in protective spells, you can't harm me," the monster said. As if to emphasize the point, two more of Julia's crossbow darts thudded into his invisible shield. "I'm protected against forged metal, against teeth (for your dragon-tooth knives), wood for the gnome's staff, and just about any spell you or your friends might have access to. Seriously, what are you going to do?"

Shiv smiled broadly as his vision cleared somewhat, and coughed up a few drops of blood. He kept his eyes on the Zanquitor, and started rummaging in one of his belt pouches, feeling for something in particular. The gnome had frozen the last gargoyle in place, and Shantel clambered out of its rock-hard but unmoving grasp.

"Let my friends go, and you and I can handle this one-on-one," said Shiv. "I'm sure if you want to you can always track them down later."

"True," said the creature, coming into focus a little more as Shiv's tears began working again. Two more crossbow bolts stopped in front of its face, not provoking so much as a blink. It shrugged, its bones crackling, and waved vaguely at the door, which opened to reveal the staircase going back to the roof. "Very well, they can go. Leave. Now."

"And the maze will let them out?" Shiv said. The creature laughed and shook its head.

"Yes, it will. Let them out."

"Alright then. Go, everyone... I'll be right behind you," Shiv said breathlessly, gesturing to the door with his left hand. The Zanquitor grinned, showing human incisors mixed unevenly with animalistic fangs.

"No," said Julia quietly. Shantel and the Doctor paused halfway to the door. Shiv said nothing, but pointed again, and met her eyes with a sympathetic but stern expression. A hundred emotions tried to show on her face at once, and Shiv saw them, his eyes finally clearing for the most part. He smiled encouragingly at her, as the vision had told him he had smiled at his father and sister.

"Dammit!" snapped Shantel, who stalked over to Julia. She was a half a head taller than the Hammerhand sister, but for some reason it had never been apparent until now. She grabbed Julia's hand forcefully and stomped over towards the door. Julia let herself be dragged. The Doctor led the way out, nodding once to Shiv before he left. Shiv nodded back, and with three magical syllables and a couple of minor gestures, his knives wriggled slowly across the floor back towards him.

"There! Now, if you'll-" began the Zanquitor.

"No, give them time to go, you'll have me to yourself soon enough," Shiv said. The Zanquitor snickered, and began cracking his knuckles again; for the first time the cracks matched up with the appearance of his hands.

"One minute, that's enough time. For them," the monster said, and Shiv nodded. Looking around the marble chamber, Shiv cleared his throat. His knives were all once again lying at his feet, and he casually began picking them up and re-sheathing them. The Zanquitor seemed amused at the various hiding places he stashed the blades.

"So, er... what exactly are you?" Shiv asked, as if trying to stall for time. The Zanquitor glared at him warily.

"I was human. My father laid enchantments on me in the womb, in my youth, to increase my magical talents. I was a prodigy, a master at fifteen. Eventually my human body, was too weak to hold the power of my spells. I worked with magic beyond the capacity of mortals, and I either risked burning myself to a cinder, or held back from my true potential. And age became a problem; human bodies only last so long. So I... altered my body."

"You're a shape-shifter?"

"No, this change was more fundamental, down to my soul. I studied magical creatures: dragons, daemons, faeries, and so forth, and I learned the fundamental differences that made them better at magic. And I made those changes to myself. I was... interrupted... by some meddlers, many parts of the spell were ruined, and I didn't turn out quite the way I had intended, physically. But my magical powers were greatly increased, so I lived with the rest. I was my first work of art. And it's been a minute."

"So it has. You're sure the maze is set to let them out?" Shiv said. His hand had long since closed on what he was searching for in his pouch. He counted the objects in his hand. There were three. He left his hand inside the pouch, but grasped the three tiny objects firmly.

"Of course," said the Zanquitor, smiling. He crooked his finger. "Come here."

Shiv pulled his hand free of his pouch and threw the three tiny vials of the Doctor's liquid fire at the Zanquitor. The shock was visible on the monster's face as he registered the flying glass passing through his shield. Shiv did not wait to see them impact, but turned and stumbled towards the open door, his legs nearly giving out on him. He did hear the sound of breaking glass and the shriek of the intended target as the little bottles of liquid fire burst into flame.

"YOU UNGRATEFUL LITTLE..." screamed the Zanquitor behind him as he staggered up the stairs. "UGH! MY FACE! MY-"

Shiv didn't bother to learn what cut off the Zanquitor's screams, knowing the creature would be after him in a moment. The stairs curved around tightly as they rose, but he used his hands as well as his feet to climb them, and he exited the trapdoor quickly. The daylight, however cloudy, overwhelmed his eyesight, but he saw enough to see the others, standing at the edge in the gap between the red-robed guards. Despite the Zanquitor's scream, the guards still stood motionless, as if at attention.

"The platform isn't there!" shouted Julia, running back to him. She stopped short of an embrace, instead checking Shiv for injuries, and nodded to herself when she found nothing new. "The Doctor said he could do something."

They returned to the edge, where the Doctor was on his hands and knees with a knife, moving it in a cutting motion in the air.

"You'll have to stay close," he said, "my arms aren't as long as Zimmiman's."

Before they could ask what he meant, the doctor put his knife away and rubbed his arm a bit, and while he was doing that a crescent-shaped slice of stone rose up to meet him. He stepped onto it and beckoned the others to follow him.

It was tight, and they all barely fit onto the platform, having to hold onto each other to avoid falling off as they descended.

"You learned that trick from Zimmiman?" wheezed Shiv, propping the Doctor on his shoulder.

"I stole it." The gnome replied, and grinned broadly.

"I'm glad you're a thief," said Shiv, and the two women nodded in agreement.

"Me too," the Doctor said, still grinning. "I don't have it quite mastered, though. I'll have to speed up to meet the ground before it runs out."

The golden wall slid past them, fortunately smooth enough that Shiv could lean on it, the Handspan Armour absorbing most of the friction; the others leaned on him instead. Despite that, the stone slab shivered and burst into fragments a few seconds before they hit the ground. They fell into the shallow depression where the slab had come from in a heap.

Shiv had to lift the Doctor off before he could stagger to his feet. Julia and Shantel seemed twisted together a little, but managed to get up as well, rubbing bruises and dusting themselves off.

Something red fell to the pavement nearby with a loud clatter; it took more than a glance to discern it was one of the red robes from the guards, and a scattering of bleached human bones. The impact had broken the skull in half.

Before any of them could comment, another clatter struck slightly further away, the red robe seeming to hold its shape until it struck, and then bursting apart in a profusion of bones on impact.

"Well, that's peculiar, said Shiv, coughing. "That's the most I've seen them move."

"A little late, isn't it?" replied the Doctor.

Several more smashed to the ground, a spear accompanying each. Shiv looked up, and saw a blue serpentine head jutting out over the edge, screaming something and pointing down at them, although the wind made the words difficult to make out.

"Look!" Julia said, pointing. One of the red robes had sprouted a skeletal arm, which reached out and grasped one of the fallen spears. The broken skull, having come from the same pile, snapped back together as if drawn by magnets.

"Hey, maybe we should leave," said Shantel.

"Might be good, yes," agreed Shiv. He gave Julia a shove past the nearest forming skeleton towards the gate of the Great Maze. From inside the stone walls came loud grinding sounds, like spinning millstones. They trotted through the gate, Shiv pausing for a single glance behind them to see a red-robed skeleton struggling to its feet, as its companions continued to clatter to the ground.

The passageway through the Great Maze, before featureless stone walls, now had regular doorways on either side. They ran faster, seeing one of the doorways slide shut, becoming featureless stone again, as they ran past it. Another stone wall rotated as if on a huge pivot, the reverse side of the stone carved with grotesque and screaming faces. As they rushed past it, a dog's face reached out from it to snap at Julia's ankle.

At the far end of the hallway, in front of the only obvious exit, a stone slab began sliding slowly across the passage. Shantel pointed and said something unintelligible in between panting breaths, and they all ran as fast as they could.

Julia was a half a step behind Shantel, and judged they could get out of the exit archway before it was blocked off. A few steps away from the exit, she looked over her shoulder, and saw the Doctor some distance behind her, his short legs skittering to catch up, and Shiv just behind him, grasping the side of his chest and staggering. Entering the far end of the maze were three red-robed guards, looking completely undamaged and walking at a slow, steady pace with their spears lowered.

"Hurry up!" Julia shouted. "I won't leave you behind again!"

The Doctor stopped, looking over his shoulder at Shiv, and after a slight pause, began running back to him.

"You hurry up!" shouted Shantel from the other side of the archway. "They can take care of themselves!"

Julia hesitated, looking towards the narrowing gap in the stone wall and then back at Shiv, staggering forward slowly, wheezing. The Doctor caught back up to her, but instead of ducking through the gap, he knelt down and pulled out his tiny knife. He nodded to her.

"Get through and make sure the other side stays clear," he said, and Julia smiled briefly at him before ducking through.

The stone gap slammed shut behind her.

Chapter Sixty

> *Skullguard: The standing army of Talisman, these are the animated skeletons of dead soldiers, dressed in red robes. They are heavily enchanted, and being dead, they are extremely difficult to deter or destroy.*
> *Doctor Unfriendly's Comprehensive Guide to Everything.*

Shiv stood guard over the Doctor, who was down on his hands and knees tracing a shape on the pavement with his belt knife. Twenty paces down the passageway, three red-robed guards advanced at a walk with spears pointed towards them. Behind the three was another group of five, and behind those, more were still assembling in the lee of the tower. Shiv panted slowly as he could, regaining his breath, and drew his two silver daggers, one from each boot.

"You don't have any of those ghoul-bone knives left, do you?" asked the Doctor, knife working furiously.

"No," Shiv said. "Next time I try to convince Zimmiman of something, help."

"Agreed."

"Shiv!" came Julia's voice from beyond the wall. "We have more friends coming!"

The Doctor began his magical syllables and gestures over the rectangular mark. Halfway through he looked over his shoulder, and saw the guards only a half a dozen paces off. He chanted more quickly.

Shiv stepped back into the rectangle drawing, and there was a sizzling sound from the pavement.

"Dammit, Shiv, you can't step on it until I'm done!" the Doctor screeched. He immediately yelped as a spear thrust narrowly missed him. He scrambled quickly to his feet.

Shiv swung and thrust each of his daggers at the red robes, doing little more than nicking bone and tearing cloth. The robes knit themselves together almost as fast as he could cut. The Doctor had stowed his belt knife, and swung his tiny staff at the guards, clattering against bone but doing little else.

"Shouldn't you be casting a spell?" Shiv demanded, his knives parrying spear points as fast as they could.

"That was my last platform spell, and you fizzled it, thank-you. And my shove spells don't work against these things, I tried." The second group had reached the fight now, and five of the guards were in a wide half-circle around Shiv, with the remaining three forming into a second rank. The Doctor ducked into a crouch between Shiv's boots.

"Where's that bypass wand you had?" shouted the Doctor, triggering the concealed spearhead in his staff. It was only marginally effective as well.

"Son of a- it's in my pouch! No, the left one!" answered Shiv. He had taken at least four thrusts with the spears, although the Handspan Armour had thus far absorbed the shallow strikes. Each thrust was hitting more solidly, the guards working with each other to goad their targets into position. "Ouch! They're starting to hurt here!"

"I got it!" shouted the Doctor. He cackled in victory as he drew a rectangle on the wall behind him. The section of wall vanished, and the Doctor quickly rolled through.

"HEY!" shouted Shiv. "The damn hole is too small!" The top of the exit was lower than Shiv's waist.

"The number of times I've said that," mumbled the Doctor, and then shouted, "I can only reach so high!" A larger hole appeared a moment later, and this time Shiv was able to back out while fending off spear thrusts.

On the other side of the wall, Julia held the bypass wand in one hand and one of her short swords in the other. Shantel and the Doctor had spears at the ready as nearly a dozen of the red-robed guards advanced towards them. Julia tossed the wand to Shiv, who tossed his silver dagger in the air, caught and stowed the wand, and then caught the blade again smoothly.

"This way," the Hammerhand sister said, drawing her second short sword. She parried the spear of the first guard to reach them, and then shoulder checked it onto the ground with a bony clatter. It immediately began to rise, slowly. She ran left, along the wall of the Great Maze for a few steps and then ducked down a street. Several of the guards jumped off the top of the wall, adding to the numbers closing in on them.

The guards were slow, however, never advancing at more than a walk, and the group easily outpaced them, Shiv breathing heavily again.

Most of the citizens had disappeared, however, a group of three ran into the street ahead of Shiv's group. Two had slender short swords, and one a heavy iron mace.

"Stop, invaders! We will-" shouted one, cut off by Julia's leaping kick breaking his jaw. He collapsed and she stepped on his neck, her sword nimbly darting past the second man's parry to tear open the side of his face. Before the third could move, the Doctor thrust his hand towards him, and the shove spell knocked him sprawling. The man with the bleeding face dropped his sword and ran.

"At least it works on somebody," the Doctor said.

"I can't believe I found something I can't kill with knives," Shiv mused, keeping only one of the silver daggers in his off-hand. He scooped up the iron mace from where it had fallen.

"Which way is the gate?" shouted Shantel, picking up the fallen swords and imitating Julia's stance.

"That way," said Doctor Unfriendly, pointing with his staff as the spearhead retracted. He scuttled ahead and the other three followed close behind.

"Why doesn't the shove spell work against the guards?" asked Shiv, panting, as he trotted past the Doctor.

"Why?"

"I was thinking of stealing it."

"It's an illusion," Doctor Unfriendly replied, poking his head around a corner as they emerged from behind a silversmith's shop. They quickly ducked across the street into another alley. "It makes them believe they've been shoved. Probably the skeleton guards don't have brains to believe anything with."

"Shut up, you two. The gate is just over there," Julia said. They all slowed, and she peeked around another corner. "Dammit, there are about forty of those guards waiting for us."

"This way," Shiv said, and chuckled. He led them in the opposite direction, away from the gate.

"Where are you going?" Julia snapped. "There's only one way out!"

As soon as they were out of sight of the gate, Shiv produced the bypass wand and drew a rectangle on the wall.

"Oh, right," said Julia, and they left the city.

Chapter Sixty-One

> *Finding Spell: As with magic wards, this sort of spell is rather awkwardly specific. A given finding spell might be geared towards a particular person, or a particular object, such as Marvin Tailor's favourite drinking cup. The more information known about the subject at the time the spell is cast, the more accurate the spell can be. They are tremendously useful in narrow circumstances, and a Grandmaster-level finding spell can locate a unique and well-known object anywhere in the world.*
>   Doctor Unfriendly's Comprehensive Guide to Everything.

They walked quickly into the jungle, Shiv stowing the bypass wand and retrieving the metal disc the Oracle had given him. He squeezed both sides.

Nothing happened.

"Uh... Doctor?" said Shiv. "What's wrong with this thing?"

"Let me see," the Doctor said, and took the disc. He groaned. "You should have let me look at it before- oh, dammit."

"What?" Shiv snapped. "What's the problem?"

"The square on either side: It's a void rune."

"So?"

"Look, there are a dozen runes she could use for a finding spell, but a void rune is the wrong one for that kind of magic. You'd use void magic to make something disappear."

Shiv groaned.

"What?" asked Julia. She and Shantel approached. "What's wrong?"

"It's a joke. A bad one," Shiv said. "The disc is void, nothing, except maybe a spell to make us disappear. The Oracle double-crossed us."

"It's a Talisman's Highway," said Julia.

"What's that?" asked Shantel.

"A figure of speech. Something that's supposed to be there but isn't. There are no highways in Talisman. Just jungle." Julia answered, frowning.

"Lovely sense of humour this Oracle has," said Shiv. "I have a mind to return and share the punchline with her."

"I think we've had enough of Grandmaster wizards for a while, Shiv," said the Doctor. "Perhaps Redlock would be a good idea."

"But there's no way out of Talisman, that's why we needed the Oracle's gateway to get in!" Shiv growled and stomped a few paces away, trying to stifle another fit of coughing.

"Look, we can go back through the teptkins," said Julia. "We made it once."

"The gateway might have moved," said the Doctor. "They sometimes do, but I suppose it is our best chance. If the Oracle expected us to die she might not have bothered to move it."

Julia left the others to approach Shiv. She put her hand on his shoulder.

"You okay?" she asked. In the background the Doctor and Shantel began to argue about something.

"I don't like being played. Apparently it has been happening all my life."

"Maybe, but we did escape. Here." Julia handed him a small glass vial. "It's my last healing potion. It should fix that… breathing thing when you run."

"Probably a good thing. We seem to be doing a lot of running lately," Shiv said, and laughed a little. He took the little bottle and drained it. The colour returned to his face. He smiled at her. "Thanks."

"For?" Julia asked.

Shiv brushed a strand of her hair aside, and slid his fingers into her hair. They looked into each other's eyes for a moment, and then he drew her in and kissed her slowly. She put her arms around his shoulders and kissed him back. The arguing behind them stopped, and the jungle was quiet.

"Say, shouldn't we be running for our lives or something?" called the squeaky voice of the Doctor. "As much as I approve, some skeleton guards or a monster should be along to kill us soon."

Shiv turned around, glaring at the gnome.

"Your timing is wonderful, Doctor."

"I know," the gnome answered, smiling broadly back at him. "But we should get out of here before someone discovers that hole in the wall."

They got moving again, going as close to south as they could guess. It did not take them long to return to the high rock they had rested on earlier. They stopped there, eating a bit of food and drinking the last of the Doctor's wine. At one point they heard the crashing and roaring they had heard previously, but it seemed to be moving away from them, so they stayed where they were and rested for a few hours. By the time they started moving again, the sun was low in the sky.

Chapter Sixty-Two

Chocolate Rice Crisps: I tried these once at a political function. They are apparently rice cooked in a way to make it crispy, and stuck together with chocolate, a brown concoction from Gintaftar that is rather nice. Hideously expensive, but they are worth it. If you find the recipe, let me know.

Doctor Unfriendly's Comprehensive Guide to Everything.

The white-cloaked man, his illusionary disguise restored, peered into his magic mirror. Instead of his reflection, a dark room with rough stone walls appeared in its surface. He drew his finger along its surface, murmuring, and the mirror slowly panned right, until it rested on a bulky heap of fur and cloth with dark spines protruding from it.

"Zanquitor," said the Oracle, turning her hideous face to look out through the mirror. "There is no point trying to deny it. I don't like prying."

"Quite right, Oracle," he said. A hint of mockery was in his voice. "I know you don't… you simply detected my scrying, quickly, before I had cleared my throat to speak. You are very… aware."

"I know," replied the Oracle. Her face split in what could have been a smile or a threatening display of her fangs. "What do you want? I already delivered the knife smith to you."

"Yes. Yes, you did, and thank-you, you were most helpful. He was suitably… effected… by what I had to tell him, thankfully, even on top of your own… revelations. He escaped as planned. Surprisingly, he managed to injure me. Despite my preparations, actually. He had several vials of liquid fire."

The Oracle cackled for a moment, and the white-robed man frowned and impatiently waited for her to catch her breath.

"Didn't ward yourself against glass? It's a good thing you rarely show your true face," she said. "Burn marks would not improve your looks. So why have you contacted me? Our business should be concluded."

"Yes, it should," said the Zanquitor. He pursed his lips and began cracking his knuckles behind his back. He continued in a softer voice. "Did you aid him in any way?"

"Of course not. What could I possibly hope to gain?" she walked out of the view of the mirror, and the white-cloaked man sighed in minor irritation as he adjusted it to follow her. She was now standing over a large cauldron, trailing her finger in the bubbling liquid. She looked up and smiled again.

"How should I know what you hope to gain, exactly? Why should I care? I merely contacted you as a courtesy. I would not approve if you had aided him. Perhaps... perhaps your debt to the Duke was larger than you let on?" he ceased cracking his knuckles and glared intensely at her, as if evaluating.

"That's none of your business. My debts are my own. If you are looking for some sort of confession, you are as crazy as your father was."

"DON'T TALK ABOUT MY FATHER!" screeched the Zanquitor. His illusionary form flickered and melted away, and he picked up the mirror with one gargantuan hand, flinging it against one of the marble walls. It exploded in a shower of glass and flickering sparks. The Zanquitor breathed out slowly, and returned his illusion. In irritation, he realized two slivers of enchanted glass had pierced his arm, and the bluish blood ran down onto his cloak.

Far away, in her cave, the Oracle chuckled, and tapped her clawed finger into the cauldron. It began to cast a faint light on her hideous face. A bubble popped, and another face formed in the liquid. It was the face of a blonde elf with traces of a moustache.

"You heard all of that, Master Ceborn?" she said coolly.

"I did. And it is Duke, not Master."

"Human titles mean little to me. Are we even, now?"

"My title is both human and elven. Did you exact a price from the knife smith?" the Duke asked, eyes suspicious.

"Of course I did," growled the Oracle. "He would not have believed it otherwise, would he?"

"I suppose not. However, he will believe you betrayed him, as he should. You may have to wait quite some time before you can collect."

"Yes," said the Oracle. "I don't mind. His skills improve with time, and his service improves in value. I shall have my payment with usury."

"Fine. But no hunting him down. He will come to you when he understands." The Duke frowned at her until she nodded, and then his image faded from the cauldron.

She clucked in her cheek to herself, and then walked over to another part of her laboratory. The pregnant she-troll lurked there, and looked up at her lovingly as Grandmother patted her head. One clawed thumb wrenched open the eyelid on the she-troll's bad eye. It was healing nicely, with very little of Grandmother's help.

"Some people think they are smarter than Grandmother," she said to the troll, smiling. "But no one is smarter than me, are they?"

Mother smiled back at the Grandmother, and appeared to agree.

Chapter Sixty-Three

The North Wilderness: This is a relatively small spot in between Sabosland, the Counciltowers, and the Goblin Mountain Fastness. It is populated heavily with stone giants, hill giants, and dragons. Even bears live in large packs here for safety, typically numbering over a dozen. Don't go here.
Doctor Unfriendly's Comprehensive Guide to Everything.

Shiv's group jogged through the jungle, ears alert for the sounds of the teptkins, or any other hazards, in the increasing darkness. Tiny insects like gnats swarmed in the darkness, occasionally biting fiercely. All of the group swatted regularly, not effecting the numbers no matter how many hits they scored.

"Doctor," Shiv said quietly. "Do these teptkins sleep at night?"

"I think so. At least, my sources would have indicated if they were nocturnal."

"What does-" said Shantel, a little too loudly.

"Awake at night," interrupted Julia. "How far away are we?"

"An hour or two," said the Doctor. "It should be fully dark before we get there. If they are going to be asleep they will be by that point."

"Anything else we should be worried about?" asked Julia.

"Most of the really bad stuff in Talisman stays near the coast and away from the cities. Maybe jaguars, or razorbees. I think there are some kind of bald, giant bears. That'd be it."

"Snakes?" asked Shiv.

"Well, yes, snakes. I thought that went without saying. Jungles and snakes just go together. Like ham and cheese, swords and shields..."

"Gnomes and babbling?" Julia interrupted.

"Yes, like that," answered the Doctor. "I think the snakes here are mostly constrictors. No poison, mostly, although they are awfully big. You're right, I probably should have mentioned the snakes."

"So let me ask again. Is there anything else we should be worried about?" Julia repeated.

"Well, yes. The watercats probably wouldn't be this far inland, but there are isolated cases. I wouldn't eat any wild fruit, of course. Those skeleton guards will no doubt be after us still, and there are big lizards, poison frogs, wood jackals, vine spiders, arrow squirrels, and maybe manticores. I think that's it."

"So... we're in about the worst place in the world?" asked Shantel. The Doctor laughed in response.

"No, no, the North Wilderness is far worse. And Fes is supposed to be worse than that. The worst place in the world is probably the swamp of Shiepalthun. But Talisman is pretty bad."

"We're getting too loud," Shiv said, effectively ending the conversation.

They jogged on in silence, periodically slowing to a walk to rest, and then jogging again. They made excellent time; it was barely more than an hour before they saw their first teptkin.

They skidded to a halt when they saw it; it was sleeping in a high branch, head curled against its grey-feathered chest, standing on one leg. The counting songs had gone quiet, and the only sounds were the wind in the trees and buzzing of insects.

They continued walking at a gesture from Shiv; the one teptkin gave no sign that it was aware of them, and they walked underneath it, the Doctor narrowly missing being hit by a dropping. He made a face in distaste, but said nothing.

Two more teptkins were perched a few minutes past the first, also asleep. They gave these a wider berth, still aiming for the cave they had emerged from.

The buzzing grew louder.

"What's that buzzing?" asked Shantel, again, a little too loudly.

"You are aware we are sneaking?" whispered Julia harshly. "Doctor, what's the buzzing?"

"Insects, probably."

"Thanks, Doctor," whispered Shiv. There were far more teptkins coming into view, all sleeping soundly on branches above them. He pointed towards a few of them with one of his tisken knives. "All of you shut up."

Shiv swatted one of the omnipresent jungle insects from his face, and jumped when his hand connected with something the size of a mouse. He swatted the Doctor and pointed at the retreating bug angrily.

"I mentioned razorbees," whispered the Doctor defensively. "And they aren't dangerous except in numbers."

"Did you see the size of that thing's stinger?" said Shantel, again too loudly.

"The next time you talk too loudly I'll smack you," hissed Julia.

There was a loud crashing sound only a stone's hurl to one side of the teptkin grounds, and suddenly the air was full of grey feathers and angry squawks. One of the birds scratched Julia's ear, but otherwise the swarm flew into the jungle, away from the noise.

A tree made a deafening crack, and through the brush they could see it topple partway to the ground. A deep, bass groan echoed through the area, and then the sounds of several teptkins screeching came from the direction they had fled. More crashing accompanied the screams.

"Which way do we go?" shouted Shantel, getting a slap from Julia. "Ow!"

"Same direction, only faster," said Shiv. "Whatever it is, it's welcome to the poultry." He broke into a run towards the cave, two tiskens out. Julia ran alongside him, followed by the Doctor, and Shantel in the rear. More trees crashed to their right, and as one they avoided peering into the woods to see what was responsible.

There was a series of loud knocking sounds, and several trees in their area suddenly had heart-shaped reptilian scales sprouting out of the bark, like small thrown hatchets.

"That would be a manticore," shouted the Doctor. "Running is good."

More groaning, much louder, sounded to their right, only a few paces into the jungle. Another groan, further off, sounded to their left, amid more screeching teptkins. There was no need for anyone to say that meant two manticores; in unison they all ran faster. Julia tripped and stumbled on a protruding root, but Shiv caught her wrist and yanked her upright before she had slowed. As soon as she was running smoothly again, he let go, and the tisken twirled, reappearing in his hand.

They entered the clearing where the teptkins had nested, and as they reached the middle of it a vast, sinewy shape scuttled into view behind them on sword like claws. It had a face like a bearded ape on a scaled body like a bear's, but twice as long, and flexed its stunted, leathery wings excitedly. Its reptilian tail swung and flicked, scattering sharp scales in all directions. One thudded into Shiv's armour, and both Julia and Shantel yelped as they were hit as well. Shiv skidded to a halt, glancing at the two women to evaluate their injuries.

"Doctor!" he shouted, stepping in between the manticore and the others. His tisken knives whirled and disappeared behind his cloak, and he struck his forearms on his sides, releasing his stilettoes with a metallic clang. "Find the cave! Get them in it and safe!"

"Ass," growled Julia, stepping beside him as two of her crossbow bolts thudded into the manticore's humanlike face. It shrieked, and its mouth opened wide, dozens of fangs unfolding like a snake's. Her crossbows spent, she drew her two swords, and stabbed angrily at the creature's face. It darted to the side, and Shiv slammed a stiletto into the creature's jaw.

Shiv was flung back as the creature lashed out with its scale-spiked tail, over a dozen of the bladelike things sticking into the Handspan Armour.

Shantel's spear sailed over his head, clattering off the side of the beast, and suddenly it lurched backwards, falling onto its side screeching.

The Doctor fired several more shove spells at the prone creature as the second manticore scuttled into the clearing, throwing scales in a wide swath. He tugged at Shiv's cloak, pointing behind them.

"It's over there!" he shouted. "Run!"

Shiv vaulted onto his feet, and noticed the others were all ahead of him, scurrying into a dark area of bushes. Sharp scales studded their clothes and the Doctor's top hat, but their injuries appeared to be superficial, except for a bloody slash on Julia's forearm.

They all crashed into the brush, the cave opening before them, and fled inside as the air grew thick with ricocheting scales; the manticores did not follow them into the darkness inside, and soon the group could slow to a walk.

A light flickered to life from the end of Doctor Unfriendly's staff, and they stopped, checking injuries and pulling out the bladelike scales from their armour, clothes, and skin.

"Dammit!" said Shiv, pulling several from his leather breastplate.

"What?" asked the Doctor, looking up from his work.

"These scales are too soft to keep an edge for long. I can't make decent knives out of them."

Chapter Sixty-Four

The Shersaver Mountains: A large mountain range that divides the duchies of Ghirronash and Aharonep, and is only breeched in a few places. The most notable passage is at Twinfort, a small but near-impregnable fortress that has stood for centuries.
Doctor Unfriendly's Comprehensive Guide to Everything.

"Why didn't they follow us in?" asked Shantel, gingerly poking at a cut on her arm. Julia cursed her lack of more healing potion, and began to wrap it up with a bit of bandage from her backpack.

"I wouldn't follow either if I knew the Oracle was on the other side," Shiv said dryly, and the others' nodding agreement could be seen in the dim light. "Speaking of which, she didn't think we'd escape, so she probably won't be expecting us. I suggest we stay quiet and slip past her before she figures out we're alive. Shantel, that means whispering."

The others said nothing to disagree, and followed his lead into the increasing darkness. What light there was flickered occasionally, as one of the manticores prowled past the cave entrance. Dripping water echoed as if from far off, but the tunnel appeared dry along their route.

"How much further is it?" whispered Shantel. Even her whisper was a little too loud, and Shiv shook his head before he responded.

"You were here with us the first time," he whispered through the darkness. "You know as much as us. But I don't think it's much farther."

CAMERON S. CURRIE

It did seem farther to everyone, but soon the darkness started to lighten again, this time from a somewhat gloomier source. The Oracle's archway was shaded between several large stone archways and columns, limiting the light to what reflected off of raw stone, but after the total darkness it still appeared relatively bright. As they neared the archway, they all slowed to a creeping pace.

As they approached, a black lump was visible, blocking the light in the lower half of the doorway; it didn't take long for them to realize the lump was moving, rising and falling slightly along with a low grumbling sound. The group stopped moving, except for Shiv, who drew two silver daggers and pointed to the left side of the passage; the large black lump did not quite bar the entire way, it left a small gap on the left side.

"Fog," whispered Shiv to the Doctor, pointing to the exit.

"Yes, it is, remember she has another one," responded the Doctor; even his whisper sounded a bit squeaky.

"No! Fffffffog!" whispered Shiv, somewhat more loudly.

"Too loud," whispered Shantel, earning dark glares from the others. The Doctor shook his head a bit and then began to mumble, spidery fingers contorting in the magical gestures Shiv found so difficult. A trickle of fog slithered out from his hands towards the entrance, getting wider and thicker as it travelled. Soon the archway was almost totally obscured, and Shiv beckoned them forward. They stopped again, only a few paces from the entrance, and Shiv motioned for them to stop. He sheathed his daggers and took a deep breath. Then, assuming a look of deep concentration, he made a few magical mumbles and gestures himself, remembering the Greater Rotation of the left hand, and with a barely audible pop, the illusionary elephant appeared.

Soundlessly, the elephant walked forward into the fog, Shiv frowning with concentration and moving his hands in a complex pattern. As the elephant began to fade, Shiv crept after it, jerking his head for the others to follow. One of the elephant's illusionary feet stepped on the black lump, but did not appear to disturb it. As they approached, his hand motions changed and the elephant veered left, around the lump, and Shiv jerked his head once to the right with a look at the others. The others drew their weapons quietly.

Shiv was the first to reach the breathing black lump. It bristled with metallic quills and stank of sulfur, but its loud breathing maintained a steady rhythm. He had to press his back up to the wall to inch past without touching the beast, but Shiv managed to get clear. He let the elephant walk to just in front of the sleeping beast's nose and left it there, and then crept backwards. Shiv's leather-armoured back hit something hard, stopping him in mid-pace. His eyes went wide, and the elephant flickered and disappeared.

The Doctor crept by, a wry grin on his face as he tapped the huge stone column Shiv had collided with. Shiv smiled back himself, let out a slow breath, and beckoned the others to follow. The path through the stones was crooked and oppressive at first, but as they left the fog, the moonlight began to shine, and their pace quickened. They cleared the labyrinth of standing stones in only a few minutes.

Staring at the line of nine moons in the sky for a moment, the Doctor nodded and pointed to the northwest. Low mountains rose up along the horizon to the north and the west, with a narrow dip in between the two ranges.

"We go that way to hit Redlock," Doctor Unfriendly said quietly. "I wasn't sure if the path to the Oracle would have moved in only a few days, but I wanted to get my bearings to be certain. We'd do well to veer north a bit to avoid the Shersaver Mountains, there. We'll pretty much be backtracking, only without a troll this time."

The others nodded in agreement; none of them had the direction sense of the gnome doctor. They hurried off as quietly as they could manage. The group kept to the twisting valleys to avoid being seen, although a number of times Shiv saw a small pack of wolves eyeing them curiously from a high ridge.

They had made several miles from the Oracle's stones before they stopped for their first rest. It was still dark, although a tenth moon had partly risen behind them, and after eating a simple meal of oatmeal and dried apples, the group decided to camp, and continue on in the daylight.

Chapter Sixty-Five

> *Baron: The rank below Count, which is, in turn, below Duke. A Baron runs a Barony, which in Nesland is an area a man can walk across comfortably in a day. A Baronet, by comparison, runs an area that can be walked across in an hour or two.*
> *Doctor Unfriendly's Comprehensive Guide to Everything.*

Shiv awoke to the sound of birdsong. A feeling of alarm rose briefly within him, fading as soon as he noticed the lack of counting notes. He crawled out of his little tent into the sunshine, and saw the others camped nearby a tiny circle of stones that housed the smouldering remains of the previous night's fire.

The others were sound asleep despite the fact it was several hours past dawn; Julia and Shantel had bedrolls side by side near the fire, and the gnome doctor had, as usual, made a nest of the contents of his backpack and a rough blanket. Shiv smiled briefly to himself, quietly placed a few bits of kindling on the smouldering fire, and then went to wash himself with the contents of a spare water skin. He frowned briefly at only being able to wash his arms and face effectively, and promised himself a bath and laundered clothes when they returned to Redlock.

The handful of twigs slowly bloomed into flame, and Shiv retrieved a battered, black tin teapot from his tent, filled it, and set it in the fire, propping a heavier piece of wood up over the coals. In only a few minutes, he had put his armour back on, stowed his knives, and packed up his tent; by the time the sound of his puttering had caused the others to stir, his backpack was refilled with his belongings, and he was sitting propped up against a small rock, drinking a little cup of tea and strumming his lyre.

Julia was the first to wake. He nodded absently to her, absorbed in his music, and pointed vaguely towards the fire, where the teapot and a second cup sat warming.

"I thought you said you didn't have any cups," Julia said, sitting up and rubbing the sleep from her eyes.

"I didn't have cups for wine. These are teacups, I'm not a barbarian." Julia studied him, looking for any telltale smirk, but Shiv's face remained focussed on his lyre, and the tiny tin cup that had probably held worse than wine. "Anyway, a toast is supposed to be shared from the same vessel, if it means anything. Better take that cup, though, I only have one spare."

Their conversation had awakened the others; the Doctor was stirring under his cat-sized blanket, and Shantel was stretching and watching Julia get the tea. When the Doctor's baldness peeked out from his nest, he sat up and wrestled the horseshoe-shaped weed patch of hair back under his signature top hat, and then noticed there were no teacups.

"I lost my tea set... I thought you said you didn't have any cups," he muttered, rummaging through his nest of clutter and emptying out his miniature tinder-box to drink from. The taste made his nose wrinkle, but he made no complaint.

"No wine cups," answered Shiv absently, and he set down his lyre to retrieve a piece of jerky from on top of his backpack.

"Good point, we're not barbarians," the Doctor said gravely, sipping from his tinder-box and spitting out a piece of grit.

The group soon had their belongings in order, and after eating a few mouthfuls from their meager provisions, they broke camp and made for the northwest.

"If we make good time, we might be back at Redlock late tonight," the Doctor replied. "I'm looking forward to a proper sleep in a bed."

"The way your bedroll looks every morning, I thought maybe you slept in a tree," Julia said.

"What happens in my bedroom is my own business," the Doctor replied smoothly. The others laughed good-naturedly.

The day went quickly and they did indeed make good time, the weather pleasant and perfect for travelling. They stopped only once for lunch, and made a point of finishing off what provisions they had left, which seemed a feast.

They moved swiftly through the foothills in between the two mountain ranges, and by the time the sun was setting in the somewhat smoother horizon to the west, they were coming up to Abner's hill. Smoke trickled, cleverly hidden, from the chimney disguised in the illusionary tree on the hilltop. Curious, Shiv approached the hidden door and knocked.

"Hello?" came a familiar voice from inside. "Who is it?"

"Master Shiv, Doctor Unfriendly, Julia Hammerhand, and Shan-"Shiv began, but was interrupted.

"People from Redlock?" the voice was excited. A door appeared in the hillside, and a short, emaciated figure staggered out of it. It may have been Abner, once, but was near skeletal with starvation, and dressed in rags. He looked briefly at Shiv without recognition, and then limped over to Julia and the Doctor, picking up the tiny gnome in a bear-hug and then hugging Julia around the hips. "It has been so long!"

"The real Abner?" asked Shiv, amid questions from both sides. Abner nodded to him.

"You must be one of Falcior's mercenaries," Abner mused. "I escaped only days ago from the kobolds, and thought I might be able to hide in my house if I collapsed the tunnel. Are you going to Redlock? I'd invite you in, but the kobolds appear to have taken all my food and drink, and left a dreadful mess as well."

"We are," Julia said. "Everyone will be glad to see you; we all thought the kobolds had killed you when we discovered the imposter."

"Yes, I assumed the Storm Kobold had done that. He asked me hundreds of questions about Redlock so he could pass as a resident. If only I had spent more time among the villagers he might have been discovered sooner."

He retrieved a rough walking stick from inside, and joined them, limping heavily as though both of his legs were injured in different places. He chatted constantly, more than Shiv had remembered, although no doubt he had only met the impostor; soon Abner had even wearied the Doctor with the constant barrage of questions and set upon Shantel. She was more receptive, having been a recent escapee herself.

"How did you escape? I managed with Master Shiv's help, but you had no aid," Shantel asked.

"The Storm Kobold went crazy trying to find you all after the escape. He killed almost all the remaining slaves. I had been working on my shackles for some time with a spell I had been developing, and managed to pick the lock; I think it took me three weeks, I had not worked out most of the kinks before I was captured." Abner stumbled on a rock and winced, but did not slow his chatter. "I inexplicably found a tunnel that shouldn't have been there, it led straight out of the complex."

"That was ours," the Doctor commented. "Master Shiv tunneled with a bypass wand."

"Clever. So I suppose you all did help my escape. I can only assume the kobolds were no longer patrolling it once they knew you had already got out that way. Anyway, after I got out of the complex itself I ran, thinking Redlock was maybe somewhere westward, and must've ran into an area I knew by dumb luck."

"Not so dumb if it got you home," Shantel said.

It was well into the night when Shiv and the others reached the cleared area around Redlock. Two guards were at the gateway, which had a rickety gate nailed loosely in place now. Shiv waved to the guards, who in turn waved back; one of them hastened to approach the group. He had a rather uncomfortable looking dent in his helmet which caused it to rest at a tilt, and a large scar on his face.

"Master Shiv! Mistress Hammerhand! Doctor!" one of the two guards shouted. "You are ordered to report to the Baron's manor as soon as you arrive! There's been… a few developments."

"Baron?" asked Shiv, frowning. "I thought Falcior was only a Baronet."

"Not sure I understand myself yet, Master Shiv, but I think the Duke had something to do with it. I'm sure they'll explain everything once you get there."

The other guard had swung the gate open. It looked like it would barely slow down soldiers of any kind, but it was an improvement over no gate at all. The group entered, and the gate was closed behind them; the guard with the tilted helmet walked ahead of them almost at a trot.

The center of the village and the manor came into view quickly, and without slowing the guard stepped up to the heavy door and knocked loudly.

"Let's hope I'm more welcome than the last time I saw him," Shiv said with a scowl. Julia nodded briefly, and just then the door opened up.

"Ah, glad to see you all," said Ironfield, his face seeming to fight between blankness and a dozen other emotions. "You are expected. This way, please?"

Ironfield turned on the spot and the guard trotted back towards the gate; the five of them followed the butler briskly. They were led into the dining room, where Falcior's family was already seated, sharing a bottle of wine. Unusually, Recia sat at the head of the table, dressed in a pink gown with lace at her wrists and neck. At her right side was her father in half armour, face blank, and at her left was Temma, in mauve silk. As Ironfield showed them in, the three all began to smile artificially.

"Er... you summoned us?" Shiv said.

"We did," said Recia, nodding to Ironfield. He retreated through the main door. "Please, sit."

They all sat along the closest edge of the table, giving the room a lopsided appearance. The Baronet nodded at Julia and then at a pitcher of wine, and she filled a goblet for herself.

"We heard you had been made a Baron," Julia said to Falcior, sipping at the wine.

"No, actually," he responded, smiling slightly. "I was demoted. I am just a regular knight, now."

There was a moment of stunned silence.

"Oh, it's not all that bad," said Falcior softly. "I had thought the Duke had forgotten about me entirely, actually. I was lax in my responsibilities, and apparently he was quite aware of me. In retrospect, I think my elven ancestry was the only thing that kept him from having me beheaded. The Duke said he always wanted more elven blood in the nobility. Funny."

"So, who's the Baron, then?" Shiv asked.

"There is no Baron, just the office of one," replied Recia. "I am the Baroness. The new Baron will be either my husband, whoever that might be, or my son, if I have one. If I don't do either, that responsibility will fall on Temma."

The door to the dining hall opened up, and Ironfield returned, holding the door open wide.

"Sirs, Madames," said Ironfield with a mild frown. A solitary figure entered from behind him. "May I present the Storm Kobold."

Chapter Sixty-Six

> *Affairs of State: This is a human term, which essentially means the upper class doing something underhanded that the lower class is supposed to pretend is honourable.*
> *Doctor Unfriendly's Comprehensive Guide to Everything.*

Shantel shrieked, and leapt back over her chair; Shiv, Julia and the Doctor stood, hands drawing weapons. Falcior and his daughters sat, expressionless, and Abner froze in place, face pale and mismatched eyes wide.

The short, stocky creature was dressed in a regal blue robe, and carrying his bone staff. He smiled a toothy smile at them before prowling around the table to sit on the far side. A high-seated chair had been set in place there for him, so he appeared of normal height, whereas the Doctor's face was fully visible only because he was standing on his chair.

"What is the meaning of this?" growled Shiv, lip curled in just shy of a snarl.

"This actually concerns the Doctor. The Storm Kobold, here, apparently gained entrance to the gnome's cave, and now has his family prisoner. He wishes to discuss terms," Recia said with a diplomatic smile. "He also has business with the Baron, which isn't really any of your business."

The Doctor leapt up onto the table, face twisted in rage. His fingers contorted wildly and he spat out a single syllable before Sir Falcior stood, sword drawn, to point across the table at the little gnome. The Doctor stopped his spell casting, eyes wide.

"You will maintain civility in our house, Doctor Unfriendly," said Recia sternly. "You gnomes have been nothing but trouble since you moved here; in this I agree with my father. One more hostile move on your part, and you will be banished from Falcior Barony, and if I have anything to say about it, Nesland as a whole."

The Doctor, stunned, was silent for a moment.

"I fought for this village while his goblins tried to burn it down!" he shouted, hands clenched.

"Ridiculous!" spat Falcior. "A ten-year old girl has more strength of arm than you! A hundred gnomes would be no match for a single knight on horseback. Your fighting has no more relevance than my skills as a seamstress."

"I had no idea you were so widely talented," Shiv said, smiling acidly. "And clearly you know much about the strength of a ten year old girl. Personally."

"That's enough!" snapped the Baroness. "Doctor, for your efforts you will be pardoned for the troubles you have caused. Master Shiv, speaking of young girls, your sister is waiting for you at the Tortoise Toe Inn, in Miss Hammerhand's quarters. I am told that Rabboni Hareth also wishes to see you in his... hut... when you are done there. I suspect Miss Hammerhand will want her room back, so you and your sister can leave. I recommend that you do it soon. Abner, you of course are welcome back, provided you stay at your previous residence; and you there, girl, I don't know who you are but you are welcome to take up residence here if you purchase the home of one of the deceased families. Julia, your mother wants you at home, you may as well go when the others do. Any questions?"

"What about my family?" said the Doctor, voice shaking in rage.

"That's your business," said the Baroness. "We are not in the business of ransoming vermin. That has been our answer since the Storm Kobold came to us. Anyone else?"

"What has happened to the Trapper?" Shiv asked.

"What do you think?" replied the Baroness levelly. "He will be judged by the laws of his own people."

"I assume you haven't confiscated my belongings or raped my mule while we were gone?" Shiv asked, pushing his chair away from the table.

"No, Master Shiv, your mule's virtue is still intact," she replied, smirking. "And we have a job for you, once your business with the girl and the Rabboni is concluded."

"I am not in the business of working for vermin." Shiv replied. The Baroness' jaw dropped in outrage. "Come on, Doctor, let's figure out how to recover your family. Abner?"

Abner stayed where he sat, smiled, and shrugged apologetically.

The Doctor, still glaring, hopped down from his chair and stomped out past Ironfield, who was still holding the door open; Shiv, Julia and Shantel walked out in turn. Ironfield followed them back to the front door.

"I am sorry this is how it has worked out," Ironfield said. "But I do think it is what's best for Redlock. A treaty with the Storm Kobold will keep this village alive."

"I hope that works out better for you than it did for the goblins." Shiv growled, letting himself out before Ironfield could reach the door. The others followed him as he walked across the square to the Tortoise Toe Inn.

Chapter Sixty-Seven

> *Magical research: Theoretically, magic should be able to do anything. However, a given spell is incredibly specific, and coming up with a new spell, or even a modification on an existing spell, requires research. When first discovered, most spells take a lot of strange materials, time, preparation, and luck.*
>
> *Doctor Unfriendly's Comprehensive Guide to Everything.*

Mother Hammerhand was putting away a tray full of cleaned mugs under the bar when the door burst open, banging loudly off of the wall.

"Where's my sister so I can get her out of this rat's-nest town?" shouted Shiv. The Doctor stalked in on Shiv's heels, looking murderous with his staff over one shoulder. Shantel stood to one side, hands on the Talismanian short swords stuck into her belt.

"Now wait one minute," Julia shouted, shouldering past them. "The whole town isn't to blame for those traitors."

"You better not be talking about who I think you are," said Forrel Hammerhand, standing up from one of the tables. His brothers stood up as well.

"Shut up, the adults are talking now," Julia replied, and turned to her mother. "Where is Caroline?"

"She's in your room," Mother Hammerhand replied, looking back and forth between her boys and Shiv's group. "I'll get her."

"Wait!" Shiv interrupted. "Do you know where they are keeping the gnomes?"

"Mother," warned Forrel. "Stay out of this."

There was a muted clang of metal on metal as one of Shiv's stilettoes sprung out from his gauntlet. Before anyone could react he had taken two steps and placed the needle-sharp point to Forrel's armoured throat.

"You stay out of this, you oaf. I am through being gentle with you. The next time you stand in my way you lose an arm," Shiv said quietly. "If you're lucky. That goes for you other three too."

"Shiv!" cried Julia. "They're my brothers!"

"My question?" he said, looking casually over at Mother Hammerhand. Her mouth worked silently for a moment, and her eyes glanced quickly over her boys, all of whom had hands on their sheathed weapons.

"The gnomes and the Trapper are in the gnome's cave, guarded by a dozen of the Storm Kobold's bodyguard." Her voice quivered. "They're waiting there until the Storm Kobold leaves tomorrow. Please... my boys don't mean it. I'll get your sister."

Mother Hammerhand gathered her black skirts up and scurried up the stairs.

"I'm going to cut your head off," Forrel said. Daryd, Ruzzio, and Thokk glared at Shiv as if they intended to beat their brother to it. Shiv merely smiled reassuringly at Julia, as if he hadn't noticed the brothers at all.

"Doctor, do you have a back way into your place?" Shiv asked.

"No, but you do. The bypass wand."

"It can't have too much power left in it," Shiv said, but drew it out with his off hand and looked at it.

"Agreed. We'll enter from the Kobold Trapper's lair."

Caroline ran down the stairs and into the room, running over to hug Shiv and ignoring the pointed stiletto. Mother Hammerhand slinked in behind her and then stood behind the bar, worriedly looking from person to person.

"Do you know what year it is?!?" Caroline shouted. "Captain Termann told me you're my baby brother!"

"Yes, I think I am," Shiv said, and smiled.

"But that means everyone else will be old! Do you think they're still okay?"

"I hope so. We'll go there after I help the doctor out here with his family. I suspect they'll all want to come with us anyway." Shiv said. The Doctor nodded in response, smiling at Caroline encouragingly, although the murderous glare remained in his eyes.

"Doctor?" Shiv asked. "Do you have any spells that can help take out a dozen kobolds at once?"

"No…" the gnome replied, brow furrowed in concentration. "But the Zanquitor seemed to think my shove spell could be modified in that respect. I'll need a half an hour or so. Maybe I can work something out."

He leaned his staff against the wall and swung the backpack off of his shoulder, and quickly had his miniature spell book on a nearby table. Soon the table was covered in loose papers, which were in turn soon covered in equations and diagrams. "I'll need a leather gauntlet."

Shiv nodded to Ruzzio Hammerhand, who removed the one of his gloves with a snarl and tossed it onto the gnome's table. The gnome snatched it up absent-mindedly and kept scribbling.

"Julia, can you keep your brothers under control? I am going to go see what Hareth wants while the Doctor is working. Shantel, we need to get you some decent armour and weapons. We'll pay a visit to the Craftsmaster while we are out."

"Pick me up some goat hair, wood chips, and the knocker from a brass bell," shouted the Doctor over his shoulder. He pointed at Mother Hammerhand. "You! Get me some tea. I'm thirsty."

"Do it!" said Shiv. He stowed the wand, and then clutched his forearm to make the stiletto snap back into its hidden place. With a final glare at the brothers, he trotted out of the door, Shantel on his heels.

Chapter Sixty-Eight

> *Armour: There are many kinds of armour, but the best kind is usually thought to be plate armour. Most types of armour are bought as full suits, covering the entire body. Many adventurers prefer three-quarter or even half suits, which are lighter and offer more maneuverability, but cover less of the body. I don't like armour myself, it makes casting spells difficult.*
>
> Doctor Unfriendly's Comprehensive Guide to Everything.

Rabboni Hareth was working in his garden, pulling weeds when Shiv approached alone. He stood up, nodding to himself.

"Good, I don't like having that thing in my house any longer than is necessary," he said, and by the time Shiv had reached him he had dusted himself off and opened the door. They entered, and the Rabboni quickly stepped around a table and produced a dull thigh bone wrapped in leather straps; it looked like it had been hollowed out, and from the open end poked a rolled-up piece of paper. "This was at my door this morning."

He slid the paper out of the bone and handed it to Shiv. The letters were large and crude-looking as the knife thrower unrolled it and started to read.

> *Rabboni Hareth: I know you are a man of integrity, if you could deliver this message to Master Shiv upon his return, it may save several lives.*

> *Master Shiv: I understand my behaviour may have jeopardized our agreement. You must understand I had prior agreements that also needed to be fulfilled. I propose an alternative agreement: in place of your time of service to me, I ask only for the jade amulet which hangs from the Storm Kobold's neck. It is a magical item which would prove more trouble to you than you would like.*
>
> *You may believe this is not an even trade, and we have little time to negotiate. As further compensation, I offer you a spell which should prove of value once you are able to master it. It is, in effect, a spell which combines the enchantments which are placed upon two objects into one of them. My arts inform me there were sixty charges left on the bypass wand when I saw you. If it has at least six charges left when it is combined with one of your adamant stilettoes, it will bypass any shield spell the Zanquitor has in place when you next meet.*
>
> *I trust this arrangement will make us even.*
> *Good Luck,*
> *The Oracle of the Gnoll Passage.*

"This scroll was in there as well. I don't like having items of sorcery in my house." Hareth said. "The Oracle is… unwholesome."

"Yeah," Shiv agreed. "I suppose she is. Thanks, Rabboni. I'd stay to discuss it, but I'm kind of in a hurry, gnomes in trouble, apprentice getting fitted for armour, kobold troubles. You understand."

"Of course, I do. These are unusual times. Creator bless you," he said, nodding, and returned to his weeds.

Shiv trotted off, looking over the spell. He couldn't understand much of it, but perhaps the Doctor could help. He passed through the town square (making sure there were no screams or clashing metal coming from the inn) and a little way down a street to arrive at the Craftsmaster's shop.

As usual, the squat building was belching smoke from two square chimneys, and sounds of grinding and hammering came from inside. The door facing the street was wide open, however, and in the front room there was only a squat, featureless stone counter with one of the Craftsmaster's dwarf apprentices standing behind it as if on guard.

"Master Shiv!" said the apprentice. "Your woman is nearly done."

"She's not my woman, she's my apprentice," he replied.

"Of course not. Someone comes to you to learn your secrets, and you demand payment by buying her armour and weapons. Even humans can't be that odd." He opened a door behind him, and shouted into it. "Master! The human dagger smith is here!"

"Bast's rusty backside! He'll have to wait!" shouted back the Craftsmaster's familiar voice. "Ask him what kind of sword she should use, she doesn't know!"

"Something light, for close-in fighting," said Shiv before the apprentice could repeat the message. "One of her Talismanian swords would probably be ideal. I thought maybe she could use a crossbow as well, though. And she wanted a couple of good daggers."

The apprentice relayed the message, interrupted only a few times by the sounds of hammering, scraping or clanking.

"Her Talismanian sword should be fine, although those rat bastards wouldn't know a decent sword from a butter knife," the gravel-voiced dwarf shouted. "And she should maybe have a crossbow! And a brace of daggers!"

Shiv smiled to himself and nodded, and began counting coins out, putting them in stacks on the counter. It was only a few minutes before Shantel walked out, looking a bit awkward, but wearing a half-suit of rather fine looking plate armour, a Talismanian sword at her side, and a complicated looking crossbow in her hands. Her opposite arm had a tiny metal shield strapped to it, along with two built-in dagger sheaths, and a quiver of crossbow bolts hung from her belt. The Craftsmaster, dressed in his usual chainmail, stomped out behind her.

"Ahem…" said Shiv. "That is a bit more expensive than I was aiming for."

"Shiboeth's crotch-purse! You said outfit her well, keep her safe, that's what I did. Half plate armour and buckler, triple crossbow, two daggers, and ammunition. Two hundred and sixty-two towers, and a better bargain you won't find anywhere."

"Two hundred," said Shiv.

"Dwarves don't bargain away their best. That's what you're getting, taking into account our close professional relationship. Be bloody glad I didn't charge you three hundred, the Pharaoh himself would pay that if he caught me grave-robbing."

"Fine," Shiv replied. "I'm in a hurry. Did you remember the goat hair and all that?"

"'Course I did! Two foundings for the lot!"

"What!?!"

"You did mention you were in a hurry," said the Craftsmaster, sly smile peering through his beard. Shiv shook his head, but added up the coins on the counter: a collection of pure gold old-marks, tower coins, and the two silver foundings. The senior dwarf watched carefully as each coin was placed, and then nodded to himself and dropped them into a strong-box he had built into the stone counter. He pushed a little bag across the counter with the Doctor's materials inside.

"I hear what the Baronet did," the Craftsmaster said. His malevolent smile broadened. "I'll make sure to charge him extra for everything for a year or so."

"Thanks," Shiv said. "I hope to never pass by this way again, but if I do, I'll buy you a drink at the Inn."

"I'll remember that," said the Craftsmaster, and then he turned to his apprentice. "You've been standing here the whole time?!? Torban's shiftless spine, get back to work, the pumps need tending!"

Shiv and Shantel left the shop and walked back towards the inn.

"It's difficult to walk," Shantel said, her step somewhat unsteady.

"You'll appreciate it the first time someone tries to stab you," Shiv replied, and took a deep breath as he approached the Inn.

Chapter Sixty-Nine

> *Map Sense: Gnomes such as myself have the best direction sense; humans need the stars or a compass to tell direction even in ideal conditions. Similarly, humans do not seem to have the ability to accurately measure a distance by walking it. Something a gnome or dwarf would do without thinking in this way often will require a human time, effort, and arithmetic.*
>
> *Doctor Unfriendly's Comprehensive Guide to Everything.*

"So you think this spell will work?" Shiv asked as they walked along the back street. The Doctor nodded.

"I think so," he replied. "It's as good a job as I can prepare on short notice anyway. It should shove at least three or four at once, maybe more, but I'll have to be the first one in the room, or one of you might get caught in the... er... pseudo-blast."

"The su-what?" Shiv stammered.

"I told you, it's a tactile illusion; it's not a real blast, it only makes people think it is. It should encompass an area about five paces (my paces) across. Once I've fired it, you all fire crossbows and so on over me, at whoever is left standing." Doctor Unfriendly fiddled a bit with the package of goat hair, wood shavings and other odds and ends. It was a tiny roll of cloth, with a bizarre geometric pattern he had drawn in charcoal, and the various tidbits carefully glued on at strategic locations. The little gnome examined it once more, and then rolled it back up. "You have the wand ready?"

Shiv hefted the stubby little wand, and looked over his shoulder at the others. Shantel was behind him, in her new armour, with her three-armed crossbow loaded and cocked. Julia walked behind her and to the side, her miniature crossbows loaded as well. She met his eyes warily. Behind them all walked Caroline, in a simple blue dress, with one of Shiv's steel knives and strict instructions not to use it.

"Remember, Caroline, to stay behind everyone. It will get dangerous," Shiv told her.

"I'm your big sister, you can't tell me what to do, you know," Caroline replied, and smiled smugly.

"I can and I will. I don't want to tie you up, but I will if I have to. And I am good at it. I'm learning elf knots."

"Humans can't learn elf knots," interrupted the Doctor. Shiv shushed him. They peeked around the corner of Gunther's woodshed, and saw the gnome cave entrance, guarded by a half a dozen kobolds. The Doctor motioned for those behind him to stop. "The Kobold Trapper's cave is over there."

They scurried past the gap and behind Gunther's huge lumber pile, crouching, and then over to the Trapper's cave. As before, it was little more than a hole leading into the ground with an overhang to keep the rain out. Making sure there were no kobolds within sight, they slunk into the hole and crawled down into the darkness. As it became harder to see, Doctor Unfriendly conjured a tiny light on his staff, and soon they came to the single door.

The door was off of its hinges, the crossbow traps disabled and burned, and three kobold corpses were shoved against the walls. Behind the door was a pit trap, open, with another kobold impaled on spikes at the bottom. They stepped around the hole gingerly. Inside the room was more darkness, and the peculiar silence of a space that is no longer lived in. The Doctor led the way, with Shiv, Julia and Shantel having to crouch uncomfortably to follow. Caroline managed to follow them standing straight, although knowing the ceiling was close to her head had her ducking occasionally regardless.

The room was surprisingly well-furnished, being shored up with rough planks and wickerwork barriers between the walls. Much of the furniture had been smashed, however, and there were signs of several other traps having killed or injured kobold invaders in several places.

"My house should be just past the pantry," the Doctor said quietly, pointing. "The earth in between should be about two staves thick. Using the wand two times should get us really close, and then we can widen out an area to attack from."

Shiv nodded and followed the Doctor to a small door in the north wall. It had no lock, and opened to a small room lined with shelves along the walls and hooks along the ceiling. Small animals hung from the hooks in various stages of butchering; to avoid colliding with the hanging corpses, Shiv had to come in on his knees, although the Doctor could stand quite comfortably. The gnome pointed to the rear wall, and they began moving bags of flour, salt and sugar along that wall to other shelves. The shelves themselves came down rather easily, being essentially planks mounted on notched vertical poles; with the back wall clear, Shiv traced a square around its edges with the wand.

The section of wall receded several paces, and handfuls of dust fell from the ceiling. The Doctor shored up the walls a bit with the sections of shelving, looking mildly nervous at the smooth earthen walls. Before he was finished, Shiv had traced the wand around the back wall of the alcove, and instantly it was twice as deep. More dust fell. Caroline stepped in with the Doctor and began helping with the walls and ceiling, both of the tiny figures chattering instructions back and forth in an argument of whispers that echoed strangely in the confined space.

Shiv used the wand to widen the inside end of the tunnel, forming a sort of T shape; by the time he was satisfied the Doctor was unrolling his cloth bundle on the floor and mumbling calculations to himself.

He was soon ready, and Shiv touched Caroline lightly on the shoulder, pointing back into the half-dismantled pantry. As she retreated, there was a muffled bang, followed by chittering sounds, coming through the earthen wall. Everyone in the group froze, but the sounds soon faded down to a barely audible murmur.

"Everyone get in place first," Shiv whispered, pointing to places on either side of him. "Doctor, put your light out. I'll see if I can see anything."

The darkness was complete as soon as the gnome's staff winked out; the murmurs from the next room became somewhat louder as they all held their breath.

SHIV

A point of light appeared in the wall, faintly illuminating Shiv poking at the wall with a black iron knife. The barrier of earth was less than a handspan thick. As he widened it enough to see through, the clumps of dust that fell became a constant trickle... the wall would come down on its own in a few minutes. Shiv shuddered in the darkness at that; his peephole complete, he peered through.

The peephole was in Dorlah's bedroom, four gnomes on the huge bed, stripped naked and bound with a mass of ropes that looked to be made of braided rat-tail leather. Old Karl, out of his bandages for the most part, was a mass of bruises and cuts, and Mrs. Unfriendly and Dorlah were equally battered, faces stoic for the nearby Little Unfriendly. A dark shape, presumably a kobold guard from the glint of metal, blotted out the peephole for a moment, passing out of the line of sight again almost immediately. There was another bang sound, much clearer this time; it was the sound of a heavy stick cracking against something. There was more kobold chittering, and the gnome child tried to stifle a whimper.

Shiv reached back, tapping the Doctor on the head to warn him, and then began tracing a square on the thin earthen wall with the stubby wand.

The chittering changed before he was halfway done, stopping very briefly and then starting more loudly; there was the sound of scuttling feet.

Suddenly the wall was gone. The brightness stung their eyes, blurring the forms of the four kobolds facing the open tunnel. There was a murmur and a sound like sizzling meat, and the four kobolds all flew sprawling. Before the creatures could rise or react, crossbow bolts sprouted from them in thick and bloody bouquets. One made a strangled sound that was cut off by a black iron knife, which Shiv retrieved and wiped on the body.

The imprisoned gnomes, eyes wide made muffled noises of relief and joy through rat-leather gags as the Doctor rushed forward to embrace them all. Shiv stepped the rest of the way into the room, and stopped before he tripped on a crumpled form on the floor.

It took several seconds to recognize the Trapper. His captors had carefully peeled the scales from his face, leaving a thin coating of the skin underneath to hold most of the remains in. The hundreds of cuts it must have taken made it impossible to tell what colour the skin should have been; now it was a mass of shredded red. His ratlike tail, wrists and ankles had been tied together behind his back, and his body twitched beside the discarded, bloodied stick they had been beating him with. One eye was swollen shut, but the other looked balefully up at his rescuers.

Shiv was on his knees and cutting ropes instantly; as the Trapper's bounds fell away his limbs collapsed, splayed across the floor. Worriedly, Shiv looked up at the Doctor, who was cutting at his family's bonds with his little knife, and then to Julia.

"Did you pick up any more of your healing potion?" Shiv whispered, and nodded his head towards the Trapper, lying limp in his own blood. Julia frowned distastefully, but pulled a small vial from one of her belt pouches. The Kobold Trapper obediently held his mouth open, silent and patient as she sprinkled a bit into his open mouth. His face shrunk as the swelling went down, strangely pink traces showing between the spilled blood. He took a deep breath, and then staggered to his feet.

"Is you killing the Storm Kobold?" he asked, voice a simple purr. Shiv nodded in response. The somewhat revitalized kobold smiled, grotesquely scarred face still pink amid the remaining slate-coloured scales. Dozens of needle-like teeth showed beneath what remained of his lips. "I helps. For no moneys. But I keeps his head."

Chapter Seventy

Sorcerors and Wizards: Although many blend a mix of the two, generally a Wizard is one who learns his magic through careful study and practise, whereas a Sorceror gains his through a mix of natural talent and the aid of various magical entities. Some of these entities are rather malevolent, which does not advance the reputation of sorcery.
Doctor Unfriendly's Comprehensive Guide to Everything.

"I am sorry," said the Storm Kobold amiably, "that you lost your rank. Perhaps this treaty, and other wise decisions, will enable you to regain it."

The former Baronet nodded as Ironfield closed the door of his manor behind them. Two more kobold soldiers, unarmoured, but with wicked-looking spears, joined them as they turned towards the north end of the town.

"I will have two platoons of kobolds here by the end of the week, and the slaves necessary to excavate the gold three days afterward," the blue-scaled creature continued. "That should be enough time to ensure none of the villagers react unpredictably."

Sir Falcior nodded, and watched the kobold soldiers nervously. Another two had joined them at some point. Two of the soldiers watched suspiciously from the parapet atop the barracks, and farmer Ticksworth pointedly led his two children onto a side street as they approached.

CAMERON S. CURRIE

Falcior led the kobolds around a corner as they passed the barracks and stopped, as he saw the Forest Nomads that had camped inside emerging with heavily laden backpacks and several pack horses. Zimmiman was with them. Falcior motioned for the kobolds to stop, and trotted over to Zimmiman.

"What's going on here?" he asked.

"It seems the Nomads no longer feel safe here," Zimmiman said, leaning on his staff. "They are going west, to the Hillman Ceremaunal. Although I have lived in towns most of my life, I was born a Hillman, so I can get them entry."

"When are you coming back? The town needs a wizard."

"I'm not. You can give my tower to the kobold soldiers, it should serve them well enough. And apparently the town has a full supply of sorcerors, now." He nodded at the kobold soldiers, who nodded back with fangs bared. Falcior paled, and looked back to the unarmoured kobold soldiers, realizing that sorcerors did not normally train with armour. The Storm Kobold nodded, toying with the jade statuette he wore as a medallion. It looked vaguely like a horse.

None of them said another word, but the wizard hobbled off on his peg leg, followed by the nomads. Apparently they were going to stop at the Inn before they left. Falcior frowned to himself, but continued on towards the gnomes' cave.

The six kobold soldiers were still standing there, apparently playing a sorcerous game where they flicked a tiny sphere of purple light back and forth as if it were a ball. Falcior hesitated as he noticed the game, but the Storm Kobold shouldered past.

"Any disturbances from the prisoners?" the blue-scaled sorcerer asked.

"Terth ken-cha," replied one of them with a respectful bow. Falcior noticed that when a kobold bowed, it curled its rat-like tail over its left arm.

"Terth poat ter honnis et-cha?" asked the Storm Kobold in response. The soldier seemed to consider for a moment.

"Poat-cha," it replied. The Storm Kobold nodded. He pointed down into the cave, and two of them scuttled down the tiny stairs.

"What was that about?" asked Falcior.

"Just because I extend you courtesy does not mean you are entitled to make demands of me," growled the Storm Kobold, his voice a menacing thrum. "You are no longer the local lord, merely a well-treated lackey. See that you remember that. Reginald learned, in the end."

Falcior's jaw dropped, and his lips moved as if they could not get any words out. The Storm Kobold smiled, showing a dozen or more of his needle-like teeth.

There were suddenly sounds of shouting from inside the cave. The two kobold soldiers clambered up the undersized stairs, panting.

"Tun poat-cha! K'tun poat cha!" the kobold in the lead shouted. The Storm Kobold's face contorted in rage.

"Bah fithto O-kan re-poat!" he shouted at the soldiers. They scattered in all directions, looks of panic on their faces. The Storm Kobold shouted after them. "Re-poat fin fithto EST!"

Falcior was still staring wide-mouthed and silent when the Storm Kobold turned to him, at least twice as many teeth showing. The creature made a slight flicker with one hand and a sound like a cough, and Falcior rose into the air. His eyes went wider, and his arms and legs began to pinwheel helplessly.

"Lackey, if I find out you betrayed me..." the Storm Kobold growled. Three more syllables escaped from his throat, and his right hand made a twisting motion with the middle finger jabbed into to centre of the palm. Falcior's left hand burst in a shower of red, and he screamed in pain. With a gesture, the kobold threw him against the wall of Gunther's nearby woodshed, and Falcior crumpled into a whimpering heap.

Chapter Seventy-One

> *The Kobold Trapper: An exile from his own kind, the Trapper is expert at building traps- a skill most kobolds are good at- and luring prey into them. I have seen him work several times, once pre-assembling traps in his lair, and otherwise using his devices for professional reasons. His profession is frightening.*
> *Doctor Unfriendly's Comprehensive Guide to Everything.*

Zimmiman smiled coldly, the business deal concluded, and motioned to the small crowd of nomads nearby. Shiv stuffed his belongings back into his baggage and watched them leave his dilapidated circus tent, with Caroline, Old Karl, and Little Unfriendly alongside them. The Doctor, Mrs. Unfriendly, and Dorlah, once again dressed and carrying the gear they had salvaged from their cave, waved to the gnome child, who sat on the shoulder of one of the nomads like a pet. He waved back, looking worried.

Julia stood nearby, looking impatient; Shantel was off in a corner of the tent, practising with her sword; both of them had been angry with Shiv for sending Caroline on ahead, although neither had come up with an argument for keeping her in danger. The Kobold Trapper, having recovered most of his gear from the gnome's cave, was fiddling with three brass boxes he had fetched from a secret cubbyhole in his lair.

"What are those things, anyway?" Shiv asked. He had seen that the various parts were hinged together, and that they unfolded into something, but beyond that he could glean little.

"They is gift for Storm Kobold. Or his...er... soldiers. If we need, then you see," said the heavily scarred Trapper. Even after the healing potion, he spat out a wad of blood and phlegm every few minutes. "I gets Storm head, you gets Trapper's help." For some reason Shiv could not fathom, the Trapper laughed at that, the grotesque hissing chuckle made no less creepy with the Trapper's half-healed injuries.

"All right, then, is everyone ready?" Shiv called out. Six voices answered, generally affirmative if nervous. He nodded, and waved everyone out through the tent flaps. Other than the tent itself, all of his gear was packed on his mule, Cornelius. The shaggy animal stood patiently tied to a peg just inside the entrance, munching contentedly on a bag of oats the Trapper had salvaged from his ransacked lair. When they returned, Cornelius would be ready to leave instantly, so long as he'd eaten his fill. Shiv patted the fat mule's yellowish neck and left the tent.

The town gate was closed and locked, but the guards who had been there hours before were now suspiciously absent. They climbed the wooden boards easily, the rickety hinges threatening to break, and as soon as they entered the town proper, they slunk into an alley off the main road.

The second building they came to was the stable behind the Tortoise Toe Inn, the stalls empty except for three horses that belonged to the Hammerhands. The Inn's back door, leading into the kitchen, was propped open to dissipate the heat from the huge stone oven, so they entered without making a sound. Before they crossed the room, Mother Hammerhand entered, a tray of empty mugs in one hand. She started upon seeing them, and made sure the door had swung closed behind her before she spoke.

"They're looking for you, you know," she hissed, nodding at Shiv. She put down the tray and briefly inspected Julia while emptying the mugs into a washtub. Without pause she filled six small bowls with a stew that was hanging over the oven, and began placing them on the tray. "They know you freed them," she nodded disapprovingly at the gnomes, "and they are angry. Since the alarm went up, more kobolds have been coming up through the well, and no one can find Termann or the guards anywhere. There's a dozen kobolds in the common room, another dozen outside last time I checked, and no doubt more coming every minute. You all should just leave town while you have the chance, or you'll be killed for certain."

"We're going to kill the Storm Kobold." Shiv said.

"You stop talking nonsense and get my daughter away from here!" she hissed. "The Storm Kobold said he is bringing in another full company of his soldiers until order is restored. You can't fight that many. Just go."

She frowned fiercely, her eyes moist, and snatched up the tray of stew. Shiv nodded to the gnomes, who scuttled alongside Mother Hammerhand out into the common room. Behind the bar, they would be completely hidden from the eating kobold soldiers. As the door still swung back and forth, Shiv crept up to it, the other three behind him.

On the third swing of the door, Shiv booted it open, and rolled into the room, knives flying. Gnomes leapt up onto the bar, darts firing from their trick staves, and Julia, Shantel, and the Trapper's crossbows tracked and fired at kobolds who leapt up in alarm. The murmur of conversation turned to shouts, and then gurgles and grunts of pain. In only a few seconds, eleven of the enemy kobolds were dead or dying, and one stood near the door, unscathed and wide-eyed, with an equally surprised Mother Hammerhand leaning over his table, still holding onto the little bowl of stew. There was a tense silence for a moment, and the kobold soldier moved one foot as if he would leap for the door.

Mother Hammerhand quickly set down the tray during the creature's pause, and then smashed one of the little clay bowls into the scaly face, knocking the creature backwards off of the chair. She calmly picked up another bowl, and knelt beside the prone kobold as it shook its head to clear it.

The second bowl of stew clubbed into the creature's face, splattering more stew, and again, knocking the kobold to the floor. Without a pause, the innkeeper slammed it down into the unconscious face again, and again, and again. The soldier did not move.

She got to her feet slowly, shaking, and got a towel from the tray to dab at the stew on her dress.

Wordlessly, the others began reloading crossbows and trick staves, Shiv recovered his knives, and Mother Hammerhand peeked out of one of the shuttered windows.

"There's at least twenty out there," she murmured. "If even one of them comes in here, we're done for!"

She turned around, and saw Shiv and the others quickly dumping bodies behind the bar.

"You'll want to mop up as much of the blood as possible," Shiv said casually, dragging a kobold corpse in each hand. "Are there other squads patrolling the town?"

"Er..." she said, eyes even wider as she took in the sudden start and stop of violence. "Yes. Yes, I forgot those. There's two teams of around five or six looking for you, checking each street. I don't think they've checked them all, yet, but they will, and I imagine then they'll check your tent, start searching the houses. They'll find you, you can't-"

Julia grabbed her mother by the shoulders firmly.

"Mother, they want the gold. They say there's a gold mine beneath the town. They've already killed a lot of people, and they won't stop. Where are my brothers?"

"They went to find the Baronet," she replied. "He'll keep us all safe!"

"He's not the Baronet anymore," Julia growled. "And he's one of the ones who sold us to them." The mother's eyes squeezed shut, as if trying to block out the information.

"Where's the Storm Kobold?" Shiv asked.

"He's... over by the well, organizing the kobolds that arrive. What are you going to do? There's too many of them."

The Trapper was crouched by the door, unfolding one of the brass boxes. Most of it lay flat on the floor, except for one side of the cube, which folded back on itself to make a low sort of springboard, and a collection of wheels and cogs that seemed mechanically rigged to several wicked-looking blades. There was just enough room for the door to open before someone entering would step on the springboard. Grinning, the Trapper wound a tiny crank a dozen or more times before getting up and pulling another brass box from his sack. He set this one up to block anyone emerging from behind the bar.

"Shantel, Unfriendlies, get upstairs, you can fire crossbows or spells out of the windows; you'll be better served staying out of hand to hand. The Storm Kobold will have defensive spells on him, so shoot at the soldiers instead," Shiv said. "Start once you hear me shout."

"Mother, go with them," Julia said, giving her a gentle push towards the stairs. Mother Hammerhand obeyed wordlessly, still in shock.

"Julia, Trapper, you stay in the main room here with me. The Storm Kobold is a necromancer, which means probably not much in the way of throwing fire and lightning. The Inn is good cover."

The Trapper set up the last brass box underneath the largest window, the one that would most likely be used as an entrance. All of them could not help but notice there were still four smaller windows that were not trapped. Taking deep breaths, Shiv closed and barred three of them, the last window being one of the two that faced forward towards the kobold-crowded square.

With a shout, Shiv threw a tisken at the closest kobold, and shut the window before he could see the results.

He smiled ruefully at Julia as the shouts began outside, and she smiled back at him.

Chapter Seventy-Two

> *The Redlock Mine: Rumours have persisted for decades about gold being in the area, but it was not until the Storm Kobold's mischief that the presence of gold in the natural tunnels underground was confirmed. It is, perhaps, worth noting that when a thorough surveying was done, the veins were completely absent from the area under the Craftsmaster's foundry.*
>
> *Doctor Unfriendly's Comprehensive Guide to Everything.*

Termann slunk along the parapet of the fort, peering over to the town square, watching the battle between the occupants of the Inn and the swarm of kobolds. There were nearly three dozen kobold soldiers now; twenty or so had surrounded the Inn; any who had cover available were slinking in it, while the others were standing in the open. All of them were firing crossbows or casting simple spells at the windows and doors, and scorch marks on the weathered planking had started to smolder. The other dozen were gathering by the Storm Kobold at the well, forming into small groups as their leader directed, and moving to plug holes in the line as their comrades were hit by crossbow bolts, knives and darts fired from inside the Inn.

Backs to the stone battlements, four of Termann's town guard looked to him, expecting orders. Each of them carried a strung longbow and a half-full quiver of arrows, but they did not draw or fire until Termann gave the word.

"There's no way we can loose from here without giving away our position," Termann said quietly, his deep voice a calm, pleasant thrum. "But on the other side of the square is Fred and Melinda's cottage. If we can get on their roof we can pick them off, make it look like shots from the Inn."

The others nodded but said nothing; lately all of them had seen plenty of combat, but this battle erupting already within the town walls was beyond their experience. Termann, as usual, seemed not to notice their distress. He calmly pulled a coil of rope from his backpack and crawled over to the north side of the fort. Within a minute or two he had lashed the rope to one of the stone merlons and tossed the coil over the side. A jerk of his head indicated to the soldiers they were expected to follow him, and then he smoothly leapt over the edge, catching the rope with one hand and rappelling down to the grass with grace that suggested he had practised the maneuver for weeks.

The soldiers clambered down after him, one of them skinning a knee on the rough wood of the town wall, but managed to keep up despite the lack of their captain's agility. The five of them scurried past the town gate, slowing as they reached the southern half of the tiny village. As the guards caught up with their captain, Termann had already retrieved a second coil of rope, and was tossing a loop over the wall.

****

Zimmiman and some of the Nomads had taken several hours to loop around and return to the village; they had approached from the west side, where Zimmiman's squat tower jutted out from the wall. The rickety attic at the top had two opposing sides open to the air, and a solitary raven sat inside, watching them curiously. As Termann had said, the wall was unguarded, barring Zimmiman's black bird. Zimmiman got out a knife and cut a circle out of the turf at the base of the wall.

****

Underground, beneath the village, a squad of seven kobolds scuttled past the Oracle's hiding place. She was too large to fit into any of the tunnels, but she had constructed a pocket dimension to compensate. One end of the dark bubble overlapped her usual lair, and the other end peeked out of the side of one of the rock walls. Veins of gold ore as thick as a baby's finger ran along the walls and floor. It was understandable that the kobolds wanted it, but she paid it no mind. Gold no longer held her interest.

With a gesture, she moved the window sideways along the wall, following the kobolds' progress. They soon entered a wide cavern with a deep pool in the centre, and a shaft of light shone down from a hole in the ceiling. A rickety ladder of wicker led from the pool up to the hole, and as the kobolds waded in hip deep, they each would clamber up the shaky construction to disappear into the bright world above.

The Oracle's bubble receded deeper into the wall as she watched (bright light might pierce the ripple in space that concealed it), and she waited patiently for the last member of the squad to disappear. Then, the bubble slid upwards, along the cavern wall, and then the ceiling, and finally up the bright hole that became the well of Redlock. Her bubble receded as far as it could while still allowing vision (the window was the size of a pinhole now), as the bubble slid down the outside of the well to look at the rear end of the shouting Storm Kobold amid his henchmen.

Leaning against the well were piles of supplies: food, tools, bundles of arrows, and bags of various spell components. The Oracle, as she inspected them, noticed the kobold soldier guarding it had been shot with a crossbow bolt through the head. Either the casualty had not been noticed, or it was considered unimportant. Waiting a few seconds until all the kobolds were looking away from her, towards the Inn, she quickly widened the window and snatched the dead kobold in one clawed hand. As the window shrunk back down to a pinhole, the Oracle absent-mindedly stripped off the ragged leather the kobold wore and took a huge bite from the shoulder. The arm was severed, and most of the head, but she appeared not to notice, and sat back on her haunches to relax, watch the action, and enjoy her snack.

Chapter Seventy-Three

> *Clockworks: A rare type of mechanical device which performs various tasks, powered by a wound-up spring. The most common type, of course, is the clock, although toys for rich children or printing devices like the Saboslander Press exist as well. Although a clockwork device is expensive, fragile and cannot work for long, it makes up for it in convenience and as a status symbol.*
>   *Doctor Unfriendly's Comprehensive Guide to Everything.*

Shiv leapt out of the way as the front door blew off its hinges and flew across the common room, smoking. Three kobold soldiers stood just beyond the doorway, flickering remnants of crackling energy fading from their hands. Shiv smoothly threw the two steel knives he had been carrying, and drew another two blades. Two of the three kobold soldiers dropped, and the third made a throwing motion and incantation that launched a fist-sized ball of acid. It splashed over Shiv's midsection, the Handspan Armour insulating Shiv from all but a couple of drops, but developing a blackened, smoking pit that had the disturbing illusion of digging well into his belly. Shiv's third steel knife twirled end over end to lodge in his attacker's neck. The wiry creature dropped, convulsing and gurgling, and Shiv jumped back behind an overturned table, avoiding a volley of enemy crossbow bolts.

    Julia huddled underneath a window, reloading her wrist-mounted miniature crossbows. Her swords were not sheathed, but lay on the floor within easy reach. The darts loaded, she checked the quiver she had on each hip, and counted a total of twelve bolts left. Picking up her swords, she froze as she heard a scrabbling sound on the other side of the wall; she looked up, and the open window sill was grasped by four small, gnarled fingers. Another set of four appeared a short distance along the ledge, and a semi-reptilian head poked over the edge. The kobold was bald along the top of its scaled head, but had sideburns of stiff black hair jutting from its cheeks. It hopped up into the window, and Julia's swords stabbed into its belly. She shoved most of the creature back out the window, and then scraped the blades across the sill to dislodge it. Breathing a sigh of relief, she steadied herself for a peek of her own, when a second kobold launched through the window, two daggers bared. Julia's boot instinctively lashed out, extending the arc of its jump, so that it landed in the nearby brass trap.

There was a subtle clanking sound, and then a spatter of blood as two sharpened cogs dug furrows into the creature's screaming face, splitting the skull into three thick slices. Julia kicked the body away, and heard a series of clicks as the clockworks moved the cogs back into position.

"It wound up enough for two more," said the disfigured Trapper from beneath another window. His heavy crossbow readied, he stood up to his full height, pulled the trigger, and crouched again, all in a fraction of a second. He smiled gruesomely at her, blood oozing from the cuts reopening all over his face. He seemed not to notice. "I gets one too."

He set the heavy crossbow down, put his clawed foot into the stirrup, and began cranking back the string. A spear darted through the window above him, stabbing blindly. Julia stepped over to the Trapper's window, just out of reach of the spear, and shot the surprised-looking enemy kobold in the mouth. Just as quickly, she ducked back out of sight, and crawled back to her post.

"You doing okay?" Shiv called over, smiling and clutching two silver daggers. Julia nodded back. Shiv was about to say something more, when the trap by the bar made a clicking and whirring sound, and a kobold voice screeched. They looked around, and a kobold soldier was prone on the floor, clutching the ragged remnants of his foot, blood fountaining out. Julia's crossbow dart thudded into the little creature's side at the same time as Shiv's dagger landed its neck. Julia had no time to reload her crossbows before another kobold jumped the brass machine with a long spear in its hands. Shiv's second dagger hit it between the ribs, and it fell back onto the brass trap. Its shriek seemed louder than such a small creature could produce. Another kobold entered, stepping on his fallen comrade's chest, and still another kobold leapt directly onto the bar. Shiv leapt up out of cover, and two knives appeared in his hands, just as a kobold arrow sunk into his back. Julia screamed. Shiv appeared not to notice, and threw one blade at the kobold on the bar, whirled, and threw another out the front door. The other kobold's spear thrust into his armour near the kidneys, as two more of the vicious creatures replaced the one on the bar.

Julia launched herself across the room, the spear wielder's victorious snarl turning to shock as her short sword chopped into his neck, half severing it and adding to the red slick on the floor.

A kobold jumped through Julia's window, landing squarely on the brass trap and losing both of its feet. It fell square on its groin as a result, jerking uncontrollably until the machine wound itself down. Another leapt through behind it, shrieking at the sight of its mangled brother but advancing around the trap with a wicked-looking hatchet in each hand.

Another two emerged from behind the bar, and Julia found herself hard-pressed fending off attacks from them and the two on top of the bar as well. A large crossbow bolt knocked one off its perch and nailed it to a wooden wall. The Trapper ran by them, heading to the stairs, with two more enemy kobolds only three steps behind him. Another two arrows thudded into Shiv's back as his stilettoes clanged out of his leather gauntlets, and he punched one through the forehead of one of Julia's attackers. He looked back over his shoulder and saw two kobolds with bows stepping gingerly into through the front door, carefully avoiding the brass machine.

"Upstairs!" Shiv shouted, and two more arrows thudded into his armour, one uncomfortably close to his unarmoured neck. He kicked the corpse off of his left stiletto and backed towards the stairs, the Trapper knocking an opponent out of their way by using his crossbow as a club. Julia followed, chopping an arm off of one of their pursuers, and as she retreated up the stairs, she glanced back over her shoulder at her common room, containing more than a dozen enemy kobolds.

Chapter Seventy-Four

Crossbows: Crossbows are a popular weapon, in that they are easy to use and powerful. They suffer in that most of them need a crank or lever to pull back the string. I myself use spring-bows built into my trick staff, which fire darts with a coiled spring... it is far less powerful but extra sneaky.
Doctor Unfriendly's Comprehensive Guide to Everything.

Doctor Unfriendly fired another magical shove down at the advancing kobold line, knocking one of the soldiers out of formation. He frowned to himself as the two previous soldiers he had knocked down got to their feet, and the line continued to move forward. He was slowing them, but not by much, and he was well aware the rear of the Inn had already been overrun.

Shantel had discovered her triple crossbow was fantastic at the beginning of a fight, while it was loaded, but reloading the complicated device was turning out to be more trouble than it was worth, and the crank that pulled back the strings could not be set to pull back only one. Sighing, she set the strings for a fifth time, and began sliding the shafts into place. Fortunately, she had time, as the upper floor provided good cover. The clatter of boots on the stairs told her that time might be finally running out.

Dorlah and Mrs. Unfriendly had both been throwing hunting darts out of the windows; they had eventually run out of ammunition, but still had spearheads in their trick staves. They both sprung them and rushed to cover the stairs, and both sighed in relief as Shiv, Julia and the Trapper clambered up.

Mother Hammerhand ran to her daughter's side, checking her for injuries; other than bruises and a cut elbow, she found none. The Trapper ran over to peek out of the nearest window, hissed at what he saw, and then set about reloading his crossbow. It still appeared to function, although each turn of the crank made an ominous creak and jiggled the bow.

Below them there were sounds of kobolds clambering around, moving furniture and shoving other debris out of the way.

"What are they doing down there?" whined Mother Hammerhand, to anyone who would listen.

"My guess is they'll be loading the main floor with firewood," mused Shiv. The Trapper looked up and nodded at him.

"FIREWOOD?!?" she shrieked. "My Inn!"

"Don't worry, you won't be in a position to miss it," Shiv answered, and dodged a backhand from Julia.

A familiar voice came up the stairwell.

"Master Shiv...? It's me, Abner."

"Oh ye of inspiring loyalty," Shiv called back, checking his knives. He still had eight left, plus his stilettoes. "Have you been sent with a message of surrender?"

"Just yours," Abner answered.

"How did those bastards know how to find my family, Abner?" shouted the Doctor.

"Oh, that was me. Sorry." Abner replied. "I was in kind of a rough spot. They aren't that bad, you know. They'll leave the Inn standing if Shiv, Caroline and you gnomes agree to come quietly, and return the bypass wand."

"I can assure you we will stay here quite noisily, thanks," Shiv called. "And Zimmiman helped me to destroy the bypass wand." He peeked around the corner, looking down the stairwell, and saw Abner standing there alone. Several shadows betrayed the presence of kobold guards just around the corner. Shiv held up one finger for a pause, and looked over his shoulder to meet the gnome doctor's eyes, answering a question that had not been spoken.

"Here's my answer! First," began the Doctor, stepping around the corner. He regarded Abner for a moment, and then threw a vial of liquid fire. It burst on the top of Abner's head, splashing black liquid, and the undersized man's face exploded in bright flames. Abner shrieked and fell backwards out of the stairwell, the sounds of his agony receding as he fled the Inn. "And second," Doctor Unfriendly called after him, "You rat bastard, go lay with your mother!"

Doctor Unfriendly turned and walked away from the stairwell, his face a wicked grimace.

"Did that make you feel better?" asked Shiv.

"No, but it sure as hell didn't make me feel worse," replied the Doctor. He retrieved his staff from near the window. "They'll be coming now."

"Yes, they will," Shiv mused thoughtfully. "I imagine there'll be about two dozen, even after all the ones we killed. But at the top of the stairs they can only come two by two, unless they do burn the whole Inn down."

"Do you have a plan, Shiv?" Julia asked, meeting his eyes. "Tell us you have a plan."

"I did have a plan," he replied, shrugging. "It might still work, although our part in it is looking increasingly less enjoyable."

Julia snarled in response, turning away and rejoining her mother. The Trapper, ignoring the conversation for the most part, fired his crossbow out of the window. He started to duck back below the window sill, and stopped in place, beckoning Shiv to join him.

Outside, the Storm Kobold was shouting orders, and the kobolds that had surrounded the Inn were breaking up into small groups. An arrow hung in the air near the big blue kobold's neck, and spit flew when he shouted curses at his followers.

"They must be looking for whoever shot at him," mused Shiv.

"Termann shoots. From over there," the Trapper responded, pointing to a cottage on the south side of the village. Sure enough, Shiv could barely make out shapes slinking around the rooftop. No doubt the kobolds could not see them, yet, but with so many searchers it would not take them long.

The kobolds had broken into two groups, each about a dozen strong. One returned to circling the Inn, and the other broke up into two smaller parties to look for Termann's archers. Shiv lowered himself back into cover, and looked at them all.

"They are probably going to light the fire underneath us," he said flatly. Mother Hammerhand and Julia both made noises of protest. "But it's a good thing; we may have a way to win. It'll take guards on all four sides to keep us in here; if we kill enough of them now we can probably escape, and continue the fight outside."

"My Inn!" cried Mother Hammerhand.

"The only way we can save it is to get rid of the kobolds. This is the fastest way to do that. Start shooting, everyone."

He jumped up and threw his last tisken out the window; it was the type of knife that flew the farthest, and it managed to drop into the skull of one kobold. Shantel had been working on reloading her crossbow the entire time, and leapt up to fire three times from another window, killing two more. As she hunkered down to begin cranking her strings back, the Trapper leapt up and shot again, impaling a one-horned kobold through the arm. Not a kill, but no doubt the soldier was out of the fight. Julia fired two crossbow bolts as well, killing another.

The Doctor continued to throw shove spells, and the two gnome women guarded the stairs in case the kobolds entered that way.

After a few moments, they all stopped in cover and looked at each other.

"One," Shiv said.

"Two," Shantel said, earning nods of approval.

"One wounds," the Trapper said, busily cranking.

"One," Julia said.

"That's seven left: two kobolds per side, if you include the blue freak," Doctor Unfriendly said. "There's a staircase out of the back, or we could jump over the balcony rails on any side." The others nodded.

"They did start a fire," said Mrs. Unfriendly, a little sadly. "I can see the light from the flames in the stairwell."

"We're winning," Shiv said. Then two crossbow bolts flew through a window and thudded into a wall. He leapt up and threw two black iron daggers out at them, but both fell short; the remaining kobolds were hanging back out of throwing range, waiting for the fire to do their work. He crouched back down and frowned, but then began casting a spell.

SHIV

"What're you doing?" Julia snapped, hopping up to fire her miniature crossbows. A kobold arrow thudded into her arm, and she dropped, clutching it. Her mother ran to her, rifling through the daughter's pouches to find a healing potion. Shiv finished his spell and threw something yellow towards the stairs, and then scuttled over to her.

"Are you alright?" he asked, checking to see if the bolt could be removed. She touched his cheek, and then caught his eyes.

"One," she said, smiling. Her smile disappeared as Shiv grasped the arrow firmly, and put his boot on her elbow.

"It's an air-weasel spell, I use it to recover my thrown knives," he said, and as soon as she began to nod, he yanked the arrow through her arm and out. She shrieked.

"I gets another!" said the Trapper. Shantel frowned, just setting the strings on her triple bow.

Shiv smiled reassuringly at Julia as her mother recovered the healing potion. It had, at best, a tiny mouthful left. He then returned to peek out of the window.

"It looks like they aren't bothering with the sides, they're putting a couple out back and focussing on keeping the front held," called the Doctor, peeking above one window sill, and then running to the next. Apparently he was out of shove spells. "We might be able to take whoever is guarding the back way."

Shiv popped up to check the front, and saw the Storm Kobold and four of his soldiers, all armed with crossbows and hanging back well out of range of his knives or Julia's miniature crossbows. The blue kobold appeared to be casting a spell. The knife smith ducked back down.

"Once everyone is loaded, we'll go out the back," he said. "Everybody let me know when they are ready."

There was no sound but the whirring of crossbow cranks, and the rattle of the air weasel spell dragging knives up the stairs.

321

Chapter Seventy-Five

> *Fireball Spell: This is the sort of thing wizards are famous for- huge, flashy attack spells that cause moderate damage in a wide swath. If properly prepared, they can affect a very specific area.*
> *Doctor Unfriendly's Comprehensive Guide to Everything.*

The three of them with crossbows led the way, followed closely by Mother Hammerhand and the gnomes, and Shiv brought up the rear, two of his recovered black iron knives in hand. The door that led out onto the back balcony was unlocked, and beyond it the balcony with faded whitewash overlooked a small stable yard and a rickety tool shed. On the far side of the stable yard, leaning against the stable itself, were two kobold guards. They both leapt to attention, and then ducked behind the stable as the crossbow bolts flew.

The group was halfway down the back stairs, and Shiv cursed, leaping over the bannister to land roughly, feet already running.

"If they sound the alarm we're in trouble!" Shiv shouted. He ran for the corner the kobolds had dived behind, knives twirling between a throwing and a fighting grip.

The Trapper, moving surprisingly fast despite his injuries, scuttled around the other side of the stable, crossbow held rigidly at eye level. His tail twitched like a cat's. The others, unsure of which way to go, spread out with their weapons at the ready. Shiv passed out of their sight, nearly tripping over one of the kobolds as he did. The creature had been waiting in ambush, with an attack spell ready, and as Shiv recovered his balance a sheet of flame hit him squarely in the face.

Shiv's feet were knocked out from underneath him, and he landed squarely on his back, winded. Although his hair did not catch on fire, his face was covered in loose, red skin, his eyes wide in shock and pain. He barely had time to remember his knives were in his hands before the kobold slammed a spear into his chest.

The kobold let out a hoot of triumph that turned into a high-pitched shriek as a crossbow bolt emerged from its belly. It fell, grabbing at the injury helplessly, and was finished off by the Trapper's belt knife slicing across its throat.

"You is okay?" the Trapper said, leaning over Shiv.

"Not really, no," Shiv replied. "This spear got right through my armour and my face is on fire. No."

The kobold Trapper hissed in derision and yanked the spear out of his chest. Despite the pain, only the last inch of the blade had blood on it. The Trapper shook his head.

"My face on fire worse," the slate-coloured creature hissed, his pink, swollen face providing evidence. "Spear hole not big enough to kill little girl. Where other kobold?"

"I didn't see a second one," Shiv groaned, getting to his feet. Despite what the Trapper had said, his chest hurt a lot. At just that moment, a horn sounded. "Apparently he saw us, though. By my count there should still be eighteen troopers with the Storm Kobold, assuming the dozen sent to get Termann got back."

"Termann kills lots," the Trapper said. "Dozens not come back."

"How do you know?"

"I know elf, elf know Trapper. Elf kill lots." The Trapper slung his crossbow over one shoulder, knife at the ready. "We go finds womens and gnomes."

They ran together back around the corner, dodging a crossbow bolt from Shantel's triple-bow.

"Hey!" Shiv shouted, not slowing.

"Sorry," Shantel said, and shrugged apologetically.

"What happened to your face?" Julia snapped at him, running over to prod at the still-smoking flesh. She took off his hat with her good hand, blackened and missing most of the front brim, and tossed it to the ground.

"I took a sip of tea that was too hot," Shiv growled, "But then some girl couldn't stop poking at it and it got worse." He batted her hand away, ignoring the loaded crossbow that might have gone off.

"Well, I don't have any healing potion left, so you'll just have to live with it," Julia said, scowling. "Mum, do you have any?"

"Back in the Inn," Mother Hammerhand answered, nodding to the smoke-spewing building behind them. She was clutching a small cleaver with white knuckles. "I don't think we can get to it now."

"The Trapper thinks there are only the half dozen or so left out front, so we should attack now while we can," Shiv said, trotting away and beckoning them to follow. Julia and her mother both sighed before they fell in behind him, and Shantel, the Trapper and three gnomes followed behind.

"They should all be in a tight group near the well," Shiv said, rounding the corner of the Inn with knives at the ready. There were more than he expected.

The Storm Kobold stood by the well with a triumphant smirk on his face and a bone staff in his hand. Near him were seven of his soldiers. However, in front of them were at least two dozen ghouls, reanimated from the bodies of the dead kobold soldiers. Their little horns and fangs were longer and sharper, their fingers had sprouted hard little claws, and their dead eyes glared with angry hunger. The undead soldiers, drooling mouths at Shiv's belly height, stood motionless as if awaiting their master's word.

"You should have accepted my offer, Master Shiv," taunted the Storm Kobold. He chuckled. "A necromancer's army is never defeated, just damaged. You come quietly now, and I'll let you pick one of your group to let go. The rest of you get to feed my new soldiers. They're very hungry."

"I don't want to feed them!" Mother Hammerhand protested. She turned to run, but Julia grasped her shoulders.

"How's that plan of yours going?" Julia snarled, glaring at Shiv accusingly.

"Rather well, actually," Shiv said mildly. "You'd better step out of the square though."

Julia looked down and saw Shiv had stepped up to the very edge of the cobblestones that made up the town square, as if his toes were deliberately an inch or so back from them. Julia, her mother, and

Shantel were all standing on the stones, and Shiv, knives suddenly vanishing, grabbed them and yanked them back as a loud roaring sound approached.

Zimmiman's largest fireball slammed into the well, waves of yellow flame washing over the whole plaza; chunks of flaming kobold and kobold-spawned ghoul scattered across the grass nearby, but the flames came up so far as the edge of the stones and then stopped. The wall of flames burned in front of them for only a split second, and then was gone, leaving the whole square covered in a thick coating of black soot, except for a circle, about three paces wide, around the Storm Kobold, which was untouched.

One lucky soldier was standing close enough to his master to be unharmed; on the opposite side, about one third of a kobold stood on one leg for another brief second, the remaining two-thirds shrivelled and black. Then the blackened parts fell apart into well-cooked chunks, and the remaining pieces of uncooked soldier fell, sending up a small cloud of black dust.

Zimmiman and his bodyguard of Forest Nomads stood atop one cottage at the edge of the square, and on the next cottage, Termann and his town guards stood up as well. As one, the three groups of fighters looked back to the seething Storm Kobold.

Chapter Seventy-Six

> *Shades: Most undead are rather like zombies or vampires- an animated corpse. Shades, on the other hand, are rather like ghosts, being comprised mostly of polluted life force. They are exceptionally deadly in that they can reach through armour as easily as they can walk through a wall.*
> *Doctor Unfriendly's Comprehensive Guide to Everything.*

"YOU!" The Storm Kobold shouted, pointing at Shiv, mostly, but seemingly directing his shout at all of them. "Take your victory, such as it is. You can't hold me here, and you can't harm me. I have hundreds of kobolds still at Terrikota, and your village here is crippled. Another third of a company will be here momentarily. How many peasants do you have left? Fifty?"

"You aren't going to Terrikota," Shiv said, stepping forward. Two silver knives appeared in his hands. "You're not going anywhere."

"Silver?!?" The Storm Kobold sputtered out a laugh of derision. The creature barely flinched when the thrown silver blades lodged in the same series of barriers that had stopped the fireball. "I'm warded against all metal, and many other things."

Shiv stepped closer, two black iron knives appearing in his hands. They flew as quickly as they had appeared, stopping in front of the blue kobold, right beside their silver brothers, but closer to their target.

The monster growled, and with three muttered syllables threw something not quite visible at Shiv, a shimmer passing between them that streaked towards the knife thrower's head. One of Shiv's black iron knives was out in a flash, point aimed directly forward. The shimmer struck upon the point of the knife, slowing just long enough for Shiv to plunge the blade into the ground, where the spell burst.

Shiv was flung onto his back, but rolled to his feet with practised ease; he kept the iron knife in hand and a curved ivory blade appeared in the other. With a flick the iron blade was twirling towards the Storm Kobold, and passed, somewhat clumsily, through the shield, landing a few paces away. The Storm Kobold's eyes went wide.

"There are quite a few differences between a master and a grandmaster, aren't there?" Shiv said. He walked forward as another ivory knife appeared in his hand. It flew towards the Storm Kobold just as quickly; this time, the blue-scaled necromancer dodged, the ivory knife skittering along the edge of the shield. The single kobold soldier, who had stood motionless through the entire exchange, took two steps back into the soot.

Termann's arrow thudded into the soldier's temple. The slate-scaled creature was dead long before it hit the ground. Shiv kept prowling forward, only a few paces away now. Another ivory knife appeared in his hand.

The Storm Kobold made two guttural noises and thrust his hands at the ground in an awkward spinning motion. From the bodies of two of the kobold soldiers, two black shadows rose. Despite the smoke, haze, and floating ash in the air, they were visible as kobold-shaped silhouettes of blackness.

Shiv's last silver knife slid into his hand just as he reached the first silhouette, and he rammed it into the insubstantial figure's throat. The silver knives had always been best against spirits and so on, and this was no exception; the shadow doubled over as if it had a windpipe to collapse. It a few moments it faded from view entirely. The second circled around to his left flank, and Shiv reached behind his cloak for another silver knife, remembering he had given it to Marvin Tailor just as the shadow's claws tore into his left arm. The Handspan Armour was no help at all, despite remaining in place and appearing undamaged, he could feel cold blood running down his arm into his empty hand. He leapt back, turned, and slashed his silver blade along the shadow's thigh, briefly noticing the Storm Kobold casting another spell.

One of Termann's arrows flew right through the shadow-kobold without slowing, and it seemed not to notice. Shiv squared off against it, left hand empty and dripping blood, right hand still gripping his last silver knife.

The Storm Kobold finished casting his spell, and two more shades stood up from the ashes. All of Termann's guards were firing arrows now, although if they did any damage it was inconsequential. The Storm Kobold was laughing again, and casting what looked to be the same spell, although the fierce look of strained concentration on his face suggested his magical powers were reaching their limit. Shiv slashed his dagger through the first shadow's arm, crippling it, as the Storm Kobold, gasping for breath, finished his spell. Two more shadows stood up.

The Kobold was no longer laughing, chest pumping and teeth grinding as he concentrated on maintaining control over the five shadows. Shiv could not take advantage, though; although one was crippled, he could not square off against five with only one silver knife and win. As if to prove his point, the shadows glided past his flanks, attempting to surround him. Their claws seemed to flex in anticipation. Shiv backed up in response, thrusting the silver blade into the crippled monster's chest. It shrieked and melted into vapour.

The other four were keeping pace, however, and despite the arrows that flashed through them every few minutes they seemed in far better shape than Shiv, who was backing up faster as he swung his dagger to keep them just out of reach. The Storm Kobold followed, attempting to keep the shadows in sight, his chest pumping like a bellows.

They passed the edge of the square, and Shiv backed up between the two cottages his allies were standing on. As the Storm Kobold reached the edge of the flagstones, Termann leapt off of the roof, and landed lightly in front of him, black glass sword flashing. Like the ivory knives, it veered off target when it passed the Kobold's defensive spells, but it did penetrate, and the Storm Kobold leapt back, snarling. Two of the shadows broke off their pursuit of Shiv to close on Termann, and Shiv stopped falling back, lunging at the nearest shadow blade first.

Termann whirled his sword into a reverse grip and plunged it deeply into the Storm Kobold's invisible shield; although his thrust was thrown well to the side of the creature, one blue-scaled foot slipped. Suddenly, the two shadows closing on Termann jerked, and then their featureless faces turned and towards their master. Blue-clawed hands jerked in a complicated pattern, and before the shadows reached him they melted into mist.

The Storm Kobold seemed to regain his breath somewhat, and with a glance, one more shadow broke off from Shiv to attack Termann. This one nearly reached the elf captain before he whirled around, his black sword blade passing harmlessly through the shadow's belly.

Freed from Termann's attacks, the Storm Kobold's hands wove a pattern in the air, followed by a throwing motion, and Termann's left arm burst in a shower of red. The elf captain howled and dropped to his knees, grabbing impotently at the ragged stump. The blue kobold approached from Terman's rear, and the shadow approached from the front with claws spread wide; Termann's eyes blinked away the pain, and he weakly hacked his sword at the kobold's shield, grimace screaming defiance.

Shiv's knife suddenly slipped into his opponent's neck, and before the creature had melted away, he yanked the blade back, reversed grip with a graceful flourish, and threw the blade into the last shadow's back. Both shrieking shades faded away.

The Storm Kobold stood eye to eye with Termann, one clawed hand holding a shimmering, near-invisible ball, patiently eyeing the black sword blade. Shiv's last ivory knife appeared and twirled through the air, glancing off of the blue kobold's shield and striking the nearby wall of a cottage. The familiar circle of ice grew out from the tooth-shaped blade and across the wood.

"Idiot," the Storm Kobold hissed. "I know that was your last ivory knife. You only carry four. Now you cannot penetrate my wards, so I'll take my time with the one-armed meddler here, and then I can focus on you. You have no more silver knives either, so perhaps I'll give you to more of the shades."

Shiv struck his forearms against his sides, and the long, adamant stilettoes clanged and slid out into view. He took two quick, purposeful steps up to the amused-looking Storm Kobold, and punched both of the dull grey blades down into the smug creature's head.

Chapter Seventy-Seven

Fealty: The human system of government is based on fealty- with the lower ranks swearing allegiance to the upper in exchange for protection. What many people don't think of is that this leaves the upper class as obligated as the lower. Protecting a lot of people is hard work.
          Doctor Unfriendly's Comprehensive Guide to
                              Everything.

Shiv sat on the edge of the Well of Redlock, stripped to the waist, as Rabboni Hareth bound another bandage around his wounded arm. He had laid his hands on Shiv's wounds, and as usual some of them had faded and others had not. The burns on his face were mostly gone, although he would have a fine set of scars. The shadow's claw marks in his arm were still there, but the freezing numbness was gone entirely. His missing finger, the one the Oracle had bitten off, was at least healed over, but the stump that was left still looked ragged.

Zimmiman hobbled up, panting; evidently climbing down from a cottage roof was not the easiest activity for him.

"The stilettoes worked perfectly," Shiv said. "Thank you. You'll still teach me that combination spell? I can't make any sense of it."

"When you're ready," Zimmiman said, nodding. "In the meanwhile I'll find it very useful."

Hareth tied off Shiv's bandages, and looked at the prone figure of Terrman. He knelt and placed his hand on the slender elf's chest, and bowed his head only briefly. Both Shiv and Zimmiman jumped when Termann's arm suddenly reappeared, entirely untouched and unscarred, except for the armour and sleeve that had disintegrated with the Storm Kobold's spell.

"You puts holes in it!" came a gravelly shout from a nearby alley. Not having time to react to Termann's healing, they looked and saw a bedraggled Kobold Trapper padding towards them, a disembodied blue head in his hands. As he walked he was working with his belt knife, peeling off the fleshy parts like a piece of fruit. "And there is crack. Here. And here! You kills him too hard."

"Sorry about that," Shiv said, smiling. Now the others were approaching: Julia and her mother, the three gnomes, now rejoined with Karl and Little, Shantel walking hand in hand with Caroline, Shiv's ten-year old big sister, and the town guards and Forest Nomads. They all crowded around him, clapping him on the shoulders and ignoring it when he winced.

"What's that?" Zimmiman said, pointing at a crude jade horse that sat beside Shiv on the lip of the well.

"One last debt I need to pay," Shiv said.

"Won't you ever be done for a minute?" Julia snapped. "You've done more than anyone here! Take a break for once. You owe a debt to yourself!"

Shiv stood, and buried his hand in her long red hair. Most of it had fallen free of her braid. He drew her in close, and held her gaze for a long time, his lips a hair's breadth from hers. Neither was certain who began the kiss, or how long it lasted, but Julia realized, after a moment, that she was making a soft sighing noise, and broke away. She frowned at him, but said nothing. As she turned and walked away, for just a moment, it appeared her frown disappeared entirely, and she trotted back to her mother, each step with a little bounce in it.

"Master Shiv!" called another voice. Shiv turned and saw the princesses, Recia and Temma, emerging from the Baronet's Manor with their father close behind. Shiv groaned and rolled his eyes. Temma continued as she approached. "We would like to thank you for getting rid of the Storm Kobold so... expediently. We hadn't realized your abilities were so great. I hope you realize that our offer still stands."

Shiv rubbed his temples, mixed emotions playing across his face. Others were coming into the square; the Hammerhand Brothers were approaching from behind the two princesses; Farmer Ticksworth and his family, the two elves from Termann's family, Marvin Tailor and his wife and many others crowded around him, opposite the Manor.

"Actually, I am leaving this town," Shiv said. "I'm done with it. Any who want to come with me, can. I'm going looking for my first family, and no doubt we can settle there."

"You cannot steal our subjects," Recia snapped, looking over to the town guards. They remained motionless. "They owe fealty to us, not you! You attempt that, we'll have your head!"

"If you think you can take my head," Shiv said, standing up to his full height and looking down on Recia. Shiv was not especially tall, but his compact, knotted muscles criss-crossed with scars were easily visible. Recia took a half a step back. "Then take it. Or, you can take it up with the Duke. He seemed to think he owed me for what I did before. The Storm Kobold has been causing you problems for decades; I think the Duke and I will probably break about even. Whoever wants can stay with you, I'm sure your illustrious leadership will inspire many to bask in your providential radiance."

She turned away, and her sister and father followed, saying nothing but looking daggers at him. Shiv smiled at the others present, and they smiled back. Apparently, he would have a large entourage when he left. He looked Julia in the eyes for a long moment.

"Come with me," he said. Julia smiled broadly.

Chapter Seventy-Eight

> *Astrology: Reading the relative positions of the moons, and to a lesser extent, the stars, is believed by many to be hogwash. Despite this sort of ignorance, many learned people (such as myself) continue to use it to forecast the future. Each moon in the sky says a particular message- the Five Brothers mean balance, whereas Kremosh's moon means both loyalty and doom.*
>
> *Doctor Unfriendly's Comprehensive Guide to Everything.*

The caravan numbered around four dozen. Most of the horses in the village had been brought, and were loaded with every scrap they could carry. There were children, aged, and able-bodied adults in equal measure; the crowd included three elves, five gnomes (all mounted on Cornelius, on top of his pack saddle), the kobold Trapper, and even one of the Craftsmaster's apprentice dwarves. Along with Termann were all of the remaining town guards and their families, Zimmiman and his Forest Nomad companions, and even all six of the Hammerhands.

Most of those who were staying lined the street to see them off, with the notable exception of Falcior and his family. The town was down to its bare bones, now, no more than three dozen residents; but those who had elected to stay had looks of steely determination on their faces, and no small children to worry about.

Termann approached the lead portion of the caravan, where Shiv and the gnomes stood by Mother Hammerhand, Julia, and Shantel. Mother Hammerhand kept looking back to the burnt-out wreck that had been her inn, Julia looked to her mother, and the Hammerhand brothers glared at Shiv. Shiv ignored them.

"We're all ready," Termann said. "We'll move at your order."

"Shiv!" Caroline said, running over, flanked by two of the village girls. "Tell them you're my little brother!"

Shiv smiled and nodded, inspiring disbelieving looks in both of the girls.

"The village we are heading to is called Watcher's Point?" Shiv asked her.

"Yes," Caroline replied. "It's at a fork in the Whitehawk River, in between two big hills. I think it's south of a really big forest."

"That would be the southern tip of Mendin's Forest. The Nomads know it. It forms much of the border." Termann explained. "It's about ninety leagues southwest, just under two weeks travel. We should find it easily."

The caravan began to trundle away, eventually building up to a comfortable walking pace. Shiv glanced briefly at the ragged circus tent that still stood beside the town, and several emotions played across his face. With a soft chuckle, he took his spot at the lead with Cornelius and the gnomes, and began discussing plans with the Doctor about his maps of that area, and what pitfalls they might expect.

They made good time that day, covering nearly nine leagues despite the hilly terrain, and did not make camp until the sun was sinking below the horizon and twelve moons hung high in the sky.

Shiv stood off to the side of the camp, quietly scanning the rugged horizon.

"Twelve moons is a good omen," Doctor Unfriendly said. He had approached without making a sound, a skill he had been practising lately. "All the Five Brothers, Dornovigorn, Soliel, the Pharaoh, Mendin, Bast, Kremosh and Ariel are there. You couldn't ask for a better forecast."

Shiv nodded, but said nothing. He had been quiet since leaving Redlock, giving directions when they were needed, but little else. There was a rustle in some nearby bushes, although nothing appeared to have made the disturbance.

"There she is," Shiv said absently.

SHIV

"Yes, here I am," came a deep, gravelly base voice, monstrous and somewhat feminine. They both recognized the Oracle was speaking, even if they could not see any sign of her. A black speck that had been invisible in the darkness grew to form a hole of blackness roughly a pace across, and a monstrous, clawed hand thrust out, palm up. "I believe we had a deal, to cancel out that debt you owe me."

Shiv had the jade amulet out, strung on a thong that, from the right angle, looked like an overlong bridle on the rough horse-like shape. He dangled it in front of him at arm's length.

"What is it?" Shiv said. "It must be worth a fortune for you to give up eighteen months of labour from a master craftsman."

"You aren't thinking of double-crossing me, are you?" growled the Oracle's voice. The clawed hand flexed, calling attention to the fact it was nearly as long as a forearm, and the sharp nails themselves as long as human fingers. "There are many who would advise you against that. Or there would be, if they had not all been so unfortunate."

"No," Shiv snickered, toying with the amulet as it spun on its string. "I just wanted to make sure you aren't double crossing me, either."

"We had a deal," the Oracle said, the growl sounding angry.

"You know as well as I do that no deal is finished until it is finished. And don't try to threaten me, I've defeated the plans of one grandmaster wizard already this week, and frankly, I'm tired." Shiv's voice was getting somewhat irritable as well. Doctor Unfriendly backed a few steps away from the monstrous clawed hand, which was clenched in a fist and shaking slightly, knuckles a lighter shade of green than the rest of it.

"You had my help against Talisman, and defeat is a fairly strong word." The black hole was getting wider, now, and the hand had visibly relaxed, resting on the ground with one finger tapping impatiently. Within moments the circle of blackness was large enough for a person to step through. The Doctor backed up even more, and his hand was searching through one of his belt pouches.

"I have other allies. And frankly, all I'm asking for is an explanation. I didn't say I wouldn't give it to you." Shiv said with a frown.

"Oh, bugger," said the Oracle. "And I suppose you already have that spell on both of your stilettoes, now, don't you?"

Shiv said nothing, but crossed his arms. After a pause, the Oracle chuckled, the sound somewhat like a millstone grinding gravel.

"I suppose I have some responsibility for turning you into a monster, too, then," the Oracle said. "I actually never thought Zimmiman would agree to help you, or that you'd share the spell with him. Very well, I think the amulet was owned by the late Archmage Shameleah, possibly the most powerful wizard in the last ten generations or so. He was dangerous, horribly so, except that his hunger for studying ever more powerful magics kept him too busy for much else. His protégé, Donrapeus, was less studious and more ambitious, but once he had removed Shameleah, he was in turn removed much more easily."

Shiv nodded, but waited for more. The Oracle sighed.

"One of Shameleah's specialties was the storage of life force. I think Talisman created the Storm Kobold primarily by giving him this amulet."

"You think this amulet is the Archmage's Soul Object?" interjected Doctor Unfriendly. The gnome, fear suddenly overcome by professional curiosity, was at Shiv's side in an instant.

"Yes, that's what I think." The Oracle replied. The Doctor gave a low whistle, clearly impressed.

"So, what you're saying, is that you were trying to rip me off," Shiv said with a sly smile. "I'm a little bit insulted."

"I could just bite your head off and take it," the Oracle said angrily.

"You could. But you have said enough that I know you have plans for me in the future, possibly taking on Talisman again. You've made it clear that you don't think you can defeat him by yourself. If the Zanquitor gave the amulet to the Storm Kobold instead of keeping it for himself, it probably means it is not powerful enough to swing the balance in your favour by itself. Unless, of course, he didn't know what exactly it was that he had."

There was a scrabbling sound inside the black hole, by this time as big as the side of a barn. It stopped growing, and the Oracle's immense head thrust out, narrowed yellow eyes focussed on Shiv. The Oracle's monstrous mouth, full of mismatched tusks and fangs, was half open, drool hanging all the way to the ground in greasy strings.

"Are you blackmailing me?" the Oracle said incredulously, heaving her bulk out of the hole in the air.

"Truly I say unto thee, that I am, madam. You have grasped the core of the truth, the nugget, as it were, firmly, as a bear with a trout." Shiv said, looking up at her, arms crossed and face impassive.

"You little... I haven't been... you are a monster, Master Shiv, and a worse one than I thought. Perhaps young Zachary Talisman has met his match after all. Alright, then, what is your price?"

"That combination spell was very handy. Perhaps you have more spells I could use. Anything I can place on a knife. Maybe some rune magic, for example."

The Oracle slumped, which still made her twice Shiv's height, with room to spare. She shook her head.

"You aren't a wizard. How much of it will you understand?" the Oracle asked, misshapen frown thoughtful. Her clawed foot tapped impatiently.

"I know a few things, and I have a few wizards to help me figure it out. I don't expect anything higher than a Master wizard could comprehend. Maybe six spells, a nice variety. Use your judgement; after all, I may end up being your weapon, I had best be as sharp as possible."

"Very well," the Oracle said, "But just to be clear, I won't tolerate this sort of thing again. I don't like to be taken lightly, and there are always other weapons to choose from."

"Point taken," Shiv agreed. "Let's say... tomorrow, same time, about nine leagues south?"

"Agreed. Have a nice evening, Master Shiv." The Oracle turned, and vanished into her circle of blackness, which promptly vanished after her. The Doctor let out a long breath of relief.

"You are a dangerous person to be around," the gnome mused. "Is this how you've learned all those tricks you know?"

"More or less," Shiv said, and smiled broadly. "Let's get back to camp, I'm hungry."

Epilogue

Terrance Kobodan scratched his salt-and-pepper head as another customer left without a sale. He frowned to himself, but his crooked smile did not waver for long. He looked up at the sign over his shop. It had a picture of an anvil and hammer, both black, but rimmed in gold, and the legend 'Best Smith in Ironfield County' in large, clear letters. He nodded as if confirming the sign's authenticity. His father had been a blacksmith, and his father's father. The metal was in his blood; business would sort itself out if he did not give up.

Shrugging, he looked about the wares displayed in front of his shop as he put his leather apron back on, and then returned to the order he was working on. Cooking pots were not his favourite; he liked knives, but pots paid the bills.

The anvil was in an area open to the front, so he could see customers approach, and to let some of the heat out. He stoked the coal fire a bit, and then placed a half-finished iron skillet back on the anvil.

There was a commotion of sorts on the roadway, no doubt some large trader's caravan passing by. He paid it no mind, keeping his focus on hammering the skillet, and thus was surprised when he realized the caravan had stopped on the road in front of his forge. He didn't like caravans; they brought back unpleasant memories. Still, he remembered they might be customers, and so he laid the skillet in the coals to reheat, and hung his hammer, and walked over to meet the group that was approaching him.

There were two leading the group. The first was a man whose age was hard to determine, having white hair and a huge moustache but looking fit, and dressed in expensive performer's clothes and leather armour. His red hat had fresh scorch marks on the brim, although what could have caused them was not clear.

The smith's jaw dropped. The girl walking beside the performer was the very image of his long-lost daughter. He shook himself briefly, the very thought was ridiculous; she would be in her thirties by now.

"Greetings, milord. In the market for some pots or pans?" he asked. Despite his efforts, his eyes continued to slide back to the girl. She too, seemed shocked for some reason. Now that he thought of it, so did the performer, perhaps even terrified. Not sure how to react, he ignored it. There was an awkward pause.

"Do you have an apprentice? Apprentices? Children, perhaps?" the performer asked. He took his hat off, his long, white hair looking disheveled as a result.

"No," Terrence said, his smile disappearing fully for the first time that day. "All my children were lost, one way or another. And my wife. But I'm not in the market for an apprentice, especially one as old as yourself. Your daughter might be the right age, if not the right build for it."

Both the performer and the girl laughed loudly at that. The performer shook his head. For some reason, the rest of the caravan's people had approached, yet stayed several steps back, seeming nearly as nervous as the two he was talking to.

"No, no, she's not my daughter… she's my big sister." The performer looked intently at Terrence then, meeting his eyes as if waiting for a reaction. Terrence frowned again, at the ridiculousness of it. "You are… Terrence Kobodan? Senior?"

"There is no Terrence Junior, now. I thought I explained that." Terrence was getting angry. The sight of one so like his daughter was playing with his emotions. The performer sighed, and brushed his scarred face with one hand. The smallest finger in leather gauntlet he wore did not move, as if it was empty.

"I've handled this badly," said the performer, straightening himself as if standing at attention. "Let me start again. Terrence Kobodan, nearly thirty years ago, you sent your son away to spare him from the plague. Shortly after that, when it looked like she would recover, you did the same with your daughter."

Terrence stiffened, but said nothing, so the man continued.

"Your son was picked up by a travelling circus, and remained under the impression that you and the rest of his family were dead. Eventually, he was also separated from his adoptive family, and took up a life of wandering performer and an apprentice smith. He even wandered through this area many times, but his memories were unclear, and he did not know where his home was, or, as I said, that anyone of his family had survived."

"How… how do you know this…?" Terrence stammered.

"Recently, your son found a young girl in a wizard's laboratory, preserved in a glass bubble. That girl was your daughter, Caroline," the performer continued, clearing his throat.

Tears formed in Terrence's eyes, and he fell to his knees, looking at the girl.

"Twenty-six years." he said, not sure if the words were meant for himself or one of them. "It's been twenty-six years."

"That would make me, what, about thirty-two?" the performer said, smiling oddly. "I always wanted to know that."

Terrence's head whipped back to study the performer's face, wiping tears away with the back of his hand to see more clearly. Now that he looked closer, and ignored the white hair, there were similarities…

The performer put his hat back on, and reached out his hand (the one with all the fingers) to help his father up.

"I'm called 'Shiv', now," he said. "And, no offense, but I prefer it to Junior."

"Shiv? As in a crude knife?" asked Terrence.

"He has a weird thing with knives," Caroline said, and then threw her arms around her father. "You look so old! I thought your hair would still be brown!"

"It has more brown than my son's." Terrence replied wryly. Shiv smiled at that; it was funny. Terrence hauled them in for a fierce embrace, tears blurring his vision, his shoulders trembling; Shiv and Caroline and he held on for some time.

"Who are all these people, then?" Terrence said, wiping his eyes with a sooty sleeve and nodding to the silent crowd that waited by the road. "Shiv? Really? I'm not sure I like that. It sounds violent."

Shiv introduced Julia first, with a smile, and then began the litany of other names; it took much of the day to get through them all, and the stories that had brought them there. Terrence had stories of his own, if not ones so adventurous, as did Caroline, if not so many. As the sun began to set, Terrence and his guests set up tables, and they made an improvised feast from the provisions of the caravan. Although the forge did little business that day, Terrence could not remember feeling more successful.

Over the next several weeks, the caravan gradually found lodging and jobs within Watcher's Point; Shiv performed in the street near the smithy and aided with the production of the best knives the area had seen, occasionally finding time to go over the spells of the Oracle with Zimmiman or Doctor Unfriendly. The Hammerhands bought a larger inn, sharing ownership with a half a dozen other ex-Redlockers. The Kobold Trapper, the gnomes and the Forest Nomads settled in a little outpost they made between the Mendin Woods and the town itself, bringing more and better game, and wonderful gnomish books and maps. Soon the whole town was prospering as never before; and though there was the occasional rumour of hellhounds or exceptionally large trolls in the area, people did not worry so much under the protection of the veterans of Redlock.

And far away, a white-cloaked man watched them all in a magic mirror, chuckling to himself as his masterwork grew in knowledge and skill. Most of the time, his plans were on track, and when they were not, he took out his frustrations on the tiny necromancer with the burned face, or sent destructive orders to the remaining kobolds of Terrikota in their dead master's name.

And further away, the half-troll Oracle watched through a hole in the air or a bubbling cauldron, chuckling as her plans advanced as well. Most of the time her plans did, but when they did not she would stroke the razor-sharp quills of her hellhounds, or spend some time with her trolls, and she would soon feel better.

And further away still, another set of eyes watched them all through a complicated mechanism of bronze gears and crystal lenses, and he sometimes laughed as he watched, and scratched his snow monkey under its chin. The snow monkey would sit on his shoulder and watch as well, and occasionally pick at the patches on his master's plain brown robes. This watcher's plans were always on track. He had not, to his knowledge, made an error in several decades.

But as he watched the Oracle, and the Zanquitor, and the knife smith in the village, even he would often look over his shoulder, just in case there was a pair of eyes watching him. He had not caught anyone yet, but that proved nothing.

Printed in the United States
By Bookmasters